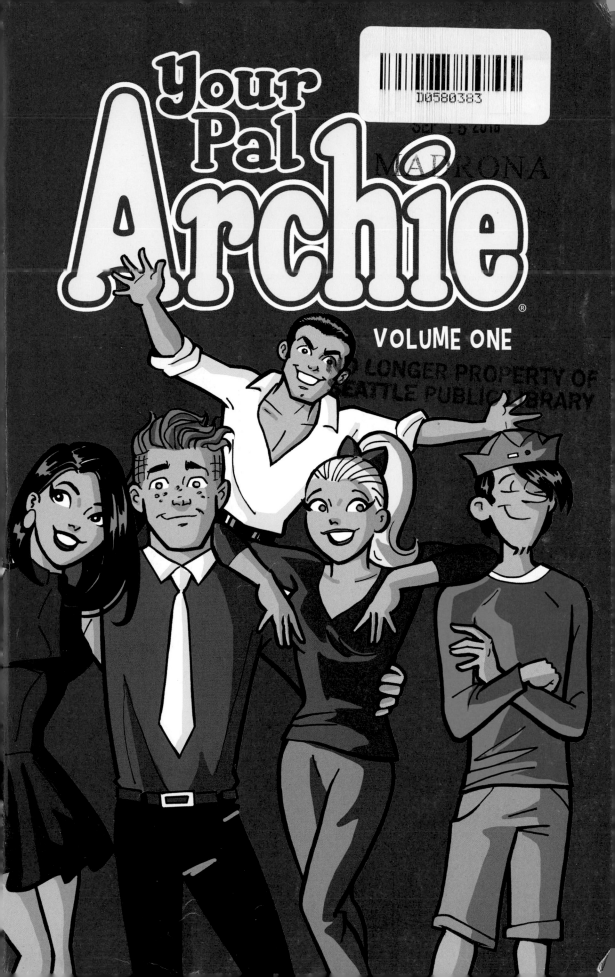

D0580383

SEP 15 2018

NO LONGER PROPERTY OF
SEATTLE PUBLIC LIBRARY

MADRONA

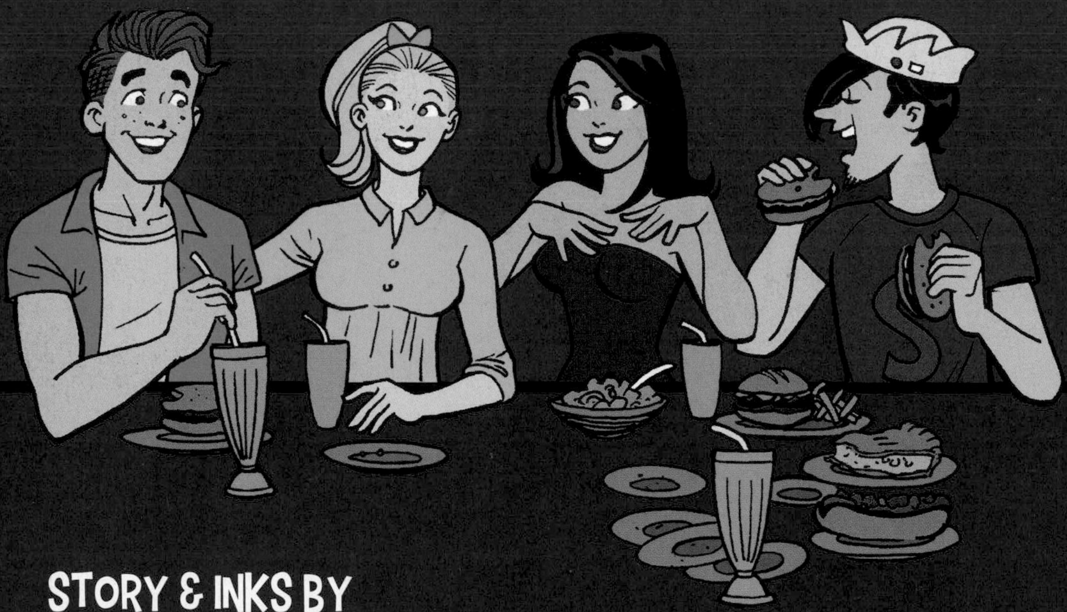

STORY & INKS BY
TY TEMPLETON

ART BY
DAN PARENT

LETTERING BY
JACK MORELLI

COLORS BY
ANDRE SZYMANOWICZ

EDITOR
VICTOR GORELICK

PUBLISHER
JON GOLDWATER

INTRODUCTION

BY TY TEMPLETON

I've been writing and drawing comics for more than thirty years and, while working on this particular series, I was able to do something I'd never done before. Something wonderful that only a small number of people ever get to do...

...live in Riverdale.

I don't mean just visit Riverdale—everyone gets to do that when they read an Archie comic—I mean LIVE in Riverdale.

All day long.

For a number of months.

It was my job.

I would think about Riverdale when I woke up, during breakfast, on a morning walk, afternoons at work, into the evening, and then some. When I wasn't plotting a story, I was inking some of Dan Parent's wonderful drawings, or I was reading comics about Archie and Jughead and Betty and Veronica, and Reggie, spending time thinking about out how far Pop's might be from Jughead's house, or which set of doors opens up towards the football field at Riverdale High or how many people make up the complete staff of the Lodge Mansion. Sometimes, I'd have Riverdale dreams.

For a writer like me, who has lived in places as scary as Gotham City or the Planet of the Apes—not to mention the real world outside my window—there is no place I'd rather be than Riverdale.

I suspect you know that, too, dear reader, or you wouldn't be this far into a foreword in the front pages of an Archie collection. There's no place YOU'D rather be than Riverdale, you can admit it. We're all pals here, come on in for a visit.

What follows is ten stories set in the best place you can be.

All featuring **YOUR PAL ARCHIE**.

CHAPTER 1

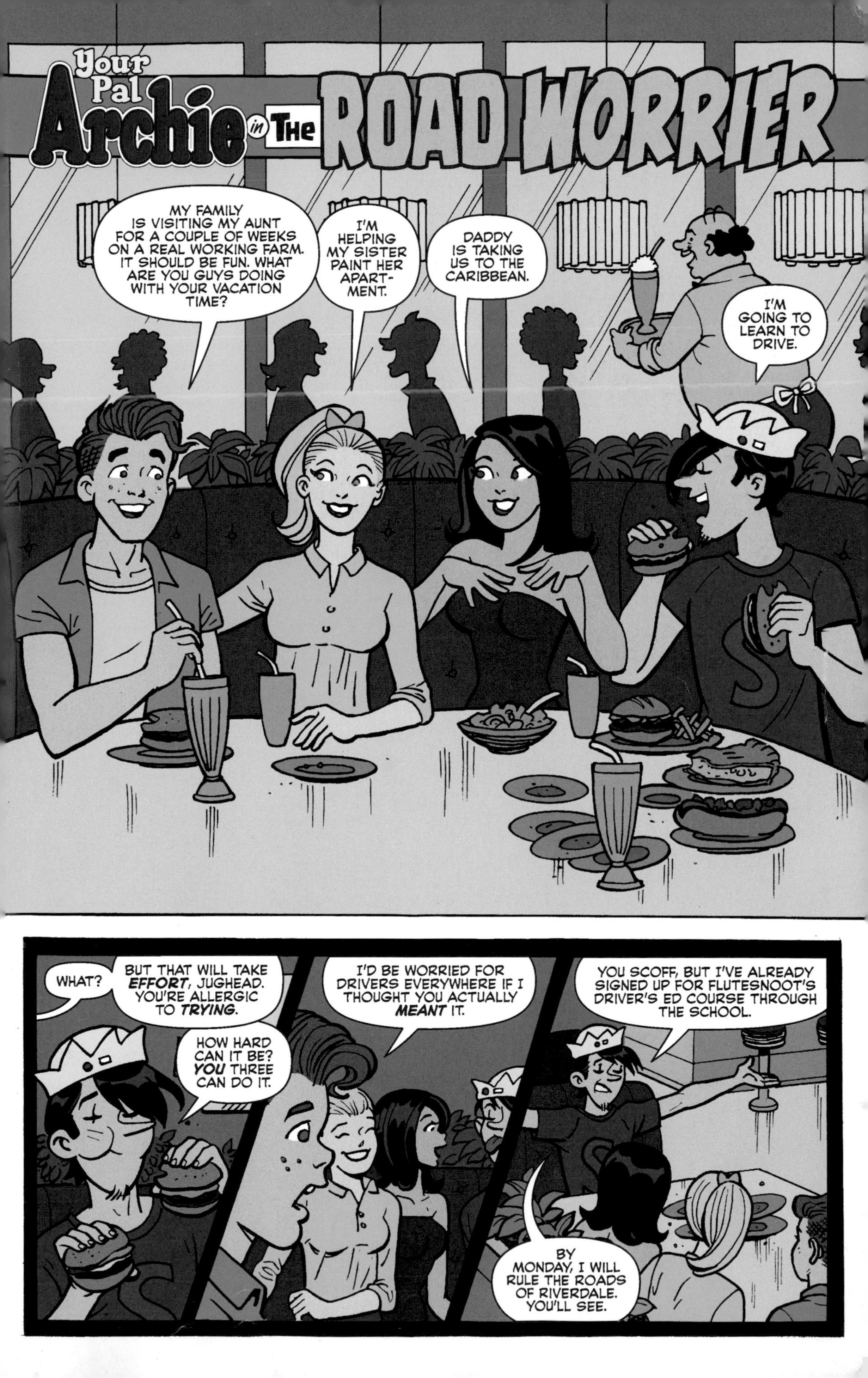
Your Pal Archie in THE ROAD WORRIER
MY FAMILY IS VISITING MY AUNT FOR A COUPLE OF WEEKS ON A REAL WORKING FARM. IT SHOULD BE FUN. WHAT ARE YOU GUYS DOING WITH YOUR VACATION TIME?
I'M HELPING MY SISTER PAINT HER APART- MENT.
DADDY IS TAKING US TO THE CARIBBEAN.
I'M GOING TO LEARN TO DRIVE.
WHAT?
BUT THAT WILL TAKE EFFORT, JUGHEAD. YOU'RE ALLERGIC TO TRYING.
HOW HARD CAN IT BE? YOU THREE CAN DO IT.
I'D BE WORRIED FOR DRIVERS EVERYWHERE IF I THOUGHT YOU ACTUALLY MEANT IT.
YOU SCOFF, BUT I'VE ALREADY SIGNED UP FOR FLUTESNOOT'S DRIVER'S ED COURSE THROUGH THE SCHOOL.
BY MONDAY, I WILL RULE THE ROADS OF RIVERDALE. YOU'LL SEE.

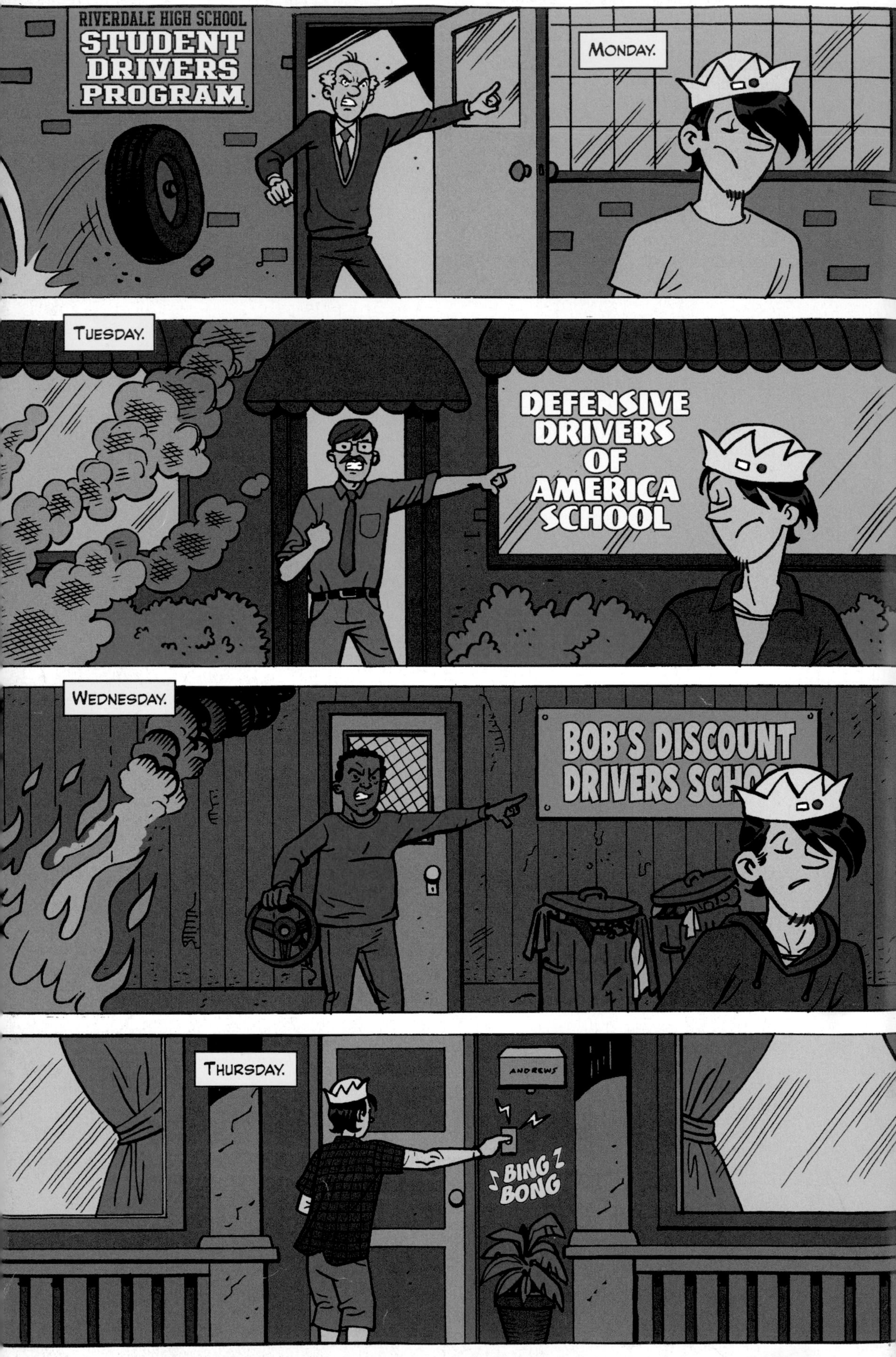

RIVERDALE HIGH SCHOOL
STUDENT DRIVERS PROGRAM
MONDAY.
TUESDAY.
DEFENSIVE DRIVERS OF AMERICA SCHOOL
WEDNESDAY.
BOB'S DISCOUNT DRIVERS SCHO
THURSDAY.
ANDREWS
BING BONG

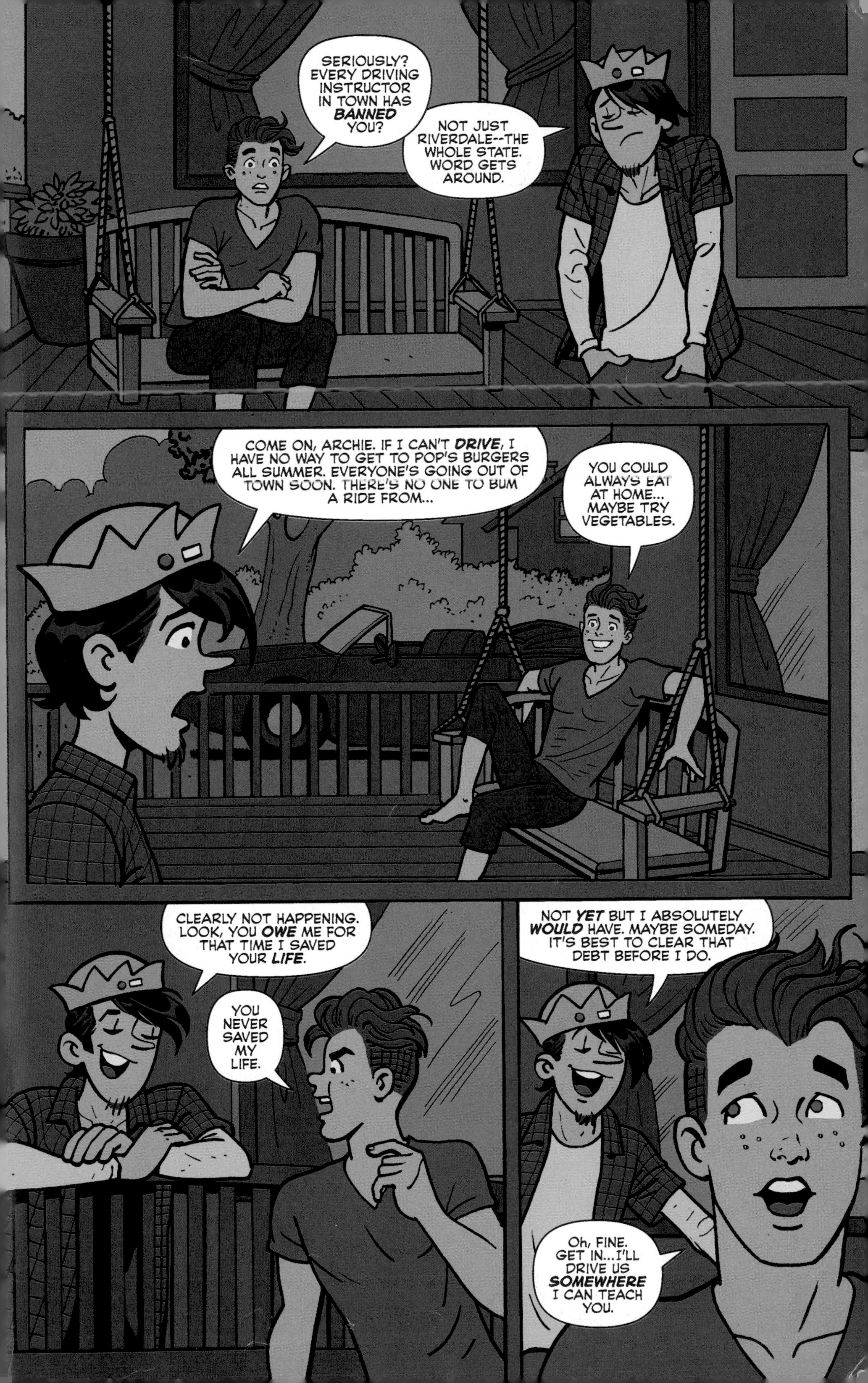
SERIOUSLY? EVERY DRIVING INSTRUCTOR IN TOWN HAS **BANNED** YOU?
NOT JUST RIVERDALE--THE WHOLE STATE. WORD GETS AROUND.
COME ON, ARCHIE. IF I CAN'T **DRIVE**, I HAVE NO WAY TO GET TO POP'S BURGERS ALL SUMMER. EVERYONE'S GOING OUT OF TOWN SOON. THERE'S NO ONE TO BUM A RIDE FROM...
YOU COULD ALWAYS EAT AT HOME... MAYBE TRY VEGETABLES.
CLEARLY NOT HAPPENING. LOOK, YOU **OWE** ME FOR THAT TIME I SAVED YOUR **LIFE**.
YOU NEVER SAVED MY LIFE.
NOT **YET** BUT I ABSOLUTELY **WOULD** HAVE. MAYBE SOMEDAY. IT'S BEST TO CLEAR THAT DEBT BEFORE I DO.
Oh, FINE. GET IN...I'LL DRIVE US **SOMEWHERE** I CAN TEACH YOU.

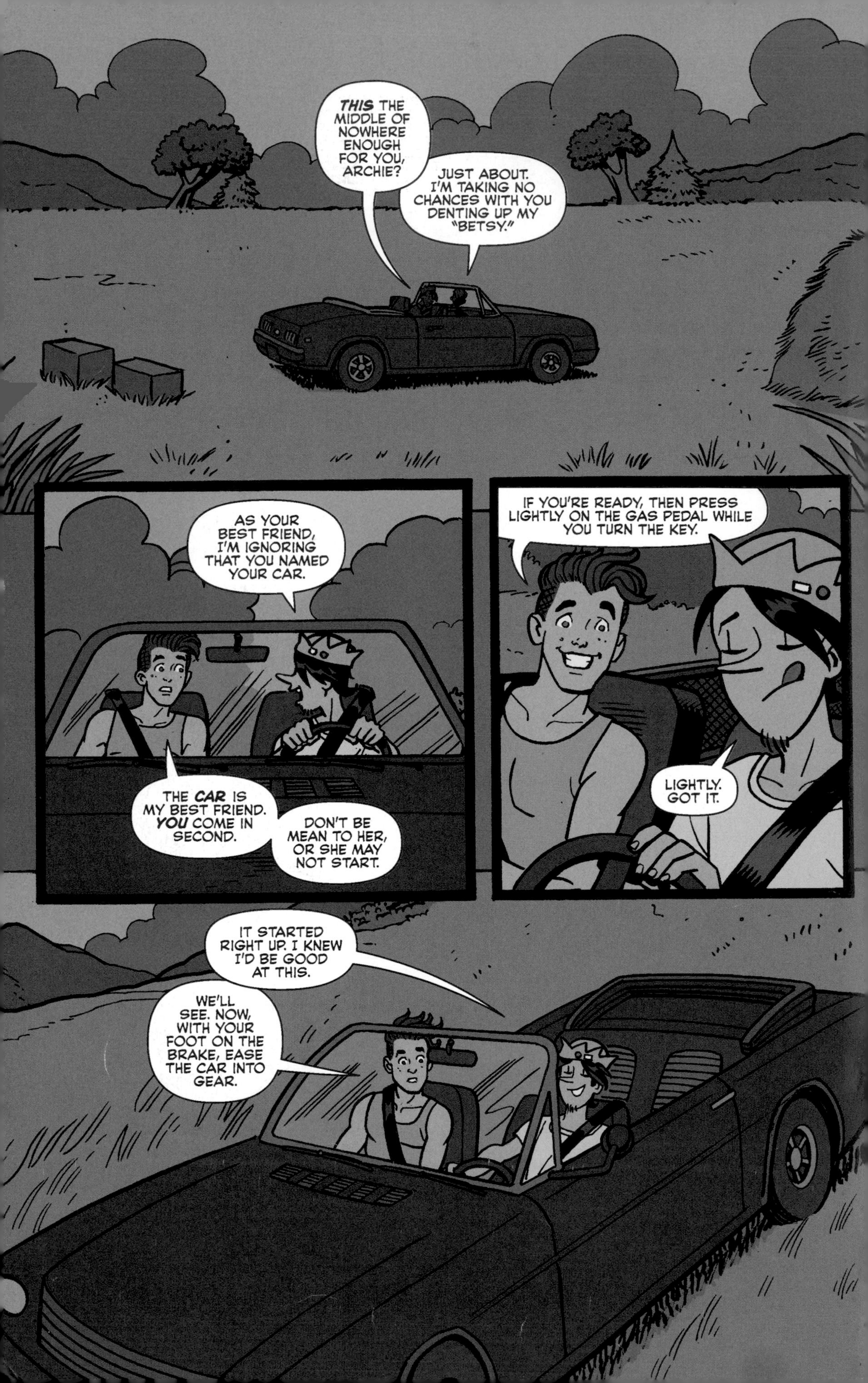
THIS THE MIDDLE OF NOWHERE ENOUGH FOR YOU, ARCHIE?
JUST ABOUT. I'M TAKING NO CHANCES WITH YOU DENTING UP MY "BETSY."
AS YOUR BEST FRIEND, I'M IGNORING THAT YOU NAMED YOUR CAR.
THE CAR IS MY BEST FRIEND. YOU COME IN SECOND.
DON'T BE MEAN TO HER, OR SHE MAY NOT START.
IF YOU'RE READY, THEN PRESS LIGHTLY ON THE GAS PEDAL WHILE YOU TURN THE KEY.
LIGHTLY. GOT IT.
IT STARTED RIGHT UP. I KNEW I'D BE GOOD AT THIS.
WE'LL SEE. NOW, WITH YOUR FOOT ON THE BRAKE, EASE THE CAR INTO GEAR.

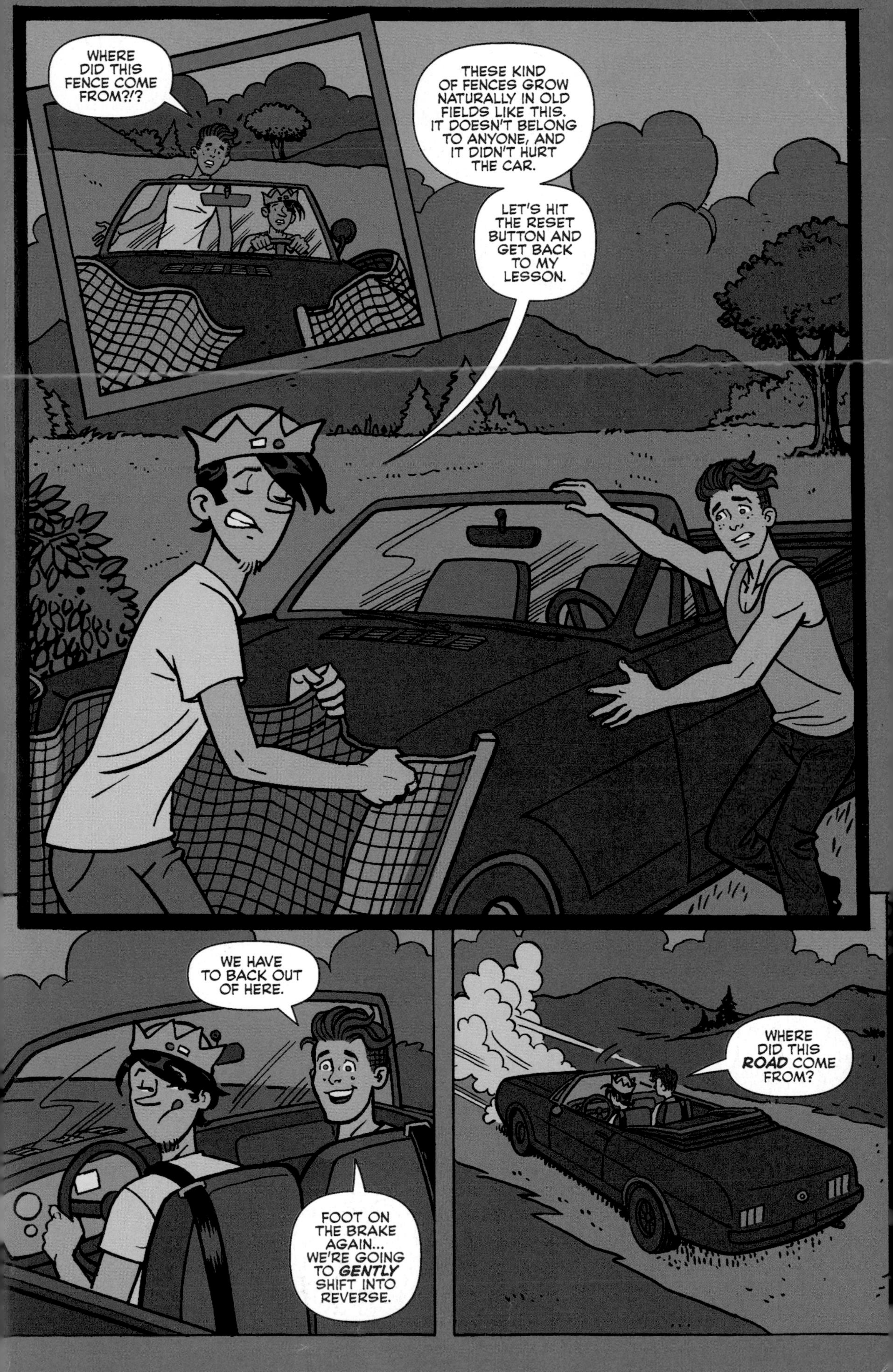
WHERE DID THIS FENCE COME FROM?!?
THESE KIND OF FENCES GROW NATURALLY IN OLD FIELDS LIKE THIS. IT DOESN'T BELONG TO ANYONE, AND IT DIDN'T HURT THE CAR.
LET'S HIT THE RESET BUTTON AND GET BACK TO MY LESSON.
WE HAVE TO BACK OUT OF HERE.
FOOT ON THE BRAKE AGAIN... WE'RE GOING TO *GENTLY* SHIFT INTO REVERSE.
WHERE DID THIS *ROAD* COME FROM?

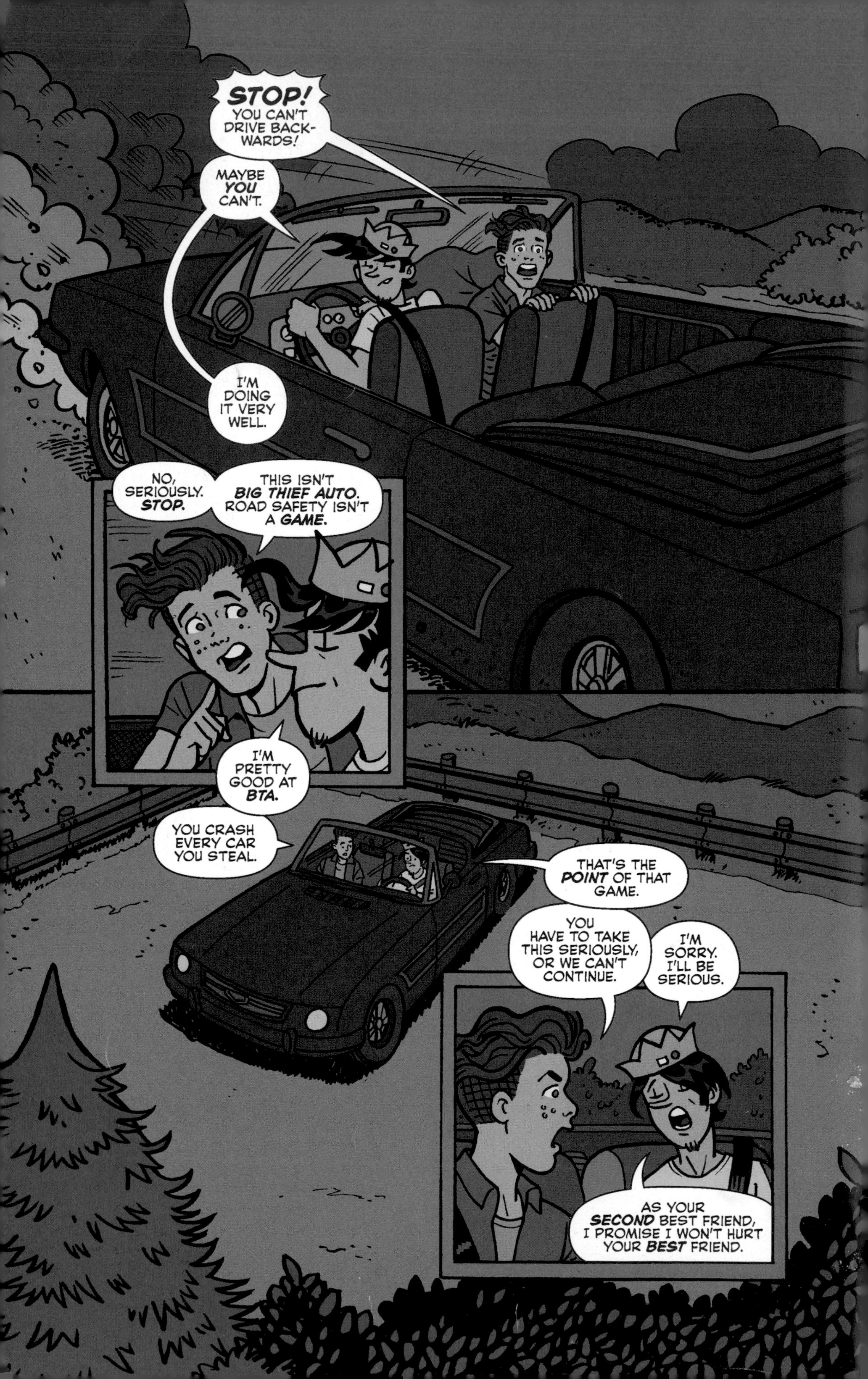
STOP! YOU CAN'T DRIVE BACK-WARDS!
MAYBE YOU CAN'T.
I'M DOING IT VERY WELL.
NO, SERIOUSLY. STOP.
THIS ISN'T BIG THIEF AUTO. ROAD SAFETY ISN'T A GAME.
I'M PRETTY GOOD AT BTA.
YOU CRASH EVERY CAR YOU STEAL.
THAT'S THE POINT OF THAT GAME.
YOU HAVE TO TAKE THIS SERIOUSLY, OR WE CAN'T CONTINUE.
I'M SORRY. I'LL BE SERIOUS.
AS YOUR SECOND BEST FRIEND, I PROMISE I WON'T HURT YOUR BEST FRIEND.

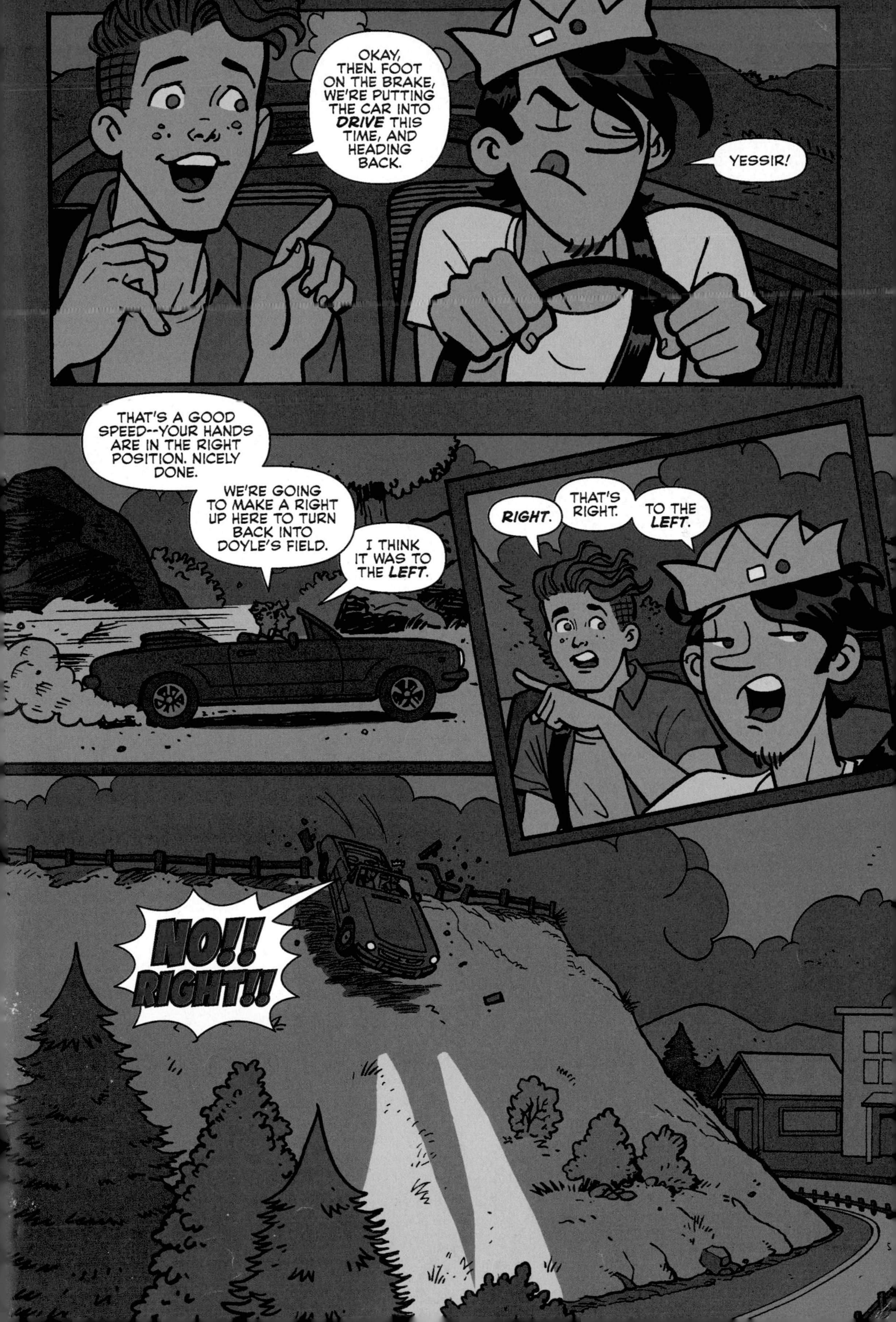

OKAY, THEN. FOOT ON THE BRAKE, WE'RE PUTTING THE CAR INTO **DRIVE** THIS TIME, AND HEADING BACK.
YESSIR!
THAT'S A GOOD SPEED--YOUR HANDS ARE IN THE RIGHT POSITION. NICELY DONE.
WE'RE GOING TO MAKE A RIGHT UP HERE TO TURN BACK INTO DOYLE'S FIELD.
I THINK IT WAS TO THE **LEFT**.
RIGHT.
THAT'S RIGHT.
TO THE **LEFT**.
NO!! RIGHT!!

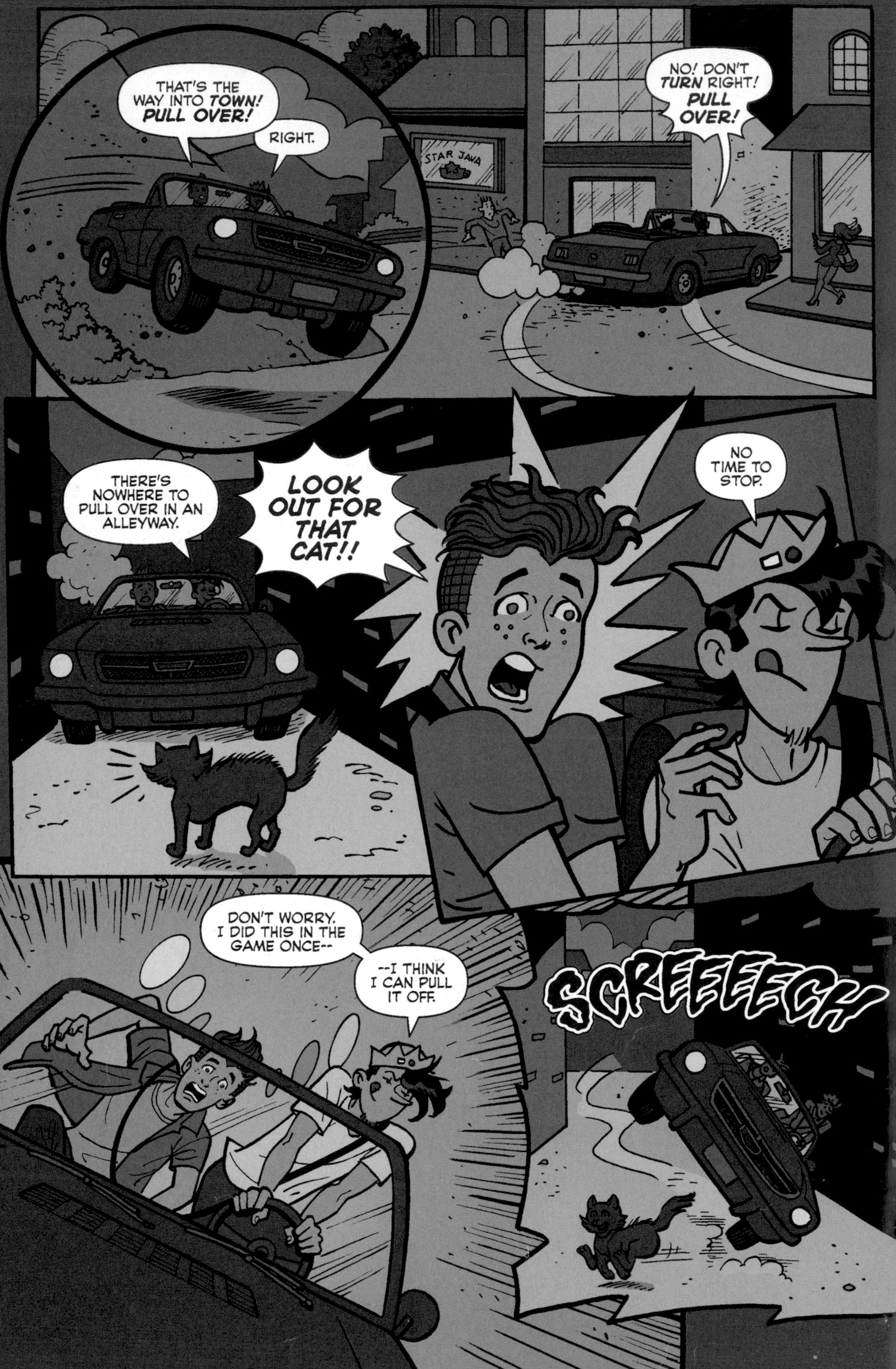
THAT'S THE WAY INTO TOWN! PULL OVER!
RIGHT.
STAR JAVA
NO! DON'T TURN RIGHT! PULL OVER!
THERE'S NOWHERE TO PULL OVER IN AN ALLEYWAY.
LOOK OUT FOR THAT CAT!!
NO TIME TO STOP.
DON'T WORRY. I DID THIS IN THE GAME ONCE--
--I THINK I CAN PULL IT OFF.
SCREEEECH

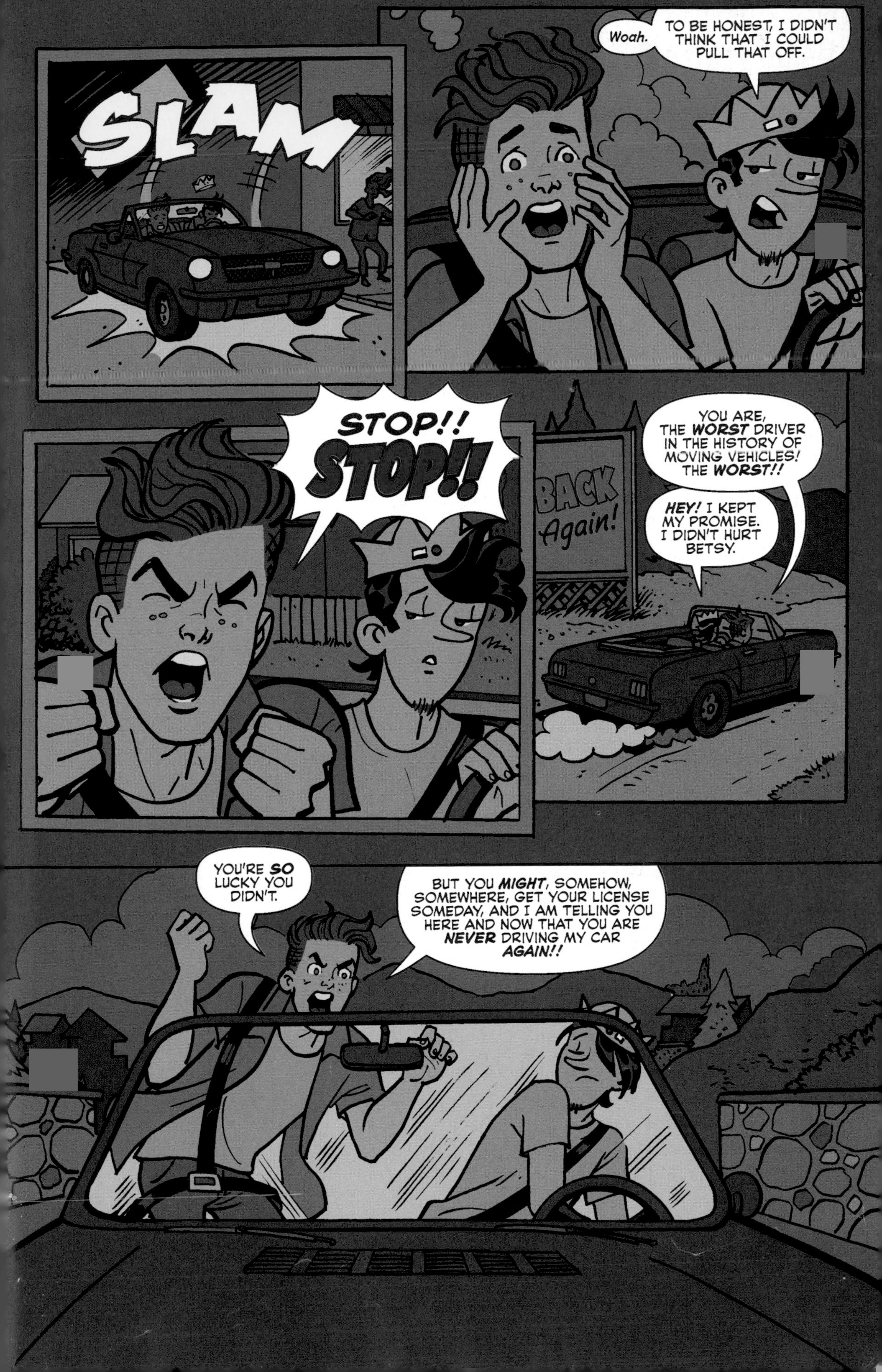
SLAM
Woah.
TO BE HONEST, I DIDN'T THINK THAT I COULD PULL THAT OFF.
STOP!! STOP!!
YOU ARE, THE WORST DRIVER IN THE HISTORY OF MOVING VEHICLES! THE WORST!!
HEY! I KEPT MY PROMISE. I DIDN'T HURT BETSY.
BACK Again!
YOU'RE SO LUCKY YOU DIDN'T.
BUT YOU MIGHT, SOMEHOW, SOMEWHERE, GET YOUR LICENSE SOMEDAY, AND I AM TELLING YOU HERE AND NOW THAT YOU ARE NEVER DRIVING MY CAR AGAIN!!

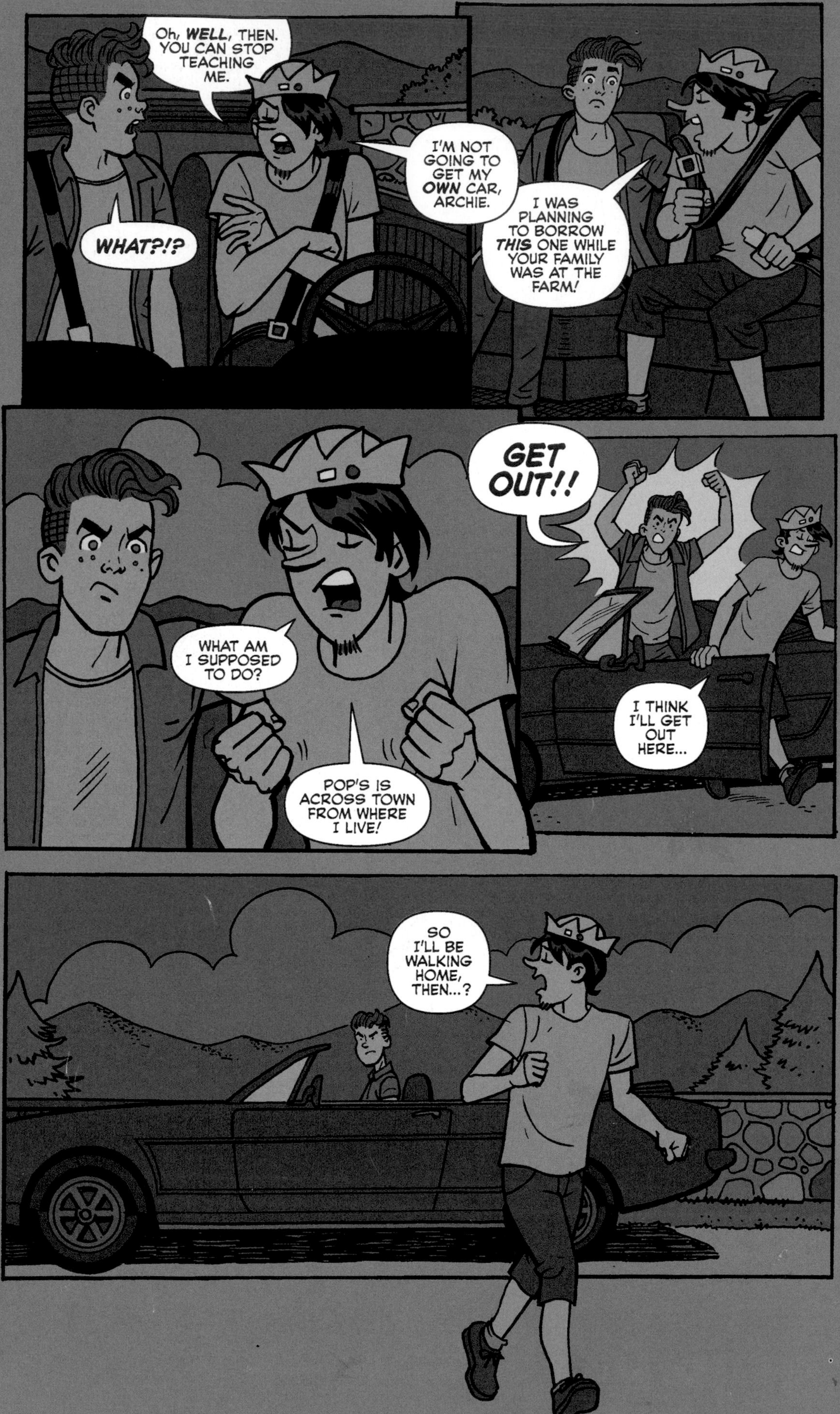
Oh, WELL, THEN. YOU CAN STOP TEACHING ME.
WHAT?!?
I'M NOT GOING TO GET MY OWN CAR, ARCHIE.
I WAS PLANNING TO BORROW THIS ONE WHILE YOUR FAMILY WAS AT THE FARM!
WHAT AM I SUPPOSED TO DO?
POP'S IS ACROSS TOWN FROM WHERE I LIVE!
GET OUT!!
I THINK I'LL GET OUT HERE...
SO I'LL BE WALKING HOME, THEN...?

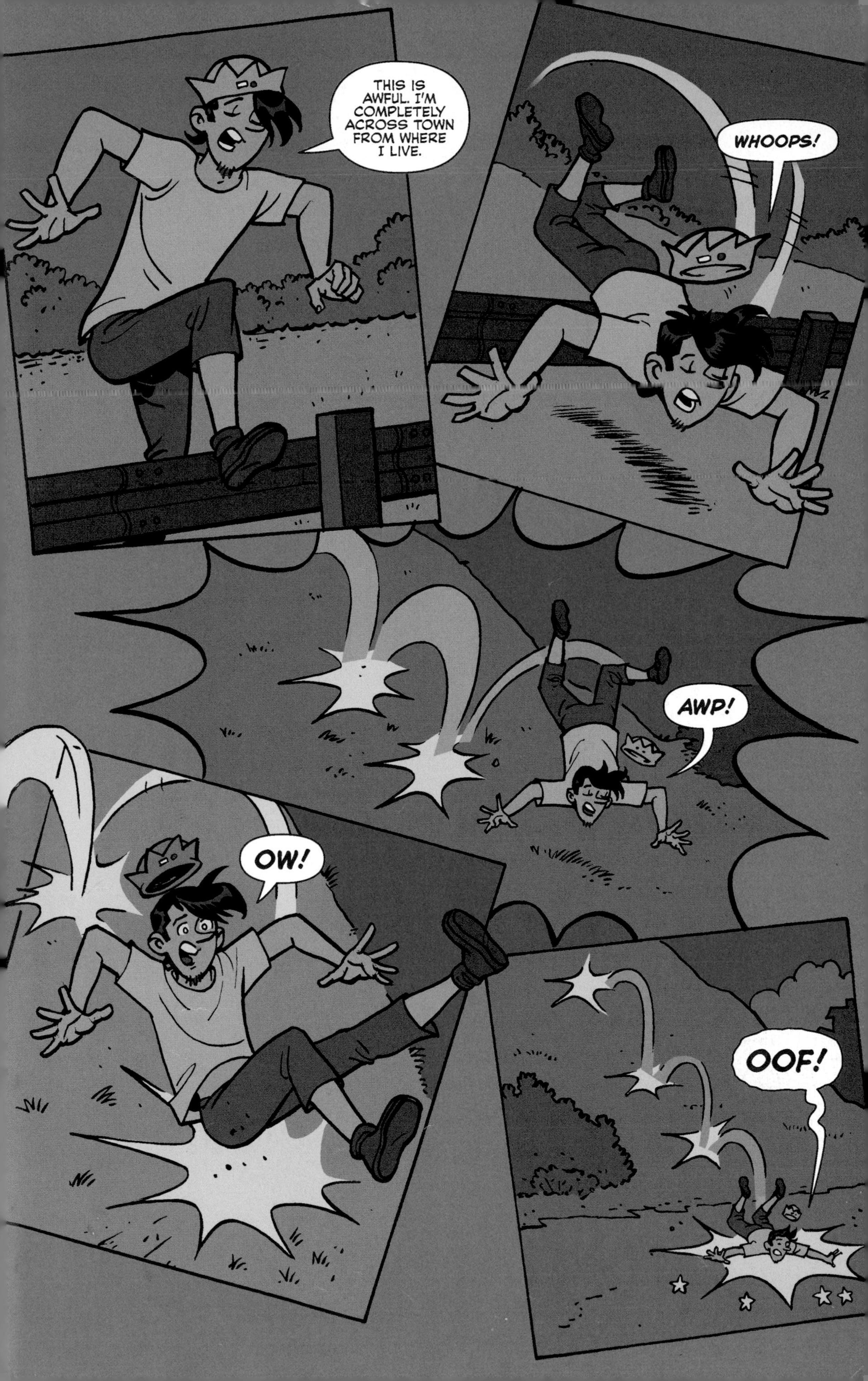
THIS IS AWFUL. I'M COMPLETELY ACROSS TOWN FROM WHERE I LIVE.
WHOOPS!
AWP!
OW!
OOF!

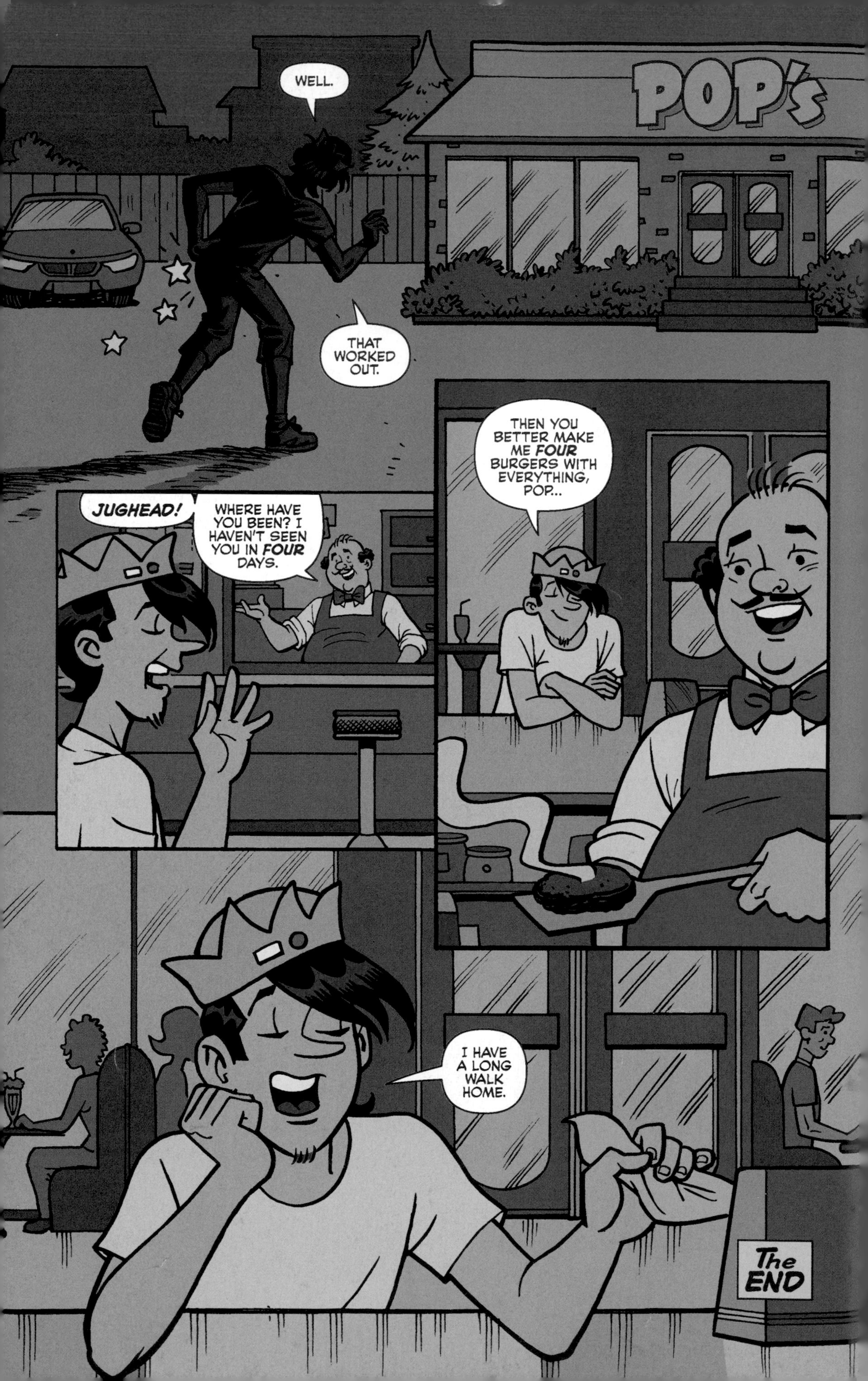
POP'S
WELL.
THAT WORKED OUT.
JUGHEAD!
WHERE HAVE YOU BEEN? I HAVEN'T SEEN YOU IN **FOUR** DAYS.
THEN YOU BETTER MAKE ME **FOUR** BURGERS WITH EVERYTHING, POP...
I HAVE A LONG WALK HOME.
The END

CHAPTER 2

PART 1

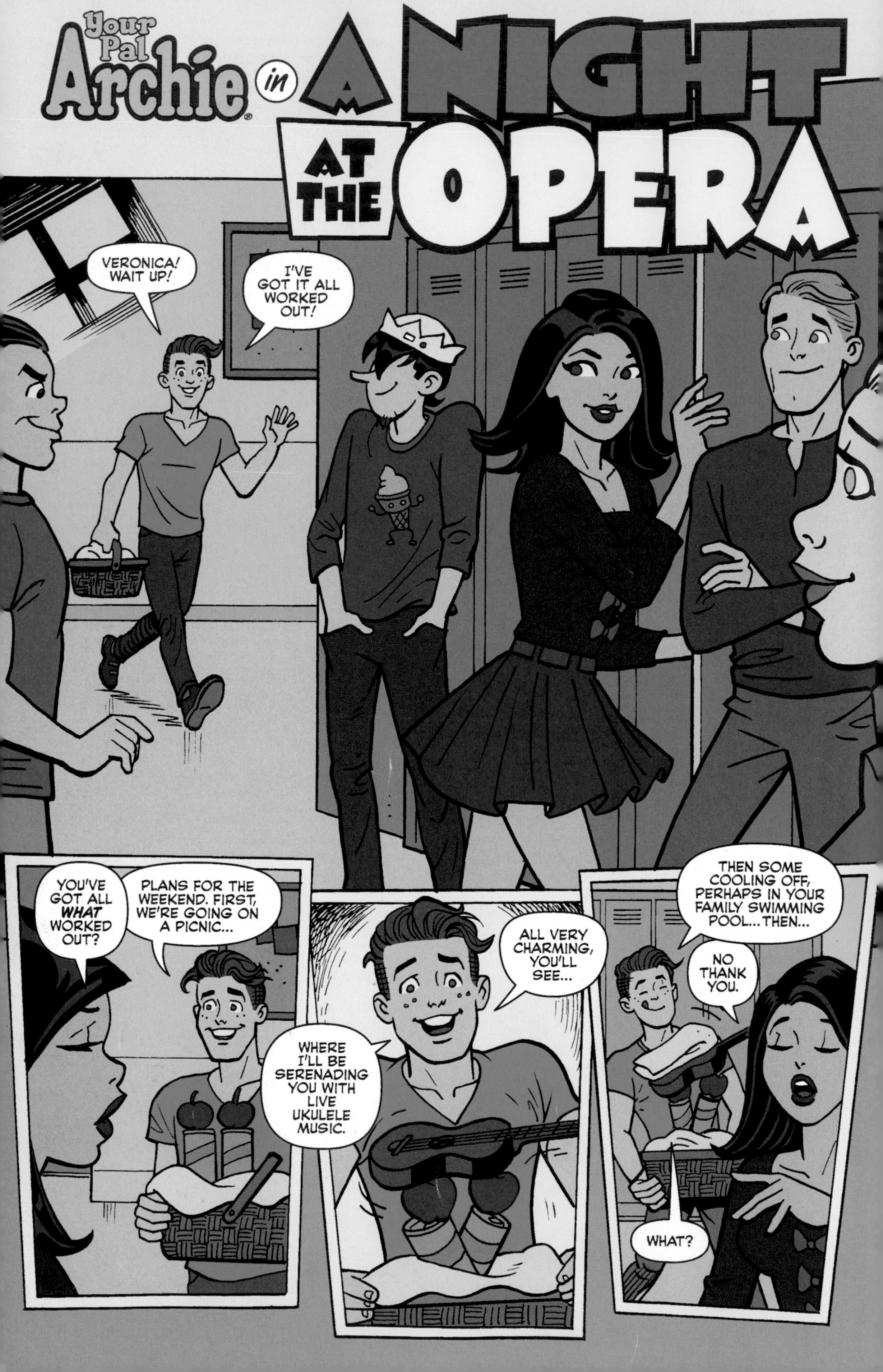
Your Pal Archie in
A NIGHT AT THE OPERA
VERONICA! WAIT UP!
I'VE GOT IT ALL WORKED OUT!
YOU'VE GOT ALL WHAT WORKED OUT?
PLANS FOR THE WEEKEND. FIRST, WE'RE GOING ON A PICNIC...
ALL VERY CHARMING, YOU'LL SEE...
WHERE I'LL BE SERENADING YOU WITH LIVE UKULELE MUSIC.
THEN SOME COOLING OFF, PERHAPS IN YOUR FAMILY SWIMMING POOL... THEN...
NO THANK YOU.
WHAT?

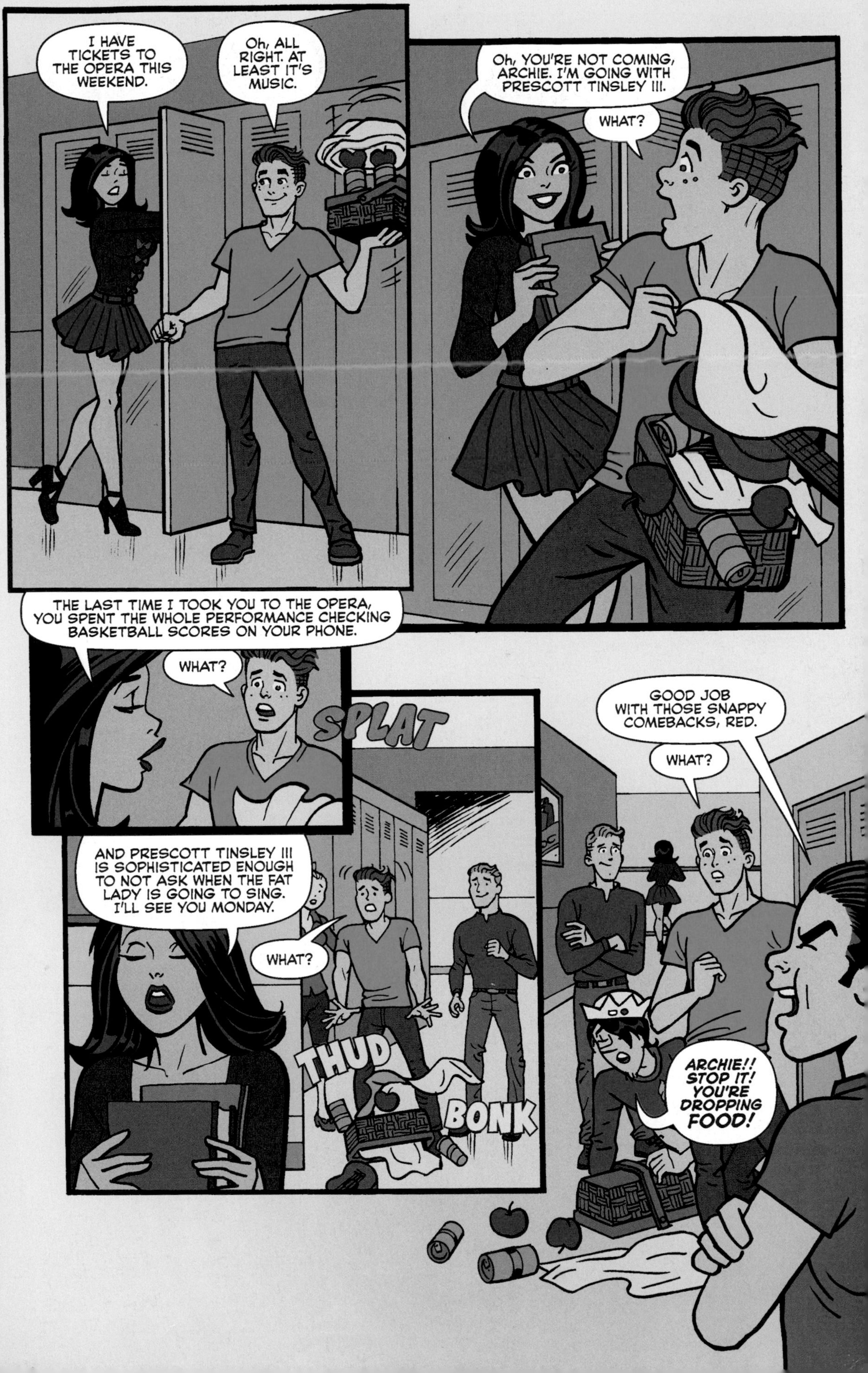
I HAVE TICKETS TO THE OPERA THIS WEEKEND.
Oh, ALL RIGHT. AT LEAST IT'S MUSIC.
Oh, YOU'RE NOT COMING, ARCHIE. I'M GOING WITH PRESCOTT TINSLEY III.
WHAT?
THE LAST TIME I TOOK YOU TO THE OPERA, YOU SPENT THE WHOLE PERFORMANCE CHECKING BASKETBALL SCORES ON YOUR PHONE.
WHAT?
SPLAT
AND PRESCOTT TINSLEY III IS SOPHISTICATED ENOUGH TO NOT ASK WHEN THE FAT LADY IS GOING TO SING. I'LL SEE YOU MONDAY.
WHAT?
THUD
BONK
GOOD JOB WITH THOSE SNAPPY COMEBACKS, RED.
WHAT?
ARCHIE!! STOP IT! YOU'RE DROPPING FOOD!

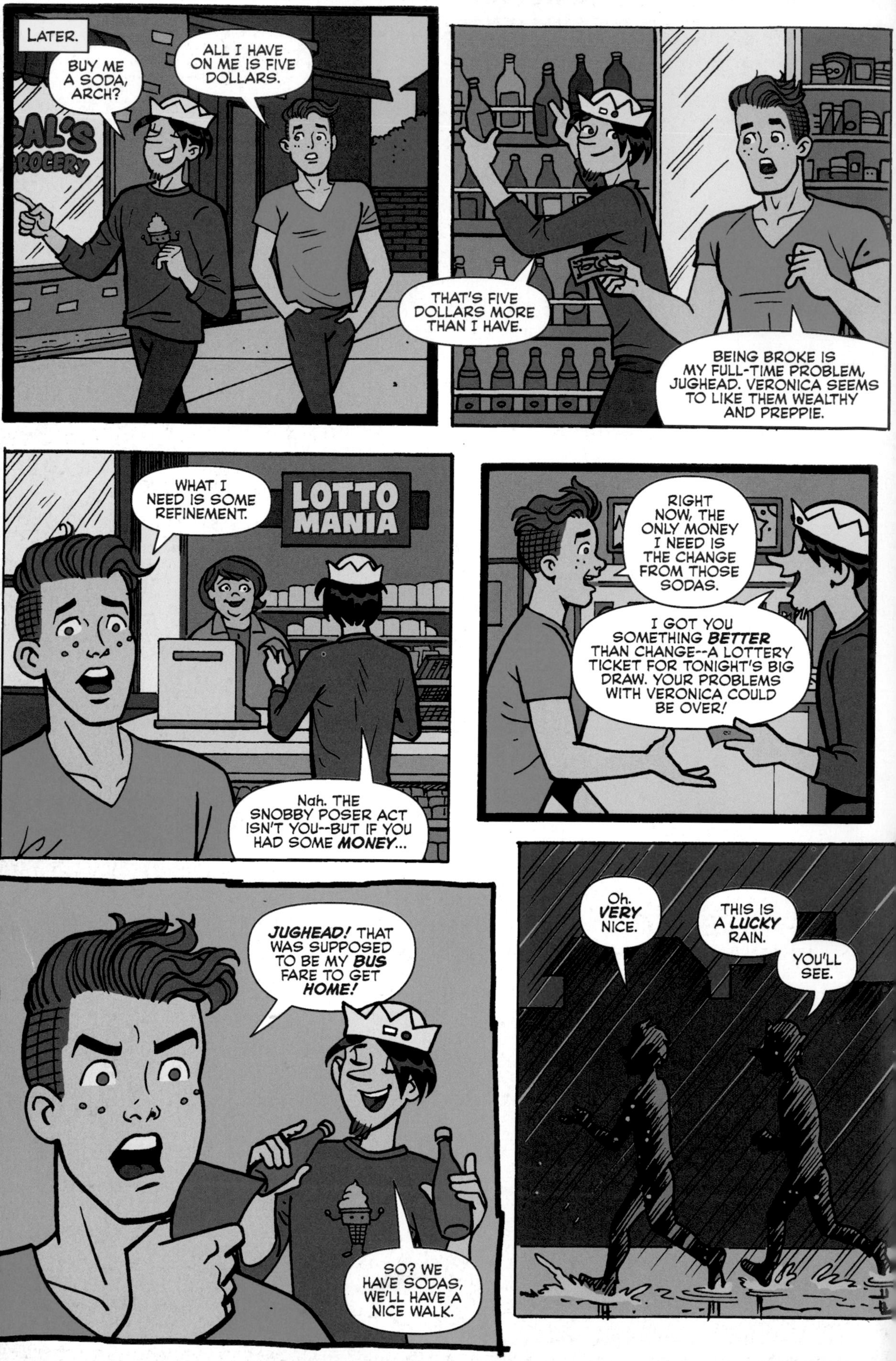
LATER.
BUY ME A SODA, ARCH?
ALL I HAVE ON ME IS FIVE DOLLARS.
THAT'S FIVE DOLLARS MORE THAN I HAVE.
BEING BROKE IS MY FULL-TIME PROBLEM, JUGHEAD. VERONICA SEEMS TO LIKE THEM WEALTHY AND PREPPIE.
SAL'S GROCERY
WHAT I NEED IS SOME REFINEMENT.
LOTTO MANIA
Nah. THE SNOBBY POSER ACT ISN'T YOU--BUT IF YOU HAD SOME MONEY...
RIGHT NOW, THE ONLY MONEY I NEED IS THE CHANGE FROM THOSE SODAS.
I GOT YOU SOMETHING BETTER THAN CHANGE--A LOTTERY TICKET FOR TONIGHT'S BIG DRAW. YOUR PROBLEMS WITH VERONICA COULD BE OVER!
JUGHEAD! THAT WAS SUPPOSED TO BE MY BUS FARE TO GET HOME!
SO? WE HAVE SODAS, WE'LL HAVE A NICE WALK.
Oh. VERY NICE.
THIS IS A LUCKY RAIN.
YOU'LL SEE.

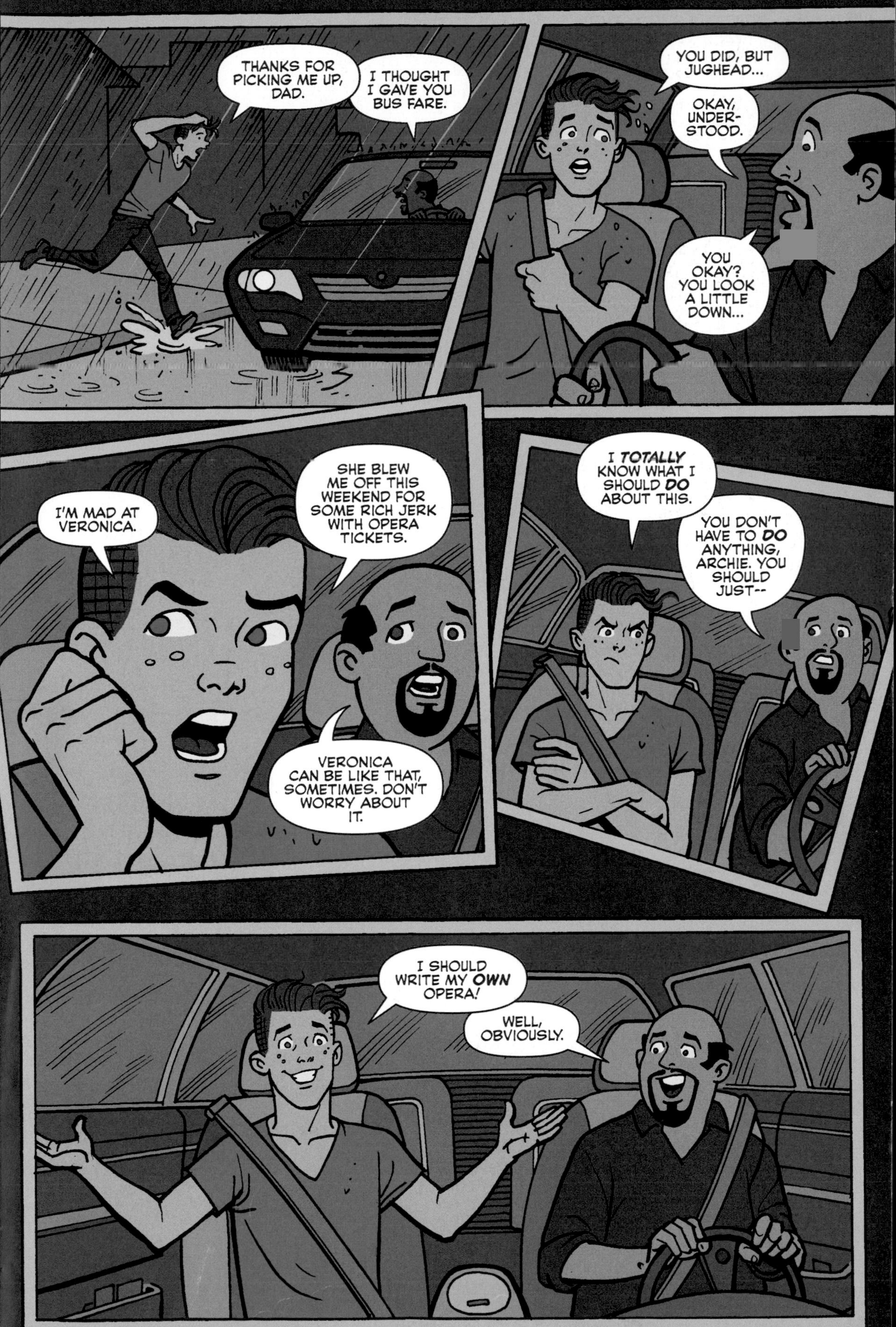
THANKS FOR PICKING ME UP, DAD.
I THOUGHT I GAVE YOU BUS FARE.
YOU DID, BUT JUGHEAD...
OKAY, UNDER-STOOD.
YOU OKAY? YOU LOOK A LITTLE DOWN...
I'M MAD AT VERONICA.
SHE BLEW ME OFF THIS WEEKEND FOR SOME RICH JERK WITH OPERA TICKETS.
VERONICA CAN BE LIKE THAT, SOMETIMES. DON'T WORRY ABOUT IT.
I TOTALLY KNOW WHAT I SHOULD DO ABOUT THIS.
YOU DON'T HAVE TO DO ANYTHING, ARCHIE. YOU SHOULD JUST--
I SHOULD WRITE MY OWN OPERA!
WELL, OBVIOUSLY.

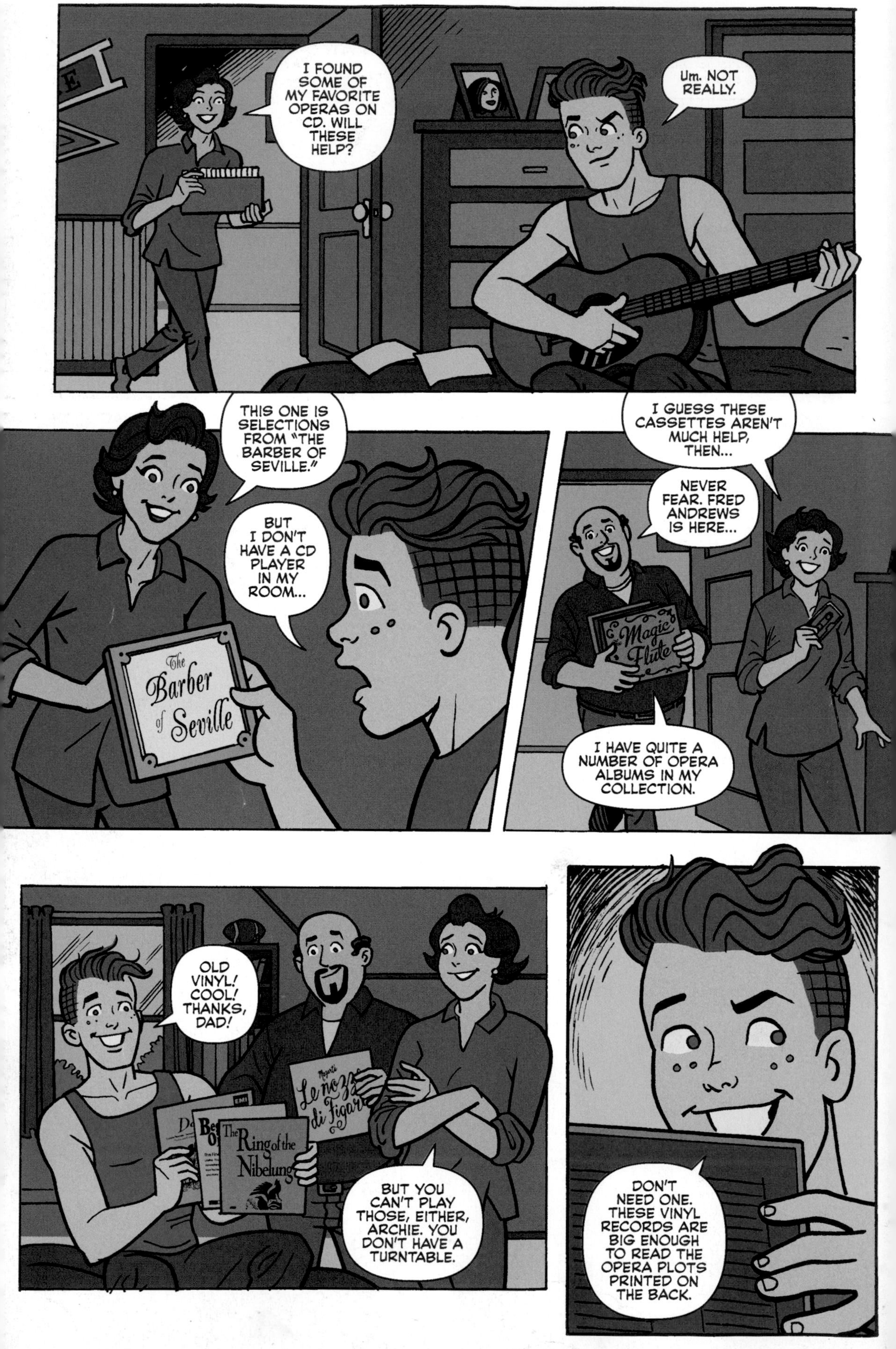
I FOUND SOME OF MY FAVORITE OPERAS ON CD. WILL THESE HELP?
Um. NOT REALLY.
THIS ONE IS SELECTIONS FROM "THE BARBER OF SEVILLE."
BUT I DON'T HAVE A CD PLAYER IN MY ROOM...
The Barber of Seville
I GUESS THESE CASSETTES AREN'T MUCH HELP, THEN...
NEVER FEAR. FRED ANDREWS IS HERE...
Magic Flute
I HAVE QUITE A NUMBER OF OPERA ALBUMS IN MY COLLECTION.
OLD VINYL! COOL! THANKS, DAD!
The Ring of the Nibelung
Le nozze di Figaro
BUT YOU CAN'T PLAY THOSE, EITHER, ARCHIE. YOU DON'T HAVE A TURNTABLE.
DON'T NEED ONE. THESE VINYL RECORDS ARE BIG ENOUGH TO READ THE OPERA PLOTS PRINTED ON THE BACK.

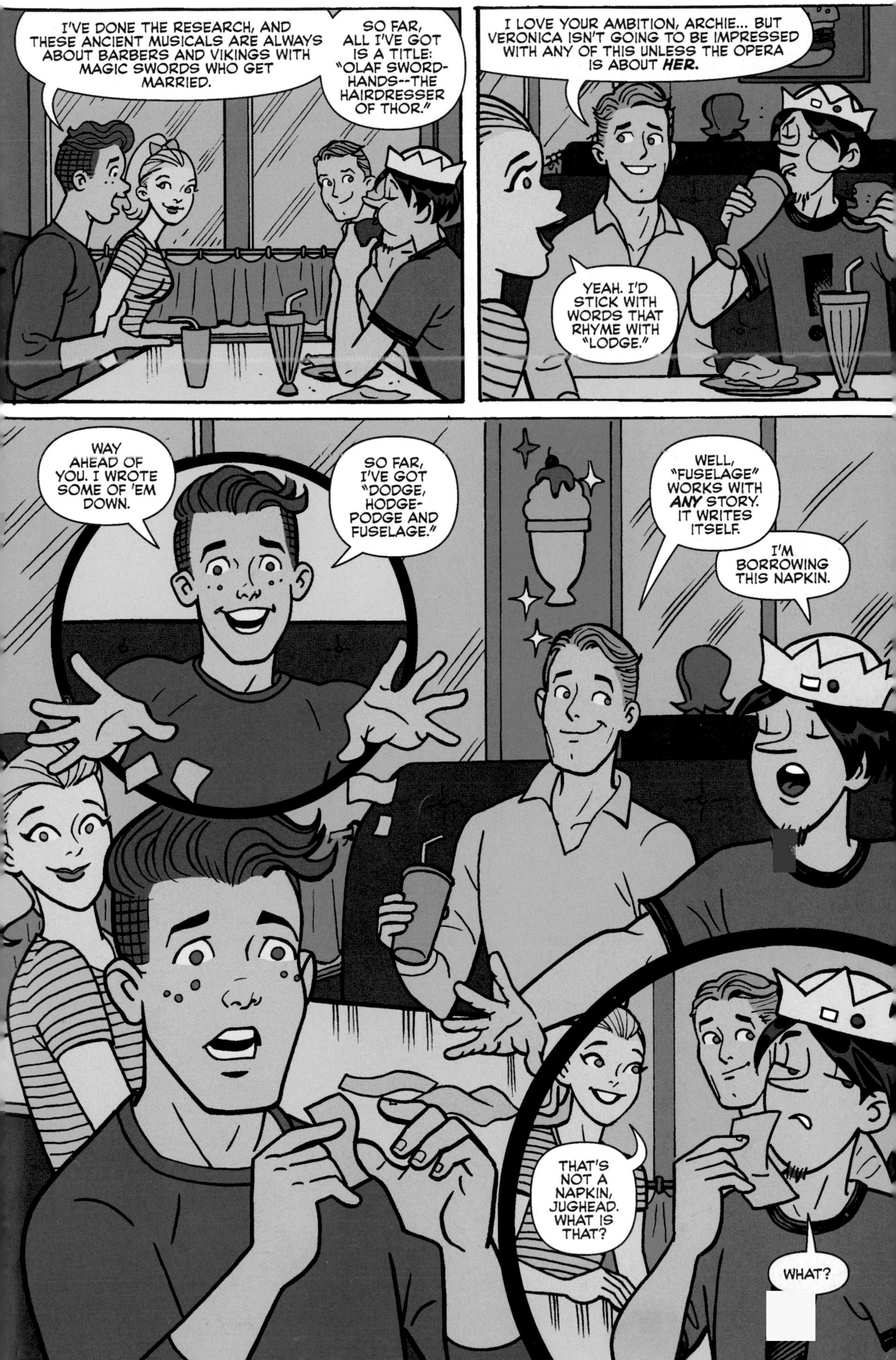
I'VE DONE THE RESEARCH, AND THESE ANCIENT MUSICALS ARE ALWAYS ABOUT BARBERS AND VIKINGS WITH MAGIC SWORDS WHO GET MARRIED.
SO FAR, ALL I'VE GOT IS A TITLE: "OLAF SWORD-HANDS--THE HAIRDRESSER OF THOR."
I LOVE YOUR AMBITION, ARCHIE... BUT VERONICA ISN'T GOING TO BE IMPRESSED WITH ANY OF THIS UNLESS THE OPERA IS ABOUT ***HER.***
YEAH. I'D STICK WITH WORDS THAT RHYME WITH "LODGE."
WAY AHEAD OF YOU. I WROTE SOME OF 'EM DOWN.
SO FAR, I'VE GOT "DODGE, HODGE-PODGE AND FUSELAGE."
WELL, "FUSELAGE" WORKS WITH ***ANY*** STORY. IT WRITES ITSELF.
I'M BORROWING THIS NAPKIN.
THAT'S NOT A NAPKIN, JUGHEAD. WHAT IS THAT?
WHAT?

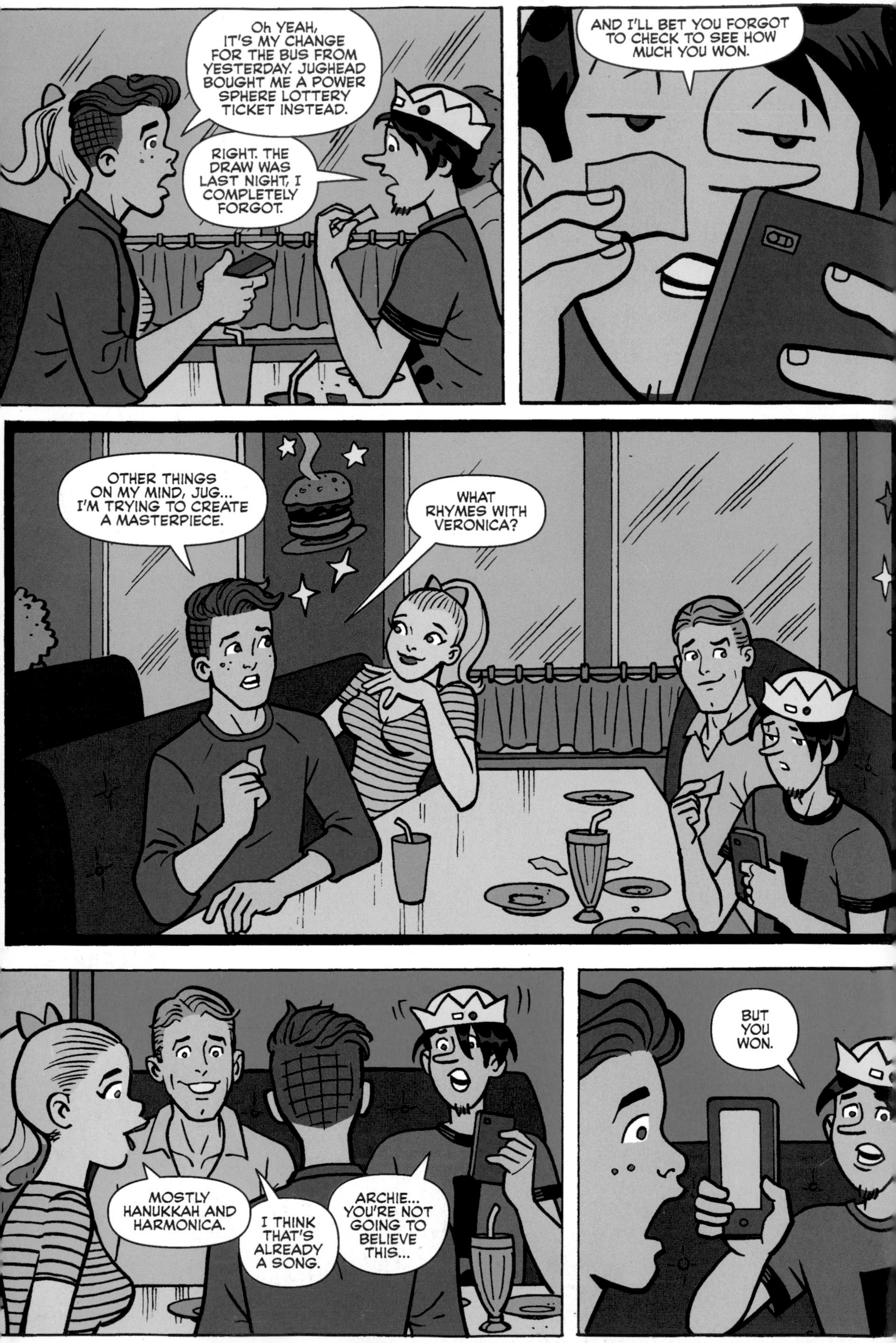
Oh YEAH, IT'S MY CHANGE FOR THE BUS FROM YESTERDAY. JUGHEAD BOUGHT ME A POWER SPHERE LOTTERY TICKET INSTEAD.
RIGHT. THE DRAW WAS LAST NIGHT, I COMPLETELY FORGOT.
AND I'LL BET YOU FORGOT TO CHECK TO SEE HOW MUCH YOU WON.
OTHER THINGS ON MY MIND, JUG... I'M TRYING TO CREATE A MASTERPIECE.
WHAT RHYMES WITH VERONICA?
MOSTLY HANUKKAH AND HARMONICA.
I THINK THAT'S ALREADY A SONG.
ARCHIE... YOU'RE NOT GOING TO BELIEVE THIS...
BUT YOU WON.

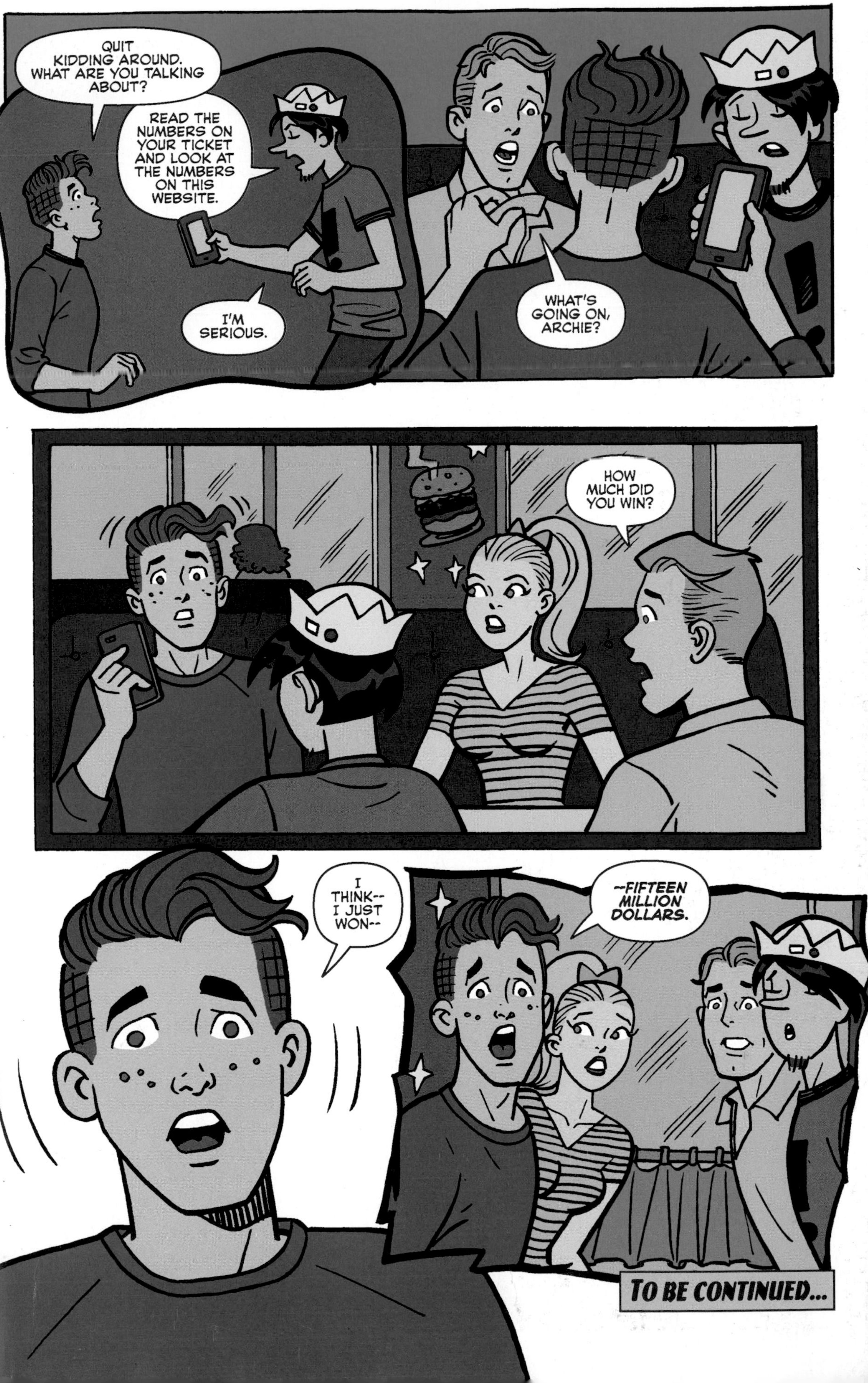
QUIT KIDDING AROUND. WHAT ARE YOU TALKING ABOUT?
READ THE NUMBERS ON YOUR TICKET AND LOOK AT THE NUMBERS ON THIS WEBSITE.
I'M SERIOUS.
WHAT'S GOING ON, ARCHIE?
HOW MUCH DID YOU WIN?
I THINK-- I JUST WON--
--FIFTEEN MILLION DOLLARS.
TO BE CONTINUED...

CHAPTER 2
PART 2

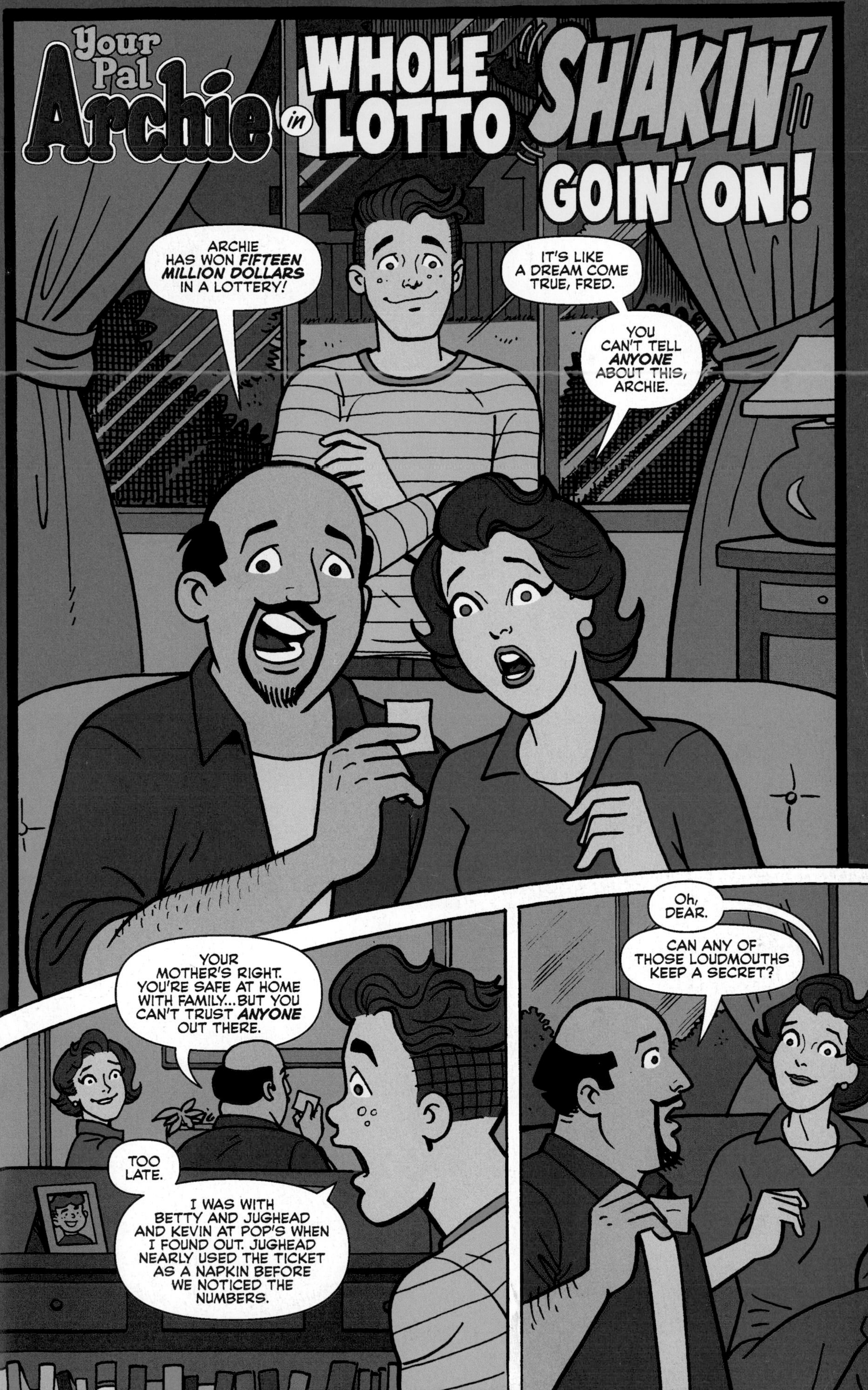
Your Pal Archie in
WHOLE LOTTO SHAKIN' GOIN' ON!
ARCHIE HAS WON FIFTEEN MILLION DOLLARS IN A LOTTERY!
IT'S LIKE A DREAM COME TRUE, FRED.
YOU CAN'T TELL ANYONE ABOUT THIS, ARCHIE.
YOUR MOTHER'S RIGHT. YOU'RE SAFE AT HOME WITH FAMILY...BUT YOU CAN'T TRUST ANYONE OUT THERE.
TOO LATE.
I WAS WITH BETTY AND JUGHEAD AND KEVIN AT POP'S WHEN I FOUND OUT. JUGHEAD NEARLY USED THE TICKET AS A NAPKIN BEFORE WE NOTICED THE NUMBERS.
Oh, DEAR.
CAN ANY OF THOSE LOUDMOUTHS KEEP A SECRET?

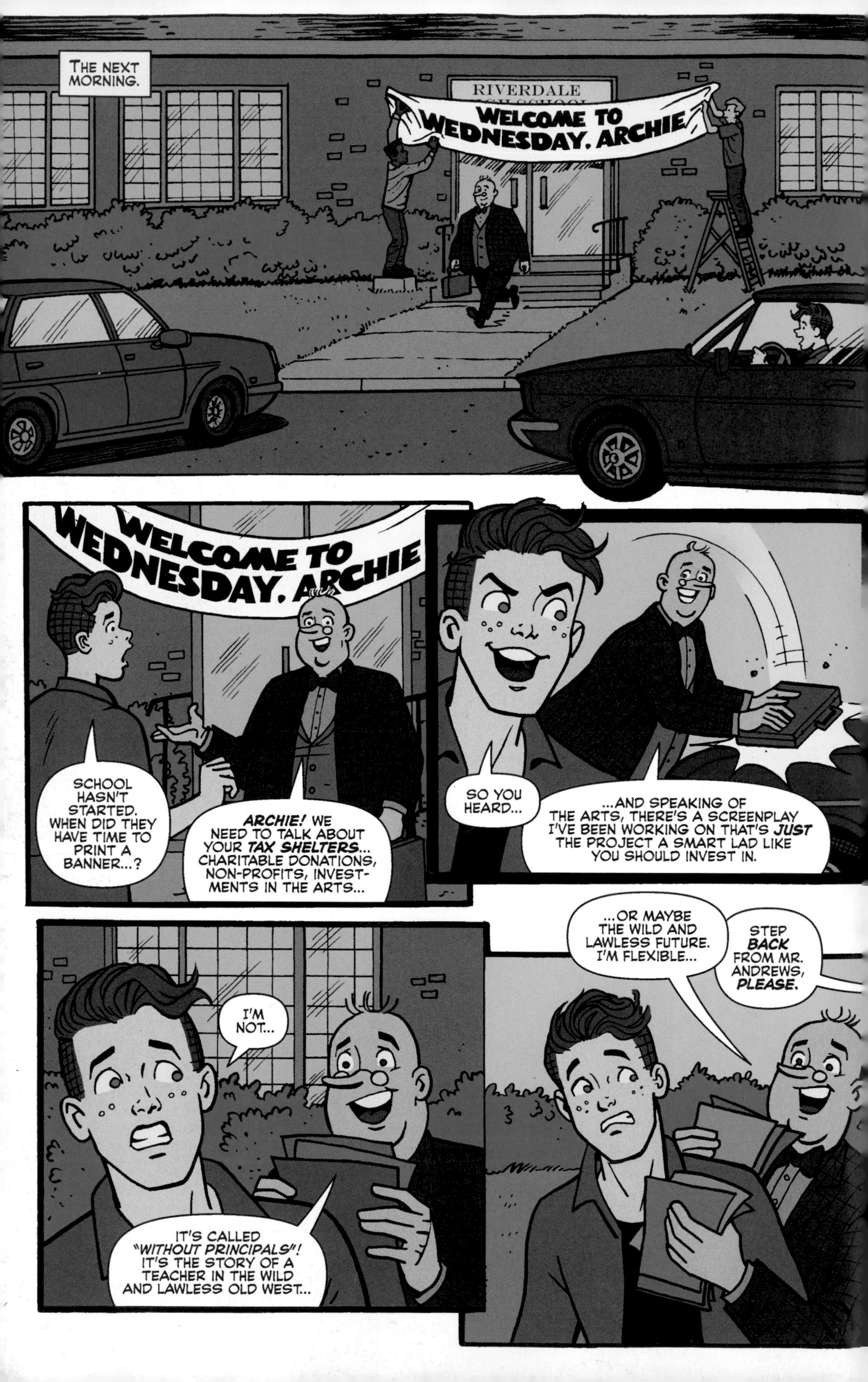

THE NEXT MORNING.
RIVERDALE
WELCOME TO WEDNESDAY, ARCHIE
WELCOME TO WEDNESDAY, ARCHIE
SCHOOL HASN'T STARTED. WHEN DID THEY HAVE TIME TO PRINT A BANNER...?
ARCHIE! WE NEED TO TALK ABOUT YOUR *TAX SHELTERS*... CHARITABLE DONATIONS, NON-PROFITS, INVESTMENTS IN THE ARTS...
SO YOU HEARD...
...AND SPEAKING OF THE ARTS, THERE'S A SCREENPLAY I'VE BEEN WORKING ON THAT'S *JUST* THE PROJECT A SMART LAD LIKE YOU SHOULD INVEST IN.
I'M NOT...
IT'S CALLED *"WITHOUT PRINCIPALS"*! IT'S THE STORY OF A TEACHER IN THE WILD AND LAWLESS OLD WEST...
...OR MAYBE THE WILD AND LAWLESS FUTURE. I'M FLEXIBLE...
STEP *BACK* FROM MR. ANDREWS, *PLEASE.*

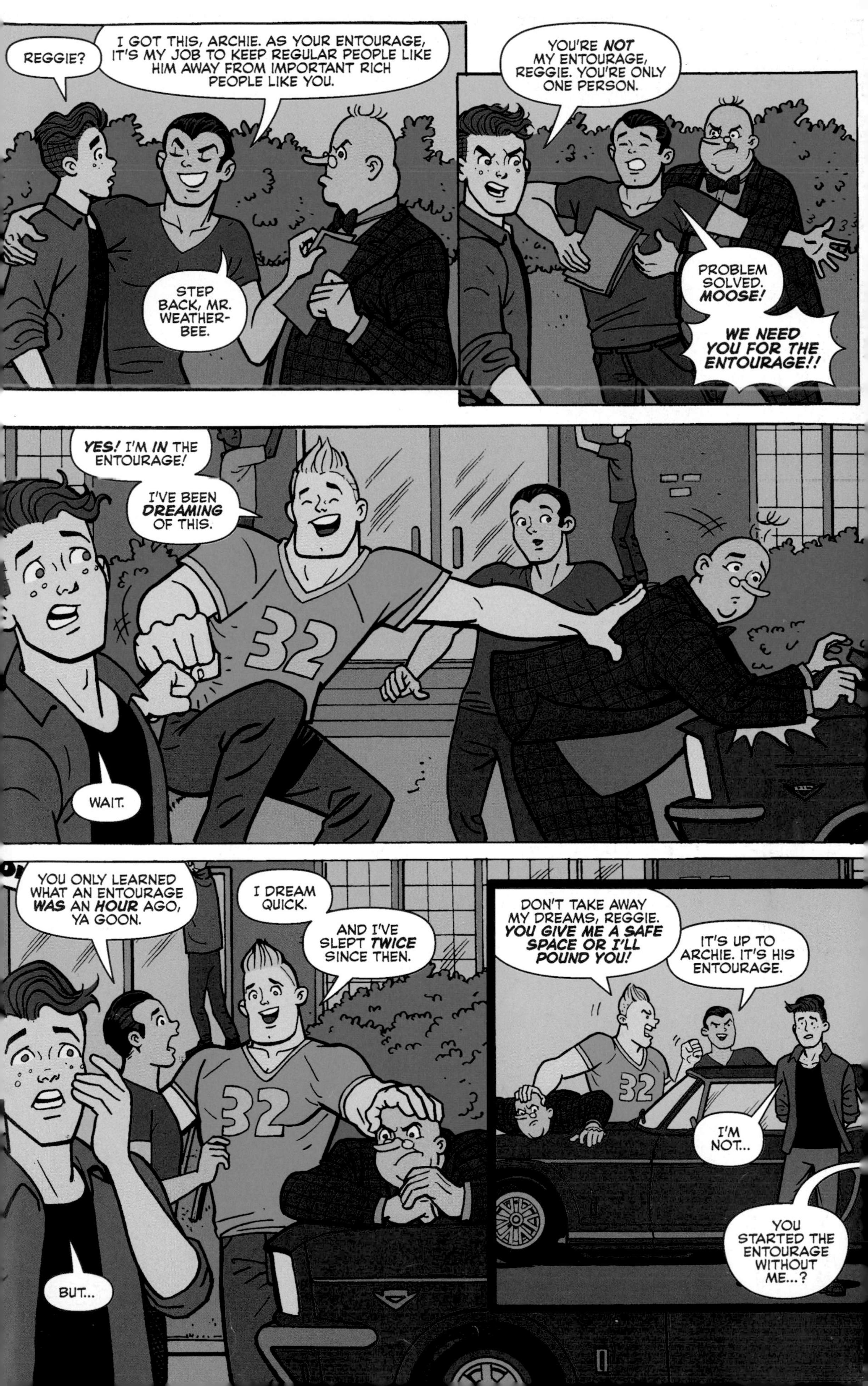
REGGIE?
I GOT THIS, ARCHIE. AS YOUR ENTOURAGE, IT'S MY JOB TO KEEP REGULAR PEOPLE LIKE HIM AWAY FROM IMPORTANT RICH PEOPLE LIKE YOU.
STEP BACK, MR. WEATHERBEE.
YOU'RE NOT MY ENTOURAGE, REGGIE. YOU'RE ONLY ONE PERSON.
PROBLEM SOLVED. MOOSE!
WE NEED YOU FOR THE ENTOURAGE!!
YES! I'M IN THE ENTOURAGE!
I'VE BEEN DREAMING OF THIS.
WAIT.
YOU ONLY LEARNED WHAT AN ENTOURAGE WAS AN HOUR AGO, YA GOON.
I DREAM QUICK.
AND I'VE SLEPT TWICE SINCE THEN.
BUT...
DON'T TAKE AWAY MY DREAMS, REGGIE. YOU GIVE ME A SAFE SPACE OR I'LL POUND YOU!
IT'S UP TO ARCHIE. IT'S HIS ENTOURAGE.
I'M NOT...
YOU STARTED THE ENTOURAGE WITHOUT ME...?

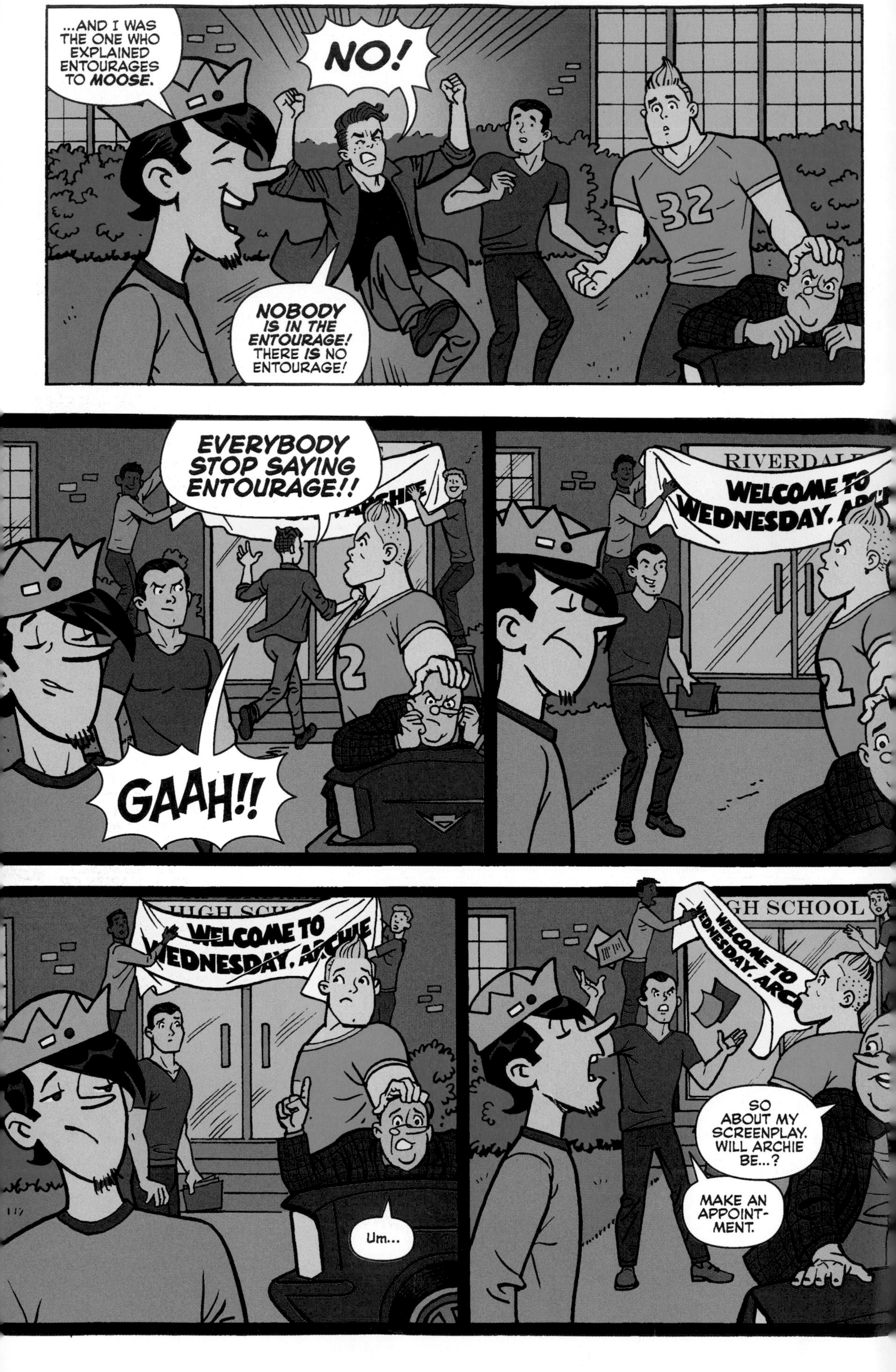
...AND I WAS THE ONE WHO EXPLAINED ENTOURAGES TO MOOSE.
NO!
NOBODY IS IN THE ENTOURAGE! THERE IS NO ENTOURAGE!
EVERYBODY STOP SAYING ENTOURAGE!!
GAAH!!
WELCOME TO
WELCOME TO
Um...
WELCOME TO
SO ABOUT MY SCREENPLAY. WILL ARCHIE BE...?
MAKE AN APPOINT-MENT.

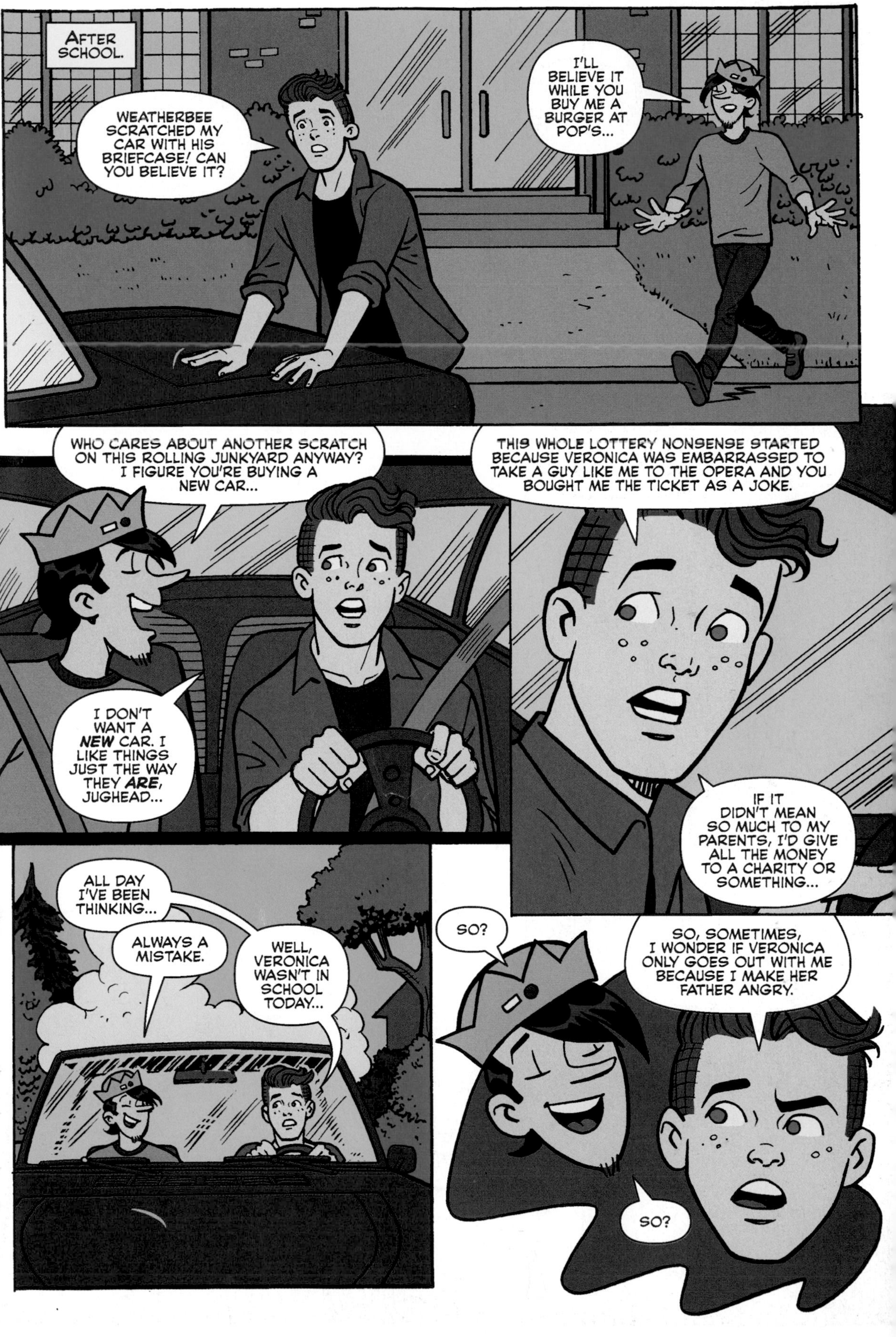
AFTER SCHOOL.
WEATHERBEE SCRATCHED MY CAR WITH HIS BRIEFCASE! CAN YOU BELIEVE IT?
I'LL BELIEVE IT WHILE YOU BUY ME A BURGER AT POP'S...
WHO CARES ABOUT ANOTHER SCRATCH ON THIS ROLLING JUNKYARD ANYWAY? I FIGURE YOU'RE BUYING A NEW CAR...
I DON'T WANT A *NEW* CAR. I LIKE THINGS JUST THE WAY THEY *ARE*, JUGHEAD...
THIS WHOLE LOTTERY NONSENSE STARTED BECAUSE VERONICA WAS EMBARRASSED TO TAKE A GUY LIKE ME TO THE OPERA AND YOU BOUGHT ME THE TICKET AS A JOKE.
IF IT DIDN'T MEAN SO MUCH TO MY PARENTS, I'D GIVE ALL THE MONEY TO A CHARITY OR SOMETHING...
ALL DAY I'VE BEEN THINKING...
ALWAYS A MISTAKE.
WELL, VERONICA WASN'T IN SCHOOL TODAY...
SO?
SO, SOMETIMES, I WONDER IF VERONICA ONLY GOES OUT WITH ME BECAUSE I MAKE HER FATHER ANGRY.
SO?

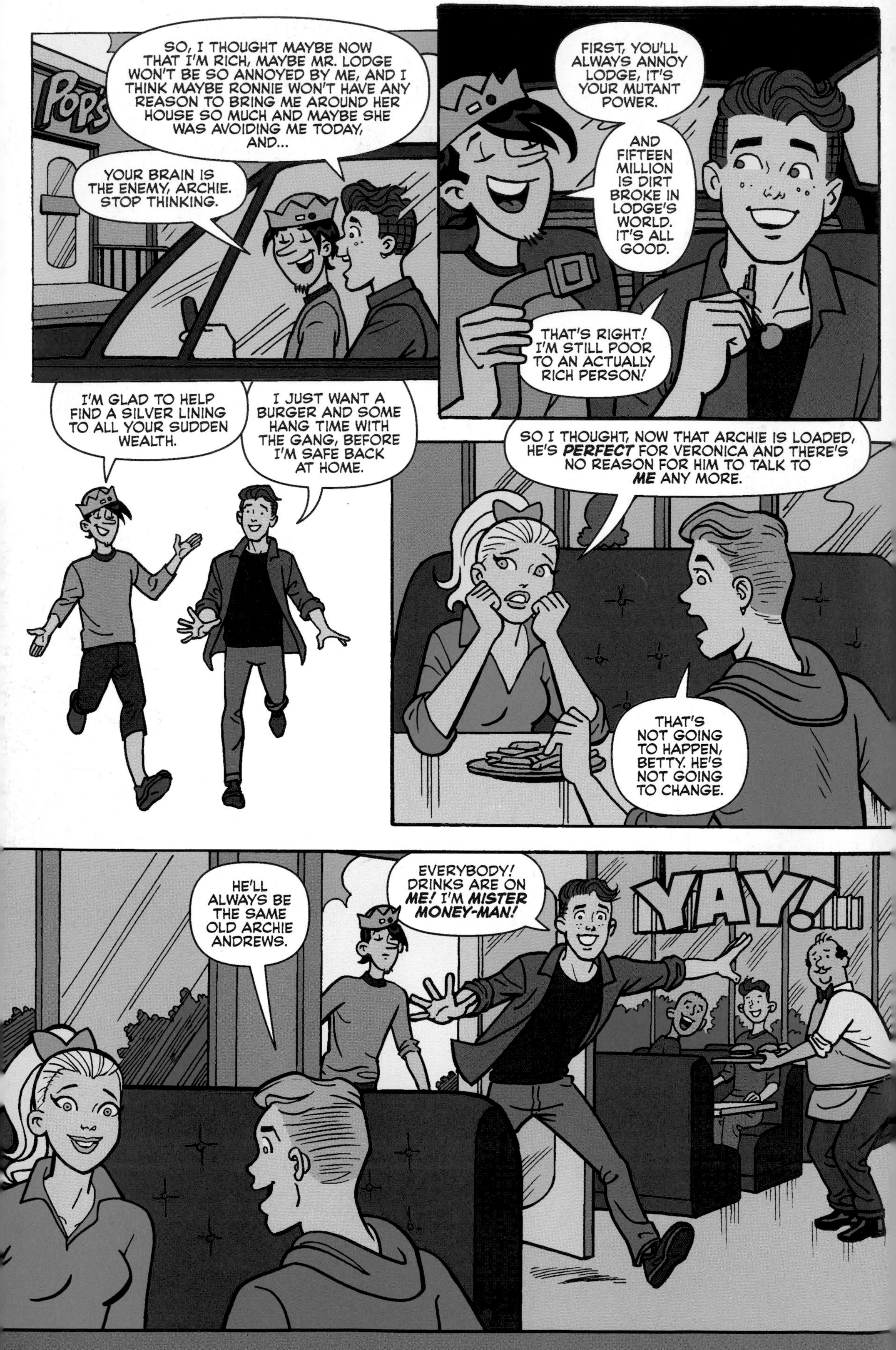

SO, I THOUGHT MAYBE NOW THAT I'M RICH, MAYBE MR. LODGE WON'T BE SO ANNOYED BY ME, AND I THINK MAYBE RONNIE WON'T HAVE ANY REASON TO BRING ME AROUND HER HOUSE SO MUCH AND MAYBE SHE WAS AVOIDING ME TODAY, AND...
YOUR BRAIN IS THE ENEMY, ARCHIE. STOP THINKING.
POP'S
FIRST, YOU'LL ALWAYS ANNOY LODGE, IT'S YOUR MUTANT POWER.
AND FIFTEEN MILLION IS DIRT BROKE IN LODGE'S WORLD. IT'S ALL GOOD.
THAT'S RIGHT! I'M STILL POOR TO AN ACTUALLY RICH PERSON!
I'M GLAD TO HELP FIND A SILVER LINING TO ALL YOUR SUDDEN WEALTH.
I JUST WANT A BURGER AND SOME HANG TIME WITH THE GANG, BEFORE I'M SAFE BACK AT HOME.
SO I THOUGHT, NOW THAT ARCHIE IS LOADED, HE'S ***PERFECT*** FOR VERONICA AND THERE'S NO REASON FOR HIM TO TALK TO ***ME*** ANY MORE.
THAT'S NOT GOING TO HAPPEN, BETTY. HE'S NOT GOING TO CHANGE.
HE'LL ALWAYS BE THE SAME OLD ARCHIE ANDREWS.
EVERYBODY! DRINKS ARE ON ***ME!*** I'M ***MISTER MONEY-MAN!***
YAY!

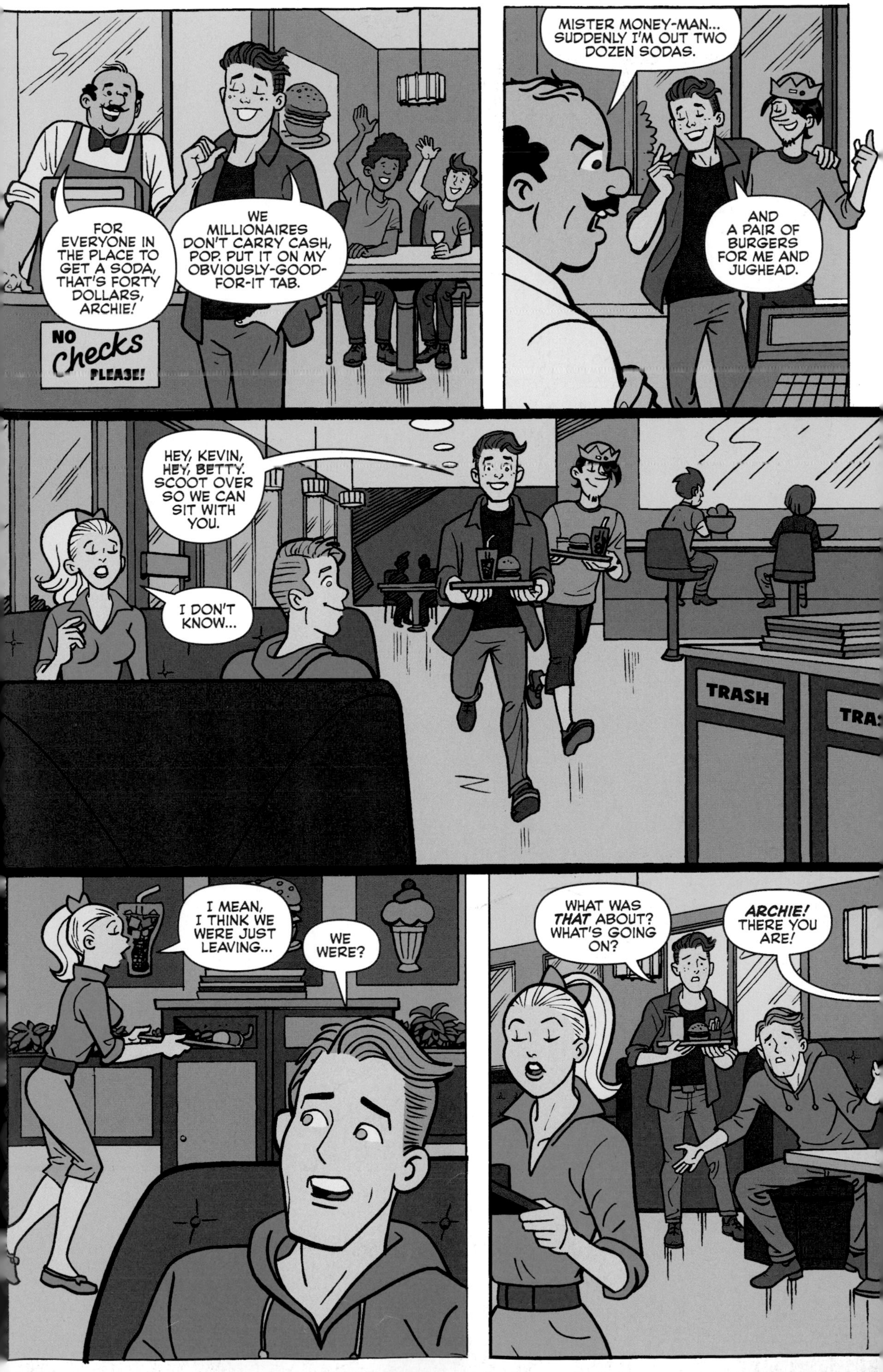
FOR EVERYONE IN THE PLACE TO GET A SODA, THAT'S FORTY DOLLARS, ARCHIE!
WE MILLIONAIRES DON'T CARRY CASH, POP. PUT IT ON MY OBVIOUSLY-GOOD-FOR-IT TAB.
NO Checks PLEASE!
MISTER MONEY-MAN... SUDDENLY I'M OUT TWO DOZEN SODAS.
AND A PAIR OF BURGERS FOR ME AND JUGHEAD.
HEY, KEVIN, HEY, BETTY. SCOOT OVER SO WE CAN SIT WITH YOU.
I DON'T KNOW...
TRASH
I MEAN, I THINK WE WERE JUST LEAVING...
WE WERE?
WHAT WAS THAT ABOUT? WHAT'S GOING ON?
ARCHIE! THERE YOU ARE!

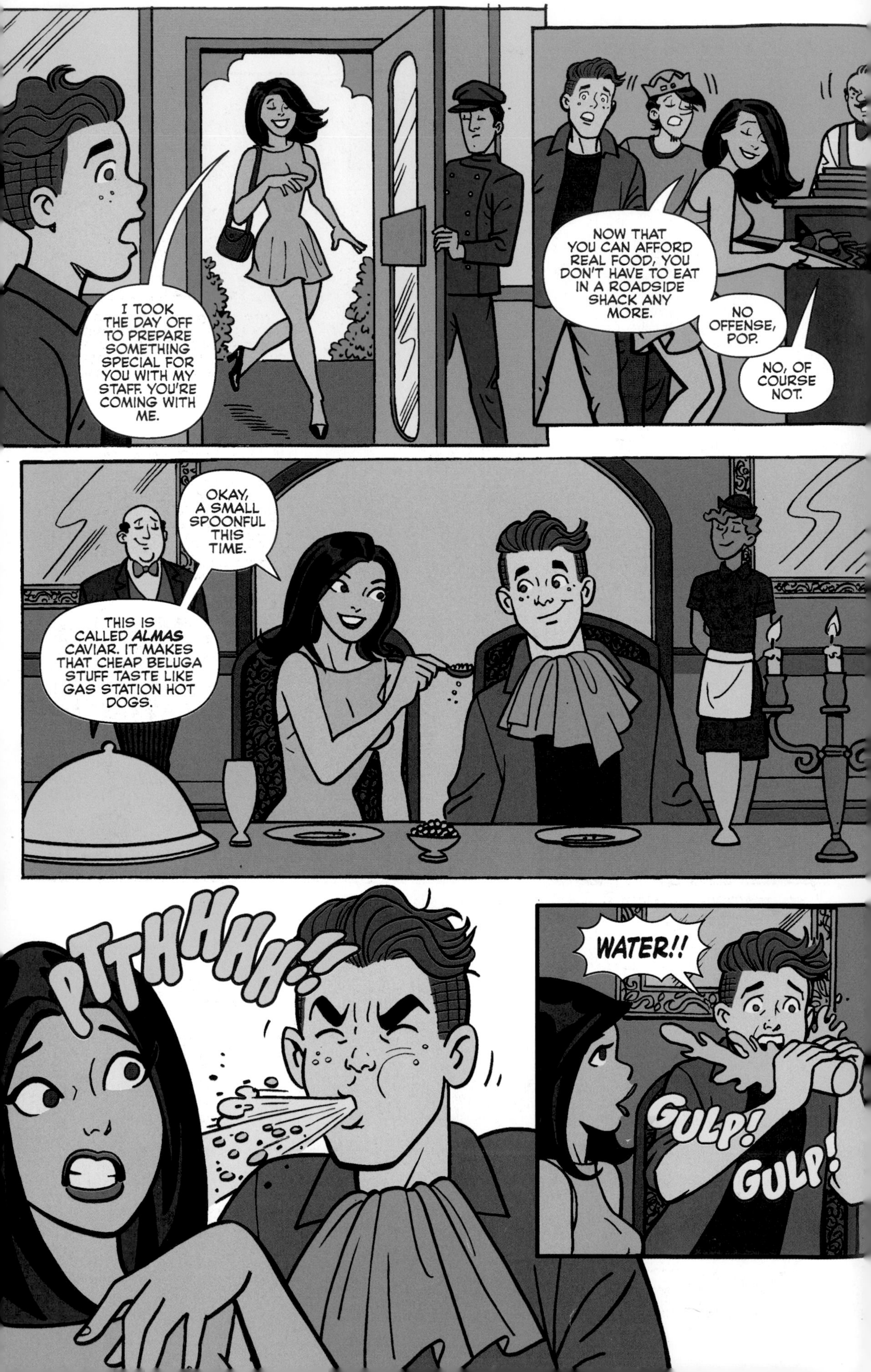
I TOOK THE DAY OFF TO PREPARE SOMETHING SPECIAL FOR YOU WITH MY STAFF. YOU'RE COMING WITH ME.
NOW THAT YOU CAN AFFORD REAL FOOD, YOU DON'T HAVE TO EAT IN A ROADSIDE SHACK ANY MORE.
NO OFFENSE, POP.
NO, OF COURSE NOT.
THIS IS CALLED ALMAS CAVIAR. IT MAKES THAT CHEAP BELUGA STUFF TASTE LIKE GAS STATION HOT DOGS.
OKAY, A SMALL SPOONFUL THIS TIME.
PTTHHHH!!
WATER!!
GULP!
GULP!

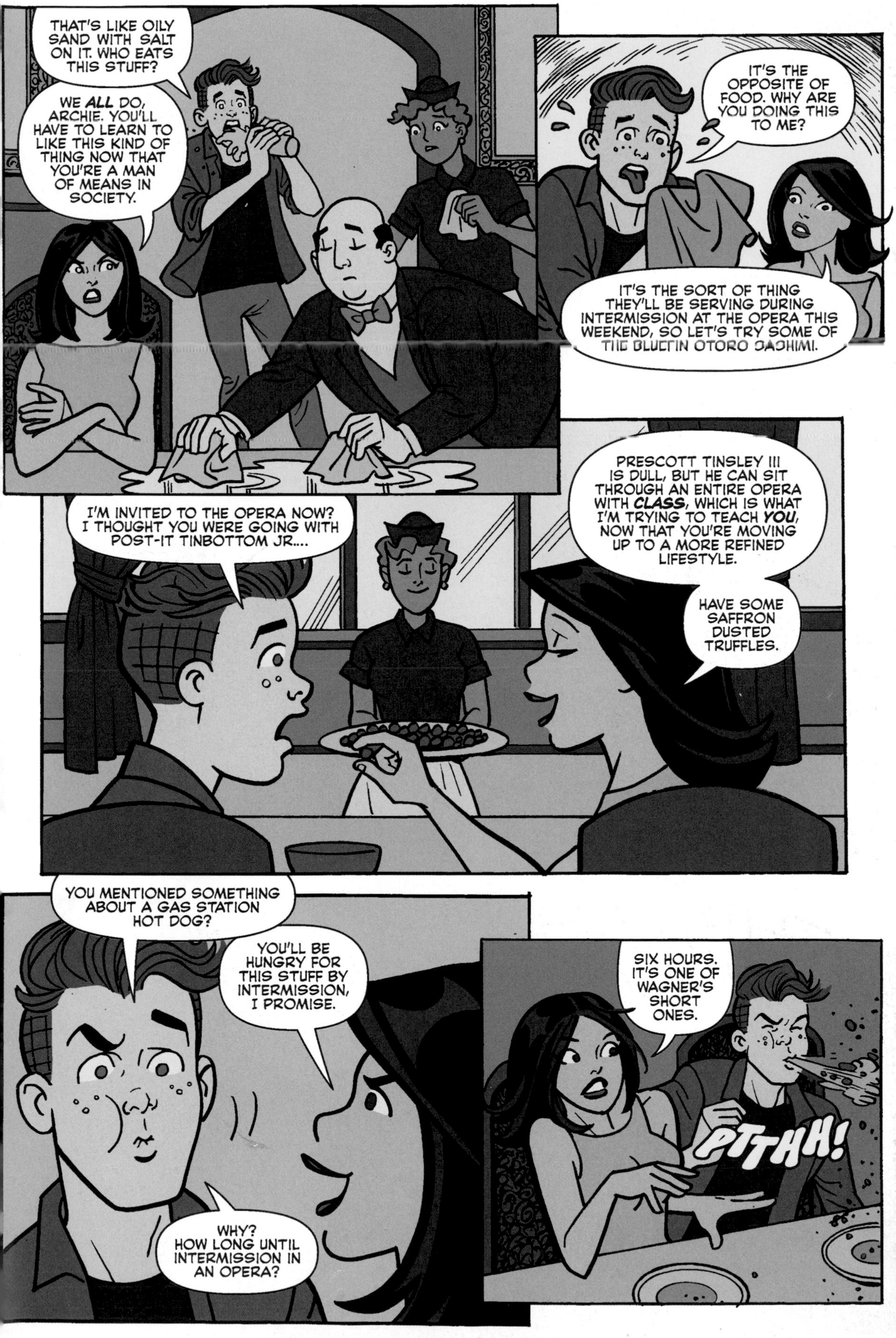
THAT'S LIKE OILY SAND WITH SALT ON IT. WHO EATS THIS STUFF?
WE ALL DO, ARCHIE. YOU'LL HAVE TO LEARN TO LIKE THIS KIND OF THING NOW THAT YOU'RE A MAN OF MEANS IN SOCIETY.
IT'S THE OPPOSITE OF FOOD. WHY ARE YOU DOING THIS TO ME?
IT'S THE SORT OF THING THEY'LL BE SERVING DURING INTERMISSION AT THE OPERA THIS WEEKEND, SO LET'S TRY SOME OF THE BLUEFIN OTORO SASHIMI.
I'M INVITED TO THE OPERA NOW? I THOUGHT YOU WERE GOING WITH POST-IT TINBOTTOM JR....
PRESCOTT TINSLEY III IS DULL, BUT HE CAN SIT THROUGH AN ENTIRE OPERA WITH CLASS, WHICH IS WHAT I'M TRYING TO TEACH YOU, NOW THAT YOU'RE MOVING UP TO A MORE REFINED LIFESTYLE.
HAVE SOME SAFFRON DUSTED TRUFFLES.
YOU MENTIONED SOMETHING ABOUT A GAS STATION HOT DOG?
YOU'LL BE HUNGRY FOR THIS STUFF BY INTERMISSION, I PROMISE.
WHY? HOW LONG UNTIL INTERMISSION IN AN OPERA?
SIX HOURS. IT'S ONE OF WAGNER'S SHORT ONES.
PTTHH!

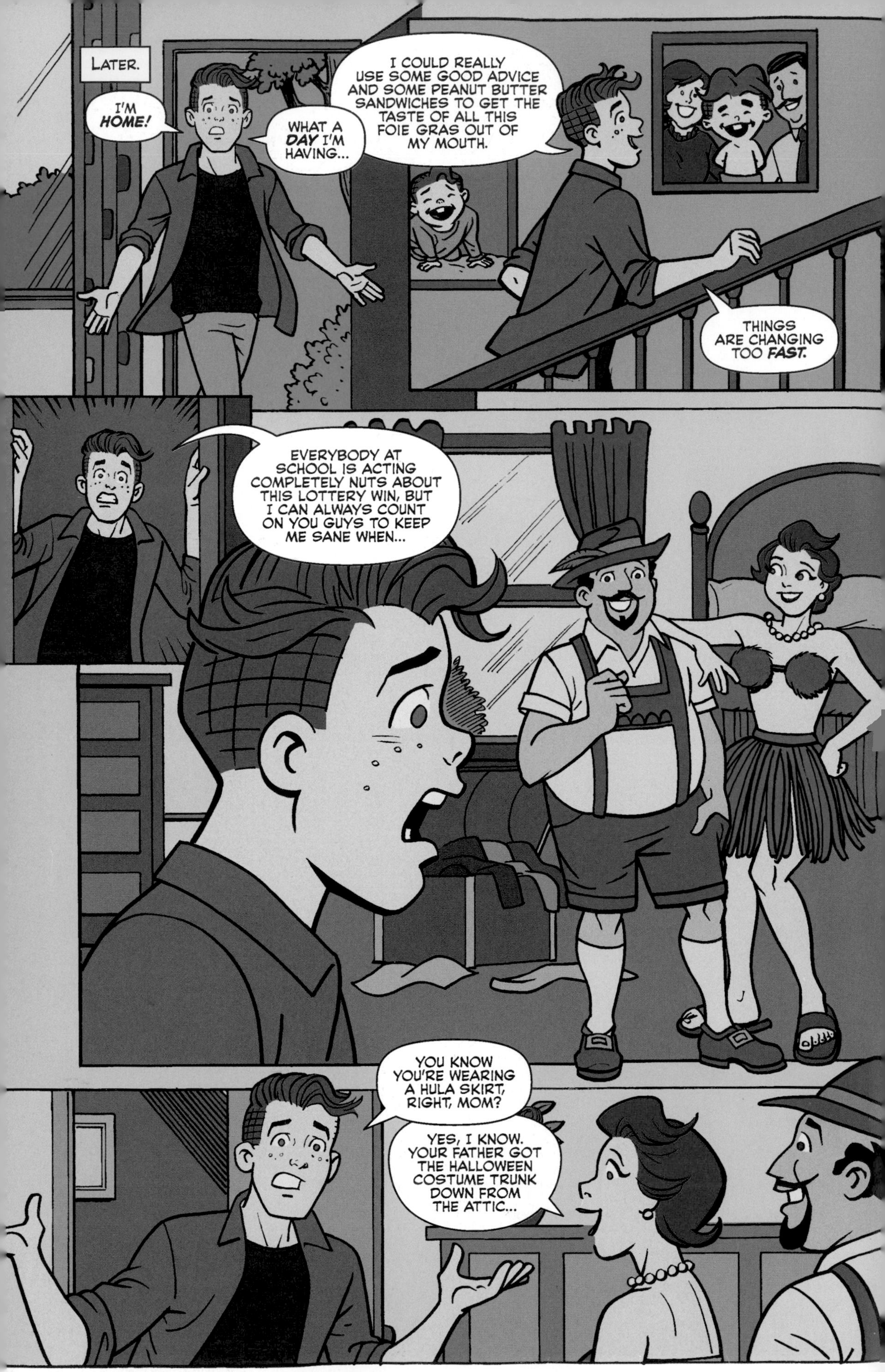
LATER.
I'M HOME!
WHAT A DAY I'M HAVING...
I COULD REALLY USE SOME GOOD ADVICE AND SOME PEANUT BUTTER SANDWICHES TO GET THE TASTE OF ALL THIS FOIE GRAS OUT OF MY MOUTH.
THINGS ARE CHANGING TOO FAST.
EVERYBODY AT SCHOOL IS ACTING COMPLETELY NUTS ABOUT THIS LOTTERY WIN, BUT I CAN ALWAYS COUNT ON YOU GUYS TO KEEP ME SANE WHEN...
YOU KNOW YOU'RE WEARING A HULA SKIRT, RIGHT, MOM?
YES, I KNOW. YOUR FATHER GOT THE HALLOWEEN COSTUME TRUNK DOWN FROM THE ATTIC...

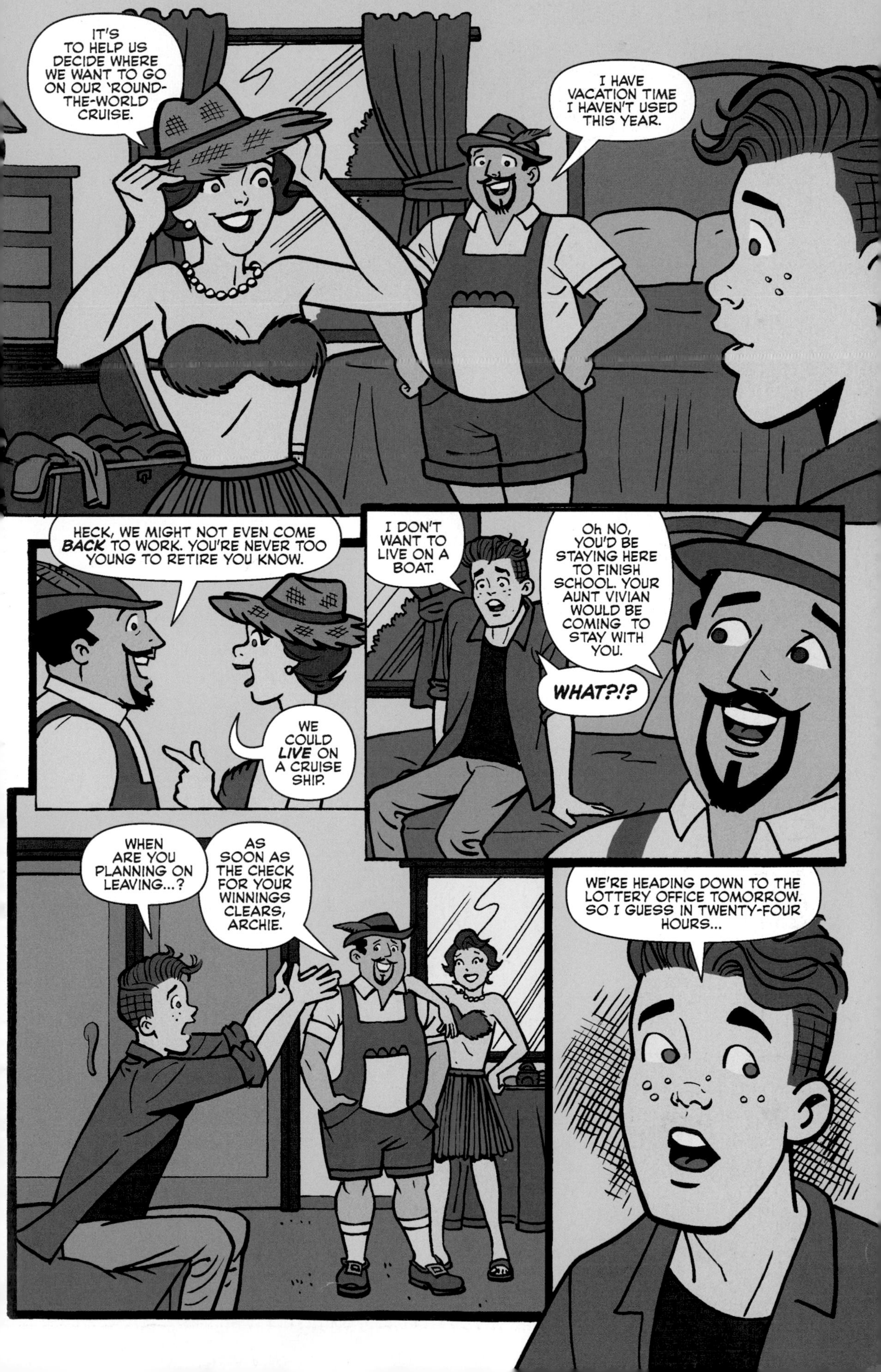
IT'S TO HELP US DECIDE WHERE WE WANT TO GO ON OUR 'ROUND-THE-WORLD CRUISE.
I HAVE VACATION TIME I HAVEN'T USED THIS YEAR.
HECK, WE MIGHT NOT EVEN COME BACK TO WORK. YOU'RE NEVER TOO YOUNG TO RETIRE YOU KNOW.
WE COULD LIVE ON A CRUISE SHIP.
I DON'T WANT TO LIVE ON A BOAT.
Oh NO, YOU'D BE STAYING HERE TO FINISH SCHOOL. YOUR AUNT VIVIAN WOULD BE COMING TO STAY WITH YOU.
WHAT?!?
WHEN ARE YOU PLANNING ON LEAVING...?
AS SOON AS THE CHECK FOR YOUR WINNINGS CLEARS, ARCHIE.
WE'RE HEADING DOWN TO THE LOTTERY OFFICE TOMORROW. SO I GUESS IN TWENTY-FOUR HOURS...

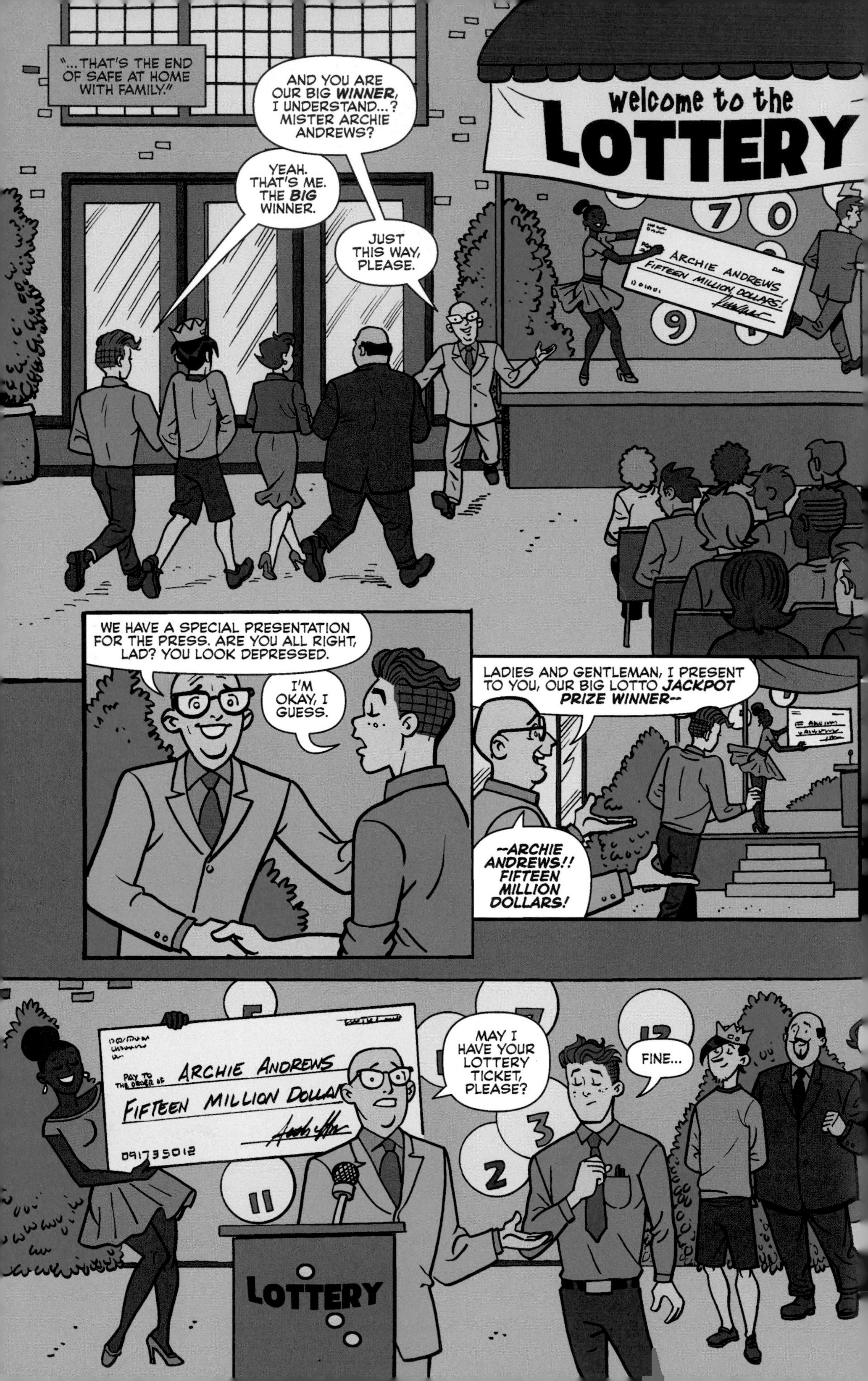

"...THAT'S THE END OF SAFE AT HOME WITH FAMILY."
AND YOU ARE OUR BIG WINNER, I UNDERSTAND...? MISTER ARCHIE ANDREWS?
YEAH. THAT'S ME. THE BIG WINNER.
JUST THIS WAY, PLEASE.
welcome to the LOTTERY
ARCHIE ANDREWS
FIFTEEN MILLION DOLLARS!
WE HAVE A SPECIAL PRESENTATION FOR THE PRESS. ARE YOU ALL RIGHT, LAD? YOU LOOK DEPRESSED.
I'M OKAY, I GUESS.
LADIES AND GENTLEMAN, I PRESENT TO YOU, OUR BIG LOTTO JACKPOT PRIZE WINNER--
--ARCHIE ANDREWS!! FIFTEEN MILLION DOLLARS!
PAY TO THE ORDER OF ARCHIE ANDREWS
FIFTEEN MILLION DOLLA
091735012
MAY I HAVE YOUR LOTTERY TICKET, PLEASE?
FINE...
LOTTERY

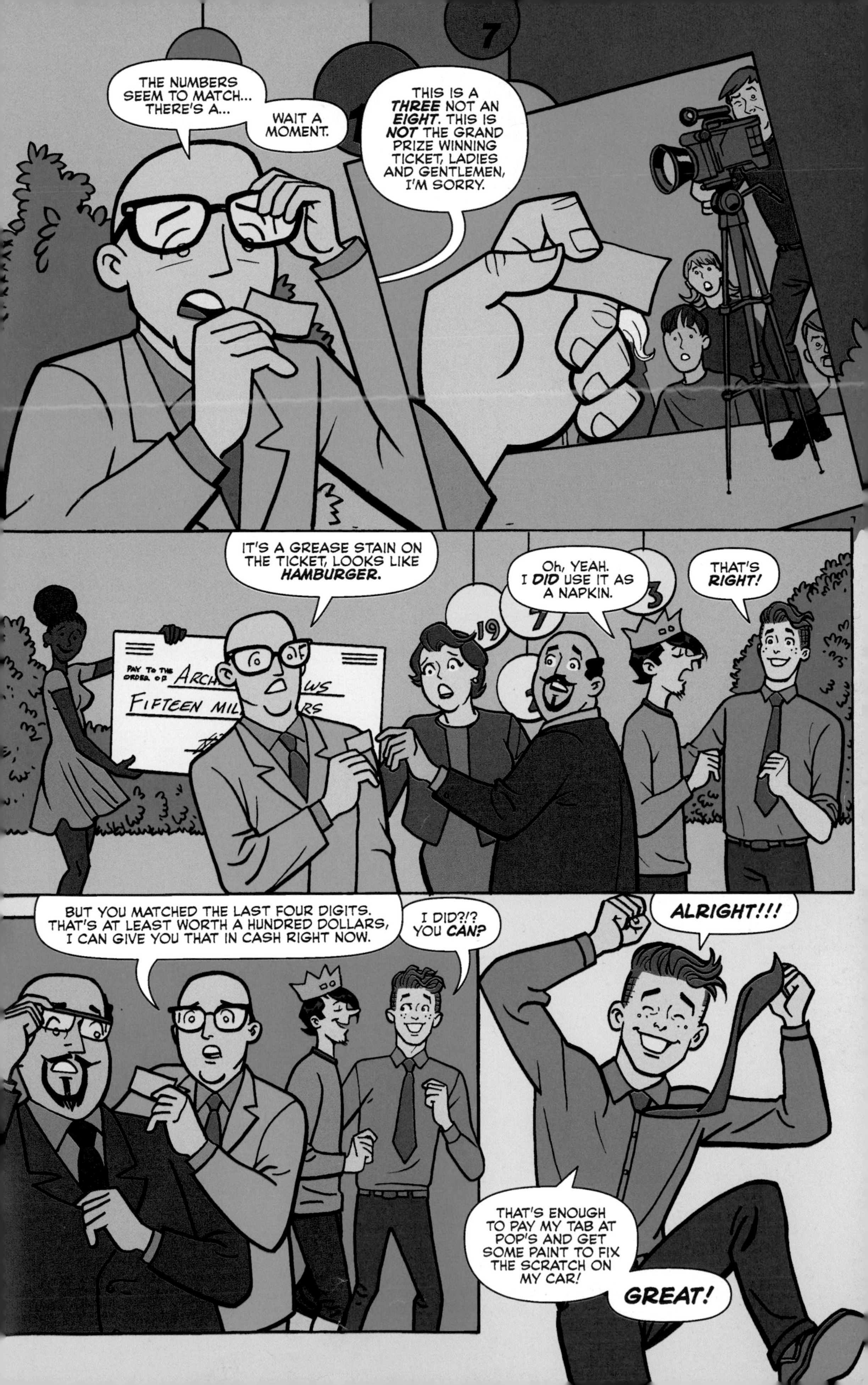
7
THE NUMBERS SEEM TO MATCH... THERE'S A...
WAIT A MOMENT.
THIS IS A ***THREE*** NOT AN ***EIGHT***. THIS IS ***NOT*** THE GRAND PRIZE WINNING TICKET, LADIES AND GENTLEMEN, I'M SORRY.
IT'S A GREASE STAIN ON THE TICKET, LOOKS LIKE ***HAMBURGER.***
Oh, YEAH. I ***DID*** USE IT AS A NAPKIN.
THAT'S ***RIGHT!***
PAY TO THE ORDER OF ARCH... WS
FIFTEEN MIL... RS
BUT YOU MATCHED THE LAST FOUR DIGITS. THAT'S AT LEAST WORTH A HUNDRED DOLLARS, I CAN GIVE YOU THAT IN CASH RIGHT NOW.
I DID?!? YOU ***CAN?***
ALRIGHT!!!
THAT'S ENOUGH TO PAY MY TAB AT POP'S AND GET SOME PAINT TO FIX THE SCRATCH ON MY CAR!
GREAT!

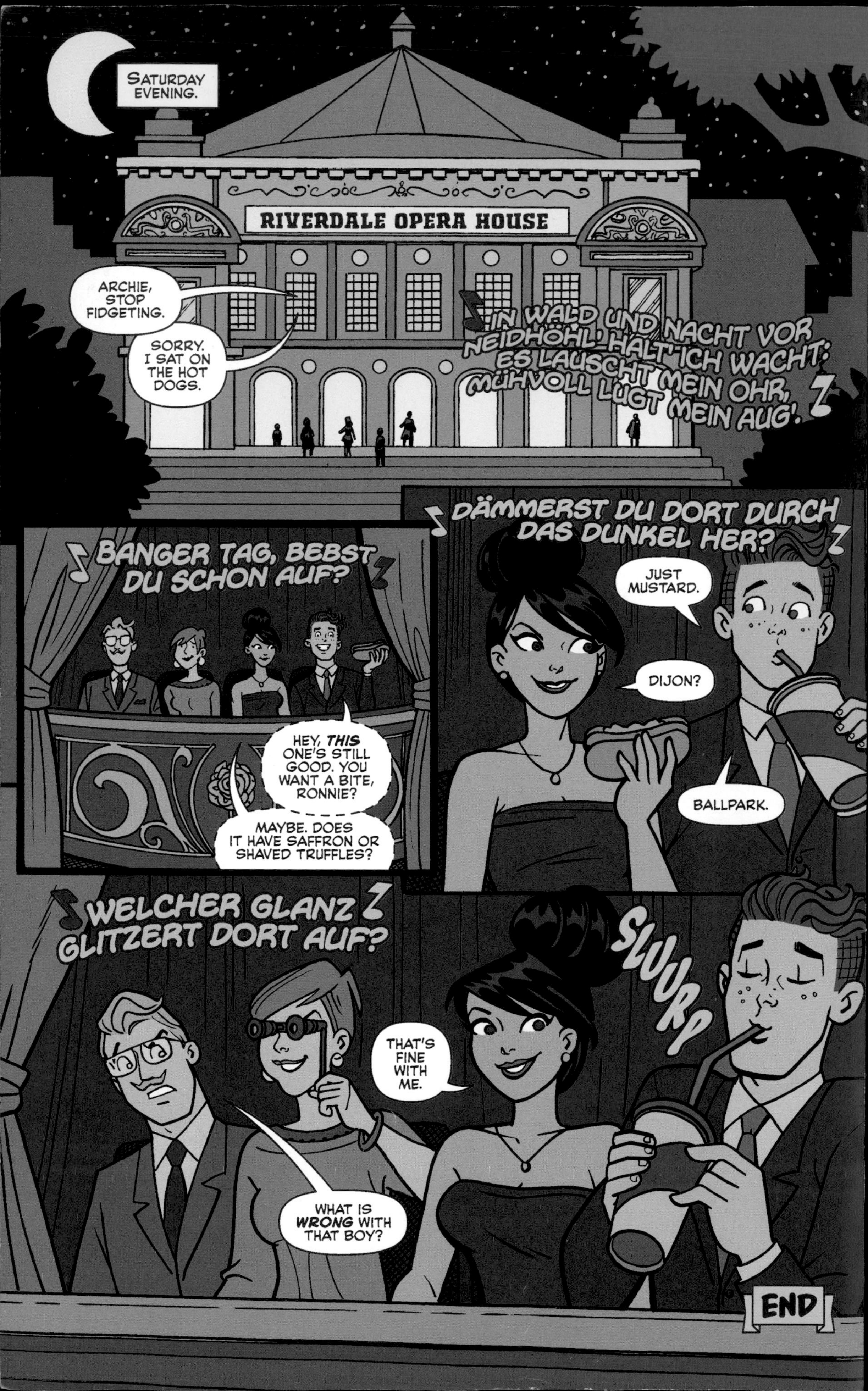
SATURDAY EVENING.
RIVERDALE OPERA HOUSE
ARCHIE, STOP FIDGETING.
SORRY. I SAT ON THE HOT DOGS.
IN WALD UND NACHT VOR NEIDHÖHL' HALT' ICH WACHT: ES LAUSCHT MEIN OHR, MÜHVOLL LUGT MEIN AUG'.
BANGER TAG, BEBST DU SCHON AUF?
HEY, THIS ONE'S STILL GOOD. YOU WANT A BITE, RONNIE?
MAYBE. DOES IT HAVE SAFFRON OR SHAVED TRUFFLES?
DÄMMERST DU DORT DURCH DAS DUNKEL HER?
JUST MUSTARD.
DIJON?
BALLPARK.
WELCHER GLANZ GLITZERT DORT AUF?
SLUURP
THAT'S FINE WITH ME.
WHAT IS WRONG WITH THAT BOY?
END

CHAPTER 3
PART 1

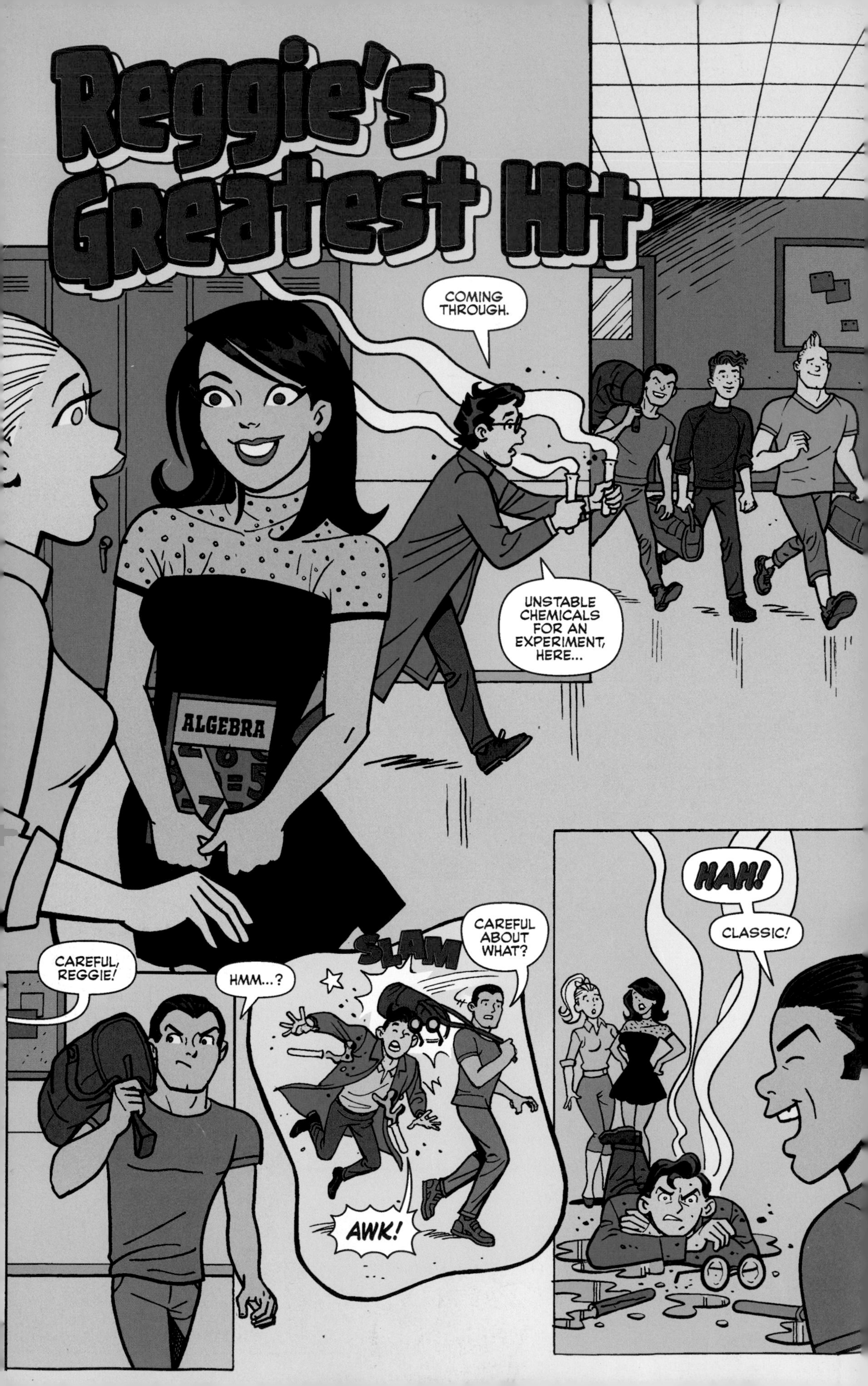
Reggie's Greatest Hit
COMING THROUGH.
UNSTABLE CHEMICALS FOR AN EXPERIMENT, HERE...
ALGEBRA
CAREFUL, REGGIE!
HMM...?
CAREFUL ABOUT WHAT?
SLAM
AWK!
HAH!
CLASSIC!

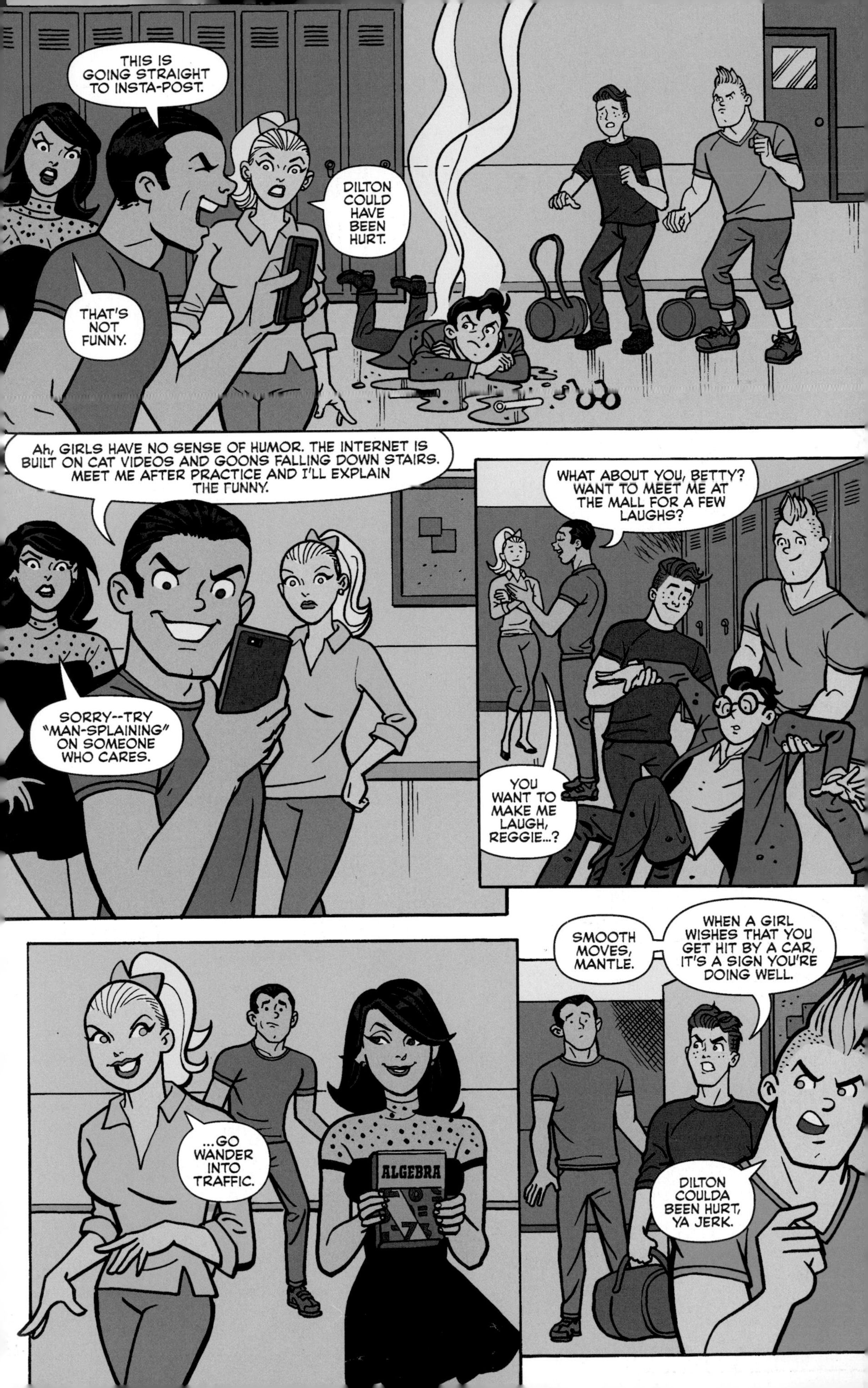
THIS IS GOING STRAIGHT TO INSTA-POST.
DILTON COULD HAVE BEEN HURT.
THAT'S NOT FUNNY.
Ah, GIRLS HAVE NO SENSE OF HUMOR. THE INTERNET IS BUILT ON CAT VIDEOS AND GOONS FALLING DOWN STAIRS. MEET ME AFTER PRACTICE AND I'LL EXPLAIN THE FUNNY.
SORRY--TRY "MAN-SPLAINING" ON SOMEONE WHO CARES.
WHAT ABOUT YOU, BETTY? WANT TO MEET ME AT THE MALL FOR A FEW LAUGHS?
YOU WANT TO MAKE ME LAUGH, REGGIE...?
...GO WANDER INTO TRAFFIC.
ALGEBRA
SMOOTH MOVES, MANTLE.
WHEN A GIRL WISHES THAT YOU GET HIT BY A CAR, IT'S A SIGN YOU'RE DOING WELL.
DILTON COULDA BEEN HURT, YA JERK.

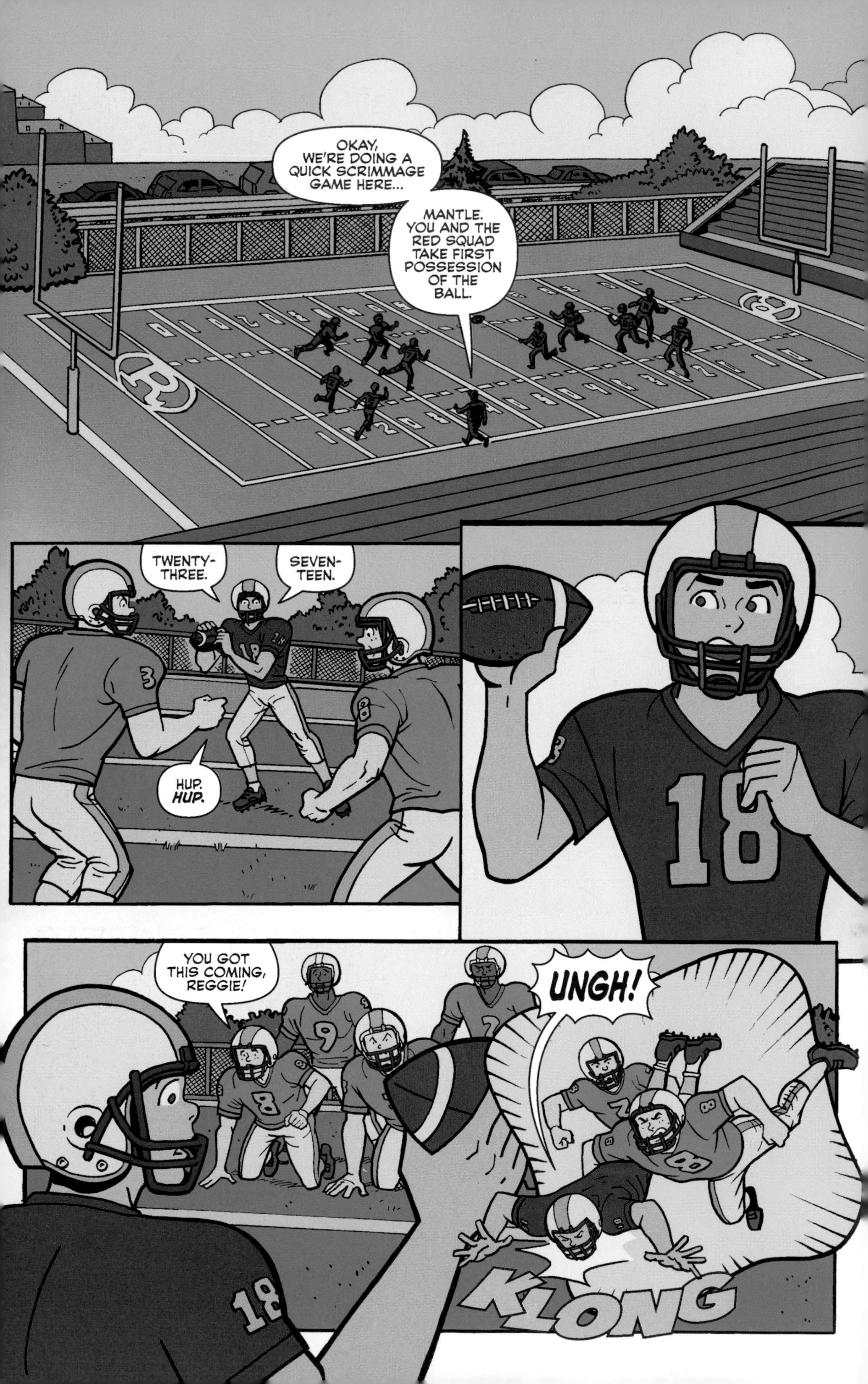
OKAY, WE'RE DOING A QUICK SCRIMMAGE GAME HERE...
MANTLE. YOU AND THE RED SQUAD TAKE FIRST POSSESSION OF THE BALL.
TWENTY-THREE.
SEVEN-TEEN.
HUP. HUP.
YOU GOT THIS COMING, REGGIE!
UNGH!
KLONG

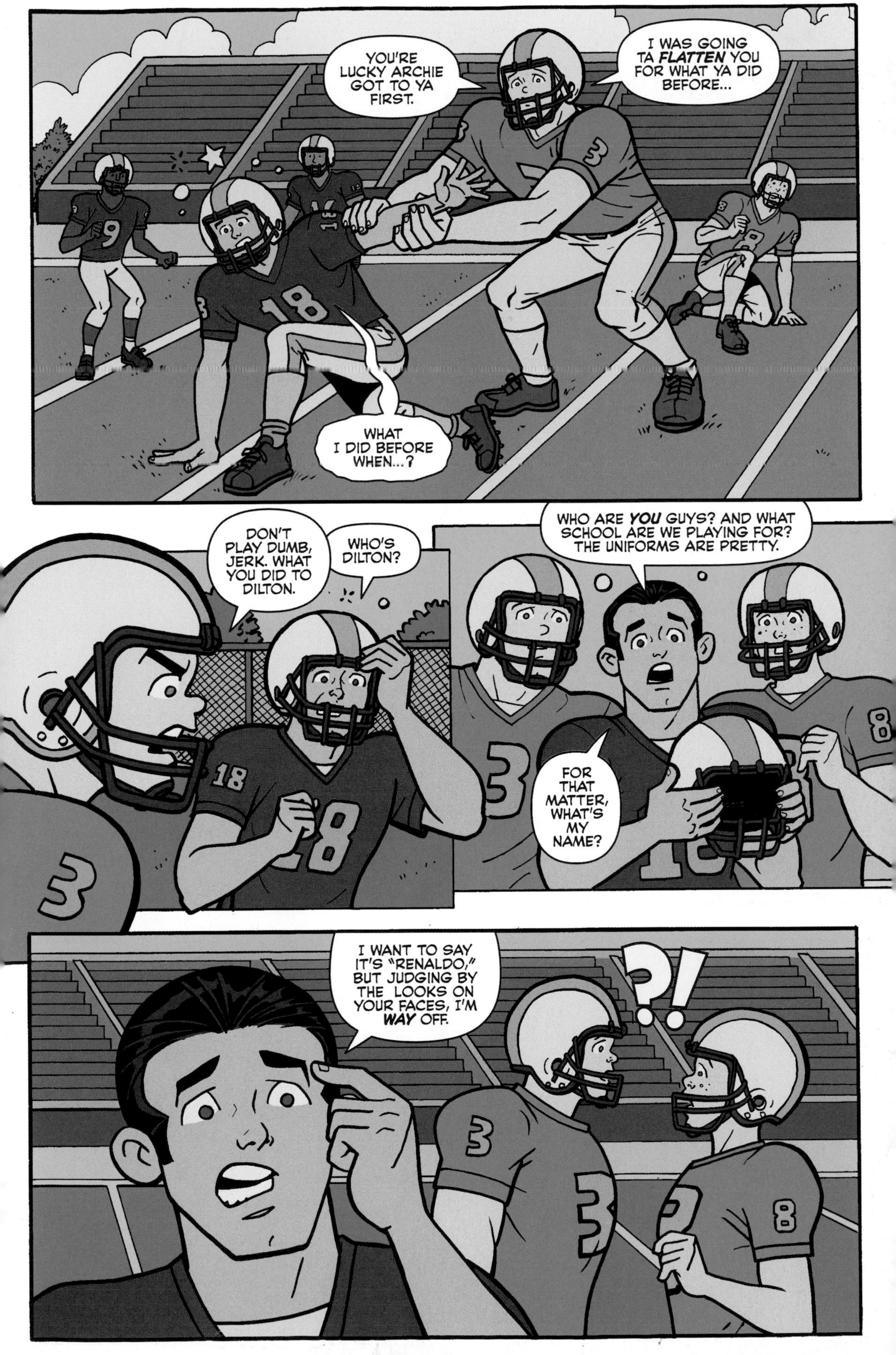
YOU'RE LUCKY ARCHIE GOT TO YA FIRST.
I WAS GOING TA *FLATTEN* YOU FOR WHAT YA DID BEFORE...
WHAT I DID BEFORE WHEN...?
DON'T PLAY DUMB, JERK. WHAT YOU DID TO DILTON.
WHO'S DILTON?
WHO ARE *YOU* GUYS? AND WHAT SCHOOL ARE WE PLAYING FOR? THE UNIFORMS ARE PRETTY.
FOR THAT MATTER, WHAT'S MY NAME?
I WANT TO SAY IT'S "RENALDO," BUT JUDGING BY THE LOOKS ON YOUR FACES, I'M *WAY* OFF.
?!

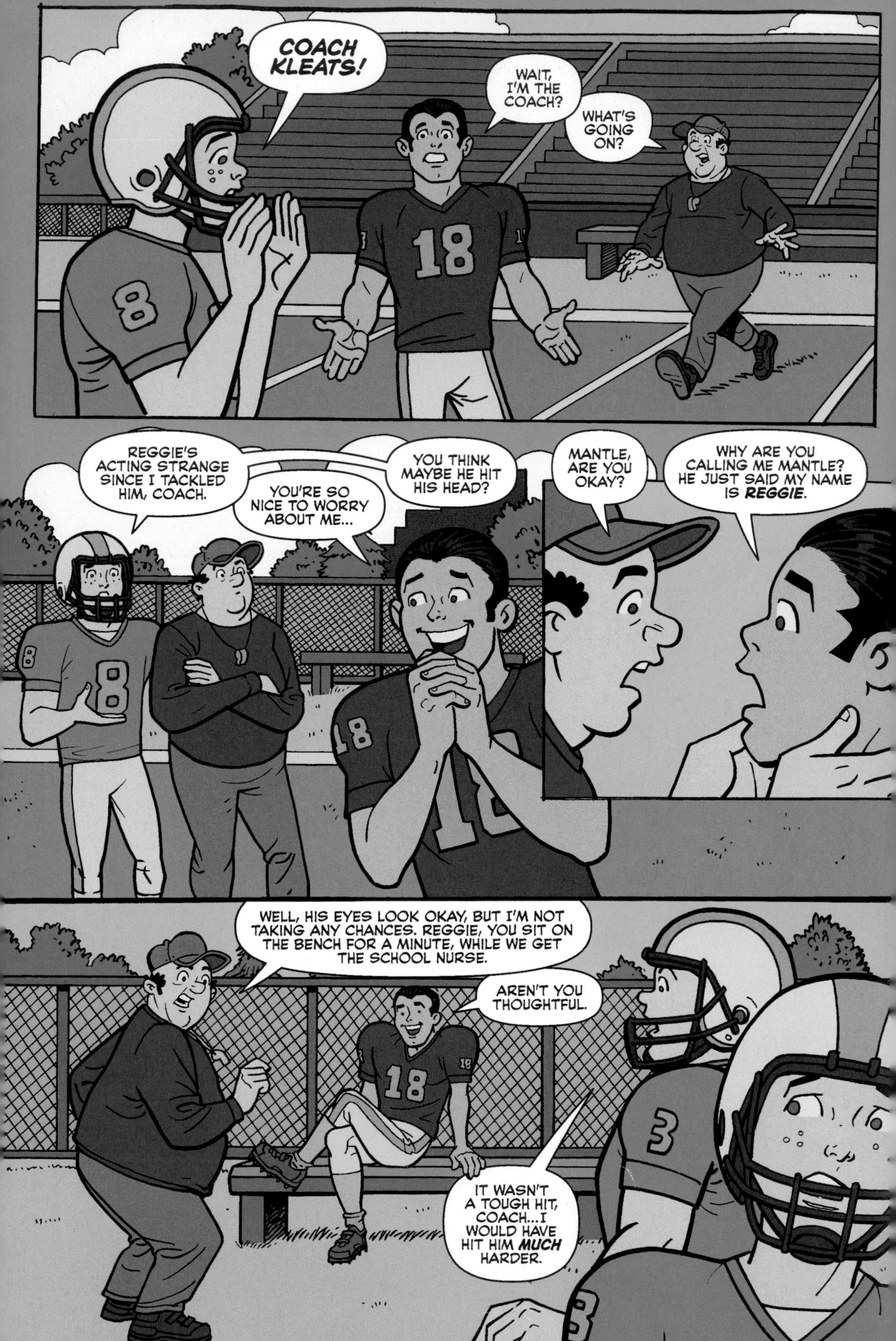
COACH KLEATS!
WAIT, I'M THE COACH?
WHAT'S GOING ON?
REGGIE'S ACTING STRANGE SINCE I TACKLED HIM, COACH.
YOU THINK MAYBE HE HIT HIS HEAD?
YOU'RE SO NICE TO WORRY ABOUT ME...
MANTLE, ARE YOU OKAY?
WHY ARE YOU CALLING ME MANTLE? HE JUST SAID MY NAME IS *REGGIE*.
WELL, HIS EYES LOOK OKAY, BUT I'M NOT TAKING ANY CHANCES. REGGIE, YOU SIT ON THE BENCH FOR A MINUTE, WHILE WE GET THE SCHOOL NURSE.
AREN'T YOU THOUGHTFUL.
IT WASN'T A TOUGH HIT, COACH...I WOULD HAVE HIT HIM *MUCH* HARDER.

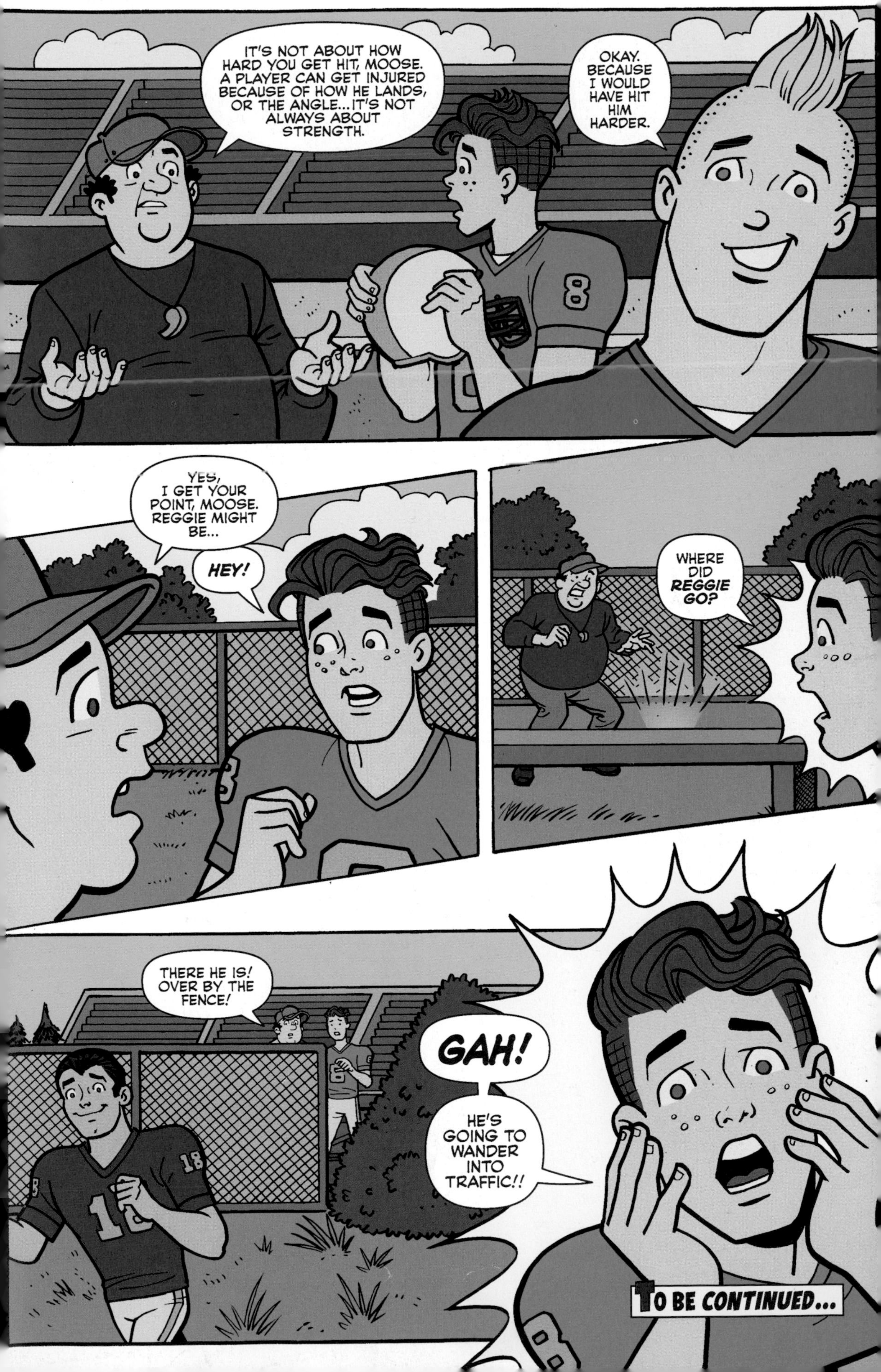
IT'S NOT ABOUT HOW HARD YOU GET HIT, MOOSE. A PLAYER CAN GET INJURED BECAUSE OF HOW HE LANDS, OR THE ANGLE...IT'S NOT ALWAYS ABOUT STRENGTH.
OKAY. BECAUSE I WOULD HAVE HIT HIM HARDER.
YES, I GET YOUR POINT, MOOSE. REGGIE MIGHT BE...
HEY!
WHERE DID REGGIE GO?
THERE HE IS! OVER BY THE FENCE!
GAH!
HE'S GOING TO WANDER INTO TRAFFIC!!
TO BE CONTINUED...

CHAPTER 3
PART 2

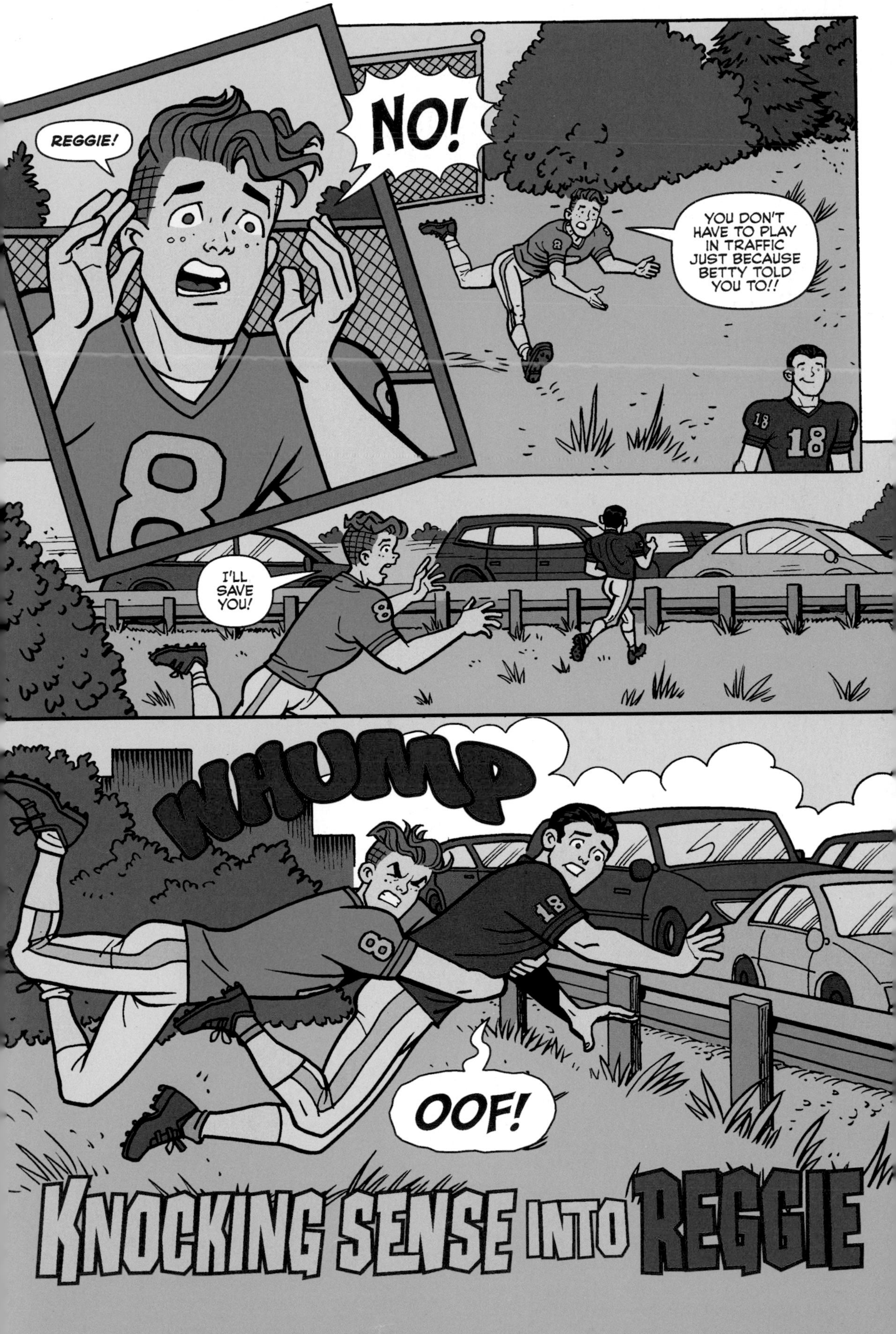
REGGIE!
NO!
YOU DON'T HAVE TO PLAY IN TRAFFIC JUST BECAUSE BETTY TOLD YOU TO!!
I'LL SAVE YOU!
WHUMP
OOF!
KNOCKING SENSE INTO REGGIE

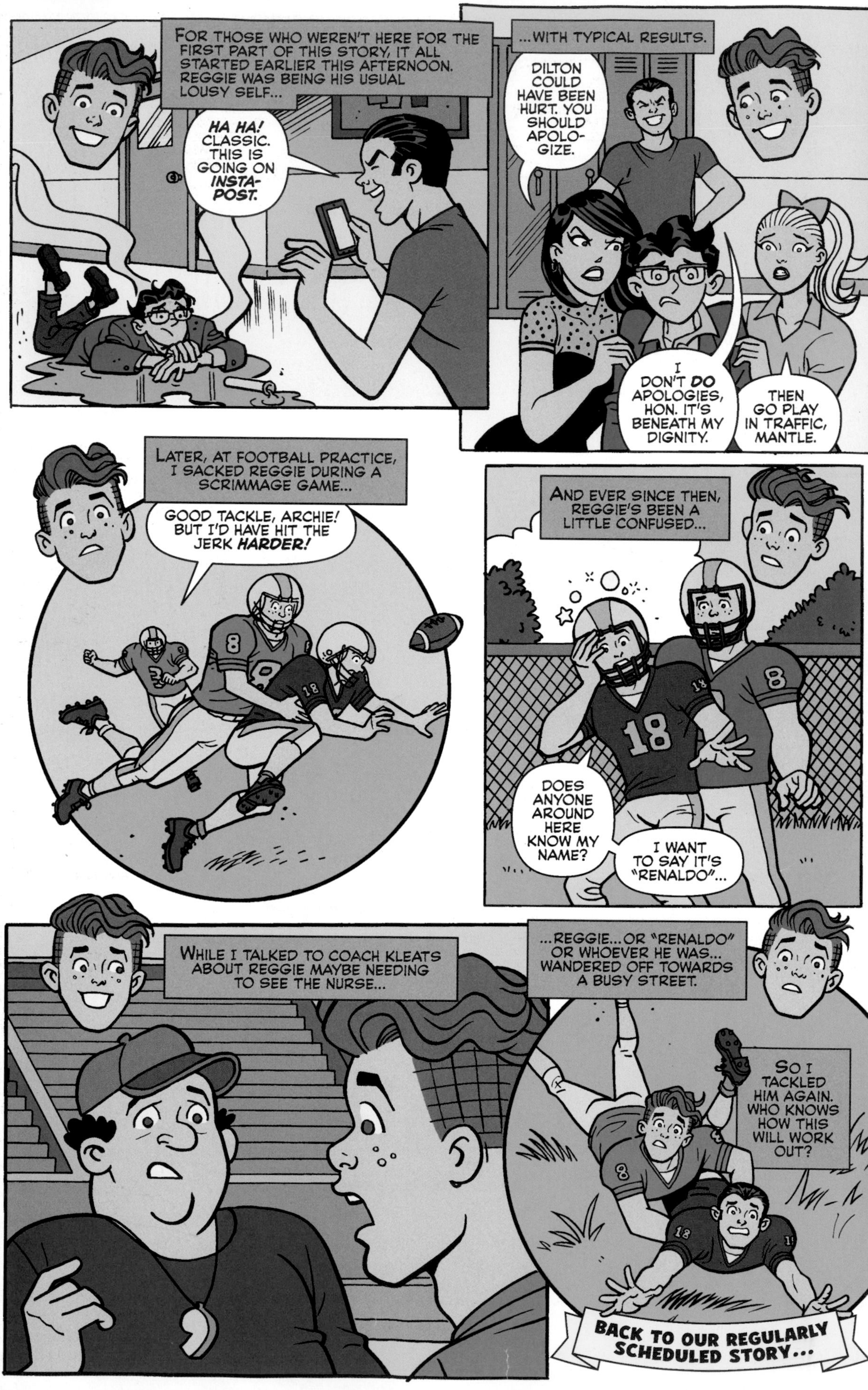
FOR THOSE WHO WEREN'T HERE FOR THE FIRST PART OF THIS STORY, IT ALL STARTED EARLIER THIS AFTERNOON. REGGIE WAS BEING HIS USUAL LOUSY SELF...
HA HA! CLASSIC. THIS IS GOING ON INSTA-POST.
...WITH TYPICAL RESULTS.
DILTON COULD HAVE BEEN HURT. YOU SHOULD APOLO-GIZE.
I DON'T DO APOLOGIES, HON. IT'S BENEATH MY DIGNITY.
THEN GO PLAY IN TRAFFIC, MANTLE.
LATER, AT FOOTBALL PRACTICE, I SACKED REGGIE DURING A SCRIMMAGE GAME...
GOOD TACKLE, ARCHIE! BUT I'D HAVE HIT THE JERK HARDER!
AND EVER SINCE THEN, REGGIE'S BEEN A LITTLE CONFUSED...
DOES ANYONE AROUND HERE KNOW MY NAME?
I WANT TO SAY IT'S "RENALDO"...
WHILE I TALKED TO COACH KLEATS ABOUT REGGIE MAYBE NEEDING TO SEE THE NURSE...
...REGGIE...OR "RENALDO" OR WHOEVER HE WAS... WANDERED OFF TOWARDS A BUSY STREET.
SO I TACKLED HIM AGAIN. WHO KNOWS HOW THIS WILL WORK OUT?
BACK TO OUR REGULARLY SCHEDULED STORY...

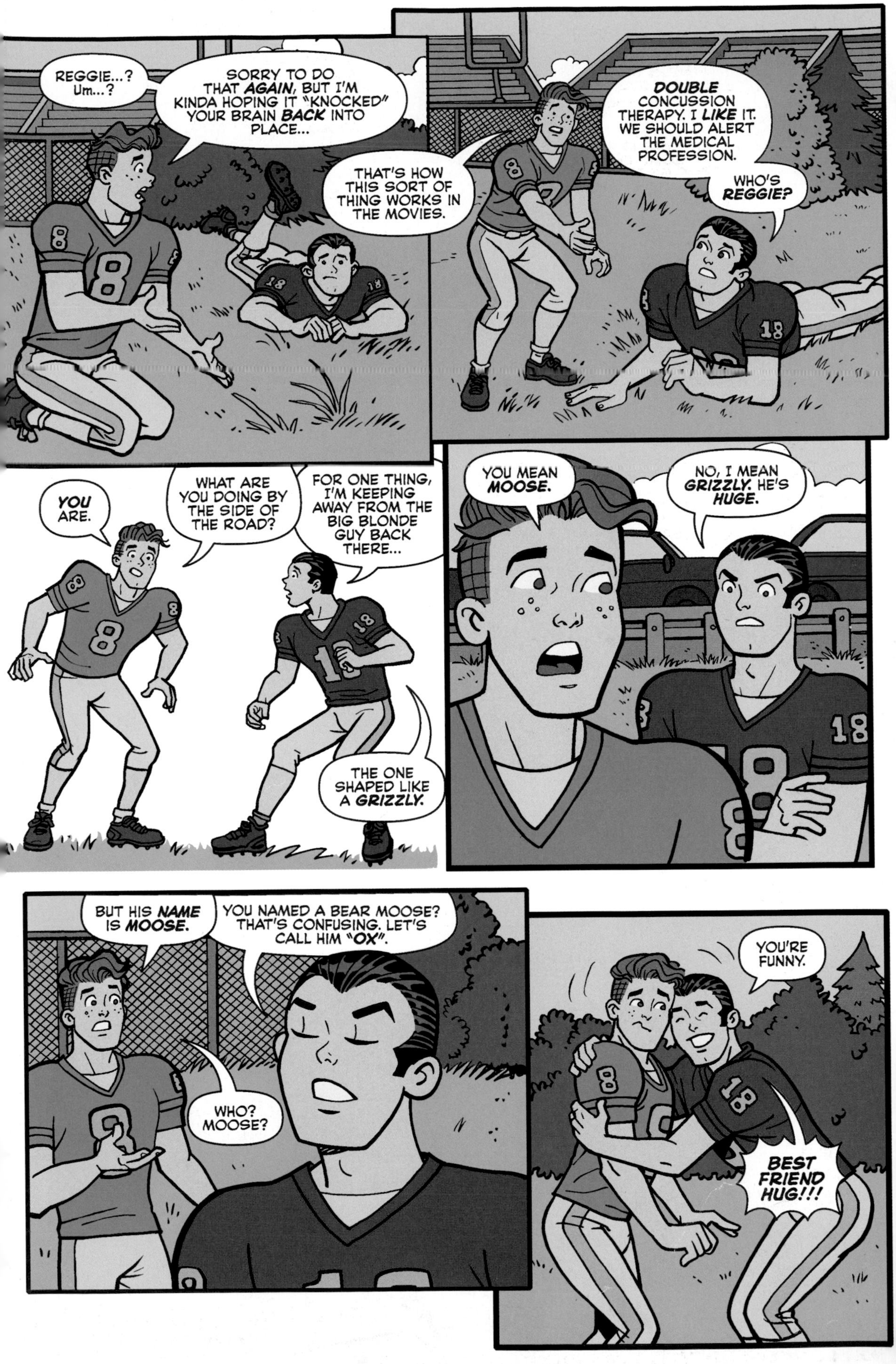
REGGIE...? Um...?
SORRY TO DO THAT AGAIN, BUT I'M KINDA HOPING IT "KNOCKED" YOUR BRAIN BACK INTO PLACE...
THAT'S HOW THIS SORT OF THING WORKS IN THE MOVIES.
DOUBLE CONCUSSION THERAPY. I LIKE IT. WE SHOULD ALERT THE MEDICAL PROFESSION.
WHO'S REGGIE?
YOU ARE.
WHAT ARE YOU DOING BY THE SIDE OF THE ROAD?
FOR ONE THING, I'M KEEPING AWAY FROM THE BIG BLONDE GUY BACK THERE...
THE ONE SHAPED LIKE A GRIZZLY.
YOU MEAN MOOSE.
NO, I MEAN GRIZZLY. HE'S HUGE.
BUT HIS NAME IS MOOSE.
YOU NAMED A BEAR MOOSE? THAT'S CONFUSING. LET'S CALL HIM "OX".
WHO? MOOSE?
YOU'RE FUNNY.
BEST FRIEND HUG!!!

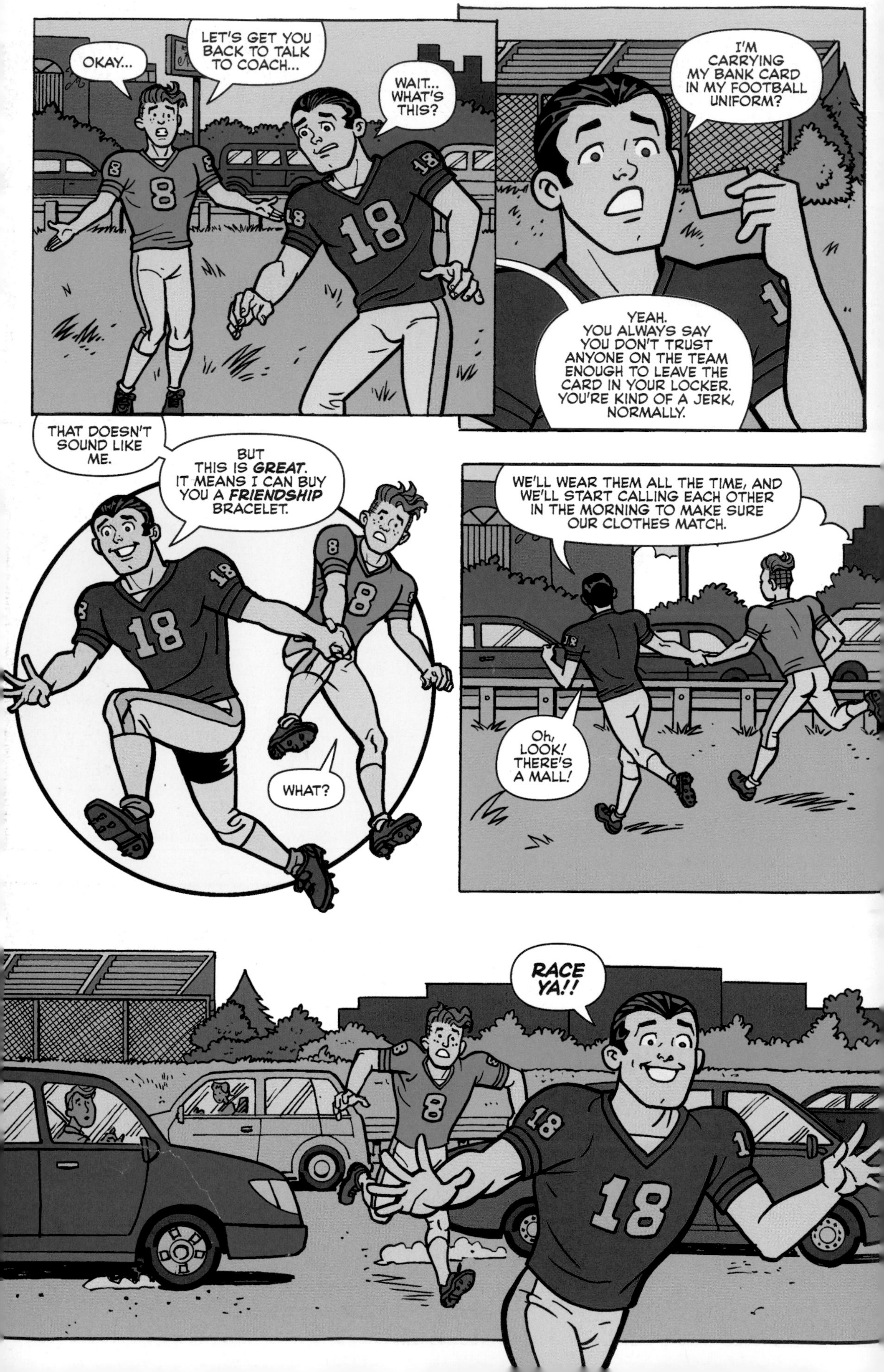
OKAY...
LET'S GET YOU BACK TO TALK TO COACH...
WAIT... WHAT'S THIS?
I'M CARRYING MY BANK CARD IN MY FOOTBALL UNIFORM?
YEAH. YOU ALWAYS SAY YOU DON'T TRUST ANYONE ON THE TEAM ENOUGH TO LEAVE THE CARD IN YOUR LOCKER. YOU'RE KIND OF A JERK, NORMALLY.
THAT DOESN'T SOUND LIKE ME.
BUT THIS IS **GREAT**. IT MEANS I CAN BUY YOU A ***FRIENDSHIP*** BRACELET.
WHAT?
WE'LL WEAR THEM ALL THE TIME, AND WE'LL START CALLING EACH OTHER IN THE MORNING TO MAKE SURE OUR CLOTHES MATCH.
Oh, LOOK! THERE'S A MALL!
RACE YA!!

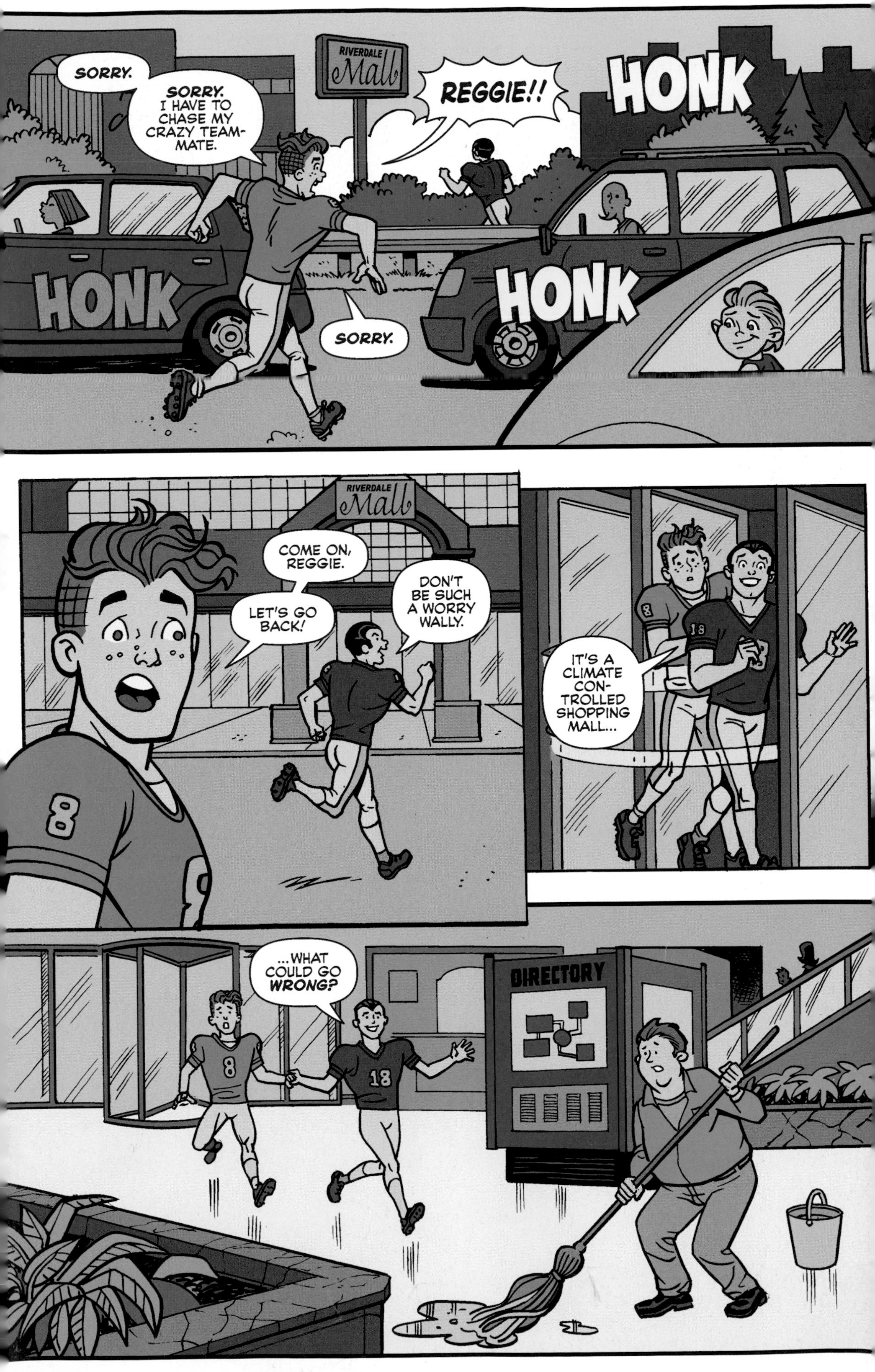
SORRY.
SORRY. I HAVE TO CHASE MY CRAZY TEAM-MATE.
RIVERDALE Mall
REGGIE!!
HONK
HONK
HONK
SORRY.
RIVERDALE Mall
COME ON, REGGIE.
LET'S GO BACK!
DON'T BE SUCH A WORRY WALLY.
IT'S A CLIMATE CON-TROLLED SHOPPING MALL...
...WHAT COULD GO WRONG?
DIRECTORY

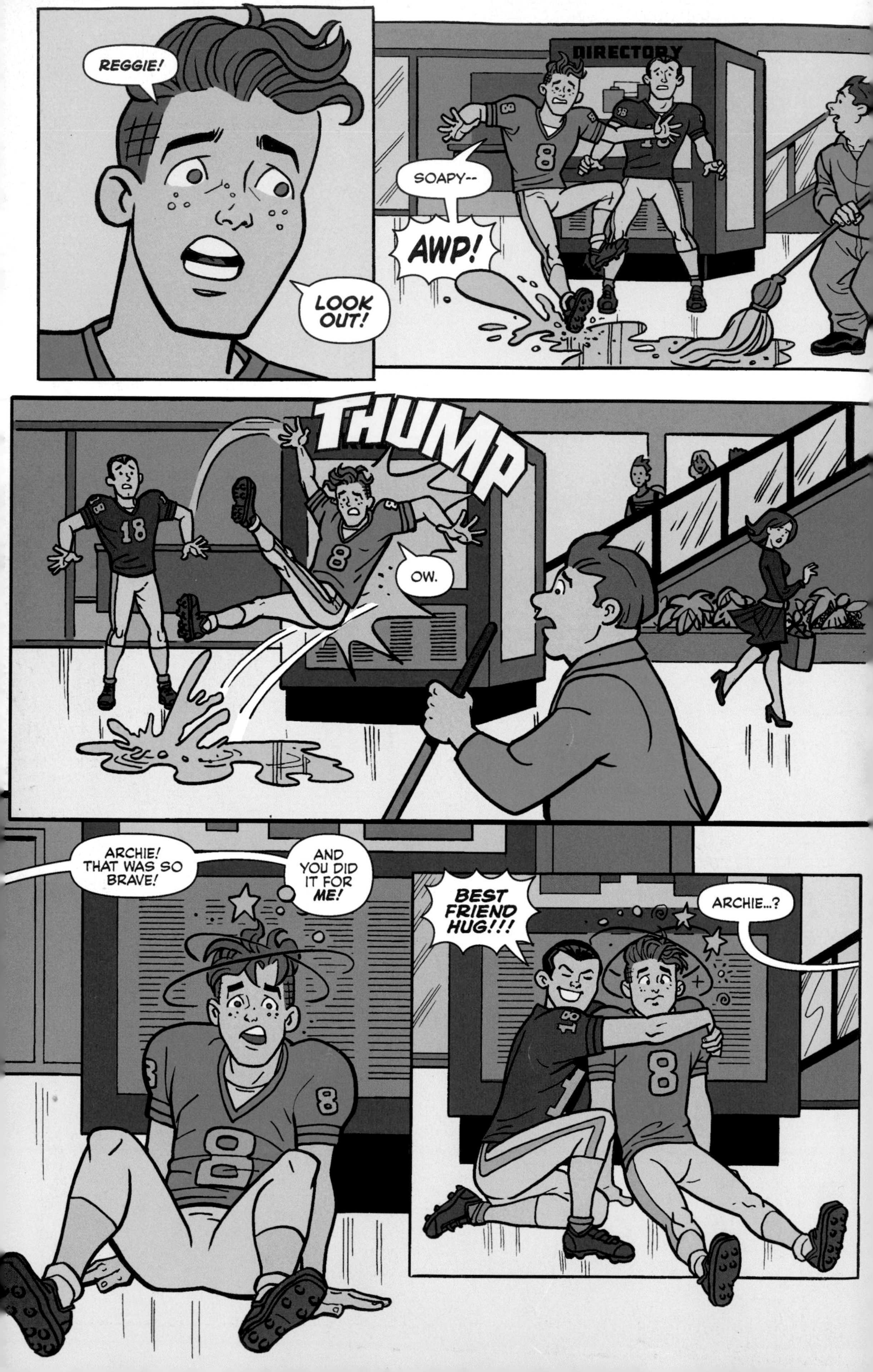
REGGIE!
LOOK OUT!
SOAPY--
AWP!
DIRECTORY
THUMP
OW.
ARCHIE! THAT WAS SO BRAVE!
AND YOU DID IT FOR ME!
BEST FRIEND HUG!!!
ARCHIE...?

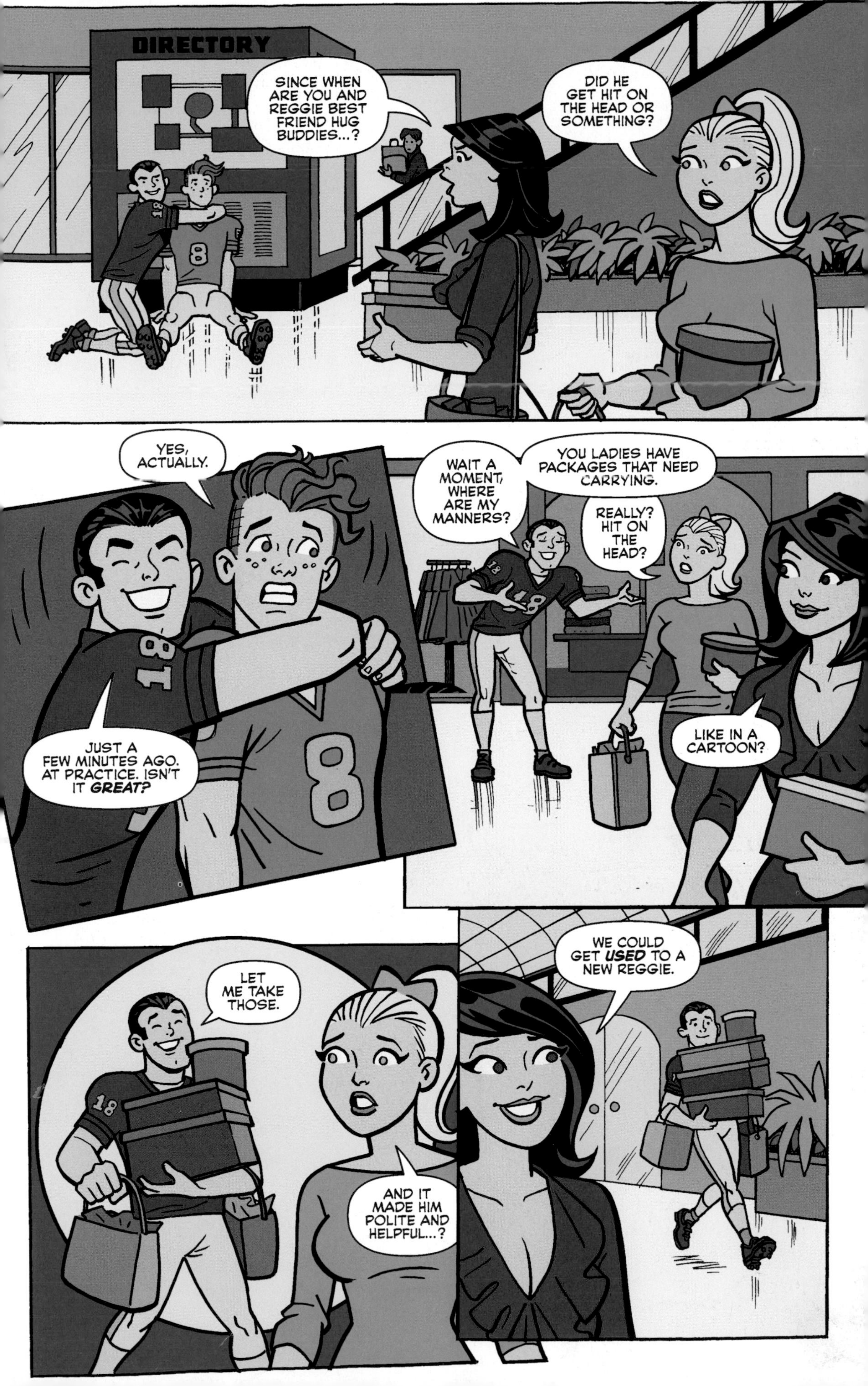
DIRECTORY
SINCE WHEN ARE YOU AND REGGIE BEST FRIEND HUG BUDDIES...?
DID HE GET HIT ON THE HEAD OR SOMETHING?
YES, ACTUALLY.
JUST A FEW MINUTES AGO. AT PRACTICE. ISN'T IT *GREAT?*
WAIT A MOMENT, WHERE ARE MY MANNERS?
YOU LADIES HAVE PACKAGES THAT NEED CARRYING.
REALLY? HIT ON THE HEAD?
LIKE IN A CARTOON?
LET ME TAKE THOSE.
AND IT MADE HIM POLITE AND HELPFUL...?
WE COULD GET *USED* TO A NEW REGGIE.

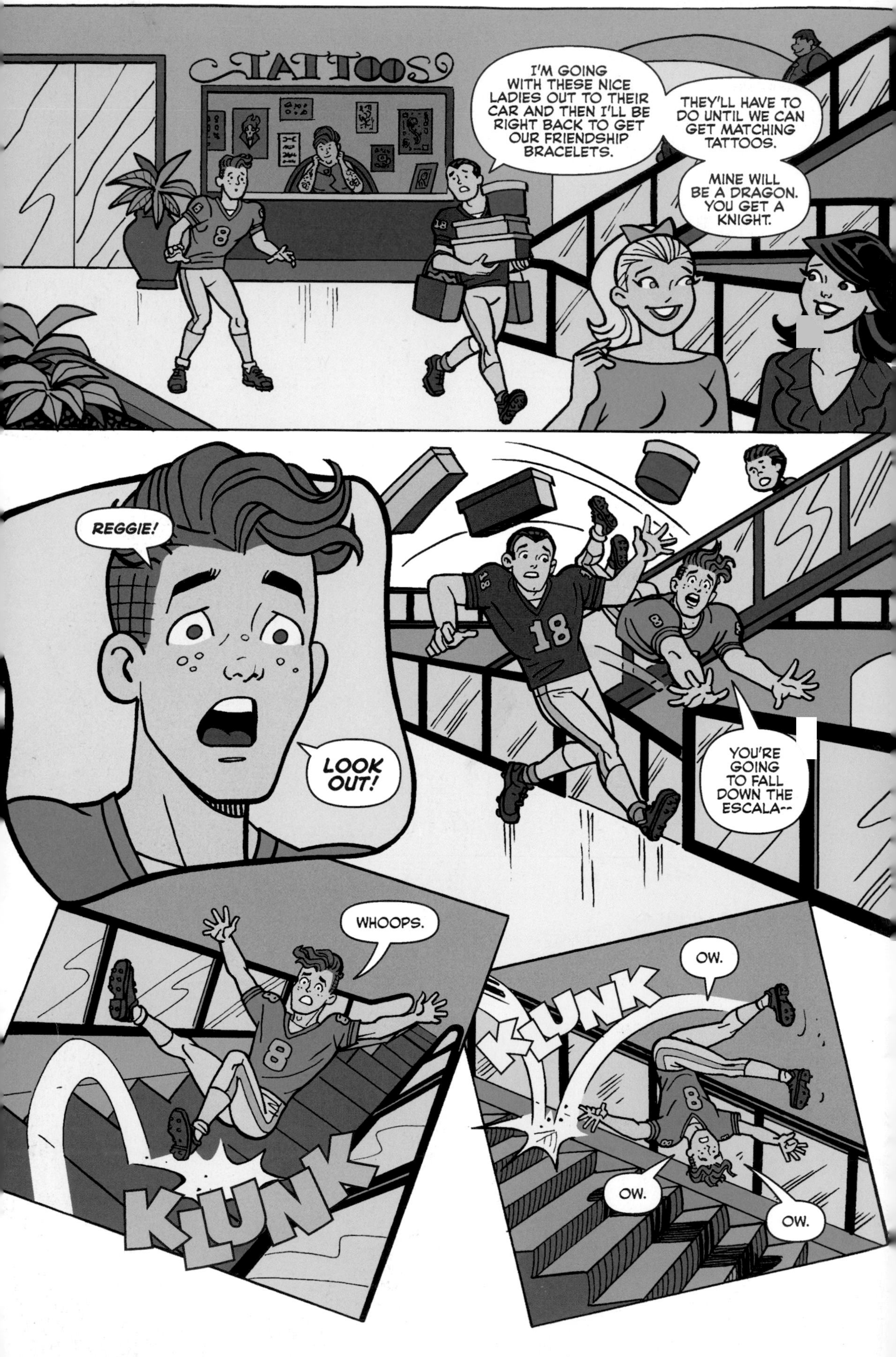
TATTOOS
I'M GOING WITH THESE NICE LADIES OUT TO THEIR CAR AND THEN I'LL BE RIGHT BACK TO GET OUR FRIENDSHIP BRACELETS.
THEY'LL HAVE TO DO UNTIL WE CAN GET MATCHING TATTOOS.
MINE WILL BE A DRAGON. YOU GET A KNIGHT.
REGGIE!
LOOK OUT!
YOU'RE GOING TO FALL DOWN THE ESCALA--
WHOOPS.
KLUNK
KLUNK
OW.
OW.
OW.

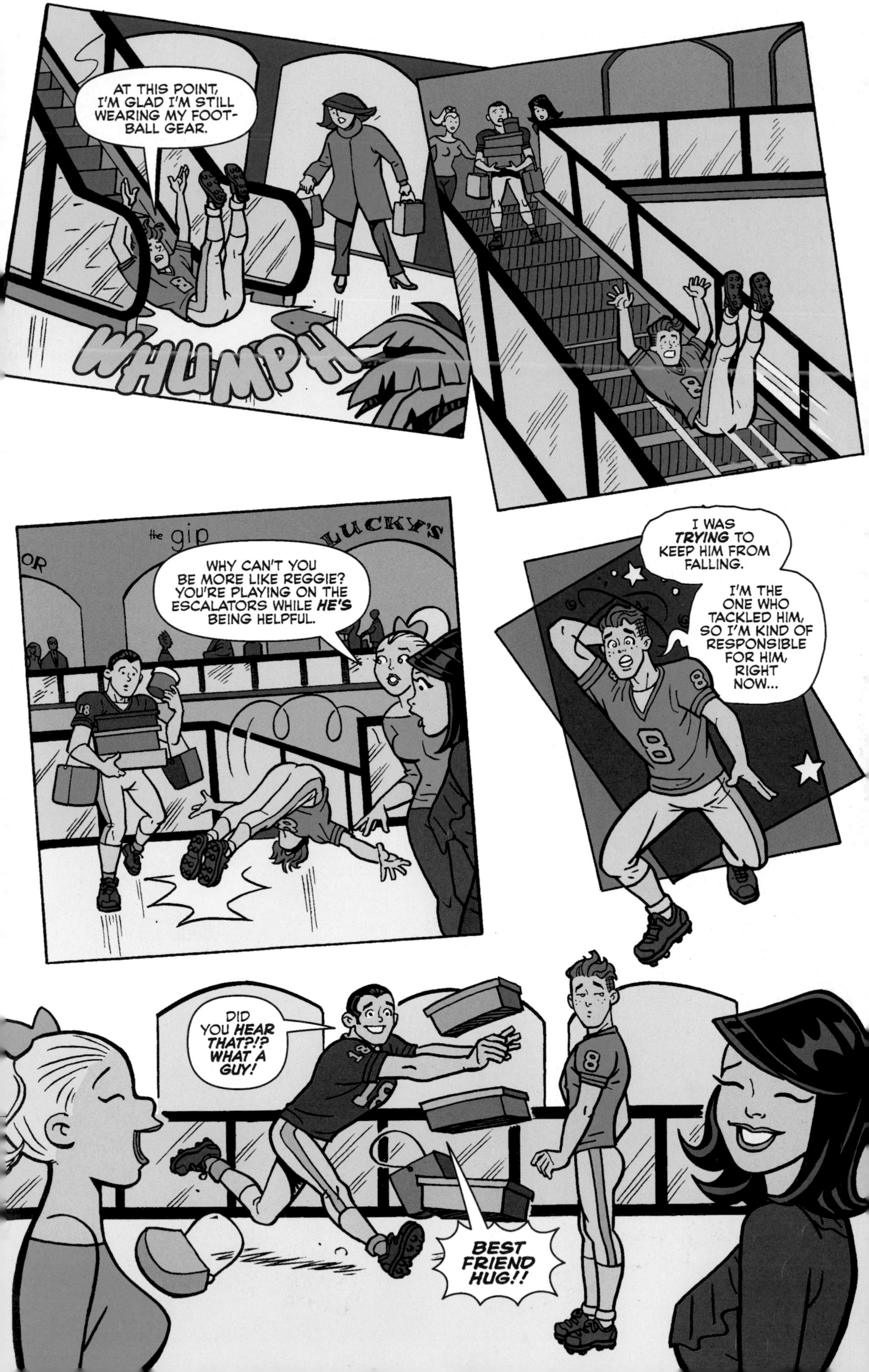
AT THIS POINT, I'M GLAD I'M STILL WEARING MY FOOT-BALL GEAR.
WHUMPH
the gip
LUCKY'S
WHY CAN'T YOU BE MORE LIKE REGGIE? YOU'RE PLAYING ON THE ESCALATORS WHILE **HE'S** BEING HELPFUL.
I WAS **TRYING** TO KEEP HIM FROM FALLING.
I'M THE ONE WHO TACKLED HIM, SO I'M KIND OF RESPONSIBLE FOR HIM, RIGHT NOW...
DID YOU **HEAR THAT?!? WHAT A GUY!**
BEST FRIEND HUG!!

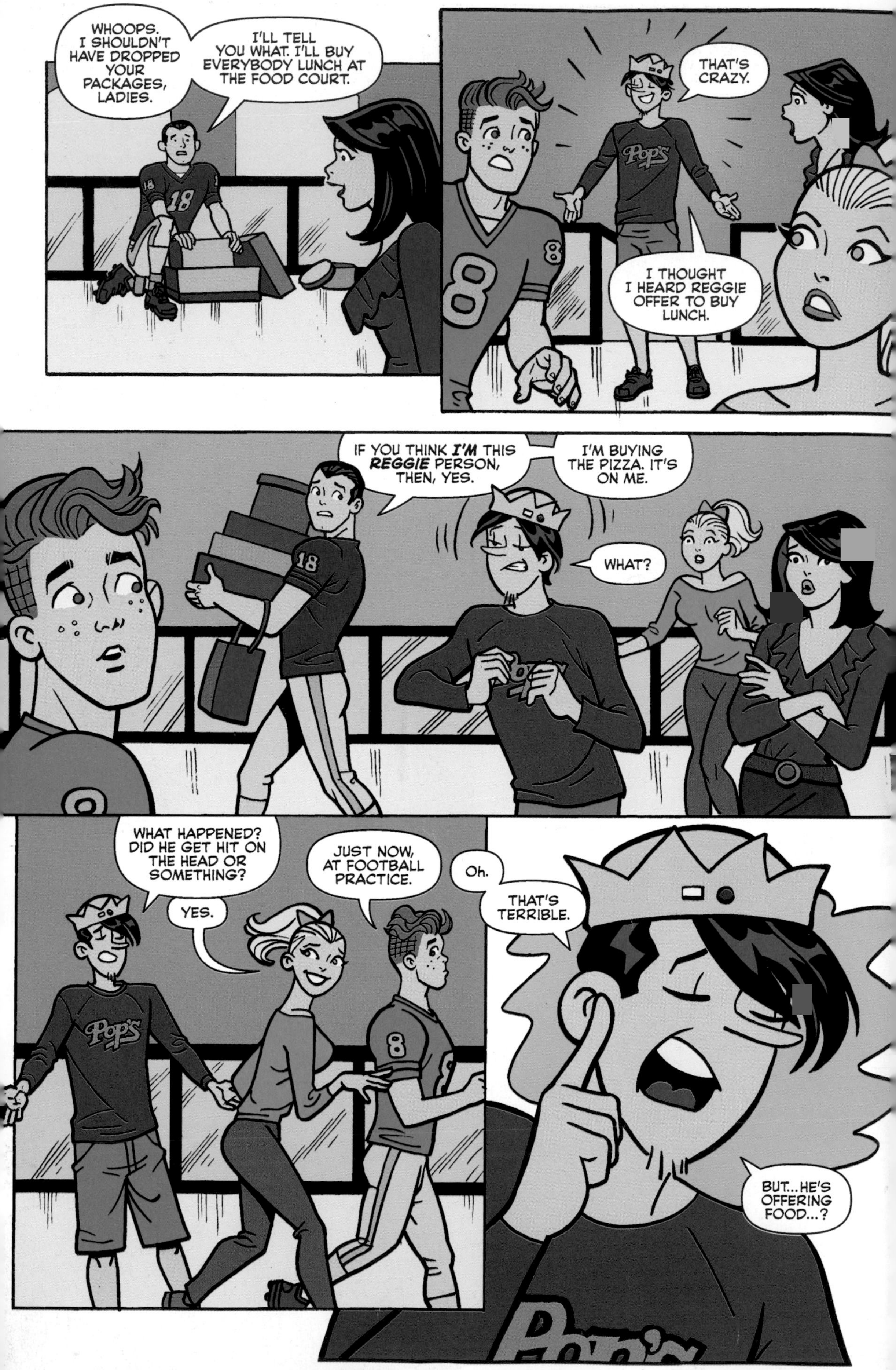
WHOOPS. I SHOULDN'T HAVE DROPPED YOUR PACKAGES, LADIES.
I'LL TELL YOU WHAT. I'LL BUY EVERYBODY LUNCH AT THE FOOD COURT.
THAT'S CRAZY.
I THOUGHT I HEARD REGGIE OFFER TO BUY LUNCH.
IF YOU THINK *I'M* THIS *REGGIE* PERSON, THEN, YES.
I'M BUYING THE PIZZA. IT'S ON ME.
WHAT?
WHAT HAPPENED? DID HE GET HIT ON THE HEAD OR SOMETHING?
YES.
JUST NOW, AT FOOTBALL PRACTICE.
Oh.
THAT'S TERRIBLE.
BUT...HE'S OFFERING FOOD...?

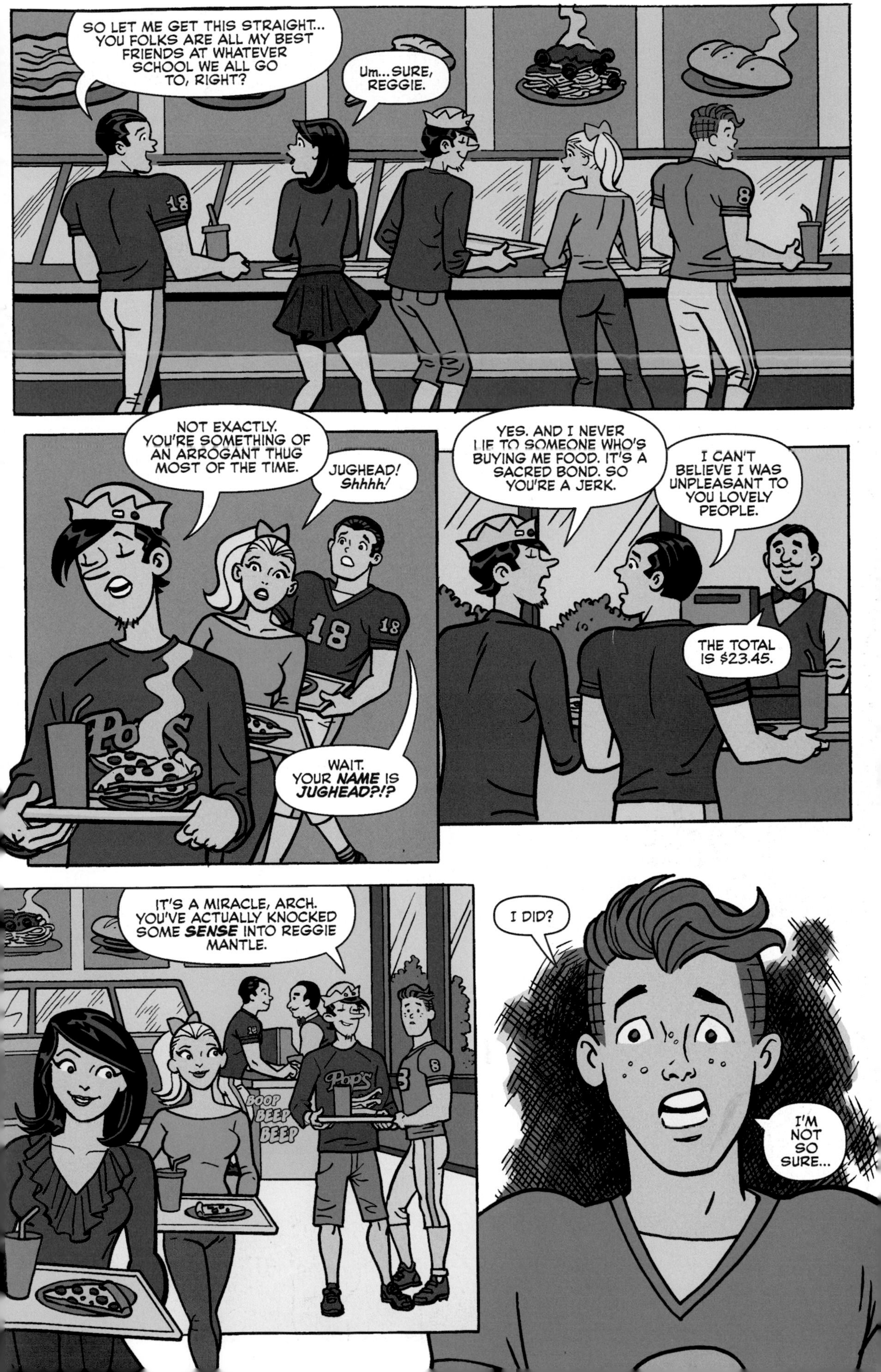
SO LET ME GET THIS STRAIGHT... YOU FOLKS ARE ALL MY BEST FRIENDS AT WHATEVER SCHOOL WE ALL GO TO, RIGHT?
Um... SURE, REGGIE.
NOT EXACTLY. YOU'RE SOMETHING OF AN ARROGANT THUG MOST OF THE TIME.
JUGHEAD! *Shhhh!*
WAIT. YOUR ***NAME*** IS ***JUGHEAD?!?***
YES. AND I NEVER LIE TO SOMEONE WHO'S BUYING ME FOOD. IT'S A SACRED BOND. SO YOU'RE A JERK.
I CAN'T BELIEVE I WAS UNPLEASANT TO YOU LOVELY PEOPLE.
THE TOTAL IS $23.45.
IT'S A MIRACLE, ARCH. YOU'VE ACTUALLY KNOCKED SOME ***SENSE*** INTO REGGIE MANTLE.
BOOP BEEP BEEP
I DID?
I'M NOT SO SURE...

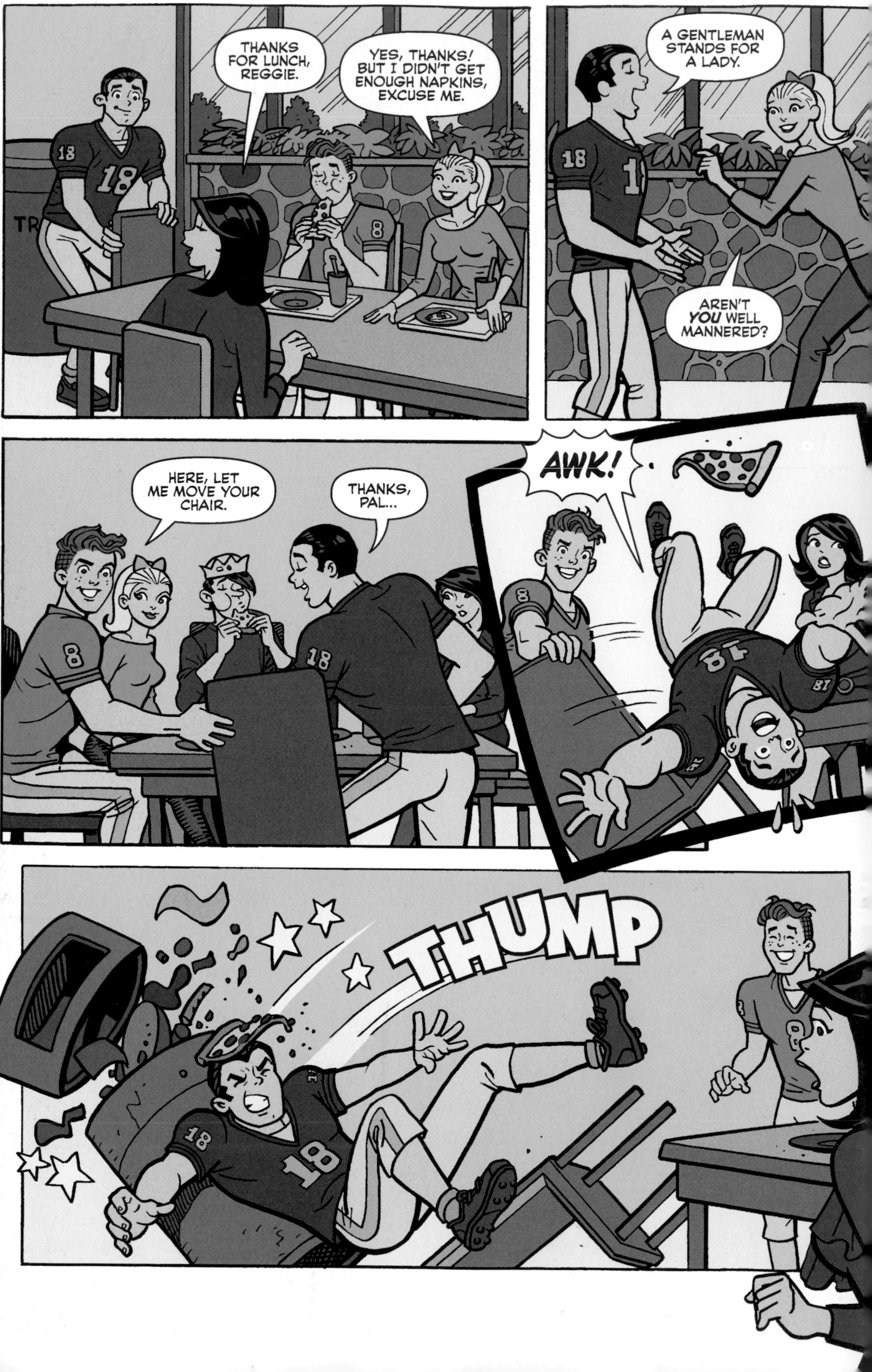
THANKS FOR LUNCH, REGGIE.
YES, THANKS! BUT I DIDN'T GET ENOUGH NAPKINS, EXCUSE ME.
A GENTLEMAN STANDS FOR A LADY.
AREN'T YOU WELL MANNERED?
HERE, LET ME MOVE YOUR CHAIR.
THANKS, PAL...
AWK!
THUMP

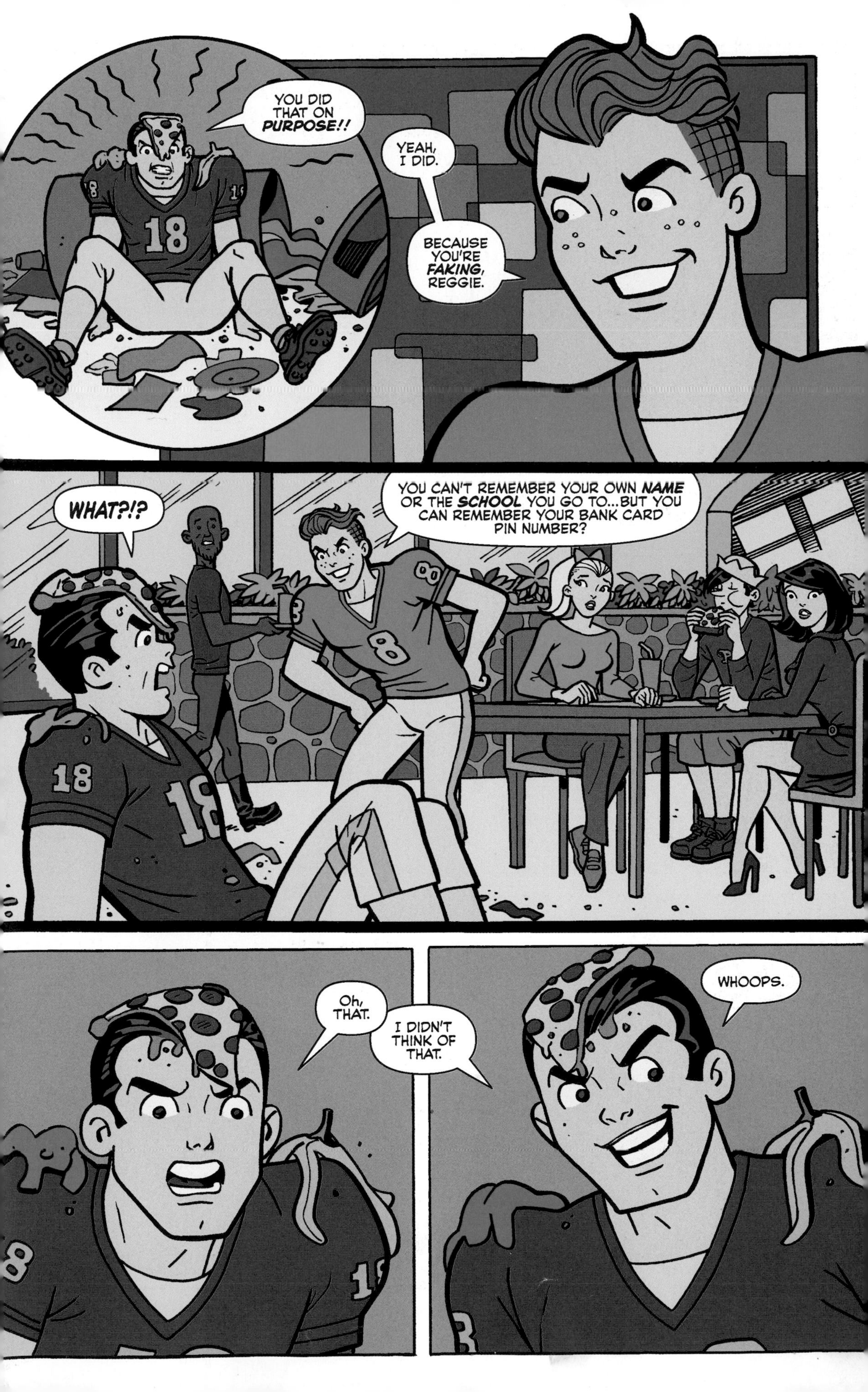
YOU DID THAT ON PURPOSE!!
YEAH, I DID.
BECAUSE YOU'RE FAKING, REGGIE.
WHAT?!?
YOU CAN'T REMEMBER YOUR OWN NAME OR THE SCHOOL YOU GO TO...BUT YOU CAN REMEMBER YOUR BANK CARD PIN NUMBER?
Oh, THAT.
I DIDN'T THINK OF THAT.
WHOOPS.

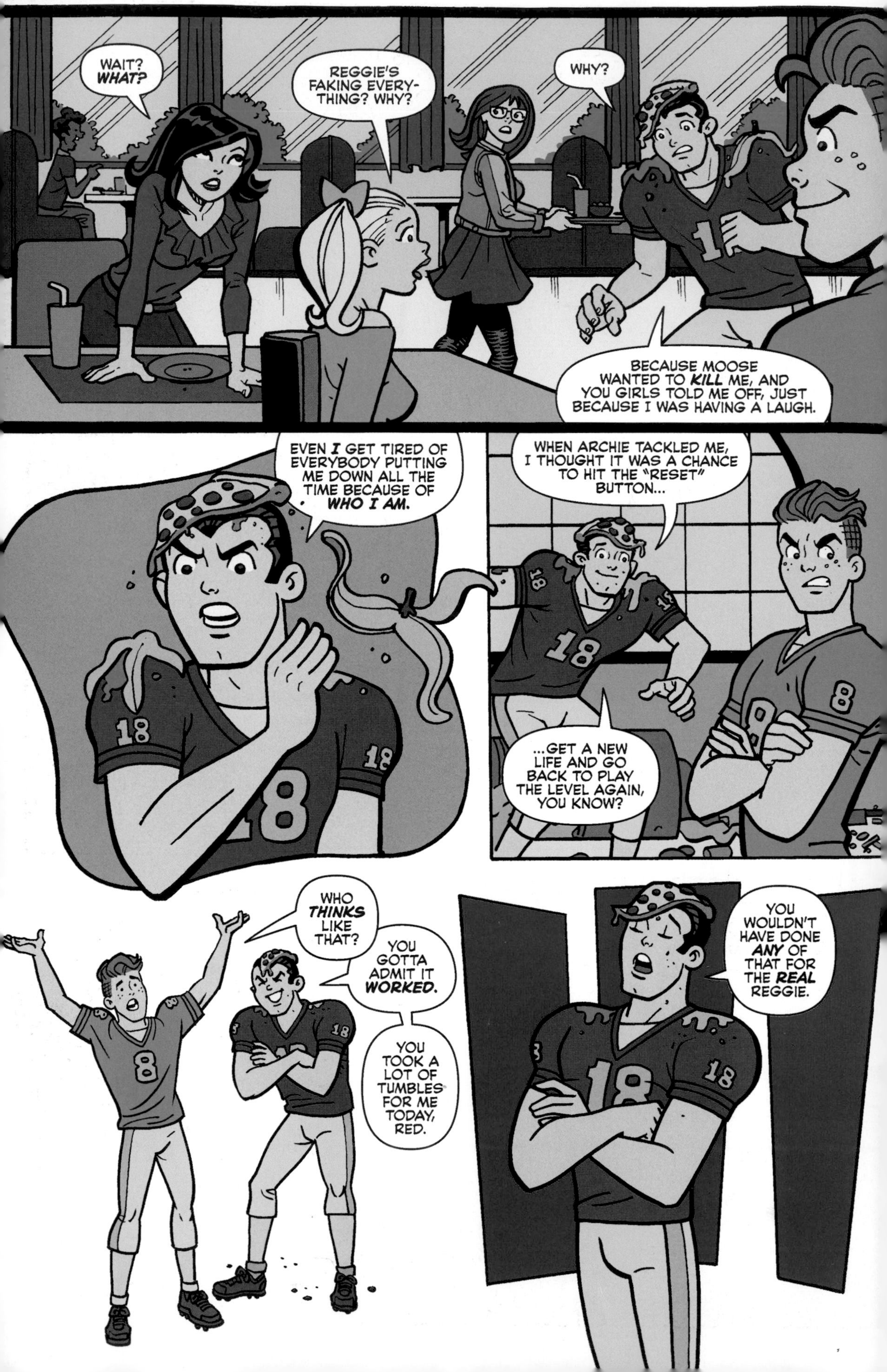
WAIT? WHAT?
REGGIE'S FAKING EVERY-THING? WHY?
WHY?
BECAUSE MOOSE WANTED TO KILL ME, AND YOU GIRLS TOLD ME OFF, JUST BECAUSE I WAS HAVING A LAUGH.
EVEN I GET TIRED OF EVERYBODY PUTTING ME DOWN ALL THE TIME BECAUSE OF WHO I AM.
WHEN ARCHIE TACKLED ME, I THOUGHT IT WAS A CHANCE TO HIT THE "RESET" BUTTON...
...GET A NEW LIFE AND GO BACK TO PLAY THE LEVEL AGAIN, YOU KNOW?
WHO THINKS LIKE THAT?
YOU GOTTA ADMIT IT WORKED.
YOU TOOK A LOT OF TUMBLES FOR ME TODAY, RED.
YOU WOULDN'T HAVE DONE ANY OF THAT FOR THE REAL REGGIE.

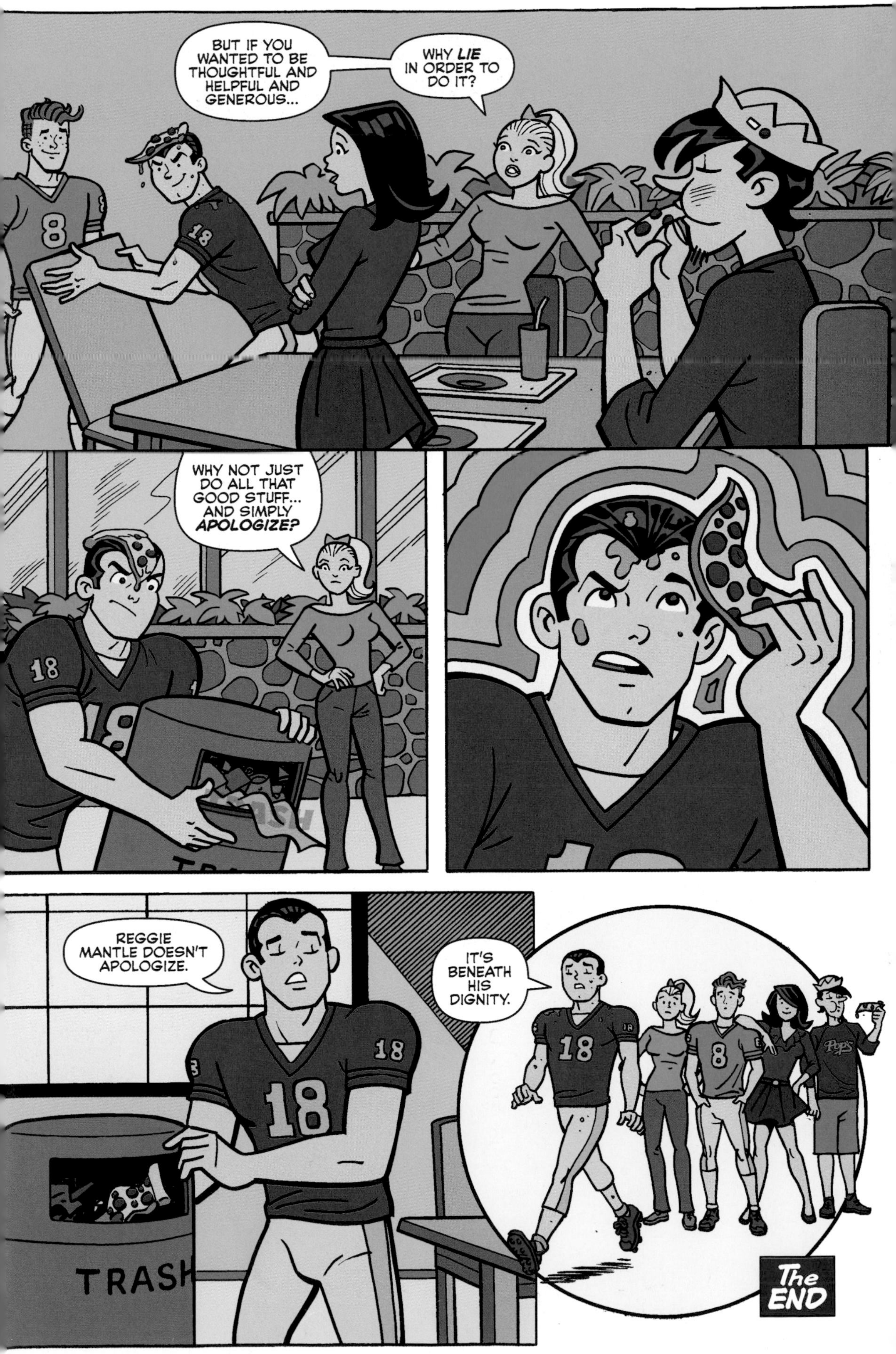
BUT IF YOU WANTED TO BE THOUGHTFUL AND HELPFUL AND GENEROUS...
WHY *LIE* IN ORDER TO DO IT?
WHY NOT JUST DO ALL THAT GOOD STUFF... AND SIMPLY ***APOLOGIZE?***
REGGIE MANTLE DOESN'T APOLOGIZE.
IT'S BENEATH HIS DIGNITY.
TRASH
The END

CHAPTER 4
PART 1

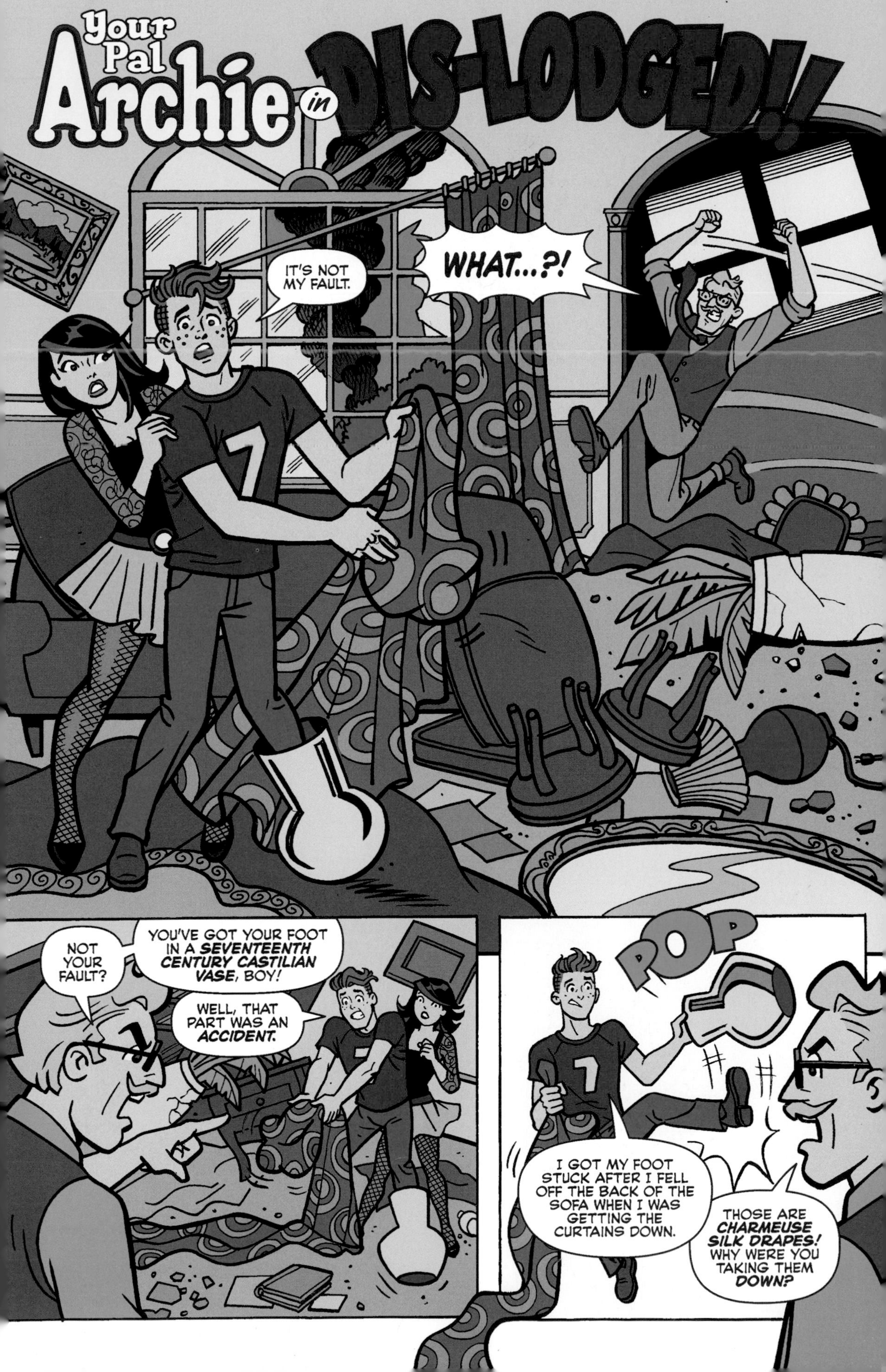
Your Pal Archie in
DIS-LODGED!!
IT'S NOT MY FAULT.
WHAT...?!
NOT YOUR FAULT?
YOU'VE GOT YOUR FOOT IN A SEVENTEENTH CENTURY CASTILIAN VASE, BOY!
WELL, THAT PART WAS AN ACCIDENT.
POP
I GOT MY FOOT STUCK AFTER I FELL OFF THE BACK OF THE SOFA WHEN I WAS GETTING THE CURTAINS DOWN.
THOSE ARE CHARMEUSE SILK DRAPES! WHY WERE YOU TAKING THEM DOWN?

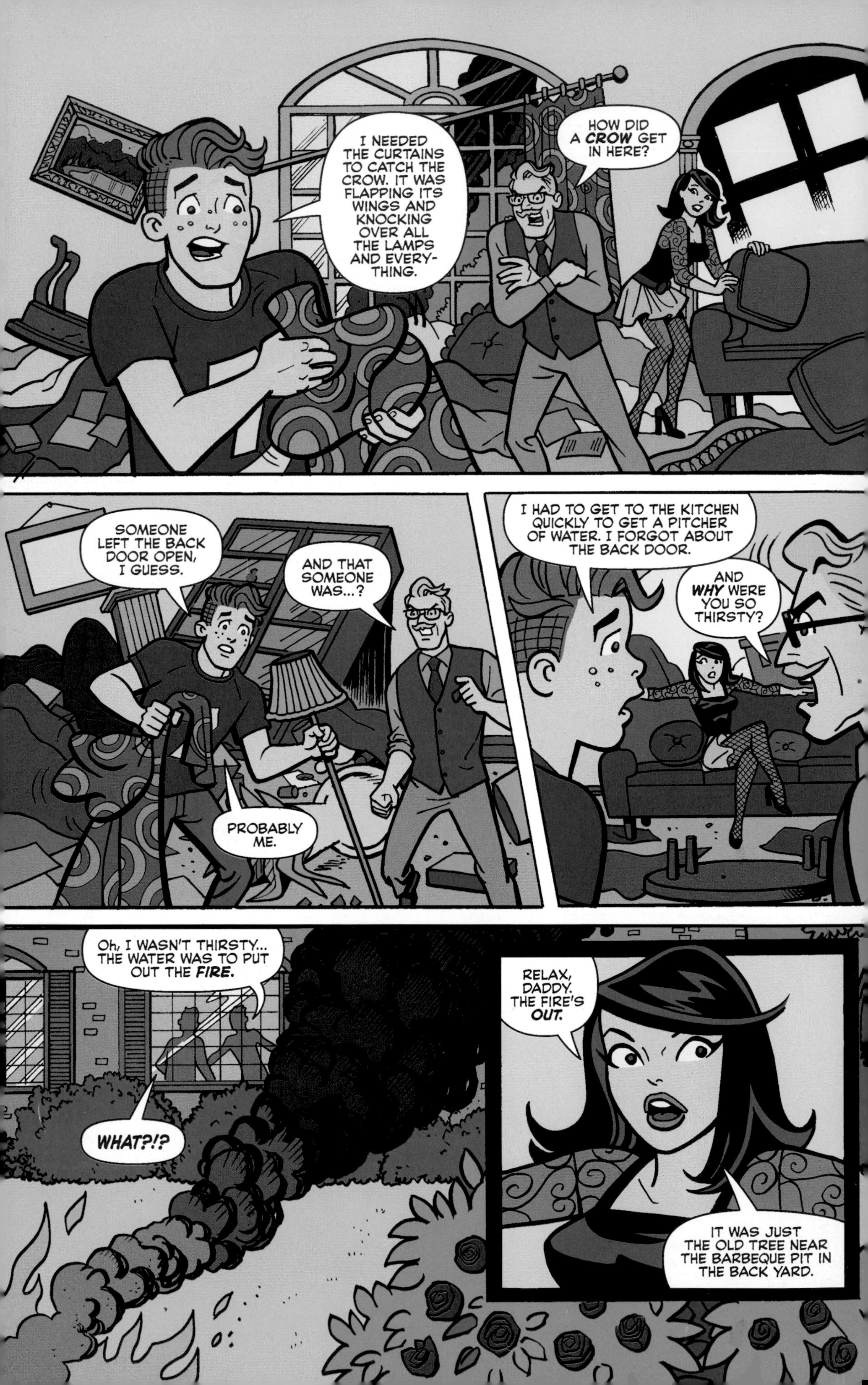
I NEEDED THE CURTAINS TO CATCH THE CROW. IT WAS FLAPPING ITS WINGS AND KNOCKING OVER ALL THE LAMPS AND EVERY-THING.
HOW DID A **CROW** GET IN HERE?
SOMEONE LEFT THE BACK DOOR OPEN, I GUESS.
AND THAT SOMEONE WAS...?
PROBABLY ME.
I HAD TO GET TO THE KITCHEN QUICKLY TO GET A PITCHER OF WATER. I FORGOT ABOUT THE BACK DOOR.
AND **WHY** WERE YOU SO THIRSTY?
Oh, I WASN'T THIRSTY... THE WATER WAS TO PUT OUT THE **FIRE**.
WHAT?!?
RELAX, DADDY. THE FIRE'S **OUT**.
IT WAS JUST THE OLD TREE NEAR THE BARBEQUE PIT IN THE BACK YARD.

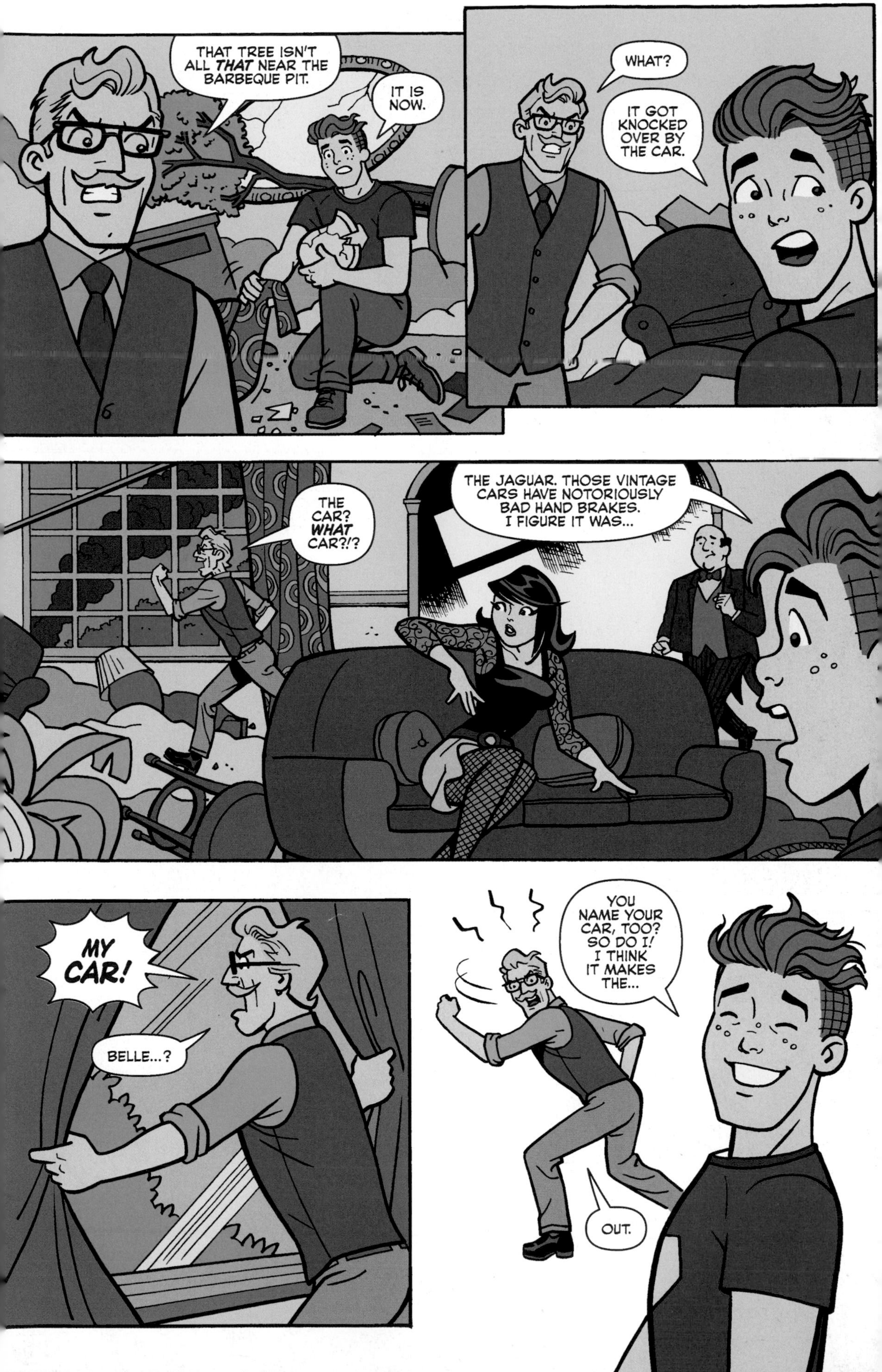
THAT TREE ISN'T ALL *THAT* NEAR THE BARBEQUE PIT.
IT IS NOW.
WHAT?
IT GOT KNOCKED OVER BY THE CAR.
THE CAR? *WHAT* CAR?!?
THE JAGUAR. THOSE VINTAGE CARS HAVE NOTORIOUSLY BAD HAND BRAKES. I FIGURE IT WAS...
MY CAR!
BELLE...?
YOU NAME YOUR CAR, TOO? SO DO I! I THINK IT MAKES THE...
OUT.

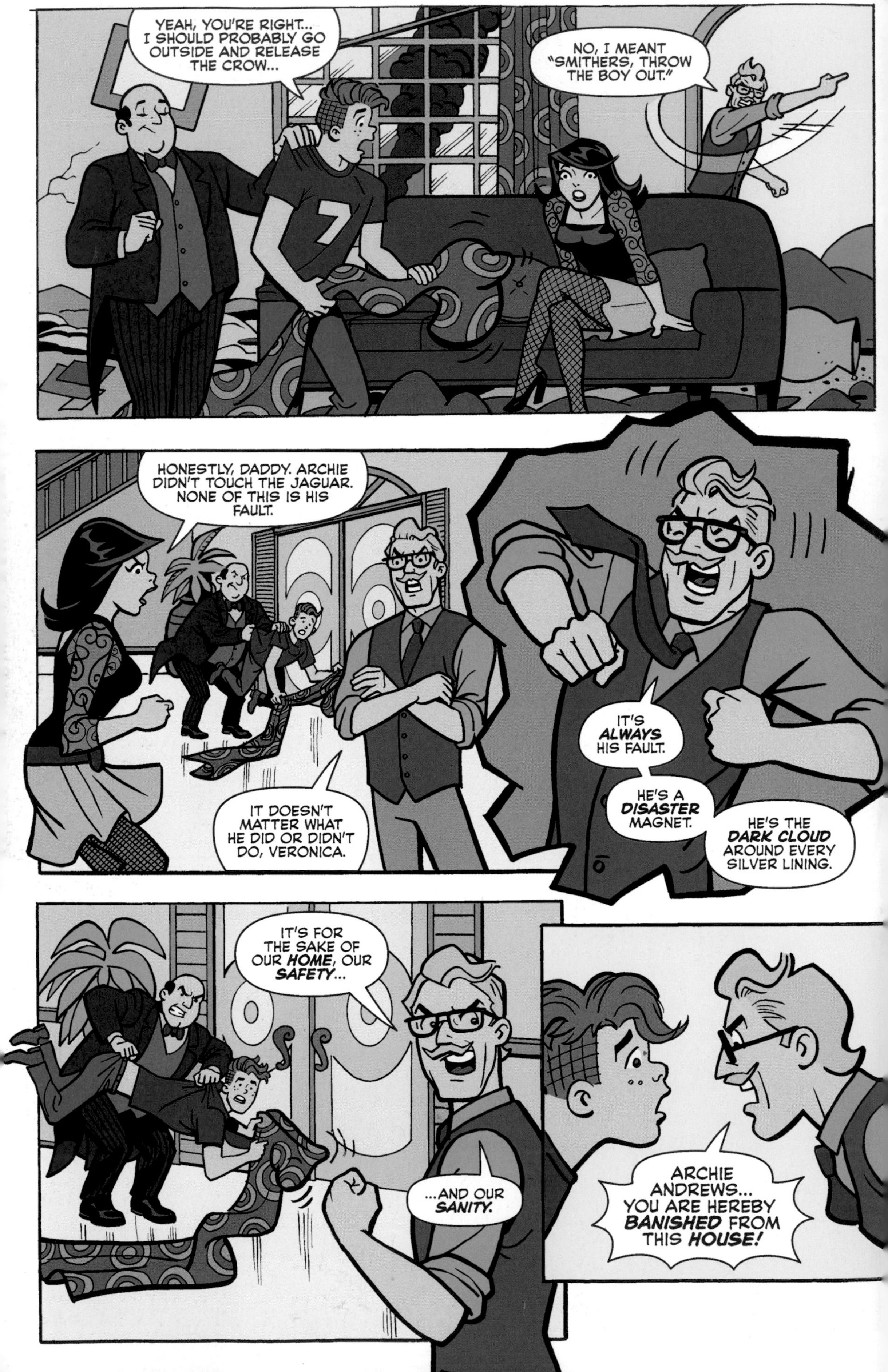
YEAH, YOU'RE RIGHT... I SHOULD PROBABLY GO OUTSIDE AND RELEASE THE CROW...
NO, I MEANT "SMITHERS, THROW THE BOY OUT."
HONESTLY, DADDY. ARCHIE DIDN'T TOUCH THE JAGUAR. NONE OF THIS IS HIS FAULT.
IT DOESN'T MATTER WHAT HE DID OR DIDN'T DO, VERONICA.
IT'S ALWAYS HIS FAULT.
HE'S A DISASTER MAGNET.
HE'S THE DARK CLOUD AROUND EVERY SILVER LINING.
IT'S FOR THE SAKE OF OUR HOME, OUR SAFETY...
...AND OUR SANITY.
ARCHIE ANDREWS... YOU ARE HEREBY BANISHED FROM THIS HOUSE!

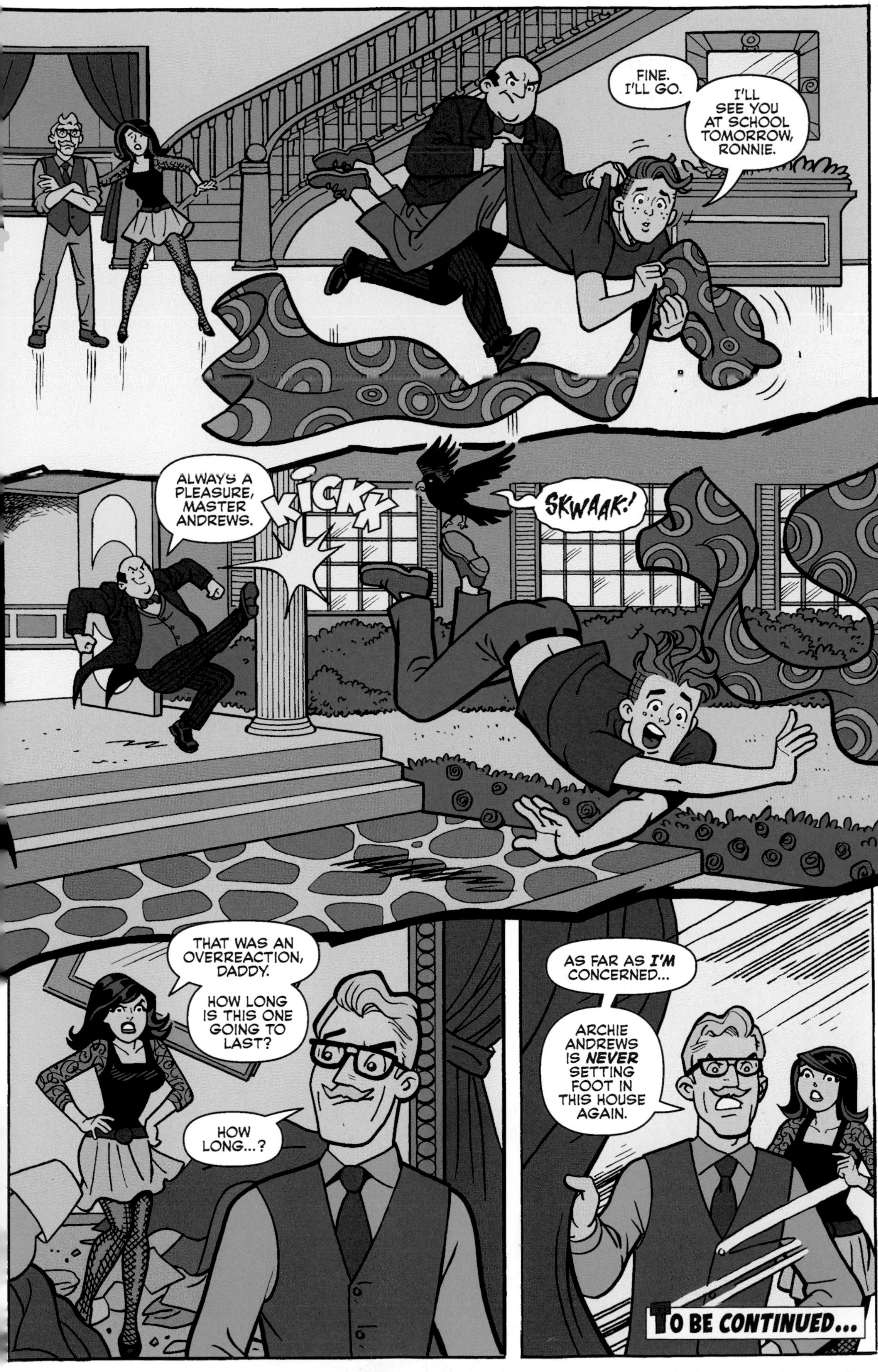
FINE. I'LL GO.
I'LL SEE YOU AT SCHOOL TOMORROW, RONNIE.
ALWAYS A PLEASURE, MASTER ANDREWS.
KICKK
SKWAAK!
THAT WAS AN OVERREACTION, DADDY.
HOW LONG IS THIS ONE GOING TO LAST?
HOW LONG...?
AS FAR AS I'M CONCERNED...
ARCHIE ANDREWS IS NEVER SETTING FOOT IN THIS HOUSE AGAIN.
TO BE CONTINUED...

CHAPTER 4
PART 2

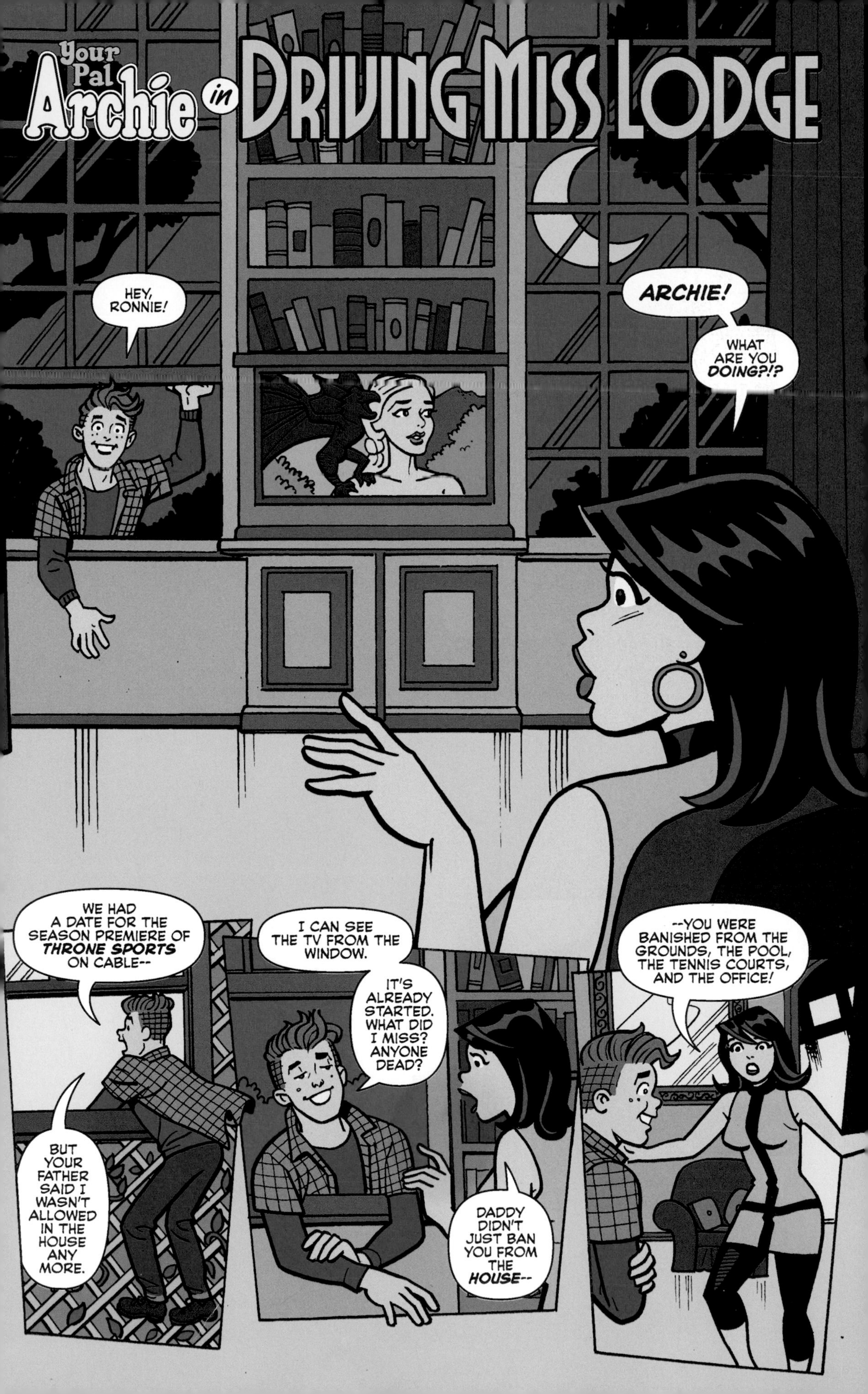
Your Pal Archie in DRIVING MISS LODGE
HEY, RONNIE!
ARCHIE!
WHAT ARE YOU DOING?!?
WE HAD A DATE FOR THE SEASON PREMIERE OF THRONE SPORTS ON CABLE--
BUT YOUR FATHER SAID I WASN'T ALLOWED IN THE HOUSE ANY MORE.
I CAN SEE THE TV FROM THE WINDOW.
IT'S ALREADY STARTED. WHAT DID I MISS? ANYONE DEAD?
DADDY DIDN'T JUST BAN YOU FROM THE HOUSE--
--YOU WERE BANISHED FROM THE GROUNDS, THE POOL, THE TENNIS COURTS, AND THE OFFICE!

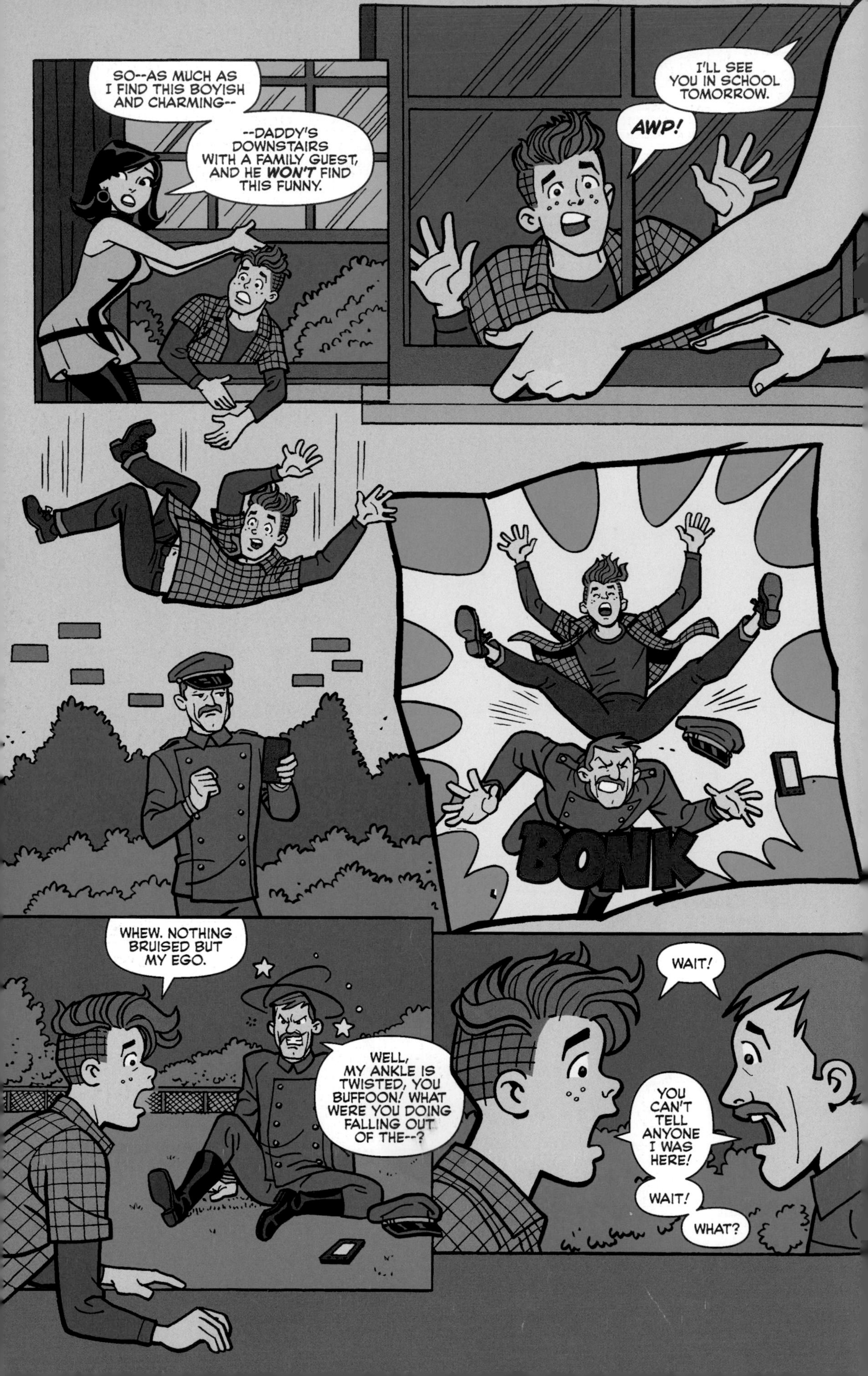
SO--AS MUCH AS I FIND THIS BOYISH AND CHARMING--
--DADDY'S DOWNSTAIRS WITH A FAMILY GUEST, AND HE WON'T FIND THIS FUNNY.
I'LL SEE YOU IN SCHOOL TOMORROW.
AWP!
BONK
WHEW. NOTHING BRUISED BUT MY EGO.
WELL, MY ANKLE IS TWISTED, YOU BUFFOON! WHAT WERE YOU DOING FALLING OUT OF THE--?
WAIT!
YOU CAN'T TELL ANYONE I WAS HERE!
WAIT!
WHAT?

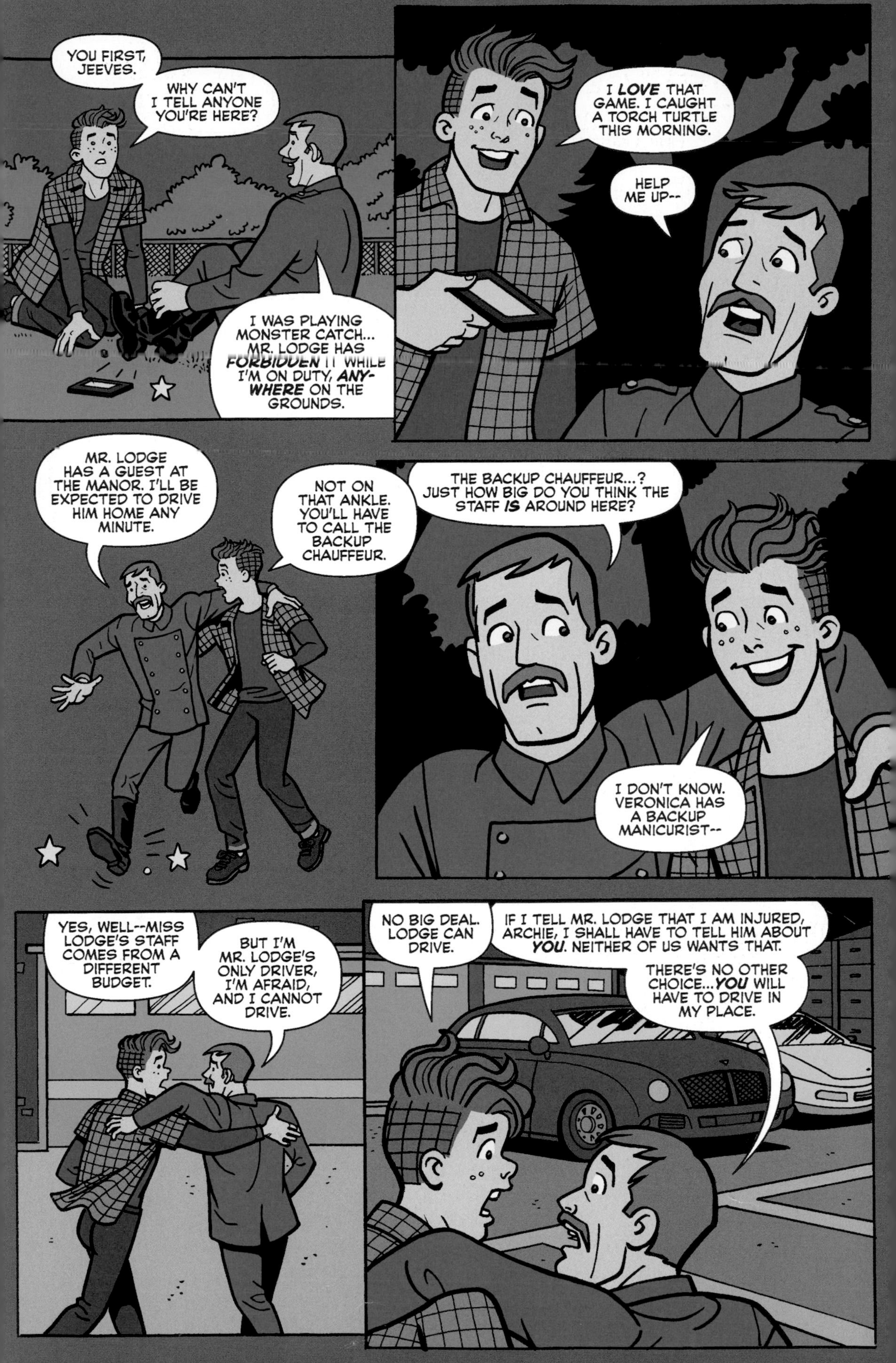
YOU FIRST, JEEVES.
WHY CAN'T I TELL ANYONE YOU'RE HERE?
I WAS PLAYING MONSTER CATCH... MR. LODGE HAS *FORBIDDEN* IT WHILE I'M ON DUTY, *ANYWHERE* ON THE GROUNDS.
I *LOVE* THAT GAME. I CAUGHT A TORCH TURTLE THIS MORNING.
HELP ME UP--
MR. LODGE HAS A GUEST AT THE MANOR. I'LL BE EXPECTED TO DRIVE HIM HOME ANY MINUTE.
NOT ON THAT ANKLE. YOU'LL HAVE TO CALL THE BACKUP CHAUFFEUR.
THE BACKUP CHAUFFEUR...? JUST HOW BIG DO YOU THINK THE STAFF *IS* AROUND HERE?
I DON'T KNOW. VERONICA HAS A BACKUP MANICURIST--
YES, WELL--MISS LODGE'S STAFF COMES FROM A DIFFERENT BUDGET.
BUT I'M MR. LODGE'S ONLY DRIVER, I'M AFRAID, AND I CANNOT DRIVE.
NO BIG DEAL. LODGE CAN DRIVE.
IF I TELL MR. LODGE THAT I AM INJURED, ARCHIE, I SHALL HAVE TO TELL HIM ABOUT *YOU*. NEITHER OF US WANTS THAT.
THERE'S NO OTHER CHOICE...*YOU* WILL HAVE TO DRIVE IN MY PLACE.

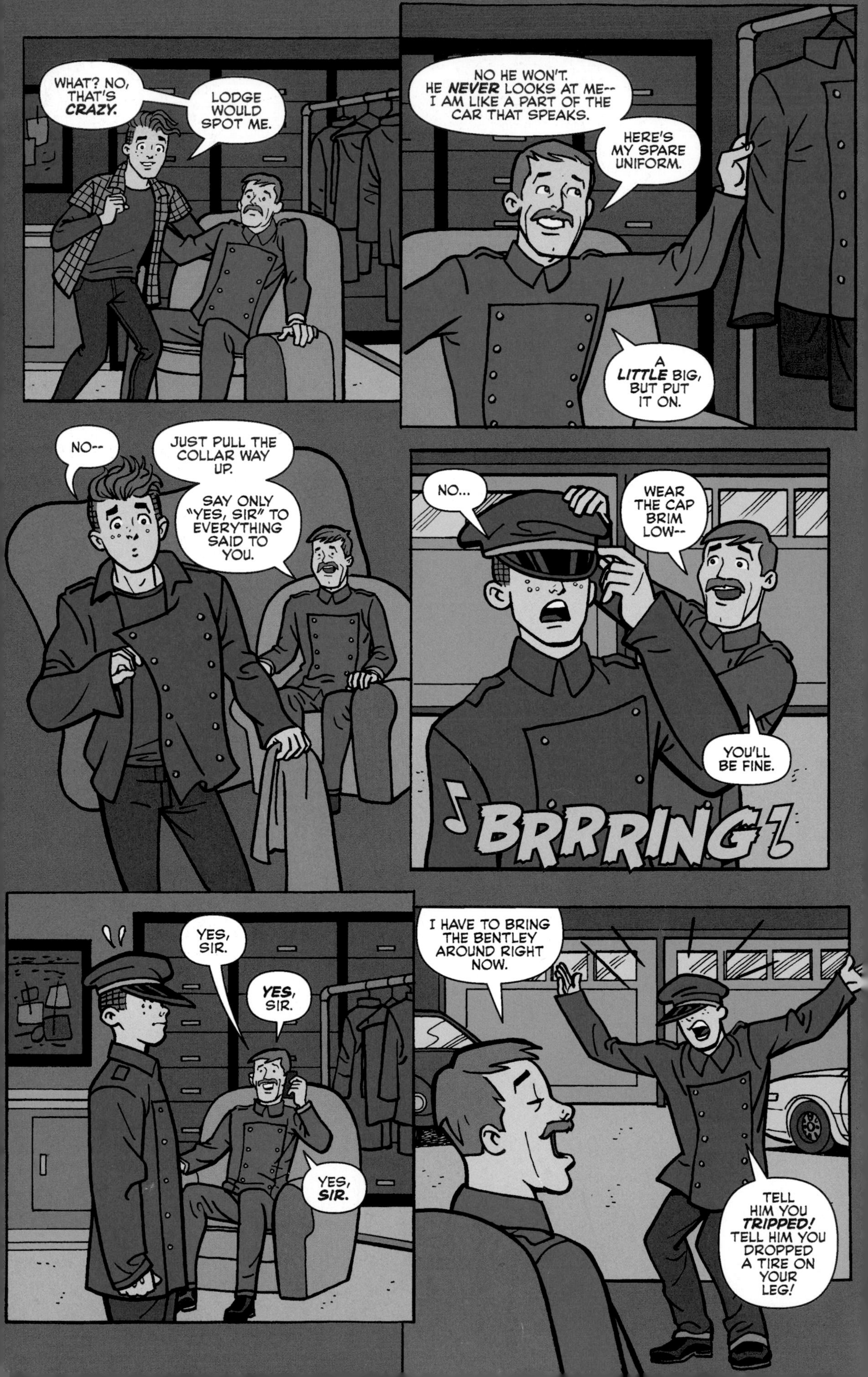
WHAT? NO, THAT'S CRAZY.
LODGE WOULD SPOT ME.
NO HE WON'T. HE NEVER LOOKS AT ME-- I AM LIKE A PART OF THE CAR THAT SPEAKS.
HERE'S MY SPARE UNIFORM.
A LITTLE BIG, BUT PUT IT ON.
NO--
JUST PULL THE COLLAR WAY UP.
SAY ONLY "YES, SIR" TO EVERYTHING SAID TO YOU.
NO...
WEAR THE CAP BRIM LOW--
YOU'LL BE FINE.
BRRRING
YES, SIR.
YES, SIR.
YES, SIR.
I HAVE TO BRING THE BENTLEY AROUND RIGHT NOW.
TELL HIM YOU TRIPPED! TELL HIM YOU DROPPED A TIRE ON YOUR LEG!

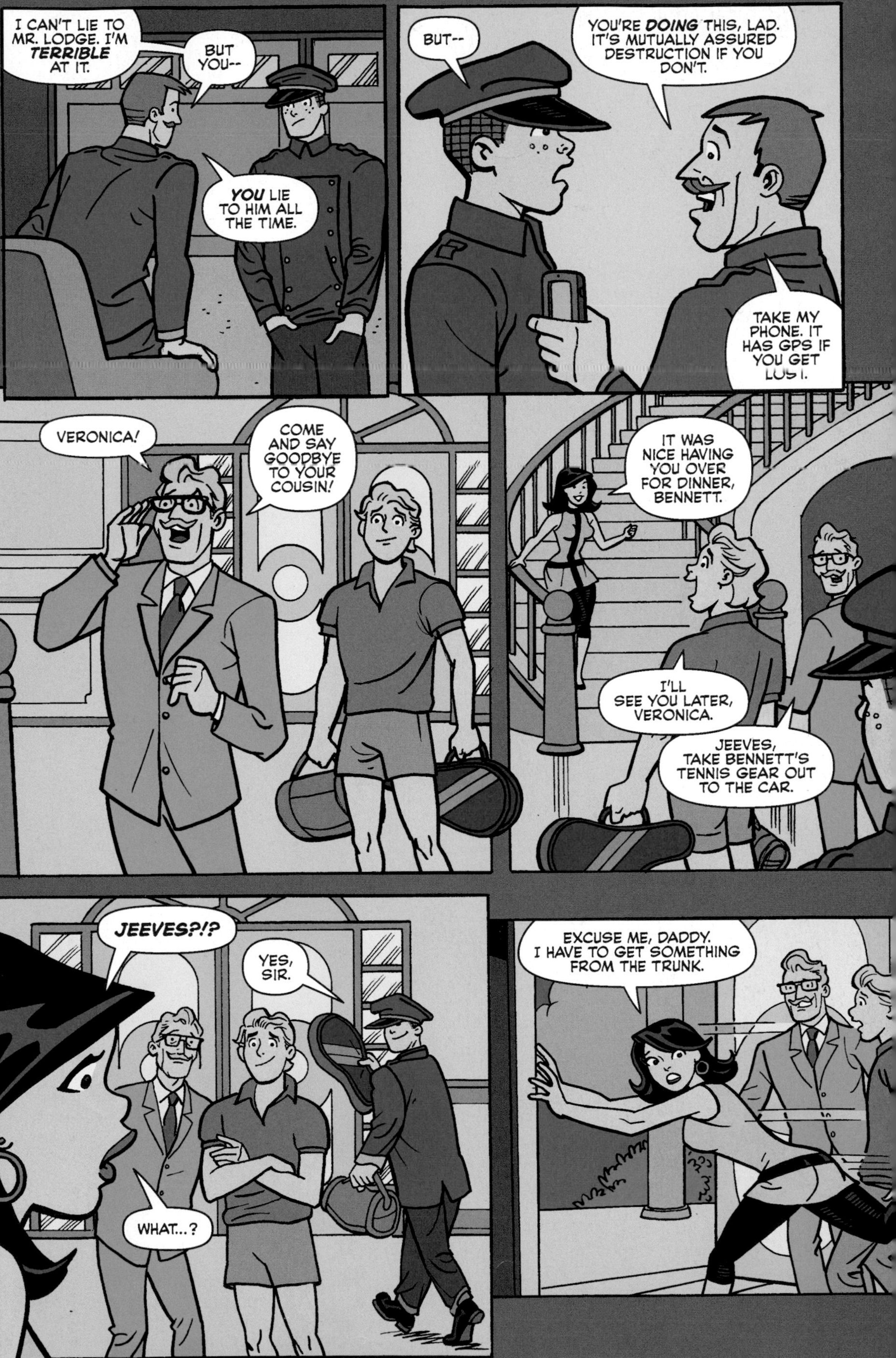
I CAN'T LIE TO MR. LODGE. I'M TERRIBLE AT IT.
BUT YOU--
YOU LIE TO HIM ALL THE TIME.
BUT--
YOU'RE DOING THIS, LAD. IT'S MUTUALLY ASSURED DESTRUCTION IF YOU DON'T.
TAKE MY PHONE. IT HAS GPS IF YOU GET LOST.
VERONICA!
COME AND SAY GOODBYE TO YOUR COUSIN!
IT WAS NICE HAVING YOU OVER FOR DINNER, BENNETT.
I'LL SEE YOU LATER, VERONICA.
JEEVES, TAKE BENNETT'S TENNIS GEAR OUT TO THE CAR.
JEEVES?!?
YES, SIR.
WHAT...?
EXCUSE ME, DADDY. I HAVE TO GET SOMETHING FROM THE TRUNK.

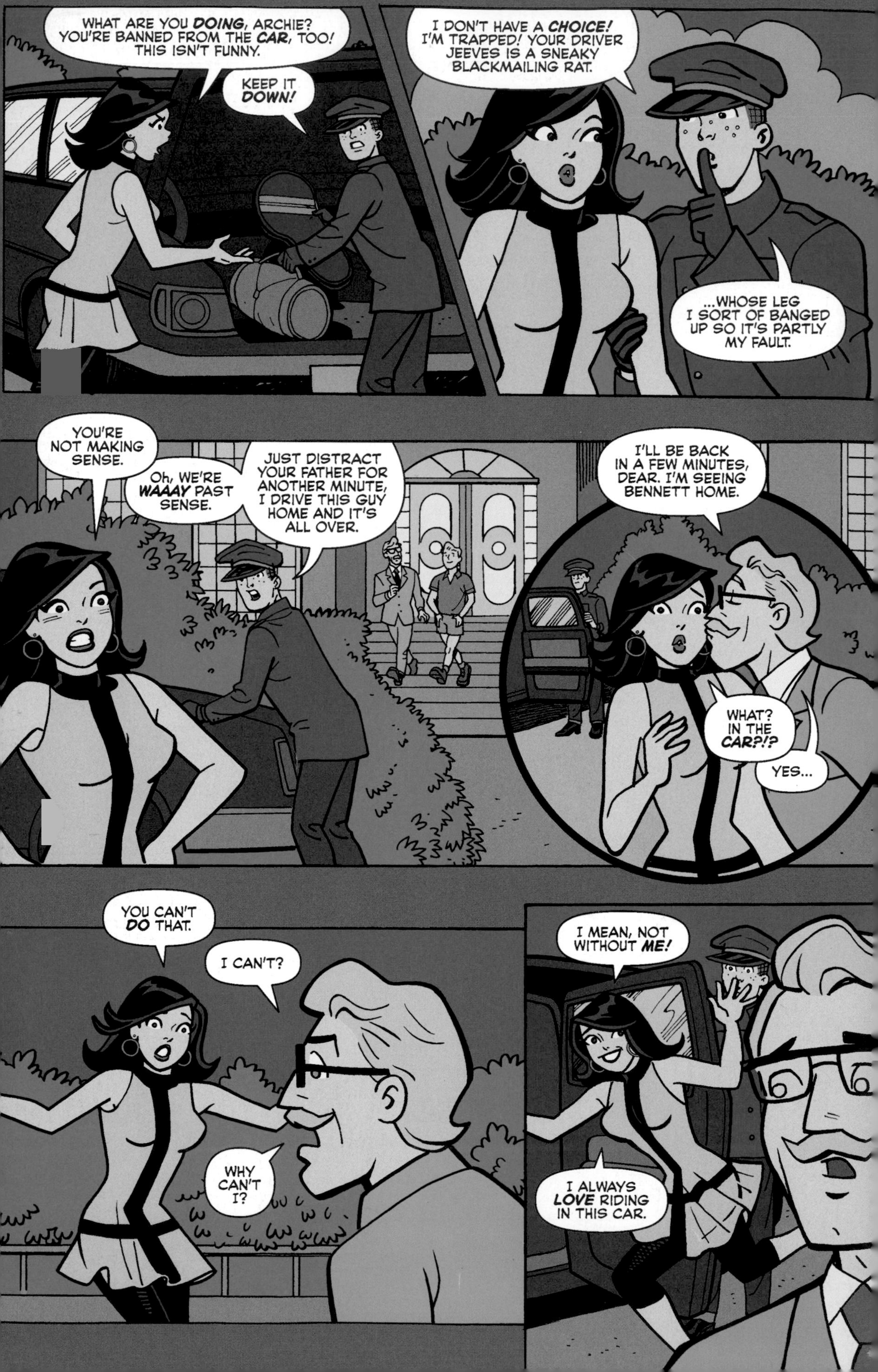

WHAT ARE YOU DOING, ARCHIE? YOU'RE BANNED FROM THE CAR, TOO! THIS ISN'T FUNNY.
KEEP IT DOWN!
I DON'T HAVE A CHOICE! I'M TRAPPED! YOUR DRIVER JEEVES IS A SNEAKY BLACKMAILING RAT.
...WHOSE LEG I SORT OF BANGED UP SO IT'S PARTLY MY FAULT.
YOU'RE NOT MAKING SENSE.
Oh, WE'RE WAAAY PAST SENSE.
JUST DISTRACT YOUR FATHER FOR ANOTHER MINUTE, I DRIVE THIS GUY HOME AND IT'S ALL OVER.
I'LL BE BACK IN A FEW MINUTES, DEAR. I'M SEEING BENNETT HOME.
WHAT? IN THE CAR?!?
YES...
YOU CAN'T DO THAT.
I CAN'T?
WHY CAN'T I?
I MEAN, NOT WITHOUT ME!
I ALWAYS LOVE RIDING IN THIS CAR.

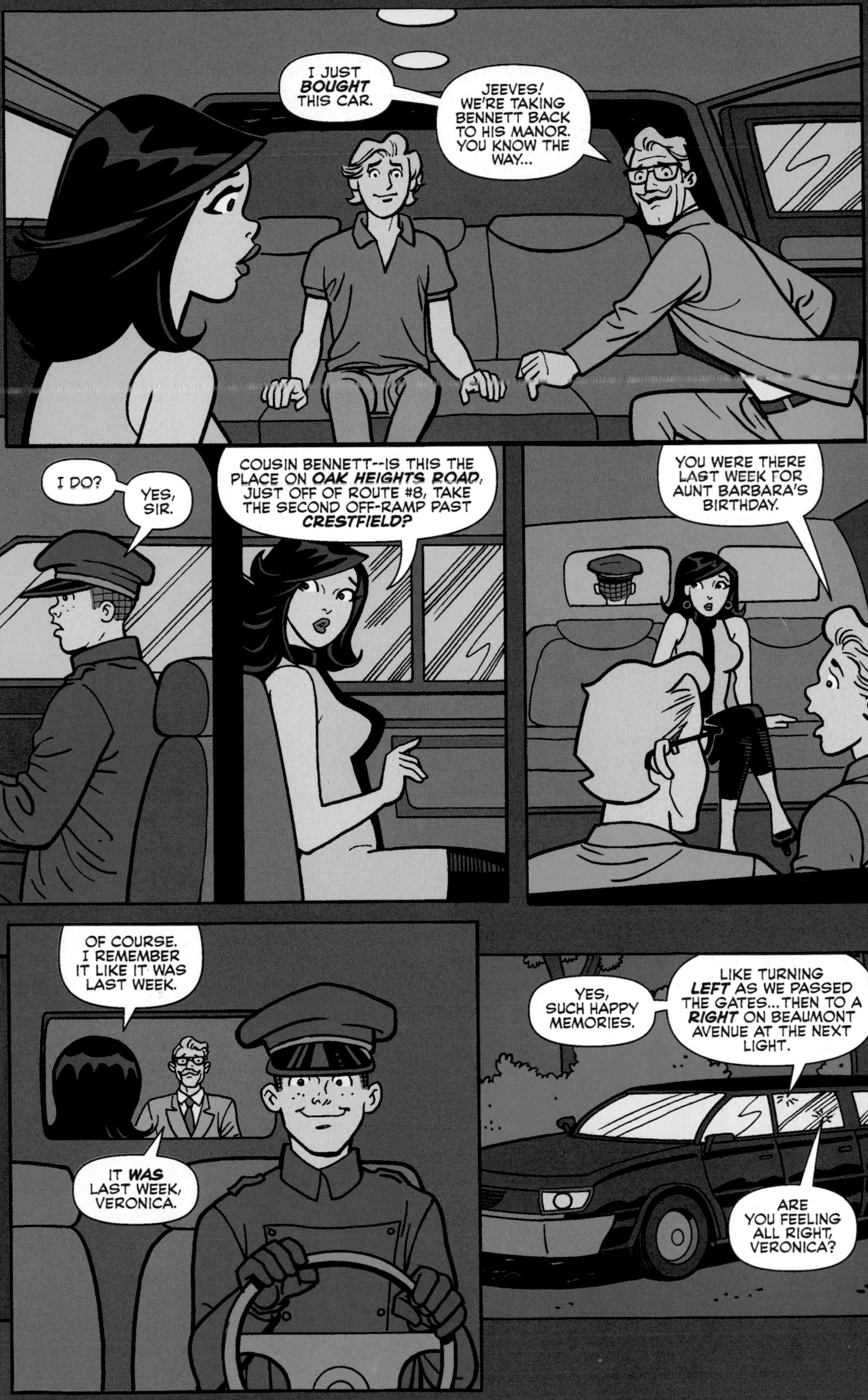
I JUST **BOUGHT** THIS CAR.
JEEVES! WE'RE TAKING BENNETT BACK TO HIS MANOR. YOU KNOW THE WAY...
I DO?
YES, SIR.
COUSIN BENNETT--IS THIS THE PLACE ON **OAK HEIGHTS ROAD**, JUST OFF OF ROUTE #8, TAKE THE SECOND OFF-RAMP PAST **CRESTFIELD?**
YOU WERE THERE LAST WEEK FOR AUNT BARBARA'S BIRTHDAY.
OF COURSE. I REMEMBER IT LIKE IT WAS LAST WEEK.
IT **WAS** LAST WEEK, VERONICA.
YES, SUCH HAPPY MEMORIES.
LIKE TURNING **LEFT** AS WE PASSED THE GATES...THEN TO A **RIGHT** ON BEAUMONT AVENUE AT THE NEXT LIGHT.
ARE YOU FEELING ALL RIGHT, VERONICA?

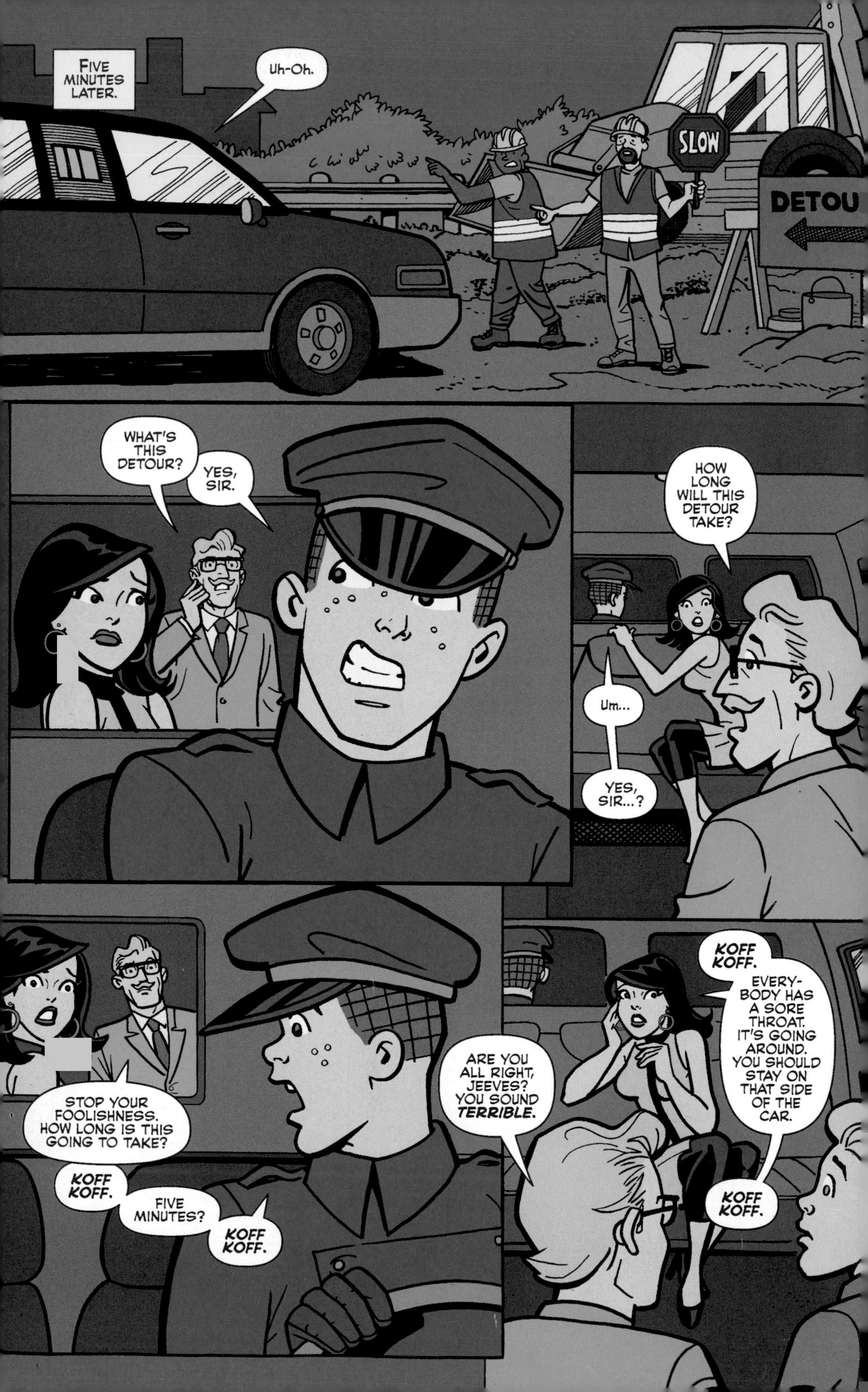
FIVE MINUTES LATER.
Uh-Oh.
SLOW
DETOU
WHAT'S THIS DETOUR?
YES, SIR.
HOW LONG WILL THIS DETOUR TAKE?
Um...
YES, SIR...?
STOP YOUR FOOLISHNESS. HOW LONG IS THIS GOING TO TAKE?
KOFF KOFF.
FIVE MINUTES?
KOFF KOFF.
ARE YOU ALL RIGHT, JEEVES? YOU SOUND *TERRIBLE.*
KOFF KOFF.
EVERY-BODY HAS A SORE THROAT. IT'S GOING AROUND. YOU SHOULD STAY ON THAT SIDE OF THE CAR.
KOFF KOFF.

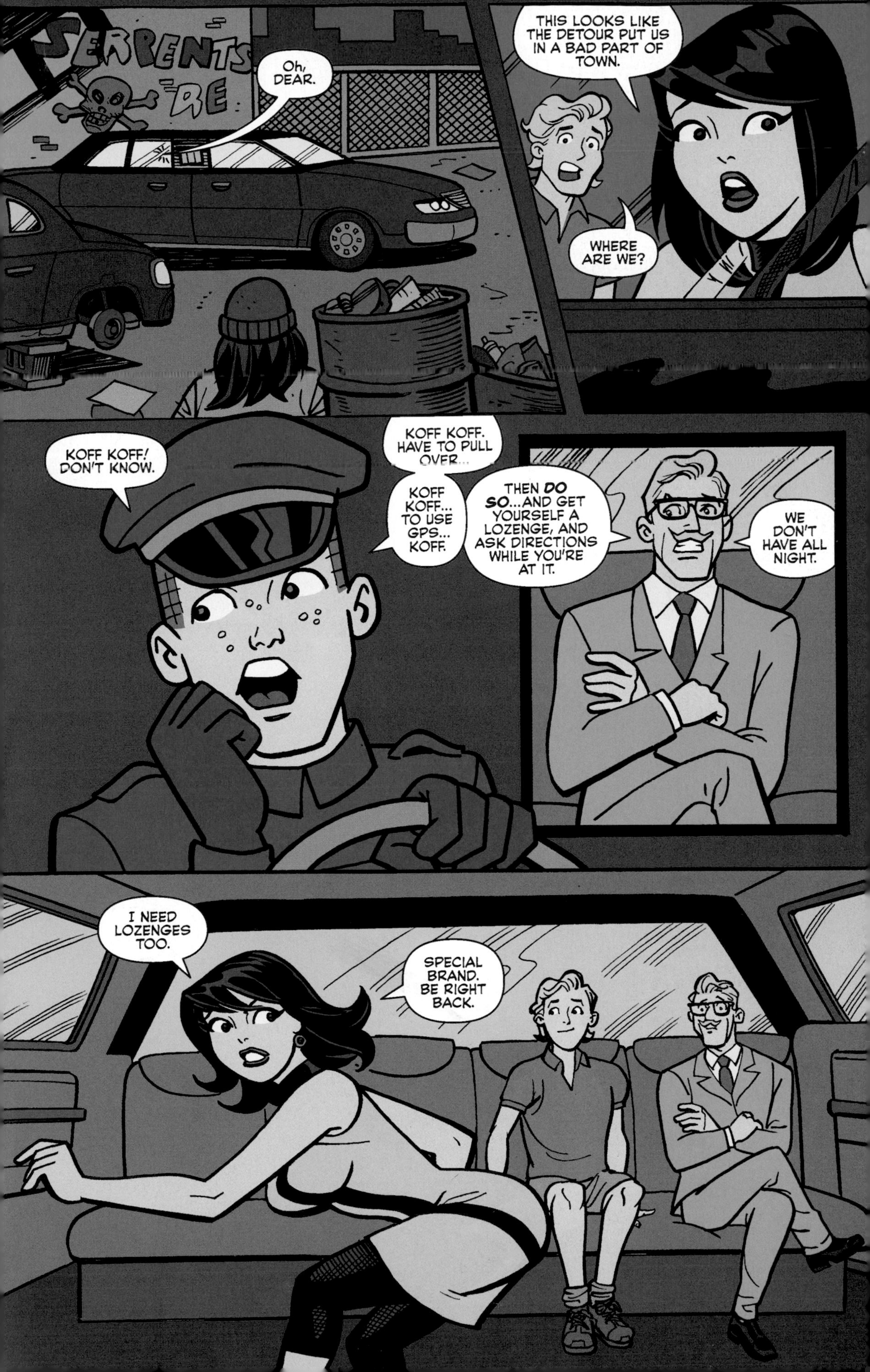

SERPENTS
RE
Oh, DEAR.
THIS LOOKS LIKE THE DETOUR PUT US IN A BAD PART OF TOWN.
WHERE ARE WE?
KOFF KOFF! DON'T KNOW.
KOFF KOFF. HAVE TO PULL OVER...
KOFF KOFF... TO USE GPS... KOFF.
THEN DO SO...AND GET YOURSELF A LOZENGE, AND ASK DIRECTIONS WHILE YOU'RE AT IT.
WE DON'T HAVE ALL NIGHT.
I NEED LOZENGES TOO.
SPECIAL BRAND. BE RIGHT BACK.

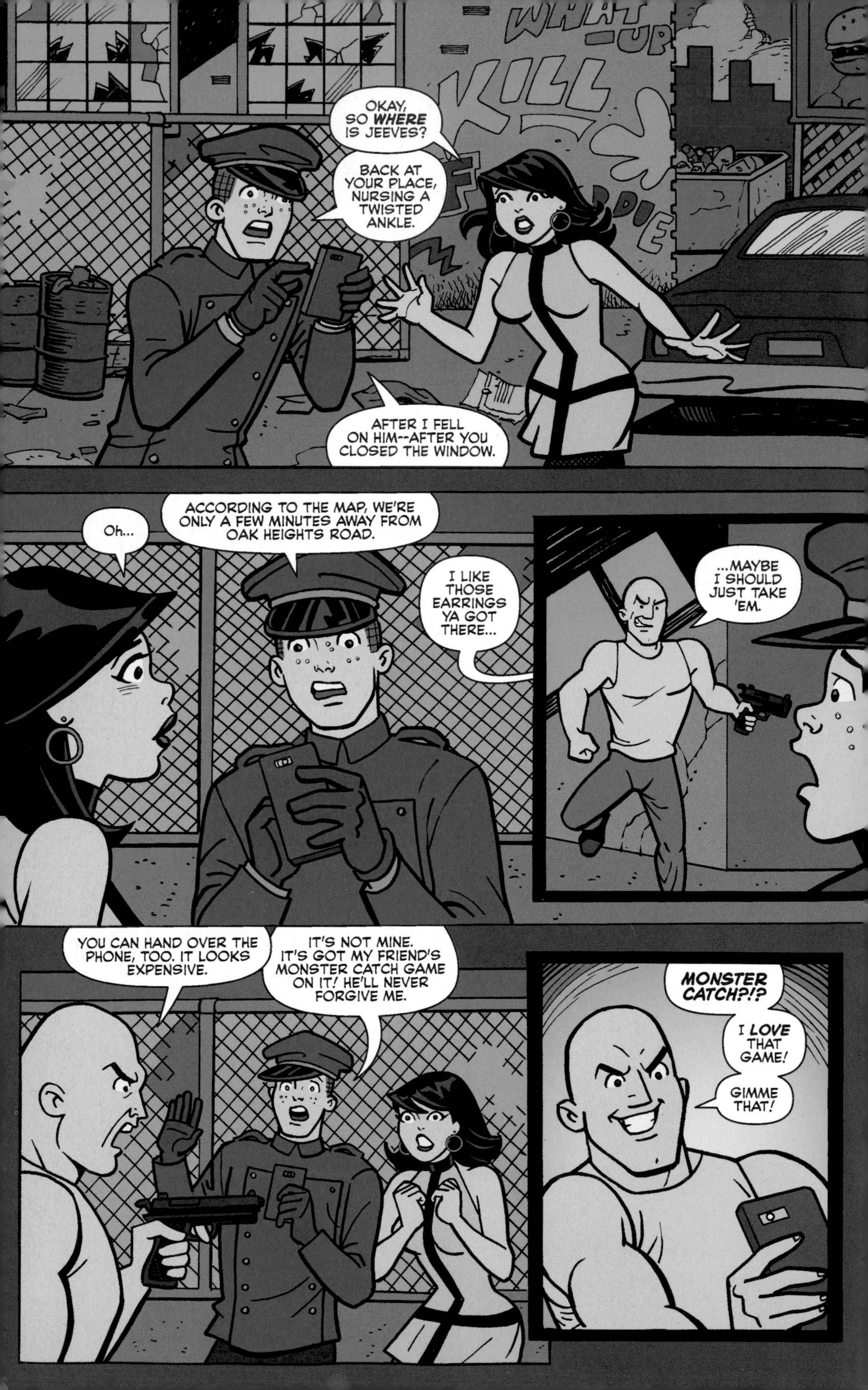
WHAT-UP
KILL
OKAY, SO WHERE IS JEEVES?
BACK AT YOUR PLACE, NURSING A TWISTED ANKLE.
AFTER I FELL ON HIM--AFTER YOU CLOSED THE WINDOW.
Oh...
ACCORDING TO THE MAP, WE'RE ONLY A FEW MINUTES AWAY FROM OAK HEIGHTS ROAD.
I LIKE THOSE EARRINGS YA GOT THERE...
...MAYBE I SHOULD JUST TAKE 'EM.
YOU CAN HAND OVER THE PHONE, TOO. IT LOOKS EXPENSIVE.
IT'S NOT MINE. IT'S GOT MY FRIEND'S MONSTER CATCH GAME ON IT! HE'LL NEVER FORGIVE ME.
MONSTER CATCH?!?
I LOVE THAT GAME!
GIMME THAT!

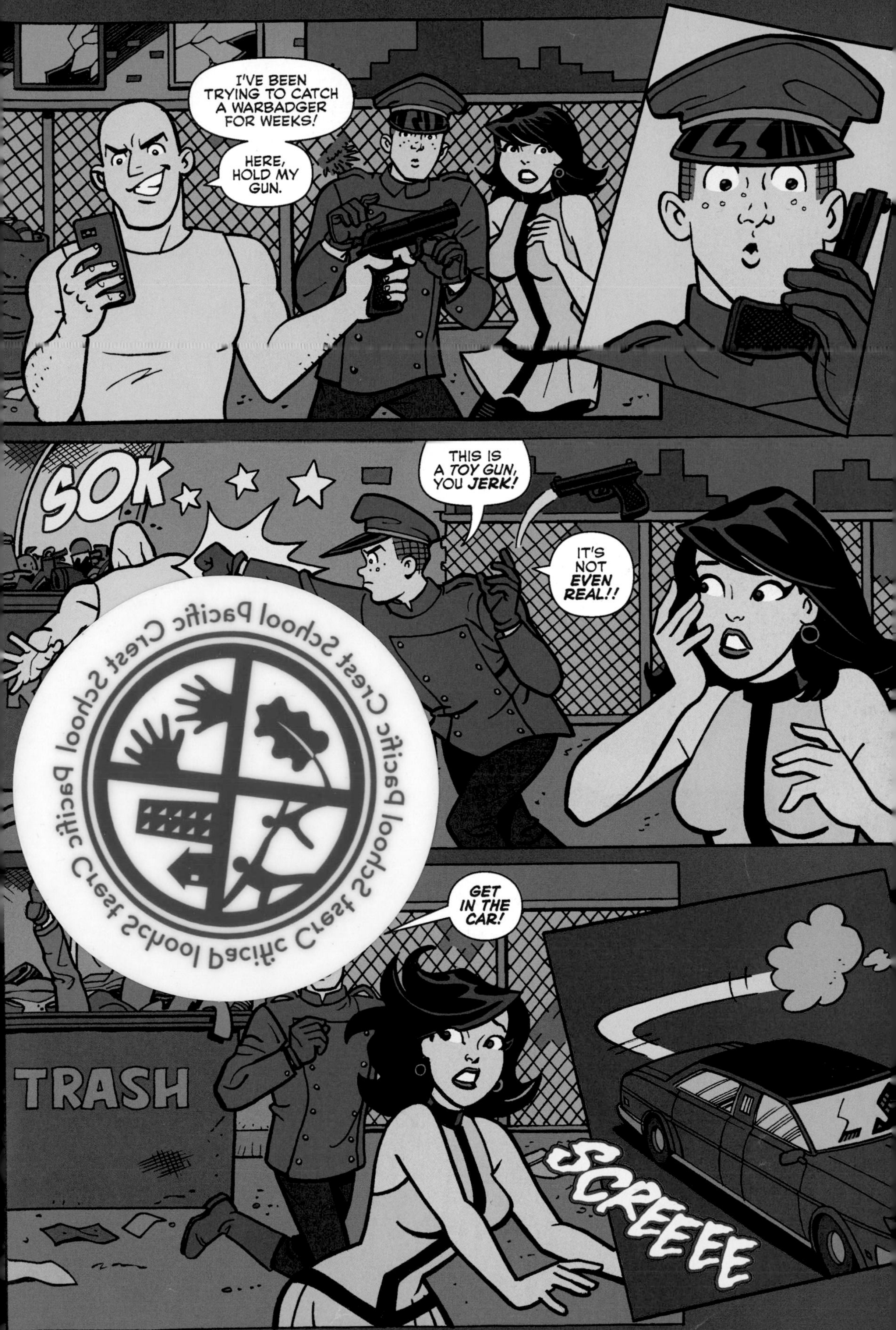
I'VE BEEN TRYING TO CATCH A WARBADGER FOR WEEKS!
HERE, HOLD MY GUN.
SOK
THIS IS A TOY GUN, YOU JERK!
IT'S NOT EVEN REAL!!
GET IN THE CAR!
TRASH
SCREEEEE

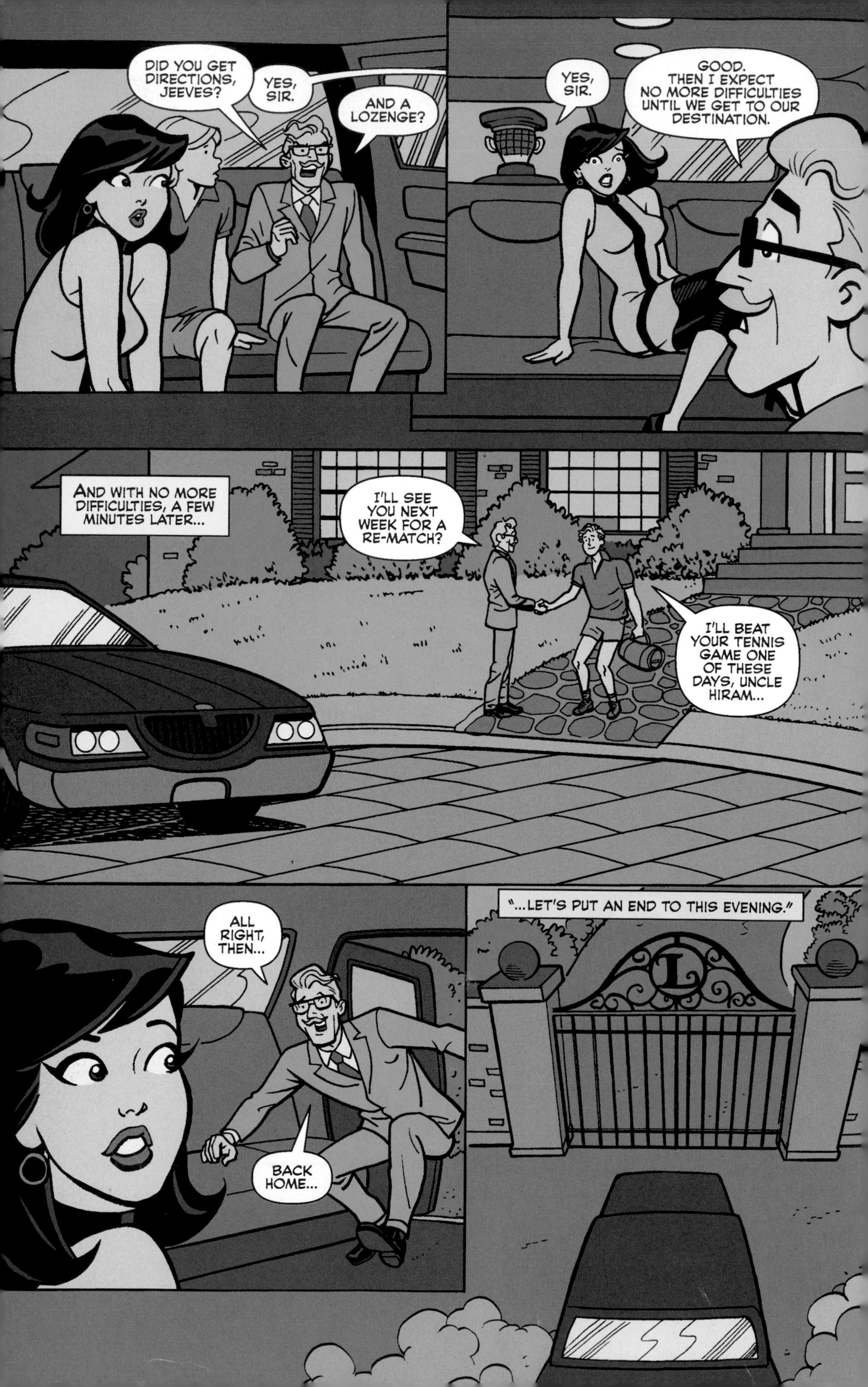
DID YOU GET DIRECTIONS, JEEVES?
YES, SIR.
AND A LOZENGE?
YES, SIR.
GOOD. THEN I EXPECT NO MORE DIFFICULTIES UNTIL WE GET TO OUR DESTINATION.
AND WITH NO MORE DIFFICULTIES, A FEW MINUTES LATER...
I'LL SEE YOU NEXT WEEK FOR A RE-MATCH?
I'LL BEAT YOUR TENNIS GAME ONE OF THESE DAYS, UNCLE HIRAM...
ALL RIGHT, THEN...
BACK HOME...
"...LET'S PUT AN END TO THIS EVENING."

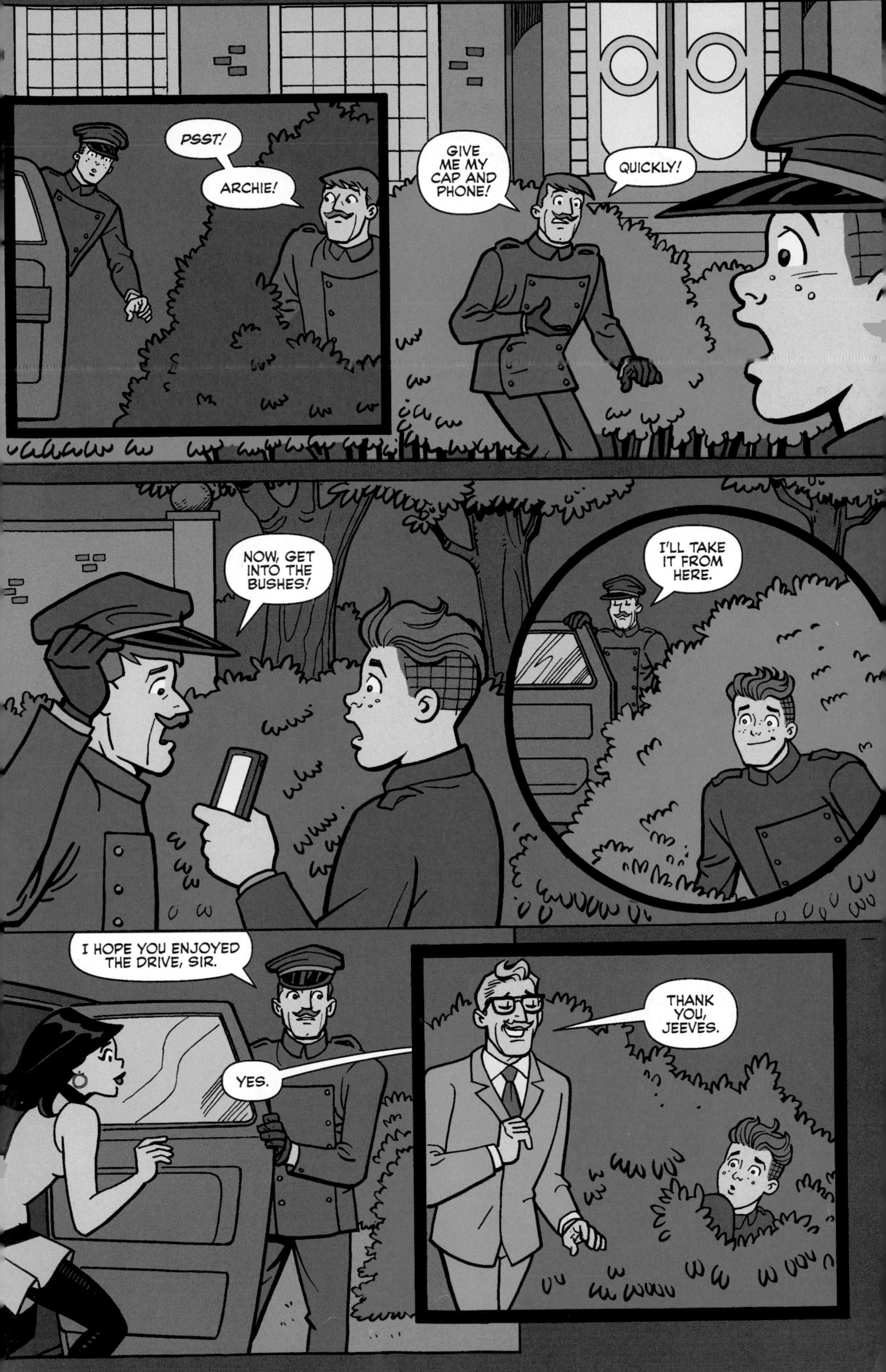
PSST!
ARCHIE!
GIVE ME MY CAP AND PHONE!
QUICKLY!
NOW, GET INTO THE BUSHES!
I'LL TAKE IT FROM HERE.
I HOPE YOU ENJOYED THE DRIVE, SIR.
YES.
THANK YOU, JEEVES.

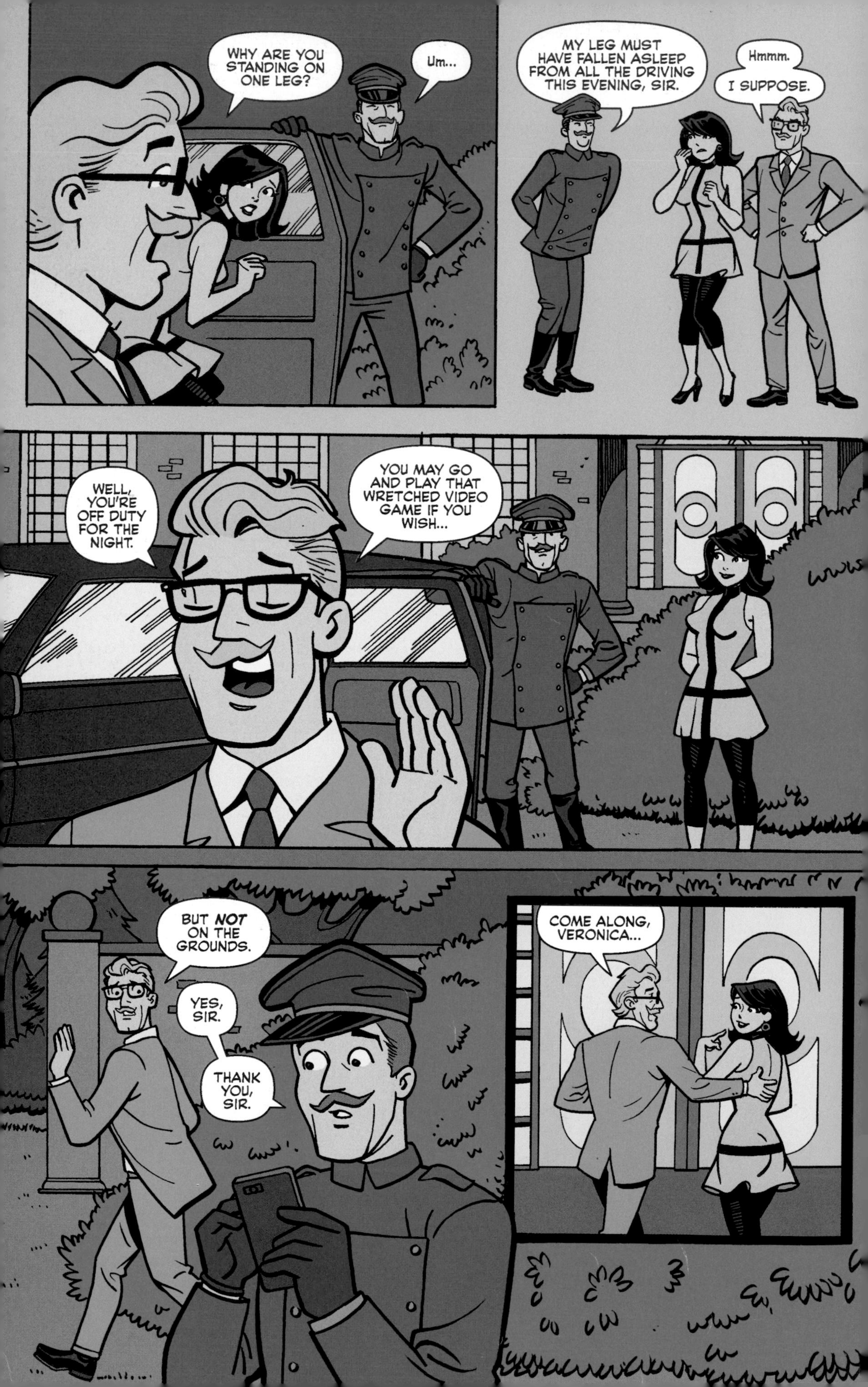
WHY ARE YOU STANDING ON ONE LEG?
Um...
MY LEG MUST HAVE FALLEN ASLEEP FROM ALL THE DRIVING THIS EVENING, SIR.
Hmmm.
I SUPPOSE.
WELL, YOU'RE OFF DUTY FOR THE NIGHT.
YOU MAY GO AND PLAY THAT WRETCHED VIDEO GAME IF YOU WISH...
BUT NOT ON THE GROUNDS.
YES, SIR.
THANK YOU, SIR.
COME ALONG, VERONICA...

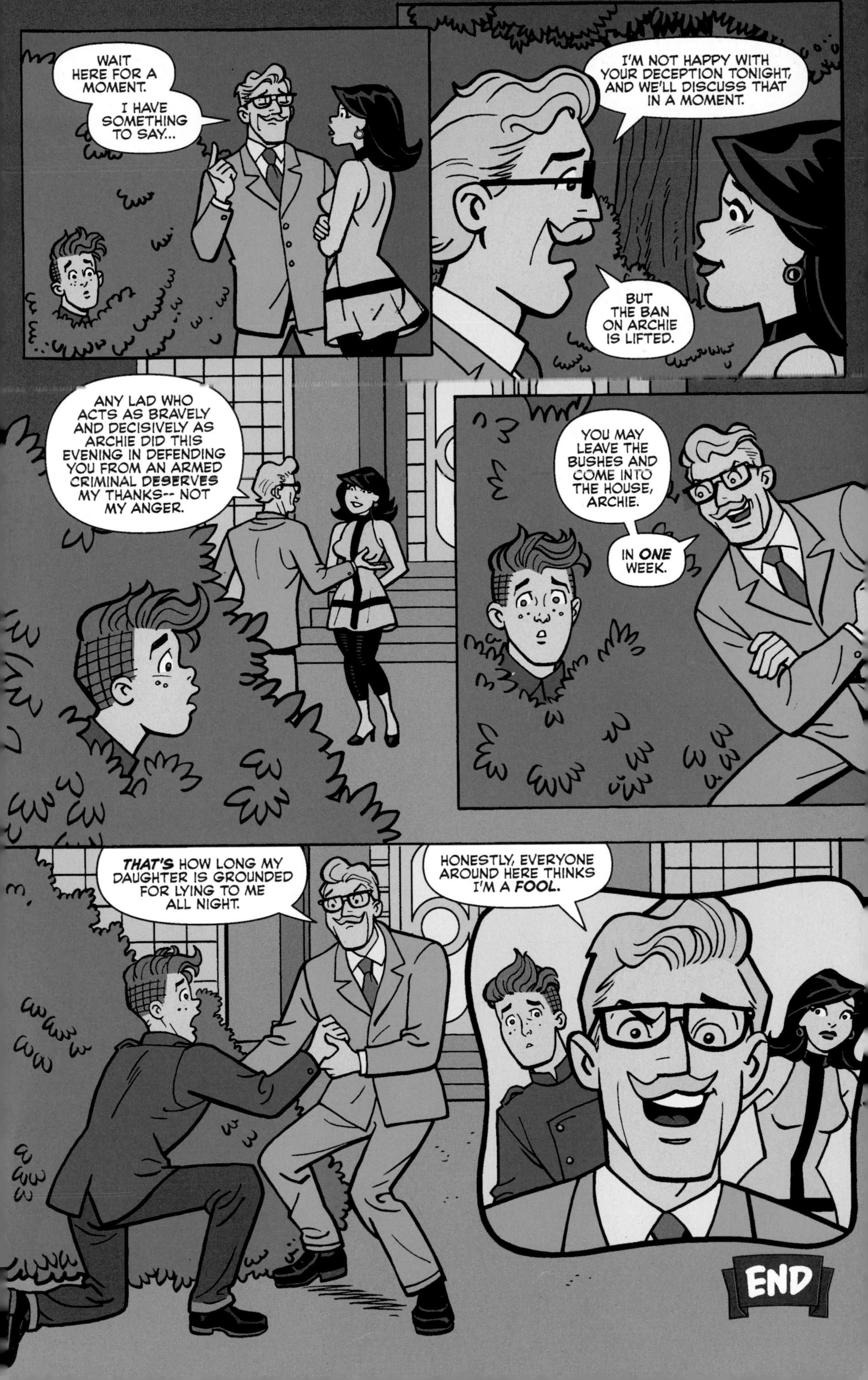
WAIT HERE FOR A MOMENT.
I HAVE SOMETHING TO SAY...
I'M NOT HAPPY WITH YOUR DECEPTION TONIGHT, AND WE'LL DISCUSS THAT IN A MOMENT.
BUT THE BAN ON ARCHIE IS LIFTED.
ANY LAD WHO ACTS AS BRAVELY AND DECISIVELY AS ARCHIE DID THIS EVENING IN DEFENDING YOU FROM AN ARMED CRIMINAL DESERVES MY THANKS-- NOT MY ANGER.
YOU MAY LEAVE THE BUSHES AND COME INTO THE HOUSE, ARCHIE.
IN ONE WEEK.
THAT'S HOW LONG MY DAUGHTER IS GROUNDED FOR LYING TO ME ALL NIGHT.
HONESTLY, EVERYONE AROUND HERE THINKS I'M A FOOL.
END

CHAPTER 5
PART 1

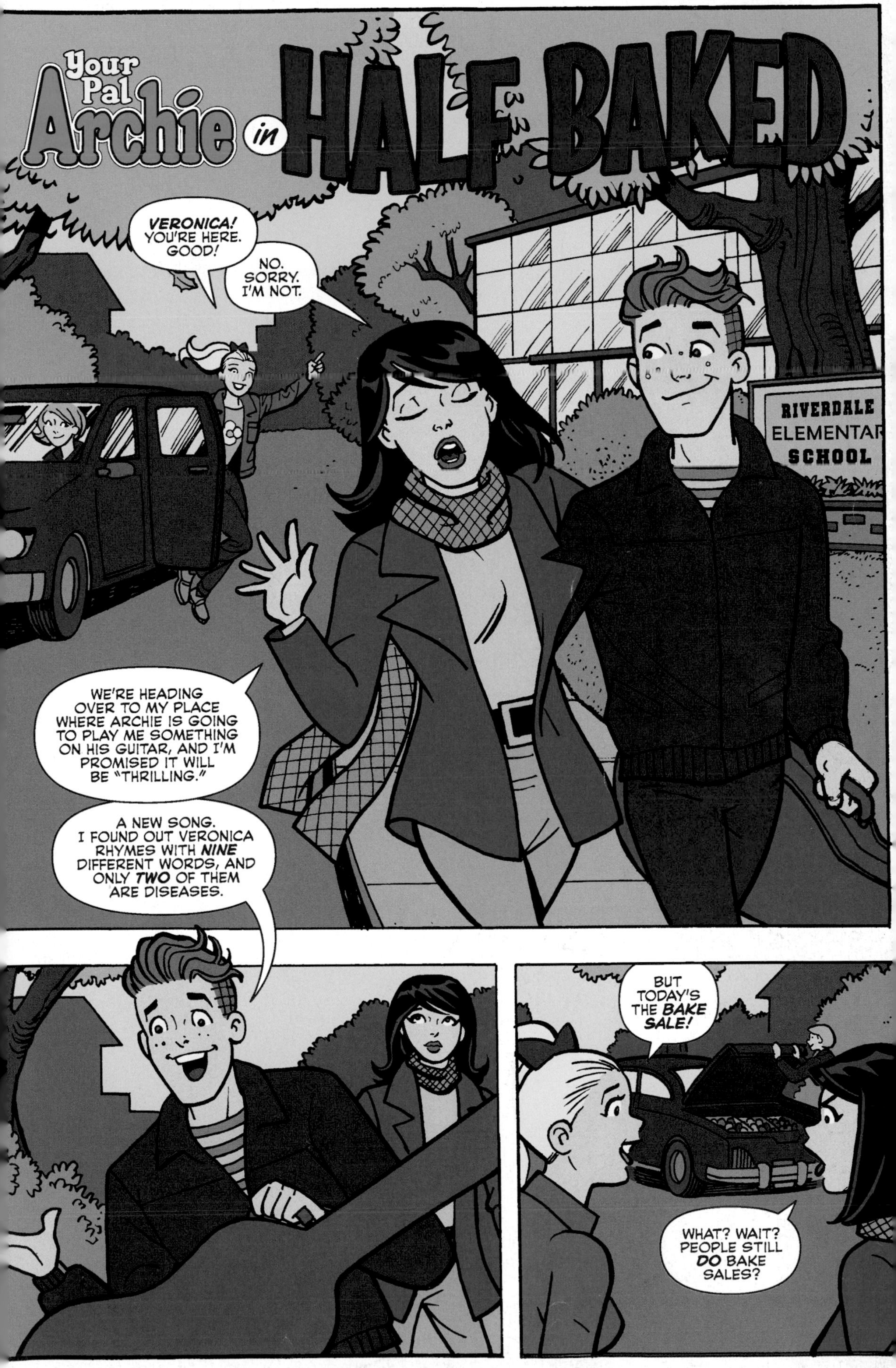
Your Pal Archie in HALF BAKED
VERONICA! YOU'RE HERE. GOOD!
NO. SORRY. I'M NOT.
RIVERDALE ELEMENTARY SCHOOL
WE'RE HEADING OVER TO MY PLACE WHERE ARCHIE IS GOING TO PLAY ME SOMETHING ON HIS GUITAR, AND I'M PROMISED IT WILL BE "THRILLING."
A NEW SONG. I FOUND OUT VERONICA RHYMES WITH NINE DIFFERENT WORDS, AND ONLY TWO OF THEM ARE DISEASES.
BUT TODAY'S THE BAKE SALE!
WHAT? WAIT? PEOPLE STILL DO BAKE SALES?

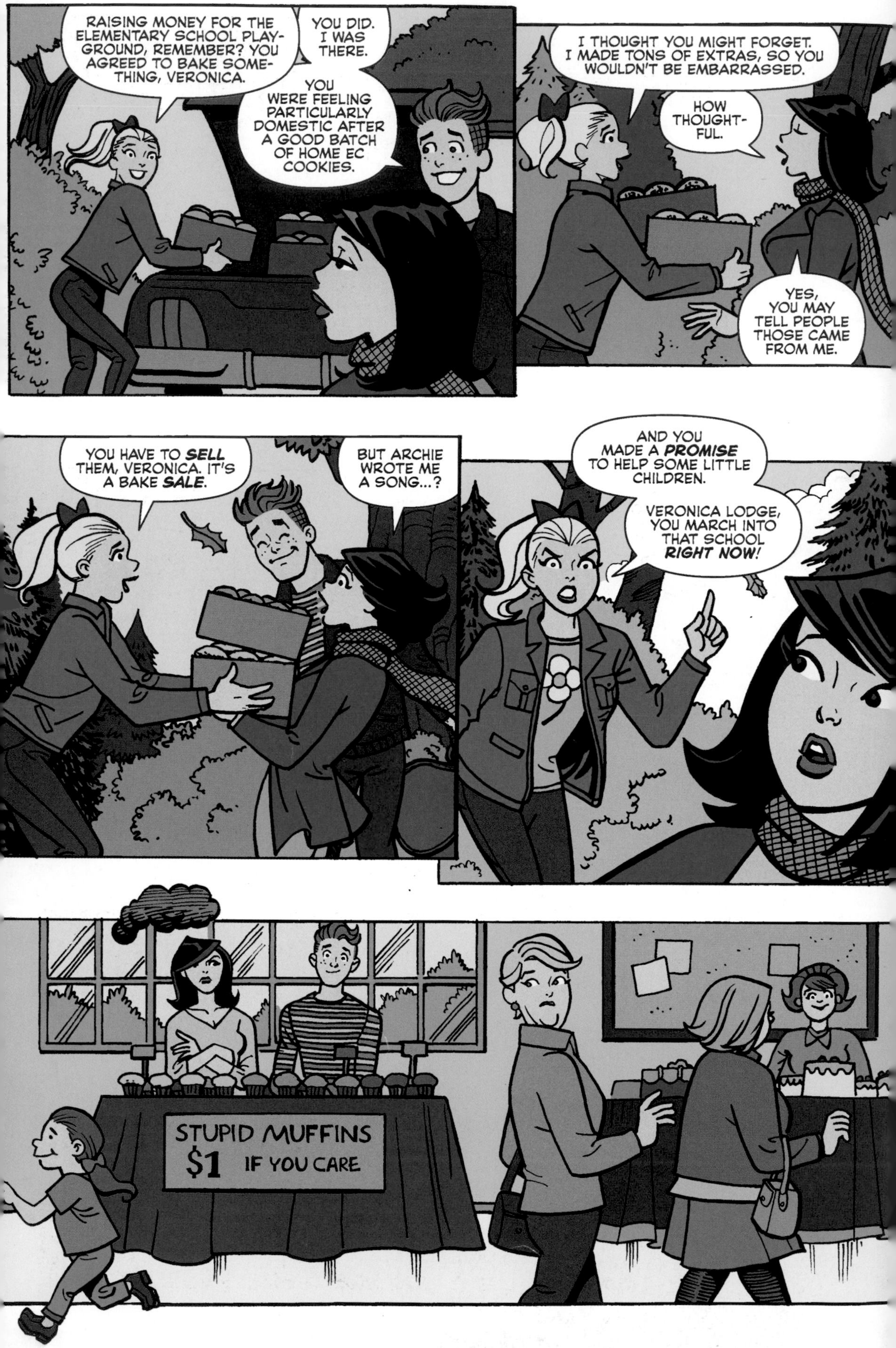
RAISING MONEY FOR THE ELEMENTARY SCHOOL PLAY-GROUND, REMEMBER? YOU AGREED TO BAKE SOME-THING, VERONICA.
YOU DID. I WAS THERE.
YOU WERE FEELING PARTICULARLY DOMESTIC AFTER A GOOD BATCH OF HOME EC COOKIES.
I THOUGHT YOU MIGHT FORGET. I MADE TONS OF EXTRAS, SO YOU WOULDN'T BE EMBARRASSED.
HOW THOUGHT-FUL.
YES, YOU MAY TELL PEOPLE THOSE CAME FROM ME.
YOU HAVE TO **SELL** THEM, VERONICA. IT'S A BAKE **SALE**.
BUT ARCHIE WROTE ME A SONG...?
AND YOU MADE A **PROMISE** TO HELP SOME LITTLE CHILDREN.
VERONICA LODGE, YOU MARCH INTO THAT SCHOOL **RIGHT NOW!**
STUPID MUFFINS
$1 IF YOU CARE

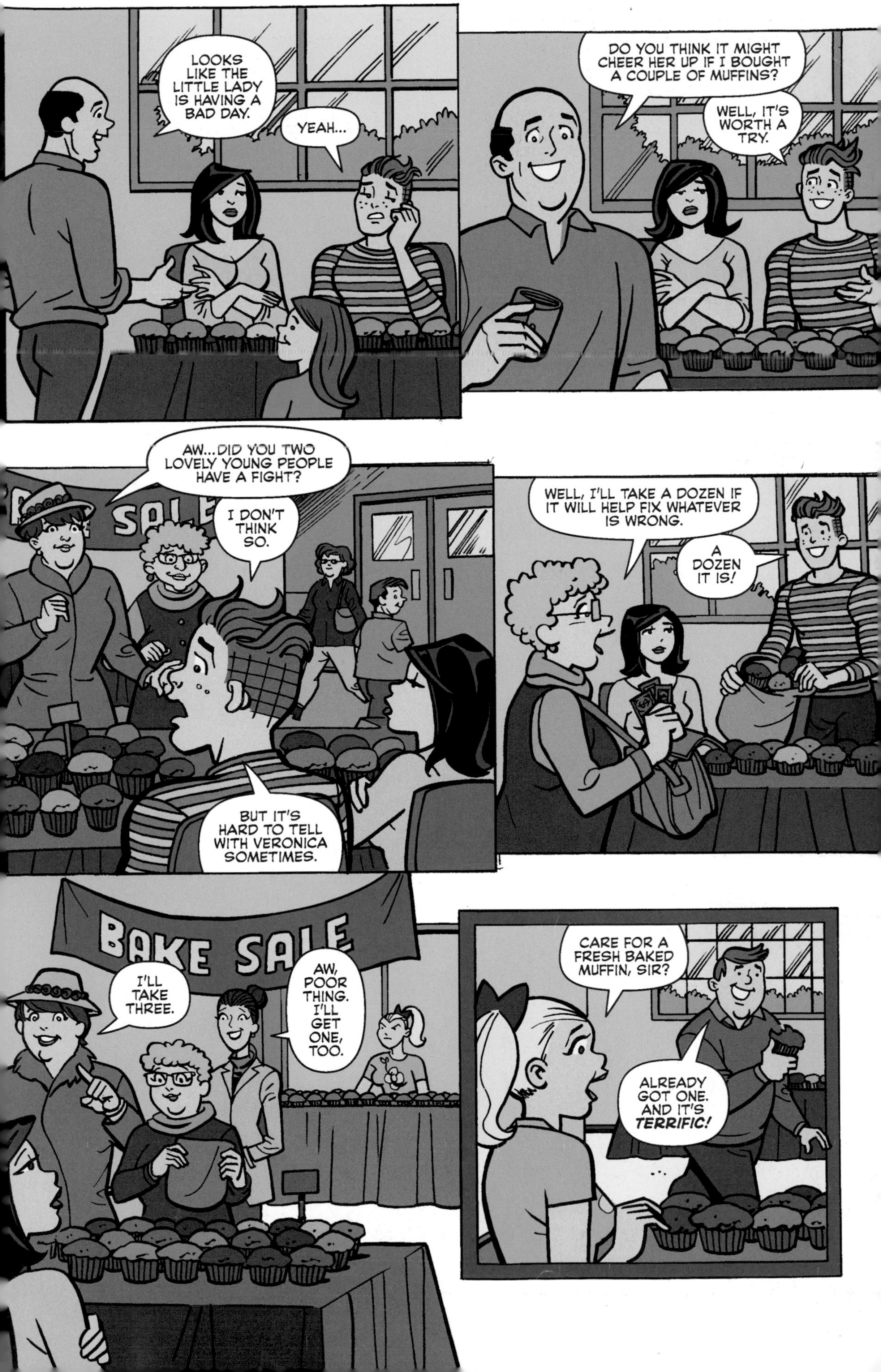
LOOKS LIKE THE LITTLE LADY IS HAVING A BAD DAY.
YEAH...
DO YOU THINK IT MIGHT CHEER HER UP IF I BOUGHT A COUPLE OF MUFFINS?
WELL, IT'S WORTH A TRY.
AW...DID YOU TWO LOVELY YOUNG PEOPLE HAVE A FIGHT?
SALE
I DON'T THINK SO.
BUT IT'S HARD TO TELL WITH VERONICA SOMETIMES.
WELL, I'LL TAKE A DOZEN IF IT WILL HELP FIX WHATEVER IS WRONG.
A DOZEN IT IS!
BAKE SALE
I'LL TAKE THREE.
AW, POOR THING. I'LL GET ONE, TOO.
CARE FOR A FRESH BAKED MUFFIN, SIR?
ALREADY GOT ONE. AND IT'S *TERRIFIC!*

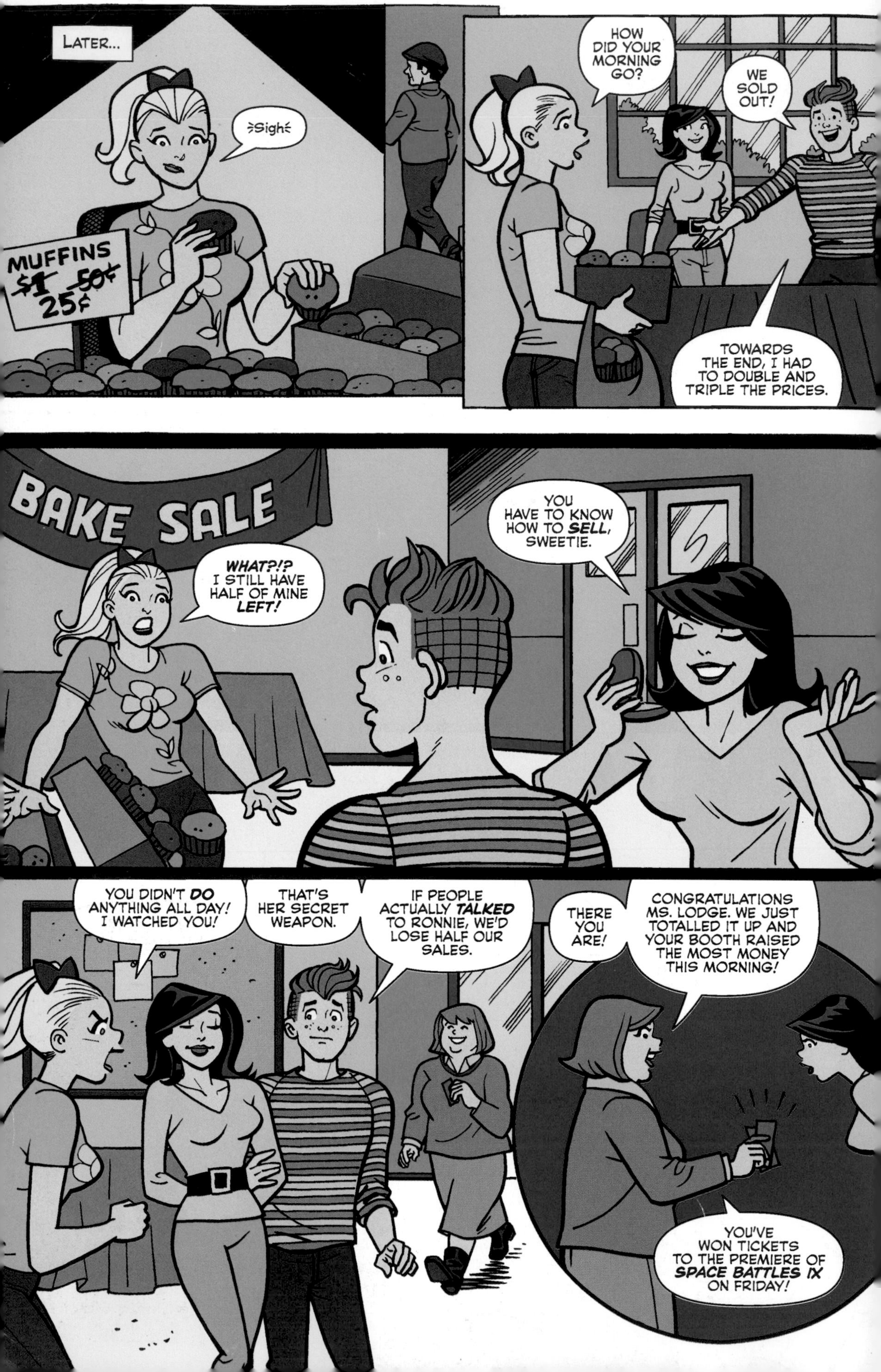
LATER...
⁓SIGH⁓
MUFFINS
$1 50¢
25¢
HOW DID YOUR MORNING GO?
WE SOLD OUT!
TOWARDS THE END, I HAD TO DOUBLE AND TRIPLE THE PRICES.
BAKE SALE
WHAT?!? I STILL HAVE HALF OF MINE LEFT!
YOU HAVE TO KNOW HOW TO SELL, SWEETIE.
YOU DIDN'T DO ANYTHING ALL DAY! I WATCHED YOU!
THAT'S HER SECRET WEAPON.
IF PEOPLE ACTUALLY TALKED TO RONNIE, WE'D LOSE HALF OUR SALES.
THERE YOU ARE!
CONGRATULATIONS MS. LODGE. WE JUST TOTALLED IT UP AND YOUR BOOTH RAISED THE MOST MONEY THIS MORNING!
YOU'VE WON TICKETS TO THE PREMIERE OF SPACE BATTLES IX ON FRIDAY!

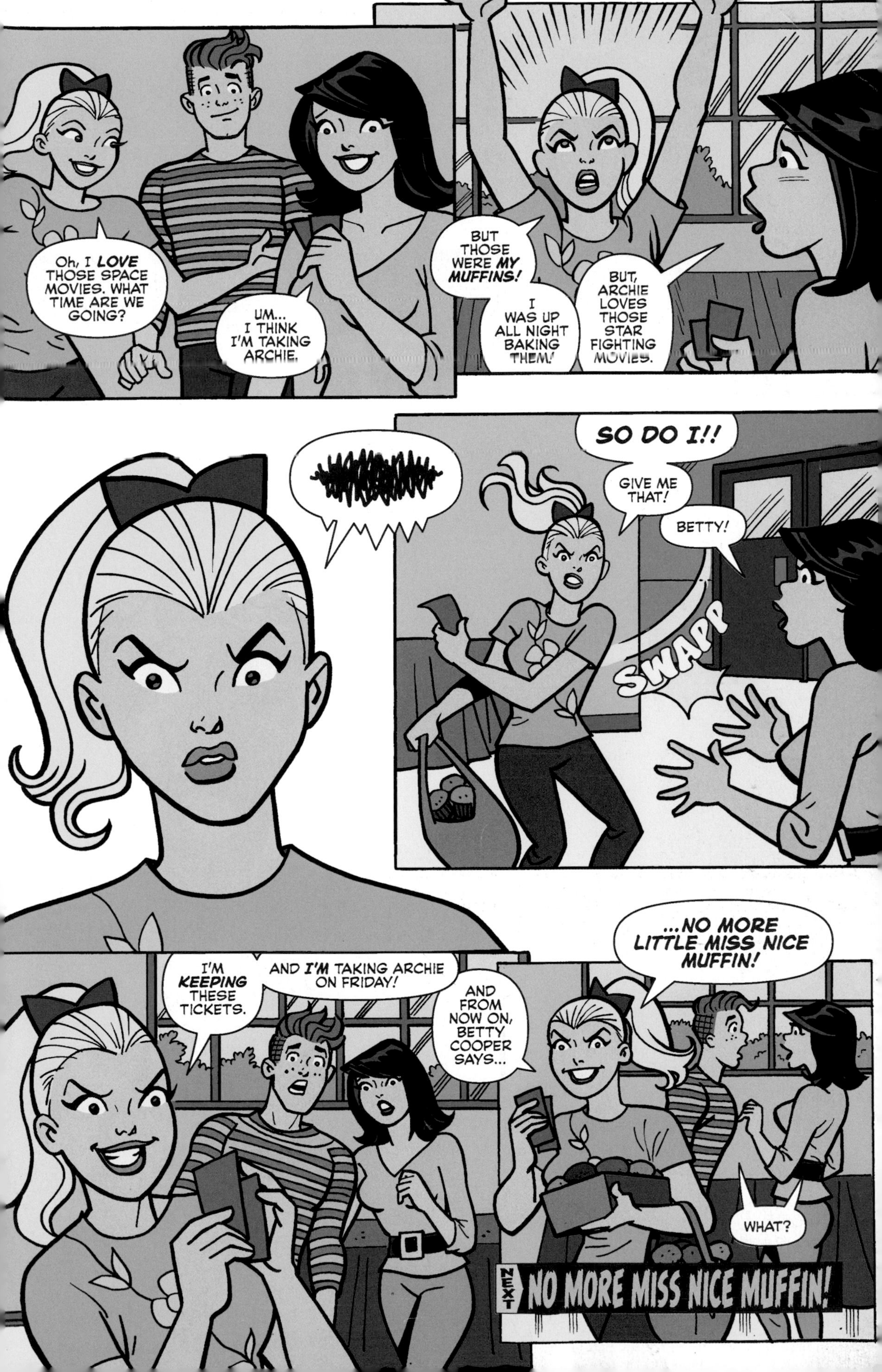
Oh, I LOVE THOSE SPACE MOVIES. WHAT TIME ARE WE GOING?
UM... I THINK I'M TAKING ARCHIE.
BUT THOSE WERE MY MUFFINS!
I WAS UP ALL NIGHT BAKING THEM!
BUT, ARCHIE LOVES THOSE STAR FIGHTING MOVIES.
SO DO I!!
GIVE ME THAT!
BETTY!
SWAPP
I'M KEEPING THESE TICKETS.
AND I'M TAKING ARCHIE ON FRIDAY!
AND FROM NOW ON, BETTY COOPER SAYS...
...NO MORE LITTLE MISS NICE MUFFIN!
WHAT?
NEXT NO MORE MISS NICE MUFFIN!

CHAPTER 5
PART 2

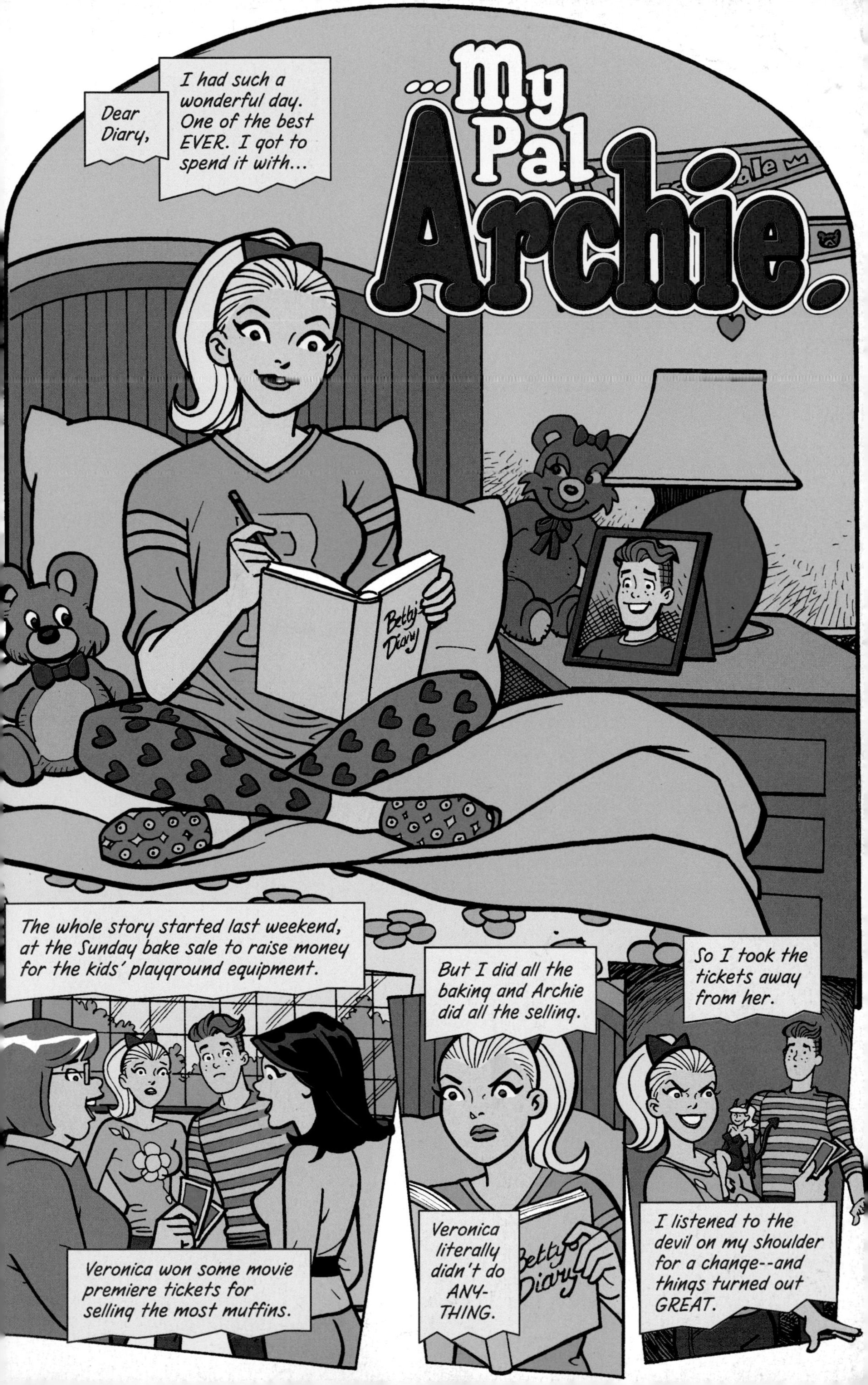
Dear Diary,
I had such a wonderful day. One of the best EVER. I got to spend it with...
...My Pal Archie...
Betty's Diary
The whole story started last weekend, at the Sunday bake sale to raise money for the kids' playground equipment.
Veronica won some movie premiere tickets for selling the most muffins.
But I did all the baking and Archie did all the selling.
Veronica literally didn't do ANY-THING.
Betty's Diary
So I took the tickets away from her.
I listened to the devil on my shoulder for a change--and things turned out GREAT.

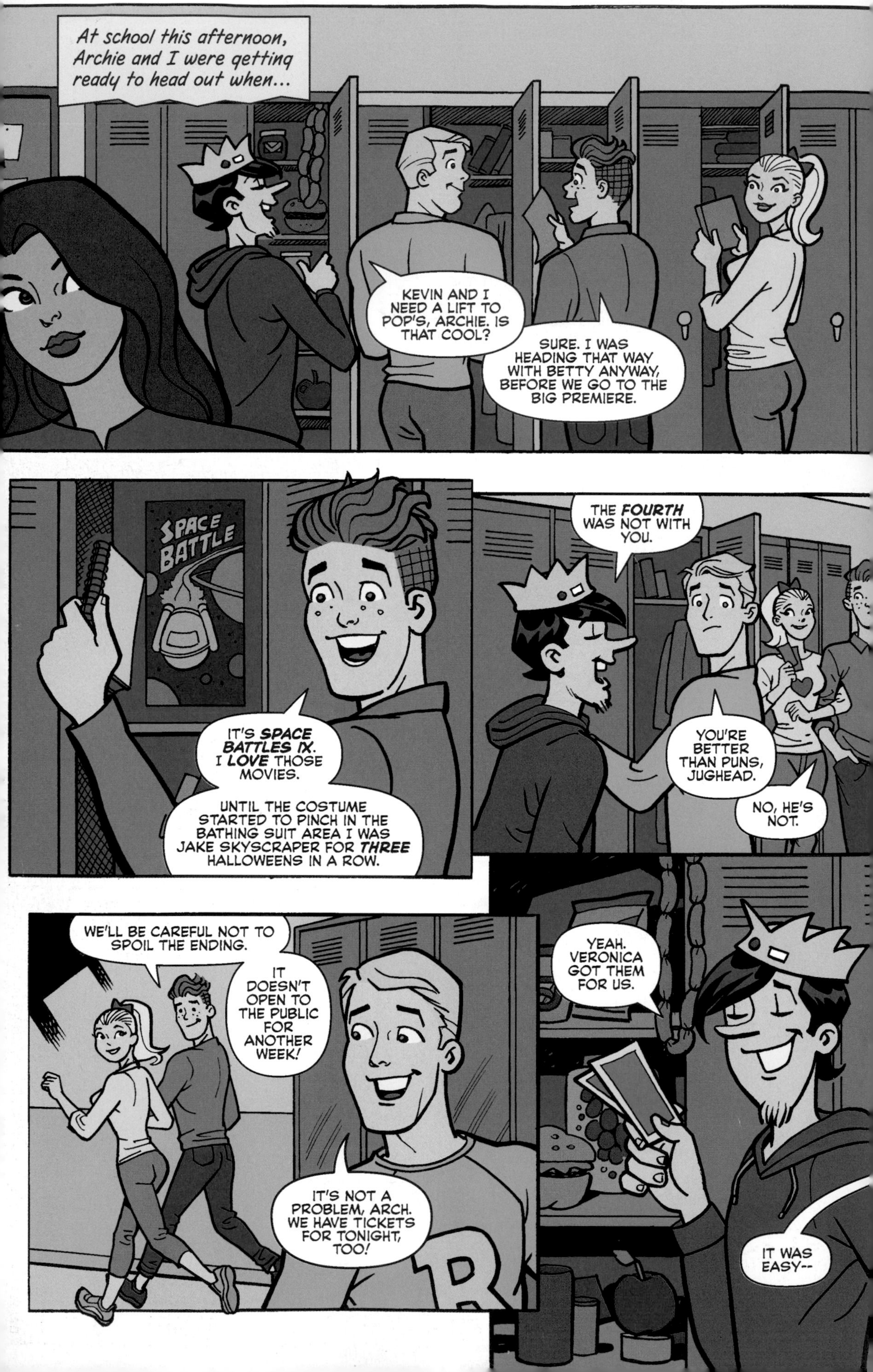
At school this afternoon, Archie and I were getting ready to head out when...
KEVIN AND I NEED A LIFT TO POP'S, ARCHIE. IS THAT COOL?
SURE. I WAS HEADING THAT WAY WITH BETTY ANYWAY, BEFORE WE GO TO THE BIG PREMIERE.
SPACE BATTLE
IT'S **SPACE BATTLES IX**. I **LOVE** THOSE MOVIES.
UNTIL THE COSTUME STARTED TO PINCH IN THE BATHING SUIT AREA I WAS JAKE SKYSCRAPER FOR **THREE** HALLOWEENS IN A ROW.
THE **FOURTH** WAS NOT WITH YOU.
YOU'RE BETTER THAN PUNS, JUGHEAD.
NO, HE'S NOT.
WE'LL BE CAREFUL NOT TO SPOIL THE ENDING.
IT DOESN'T OPEN TO THE PUBLIC FOR ANOTHER WEEK!
IT'S NOT A PROBLEM, ARCH. WE HAVE TICKETS FOR TONIGHT, TOO!
YEAH. VERONICA GOT THEM FOR US.
IT WAS EASY--

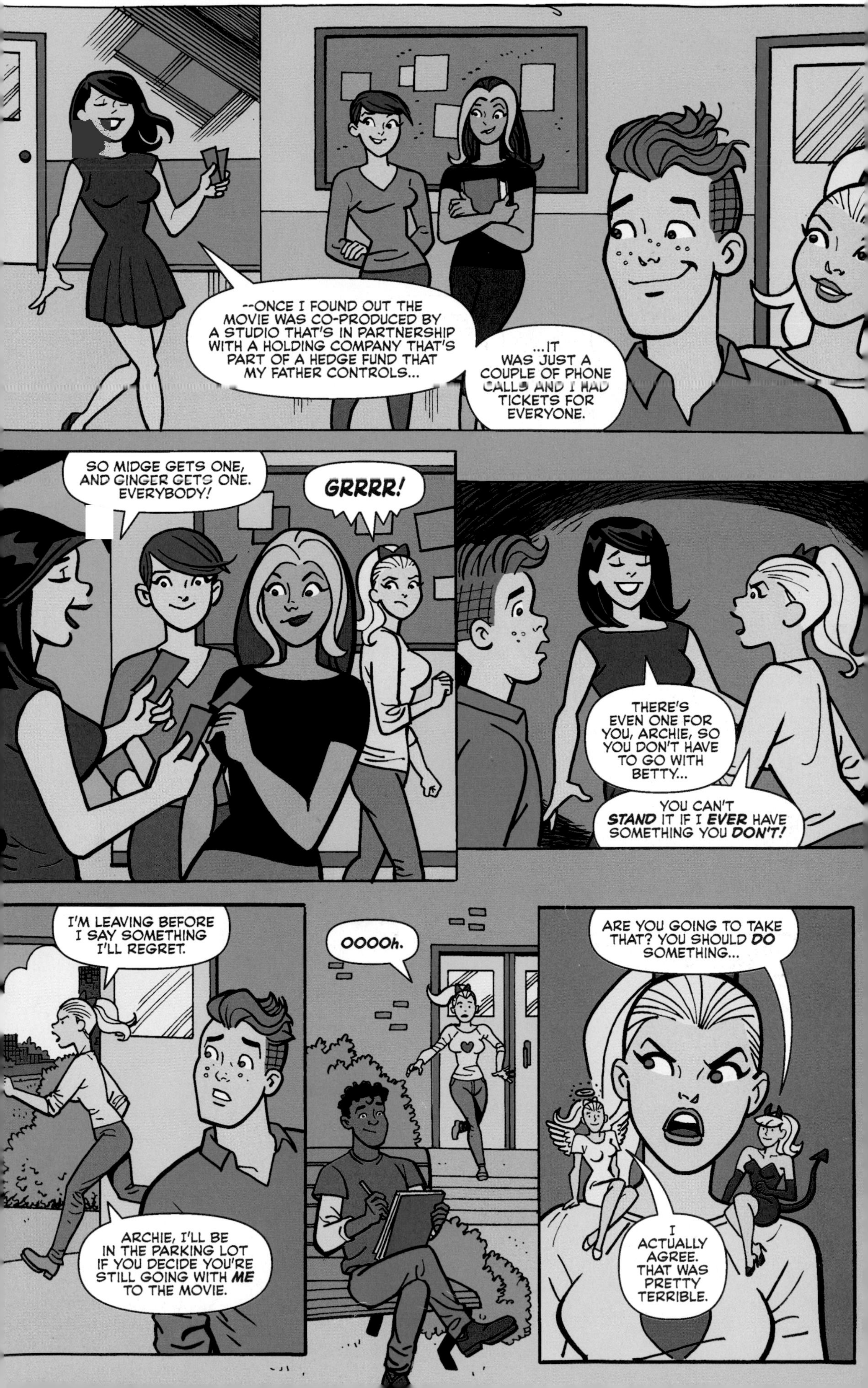
--ONCE I FOUND OUT THE MOVIE WAS CO-PRODUCED BY A STUDIO THAT'S IN PARTNERSHIP WITH A HOLDING COMPANY THAT'S PART OF A HEDGE FUND THAT MY FATHER CONTROLS...
...IT WAS JUST A COUPLE OF PHONE CALLS AND I HAD TICKETS FOR EVERYONE.
SO MIDGE GETS ONE, AND GINGER GETS ONE. EVERYBODY!
GRRRR!
THERE'S EVEN ONE FOR YOU, ARCHIE, SO YOU DON'T HAVE TO GO WITH BETTY...
YOU CAN'T ***STAND*** IT IF I ***EVER*** HAVE SOMETHING YOU ***DON'T!***
I'M LEAVING BEFORE I SAY SOMETHING I'LL REGRET.
ARCHIE, I'LL BE IN THE PARKING LOT IF YOU DECIDE YOU'RE STILL GOING WITH ***ME*** TO THE MOVIE.
OOOOh.
ARE YOU GOING TO TAKE THAT? YOU SHOULD ***DO*** SOMETHING...
I ACTUALLY AGREE. THAT WAS PRETTY TERRIBLE.

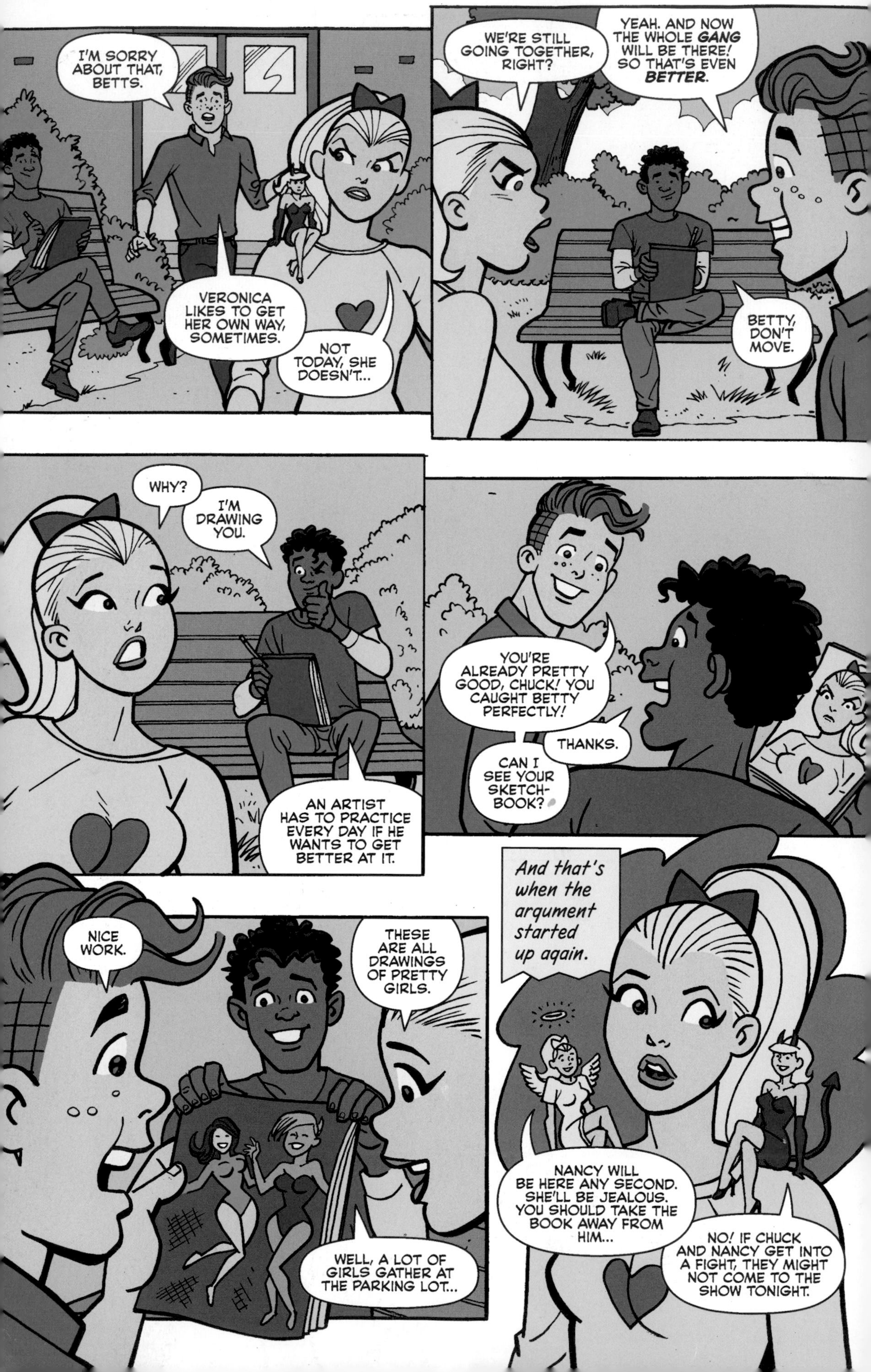
I'M SORRY ABOUT THAT, BETTS.
VERONICA LIKES TO GET HER OWN WAY, SOMETIMES.
NOT TODAY, SHE DOESN'T...
WE'RE STILL GOING TOGETHER, RIGHT?
YEAH. AND NOW THE WHOLE GANG WILL BE THERE! SO THAT'S EVEN BETTER.
BETTY, DON'T MOVE.
WHY?
I'M DRAWING YOU.
AN ARTIST HAS TO PRACTICE EVERY DAY IF HE WANTS TO GET BETTER AT IT.
YOU'RE ALREADY PRETTY GOOD, CHUCK! YOU CAUGHT BETTY PERFECTLY!
THANKS.
CAN I SEE YOUR SKETCH-BOOK?
NICE WORK.
THESE ARE ALL DRAWINGS OF PRETTY GIRLS.
WELL, A LOT OF GIRLS GATHER AT THE PARKING LOT...
And that's when the argument started up again.
NANCY WILL BE HERE ANY SECOND. SHE'LL BE JEALOUS. YOU SHOULD TAKE THE BOOK AWAY FROM HIM...
NO! IF CHUCK AND NANCY GET INTO A FIGHT, THEY MIGHT NOT COME TO THE SHOW TONIGHT.

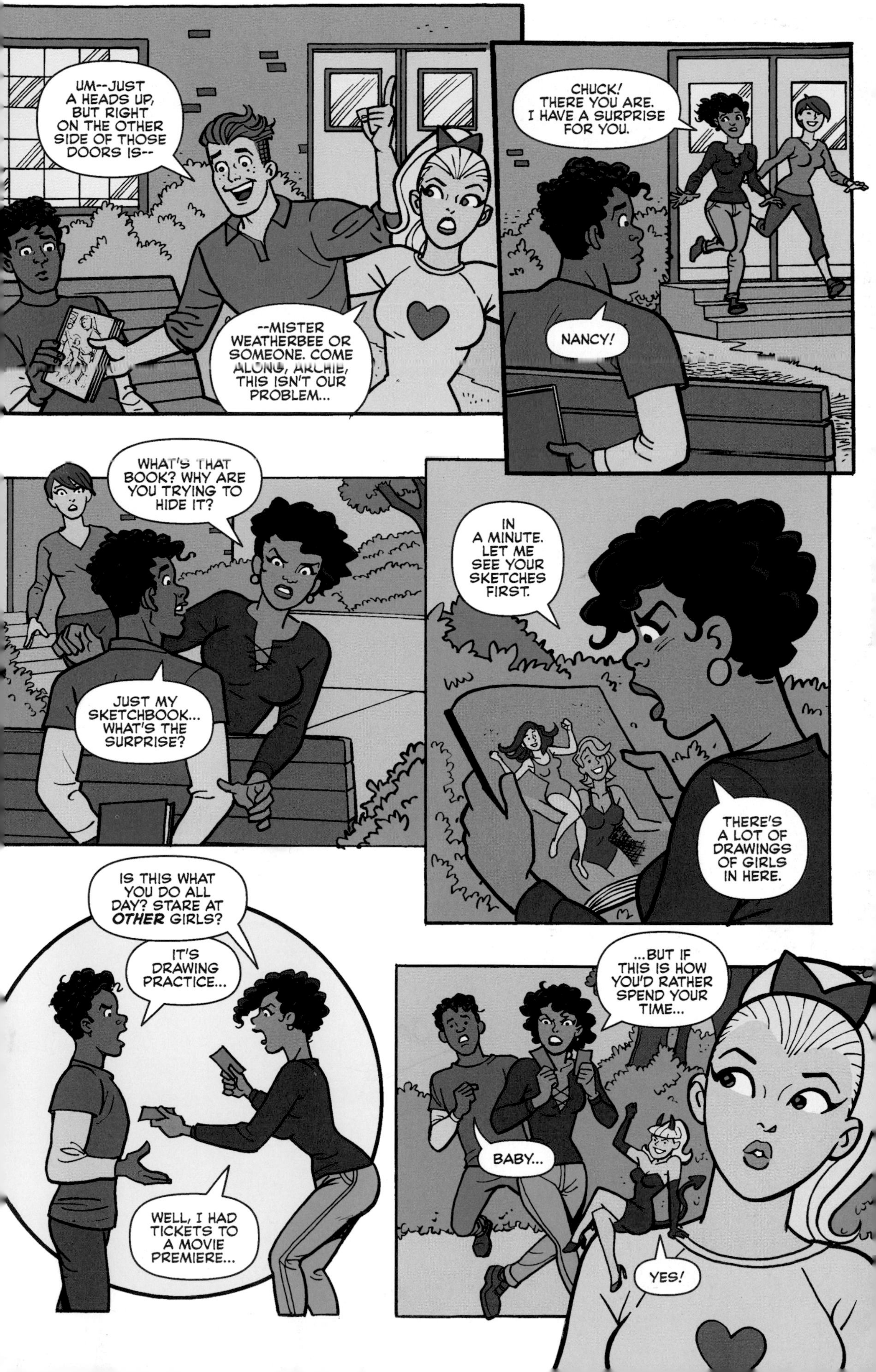
UM--JUST A HEADS UP, BUT RIGHT ON THE OTHER SIDE OF THOSE DOORS IS--
--MISTER WEATHERBEE OR SOMEONE. COME ALONG, ARCHIE, THIS ISN'T OUR PROBLEM...
CHUCK! THERE YOU ARE. I HAVE A SURPRISE FOR YOU.
NANCY!
WHAT'S THAT BOOK? WHY ARE YOU TRYING TO HIDE IT?
JUST MY SKETCHBOOK... WHAT'S THE SURPRISE?
IN A MINUTE. LET ME SEE YOUR SKETCHES FIRST.
THERE'S A LOT OF DRAWINGS OF GIRLS IN HERE.
IS THIS WHAT YOU DO ALL DAY? STARE AT OTHER GIRLS?
IT'S DRAWING PRACTICE...
WELL, I HAD TICKETS TO A MOVIE PREMIERE...
...BUT IF THIS IS HOW YOU'D RATHER SPEND YOUR TIME...
BABY...
YES!

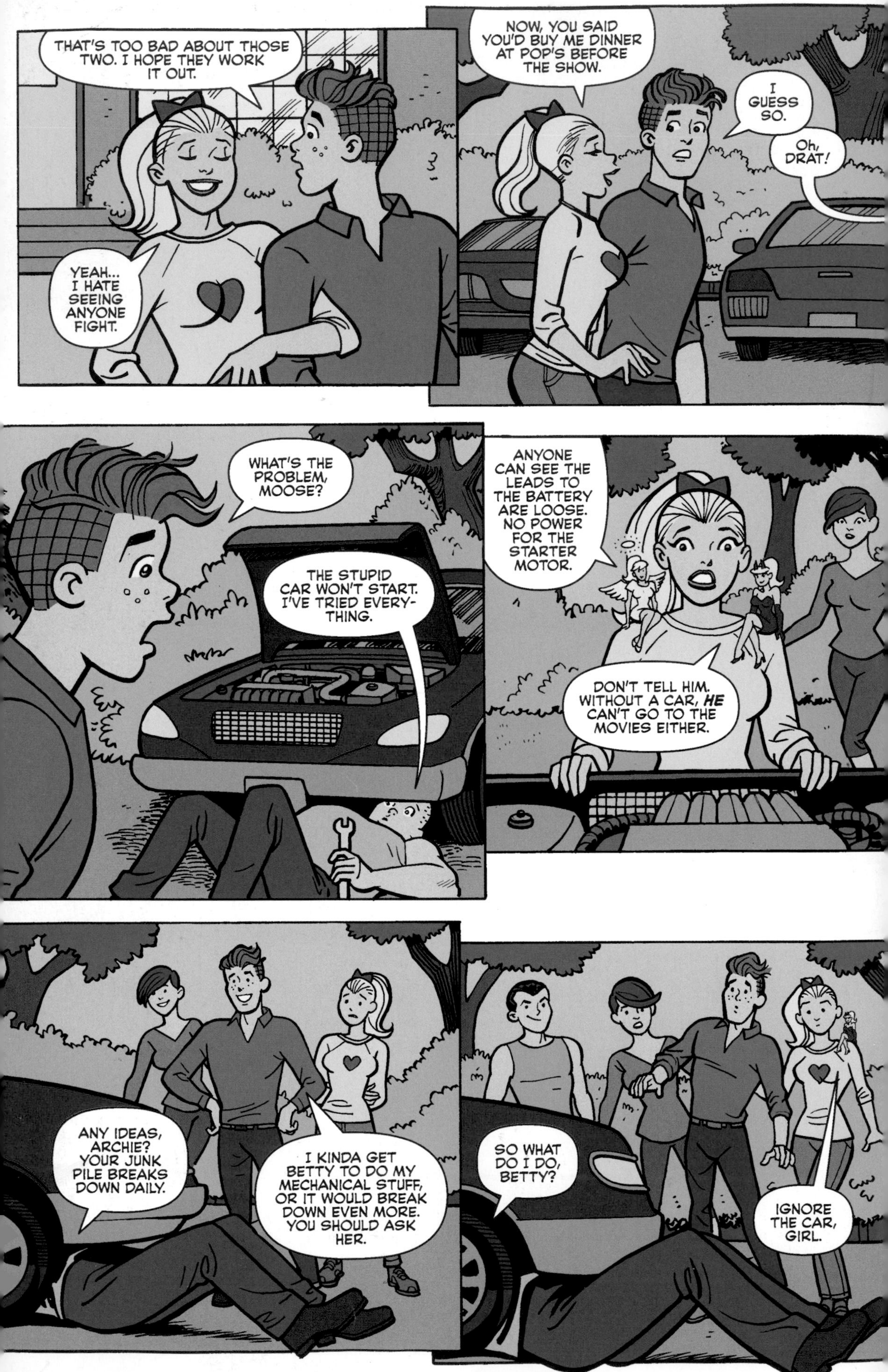
THAT'S TOO BAD ABOUT THOSE TWO. I HOPE THEY WORK IT OUT.
YEAH... I HATE SEEING ANYONE FIGHT.
NOW, YOU SAID YOU'D BUY ME DINNER AT POP'S BEFORE THE SHOW.
I GUESS SO.
Oh, DRAT!
WHAT'S THE PROBLEM, MOOSE?
THE STUPID CAR WON'T START. I'VE TRIED EVERY-THING.
ANYONE CAN SEE THE LEADS TO THE BATTERY ARE LOOSE. NO POWER FOR THE STARTER MOTOR.
DON'T TELL HIM. WITHOUT A CAR, HE CAN'T GO TO THE MOVIES EITHER.
ANY IDEAS, ARCHIE? YOUR JUNK PILE BREAKS DOWN DAILY.
I KINDA GET BETTY TO DO MY MECHANICAL STUFF, OR IT WOULD BREAK DOWN EVEN MORE. YOU SHOULD ASK HER.
SO WHAT DO I DO, BETTY?
IGNORE THE CAR, GIRL.

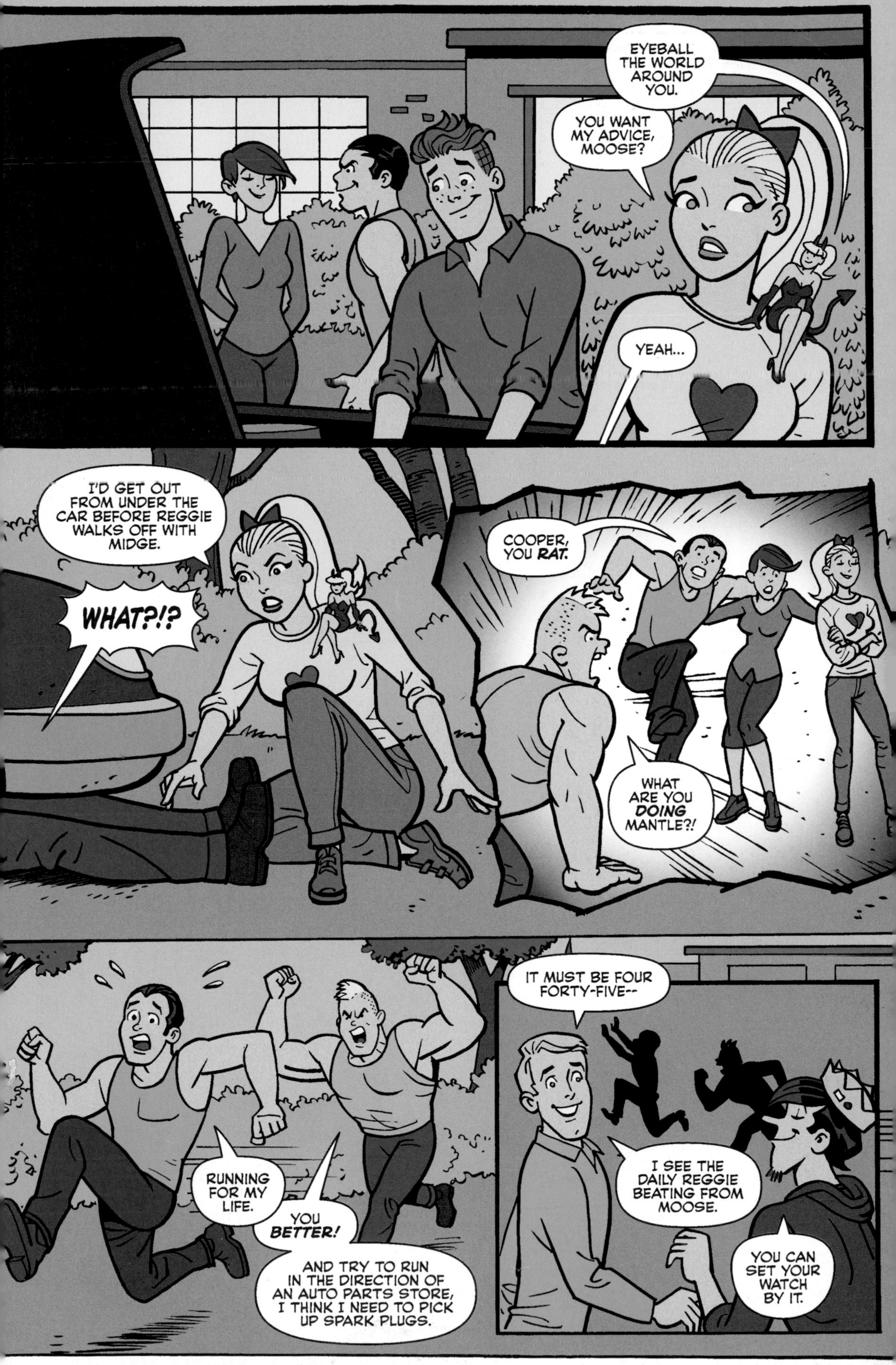
YOU WANT MY ADVICE, MOOSE?
EYEBALL THE WORLD AROUND YOU.
YEAH...
I'D GET OUT FROM UNDER THE CAR BEFORE REGGIE WALKS OFF WITH MIDGE.
WHAT?!?
COOPER, YOU RAT.
WHAT ARE YOU DOING MANTLE?!
RUNNING FOR MY LIFE.
YOU BETTER!
AND TRY TO RUN IN THE DIRECTION OF AN AUTO PARTS STORE, I THINK I NEED TO PICK UP SPARK PLUGS.
IT MUST BE FOUR FORTY-FIVE--
I SEE THE DAILY REGGIE BEATING FROM MOOSE.
YOU CAN SET YOUR WATCH BY IT.

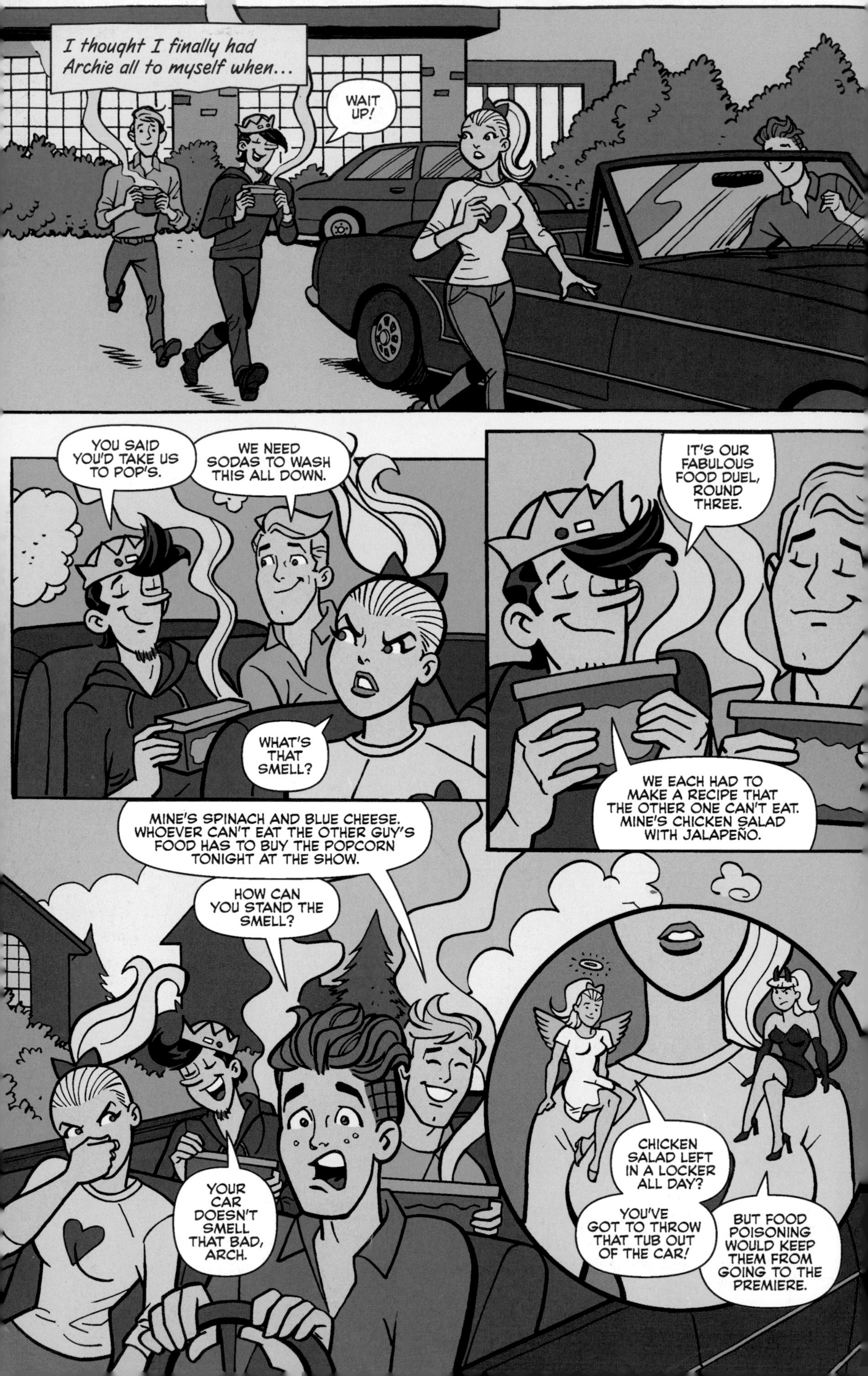
I thought I finally had Archie all to myself when...
WAIT UP!
YOU SAID YOU'D TAKE US TO POP'S.
WE NEED SODAS TO WASH THIS ALL DOWN.
WHAT'S THAT SMELL?
IT'S OUR FABULOUS FOOD DUEL, ROUND THREE.
WE EACH HAD TO MAKE A RECIPE THAT THE OTHER ONE CAN'T EAT. MINE'S CHICKEN SALAD WITH JALAPEÑO.
MINE'S SPINACH AND BLUE CHEESE. WHOEVER CAN'T EAT THE OTHER GUY'S FOOD HAS TO BUY THE POPCORN TONIGHT AT THE SHOW.
HOW CAN YOU STAND THE SMELL?
YOUR CAR DOESN'T SMELL THAT BAD, ARCH.
CHICKEN SALAD LEFT IN A LOCKER ALL DAY?
YOU'VE GOT TO THROW THAT TUB OUT OF THE CAR!
BUT FOOD POISONING WOULD KEEP THEM FROM GOING TO THE PREMIERE.

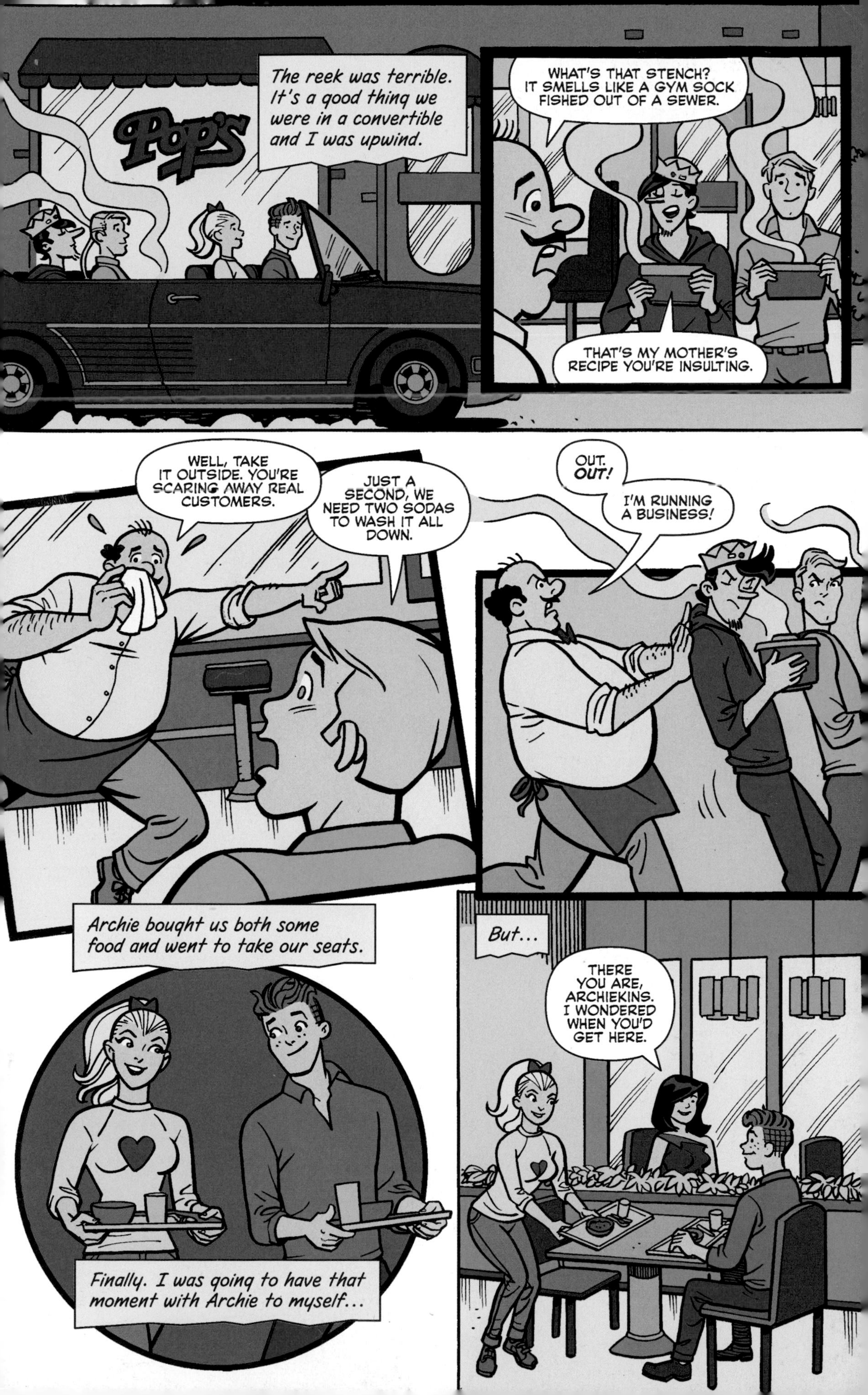
The reek was terrible. It's a good thing we were in a convertible and I was upwind.
WHAT'S THAT STENCH? IT SMELLS LIKE A GYM SOCK FISHED OUT OF A SEWER.
THAT'S MY MOTHER'S RECIPE YOU'RE INSULTING.
WELL, TAKE IT OUTSIDE. YOU'RE SCARING AWAY REAL CUSTOMERS.
JUST A SECOND, WE NEED TWO SODAS TO WASH IT ALL DOWN.
OUT. OUT!
I'M RUNNING A BUSINESS!
Archie bought us both some food and went to take our seats.
Finally. I was going to have that moment with Archie to myself...
But...
THERE YOU ARE, ARCHIEKINS. I WONDERED WHEN YOU'D GET HERE.

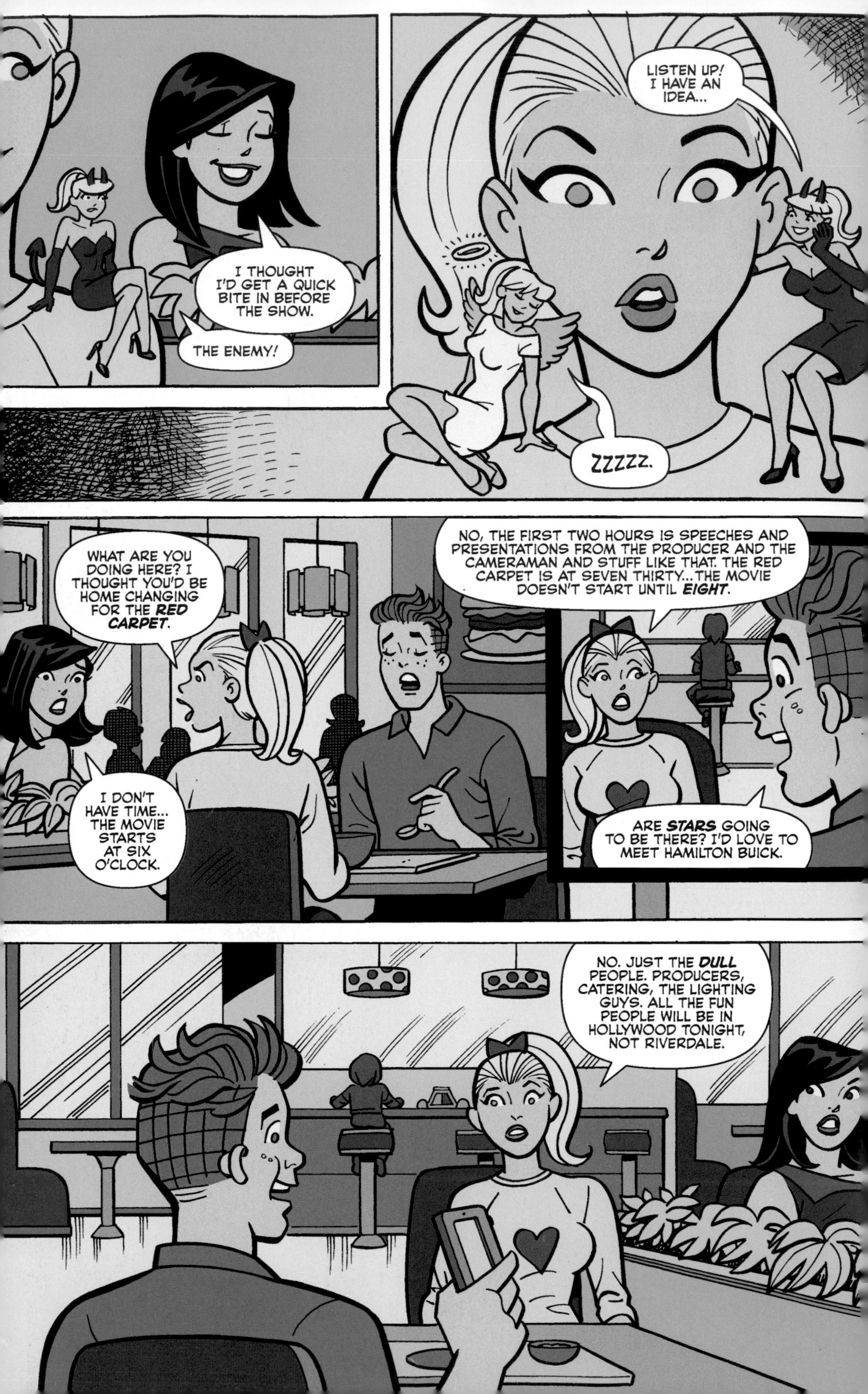
I THOUGHT I'D GET A QUICK BITE IN BEFORE THE SHOW.
THE ENEMY!
LISTEN UP! I HAVE AN IDEA...
ZZZZZ.
WHAT ARE YOU DOING HERE? I THOUGHT YOU'D BE HOME CHANGING FOR THE RED CARPET.
I DON'T HAVE TIME... THE MOVIE STARTS AT SIX O'CLOCK.
NO, THE FIRST TWO HOURS IS SPEECHES AND PRESENTATIONS FROM THE PRODUCER AND THE CAMERAMAN AND STUFF LIKE THAT. THE RED CARPET IS AT SEVEN THIRTY... THE MOVIE DOESN'T START UNTIL EIGHT.
ARE STARS GOING TO BE THERE? I'D LOVE TO MEET HAMILTON BUICK.
NO. JUST THE DULL PEOPLE. PRODUCERS, CATERING, THE LIGHTING GUYS. ALL THE FUN PEOPLE WILL BE IN HOLLYWOOD TONIGHT, NOT RIVERDALE.

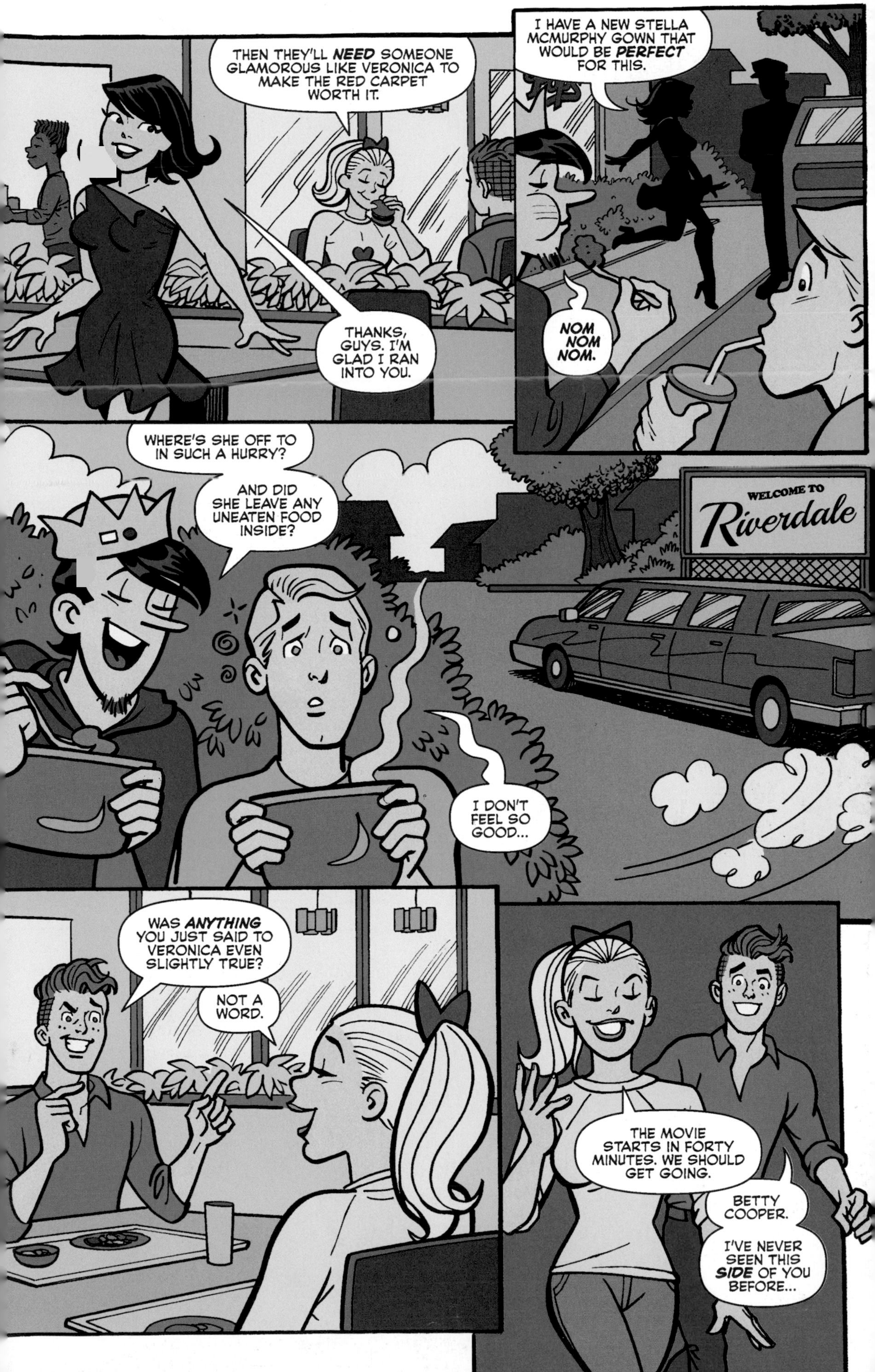
THEN THEY'LL NEED SOMEONE GLAMOROUS LIKE VERONICA TO MAKE THE RED CARPET WORTH IT.
THANKS, GUYS. I'M GLAD I RAN INTO YOU.
I HAVE A NEW STELLA MCMURPHY GOWN THAT WOULD BE PERFECT FOR THIS.
NOM NOM NOM.
WHERE'S SHE OFF TO IN SUCH A HURRY?
AND DID SHE LEAVE ANY UNEATEN FOOD INSIDE?
WELCOME TO Riverdale
I DON'T FEEL SO GOOD...
WAS ANYTHING YOU JUST SAID TO VERONICA EVEN SLIGHTLY TRUE?
NOT A WORD.
THE MOVIE STARTS IN FORTY MINUTES. WE SHOULD GET GOING.
BETTY COOPER.
I'VE NEVER SEEN THIS SIDE OF YOU BEFORE...

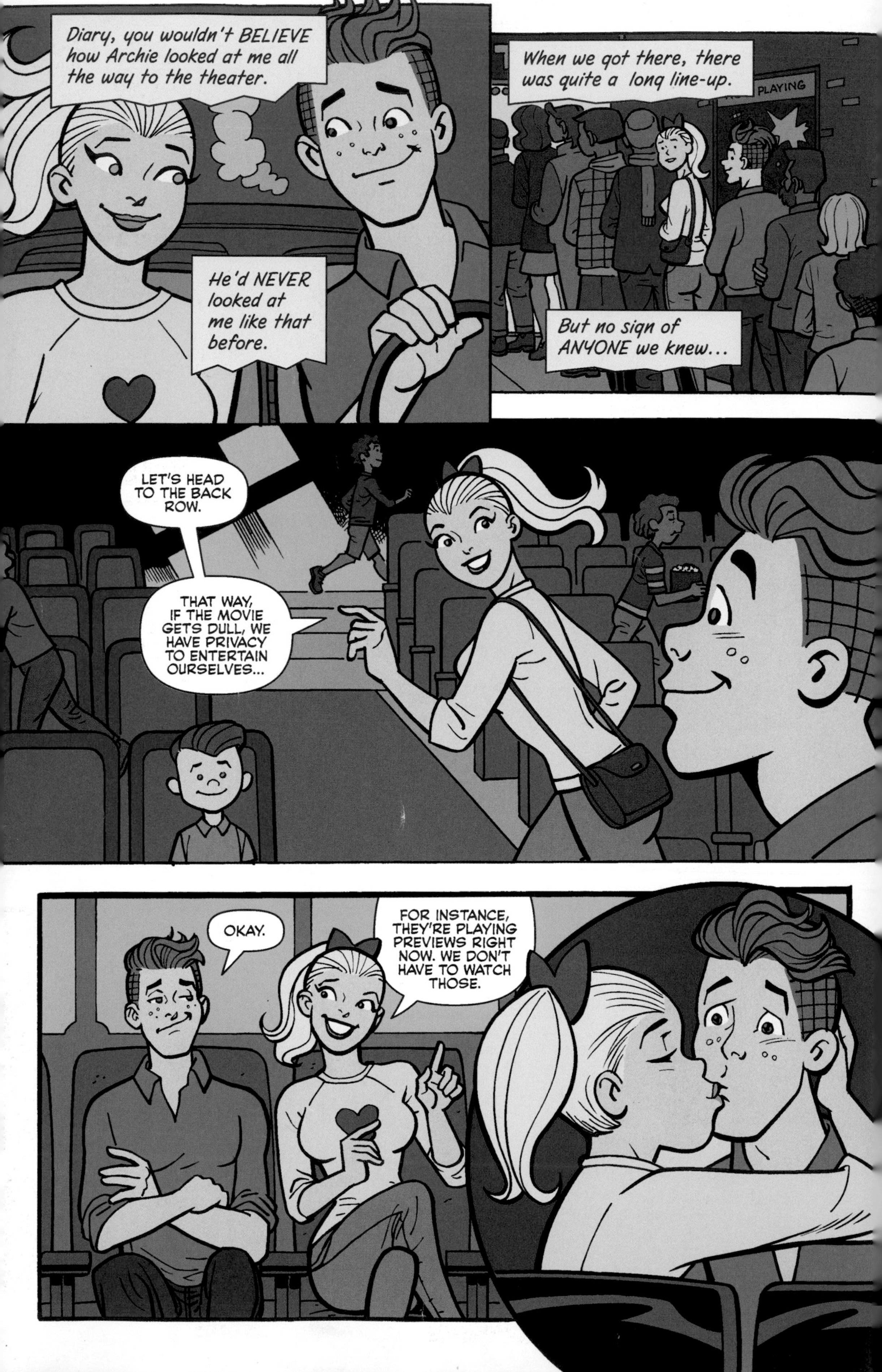

Diary, you wouldn't BELIEVE how Archie looked at me all the way to the theater.
He'd NEVER looked at me like that before.
When we got there, there was quite a long line-up.
PLAYING
But no sign of ANYONE we knew...
LET'S HEAD TO THE BACK ROW.
THAT WAY, IF THE MOVIE GETS DULL, WE HAVE PRIVACY TO ENTERTAIN OURSELVES...
OKAY.
FOR INSTANCE, THEY'RE PLAYING PREVIEWS RIGHT NOW. WE DON'T HAVE TO WATCH THOSE.

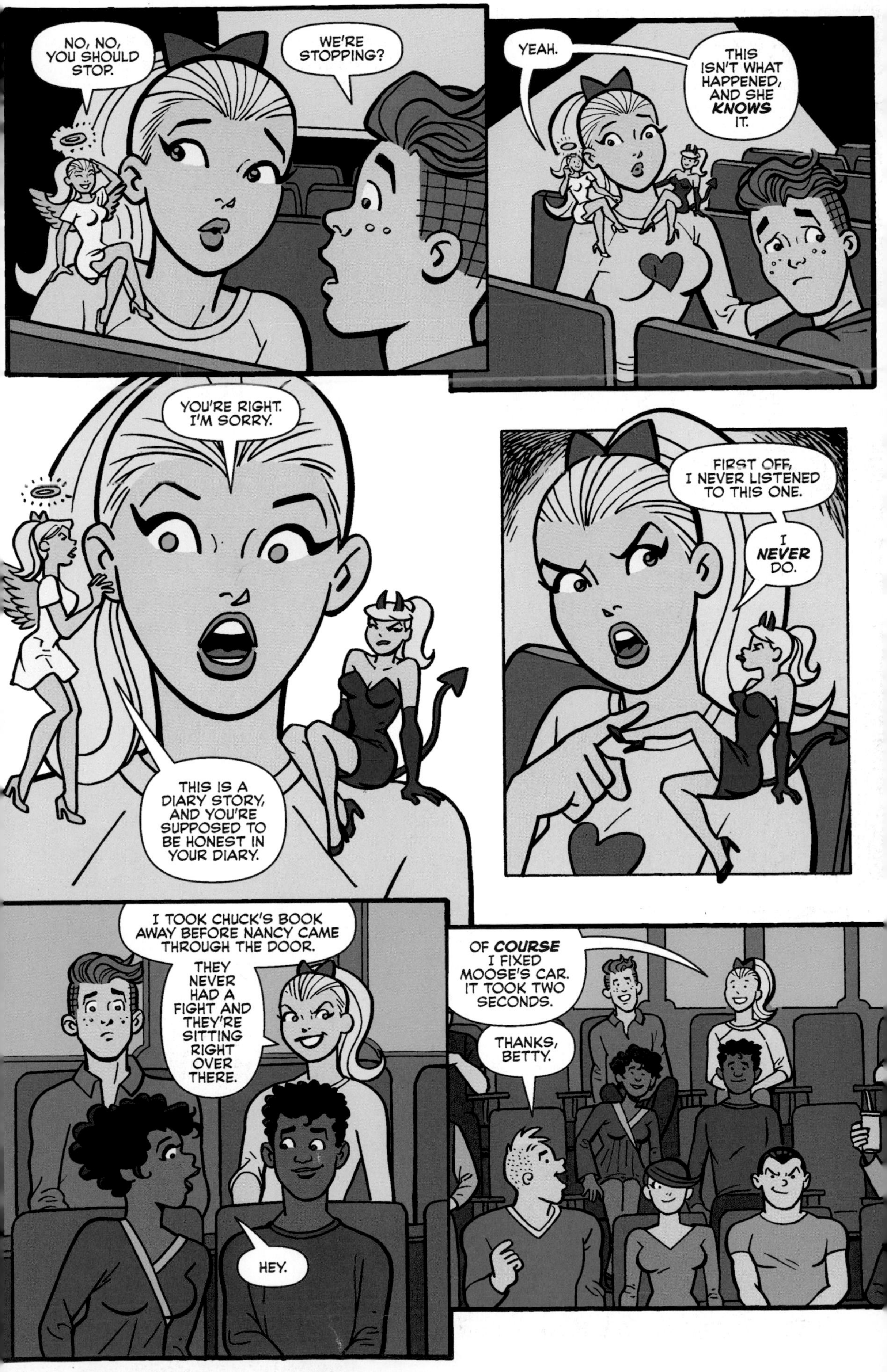

NO, NO, YOU SHOULD STOP.
WE'RE STOPPING?
YEAH.
THIS ISN'T WHAT HAPPENED, AND SHE **KNOWS** IT.
YOU'RE RIGHT. I'M SORRY.
THIS IS A DIARY STORY, AND YOU'RE SUPPOSED TO BE HONEST IN YOUR DIARY.
FIRST OFF, I NEVER LISTENED TO THIS ONE.
I **NEVER** DO.
I TOOK CHUCK'S BOOK AWAY BEFORE NANCY CAME THROUGH THE DOOR.
THEY NEVER HAD A FIGHT AND THEY'RE SITTING RIGHT OVER THERE.
HEY.
OF **COURSE** I FIXED MOOSE'S CAR. IT TOOK TWO SECONDS.
THANKS, BETTY.

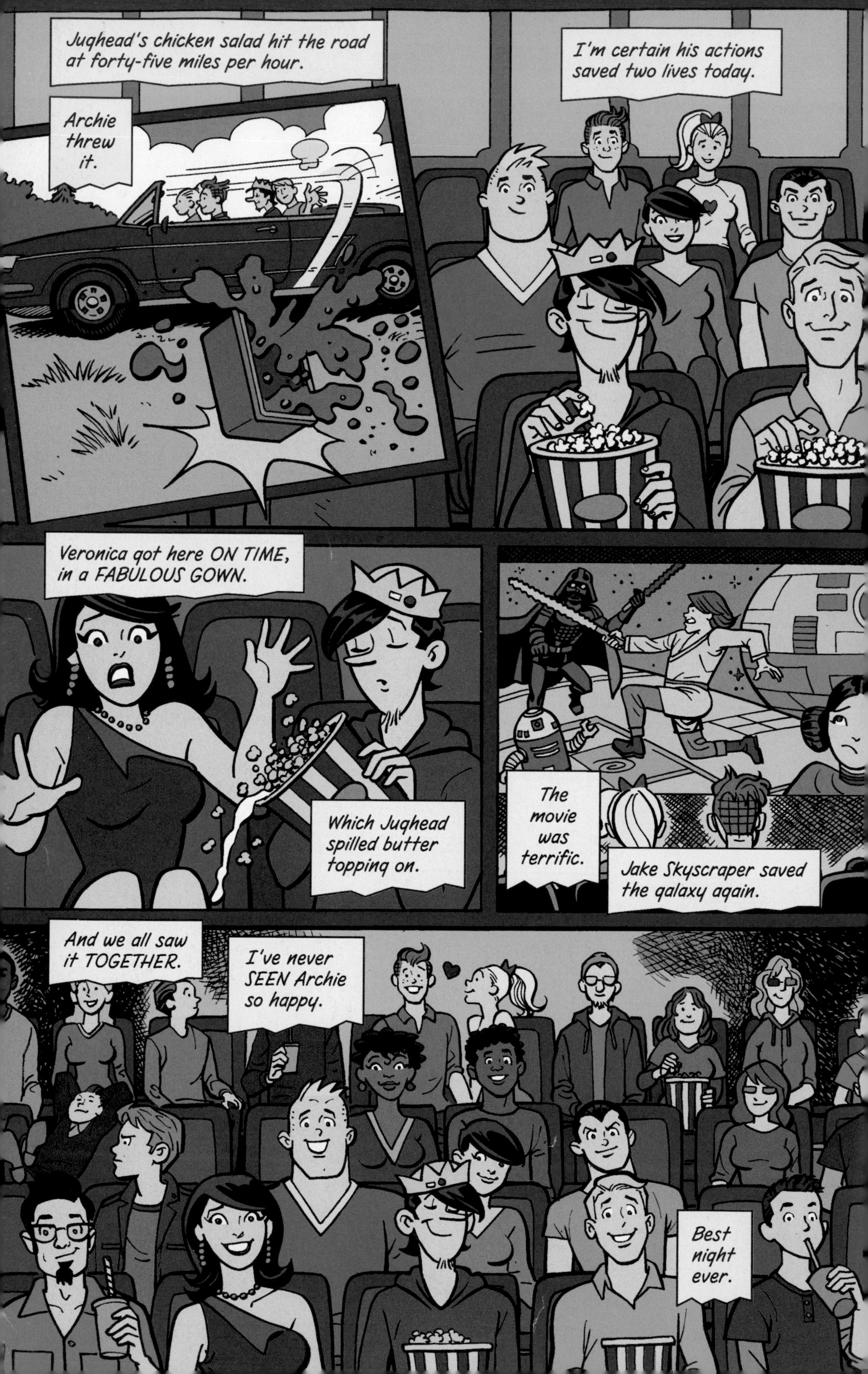
Jughead's chicken salad hit the road at forty-five miles per hour.
Archie threw it.
I'm certain his actions saved two lives today.
Veronica got here ON TIME, in a FABULOUS GOWN.
Which Jughead spilled butter topping on.
The movie was terrific.
Jake Skyscraper saved the galaxy again.
And we all saw it TOGETHER.
I've never SEEN Archie so happy.
Best night ever.

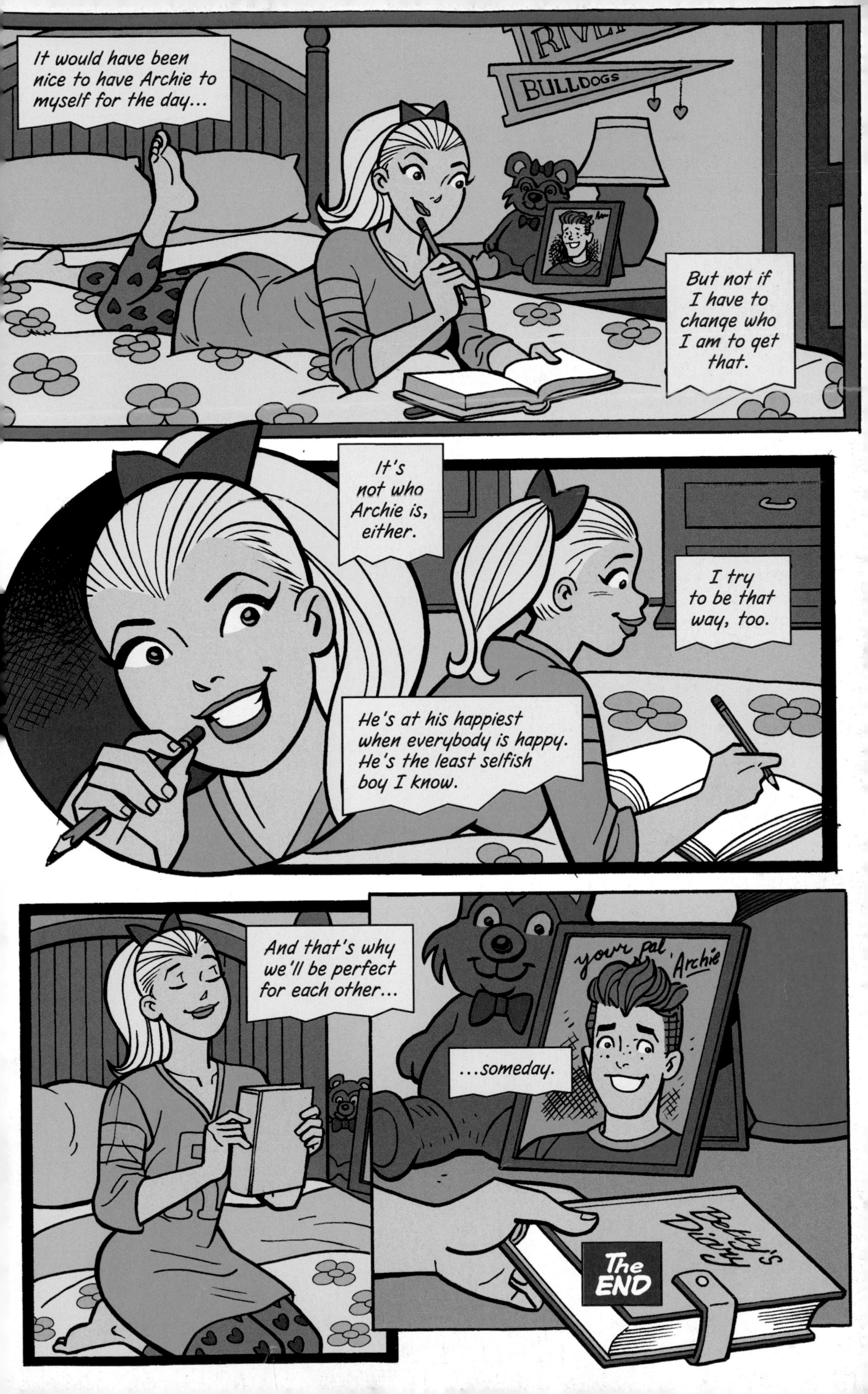
RIVE
BULLDOGS
It would have been nice to have Archie to myself for the day...
But not if I have to change who I am to get that.
It's not who Archie is, either.
I try to be that way, too.
He's at his happiest when everybody is happy. He's the least selfish boy I know.
And that's why we'll be perfect for each other...
your pal, Archie
...someday.
Betty's Diary
The END

CHAPTER 6

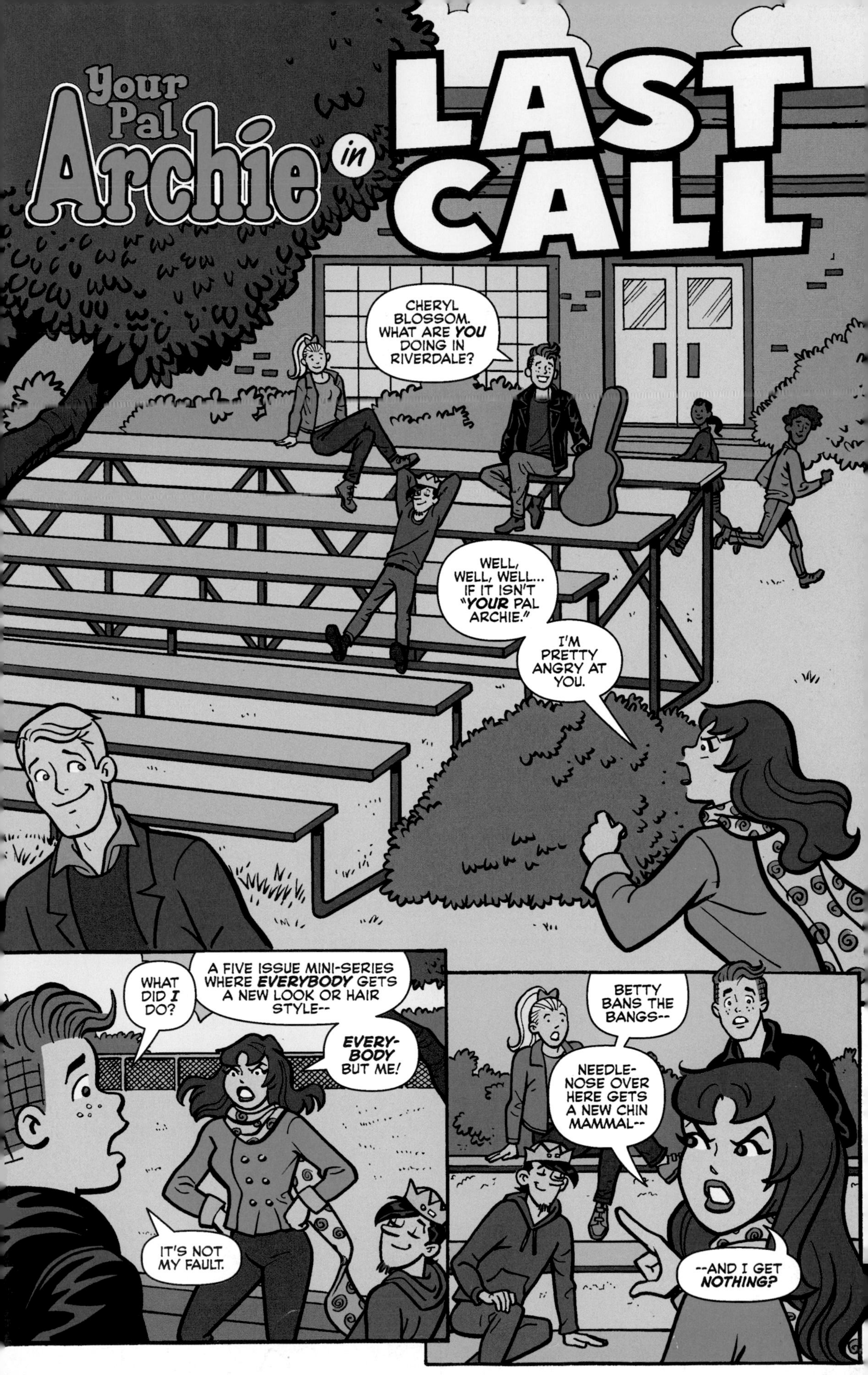
Your Pal Archie in
LAST CALL
CHERYL BLOSSOM. WHAT ARE YOU DOING IN RIVERDALE?
WELL, WELL, WELL... IF IT ISN'T "YOUR PAL ARCHIE."
I'M PRETTY ANGRY AT YOU.
WHAT DID I DO?
A FIVE ISSUE MINI-SERIES WHERE EVERYBODY GETS A NEW LOOK OR HAIR STYLE--
EVERY-BODY BUT ME!
IT'S NOT MY FAULT.
BETTY BANS THE BANGS--
NEEDLE-NOSE OVER HERE GETS A NEW CHIN MAMMAL--
--AND I GET NOTHING?

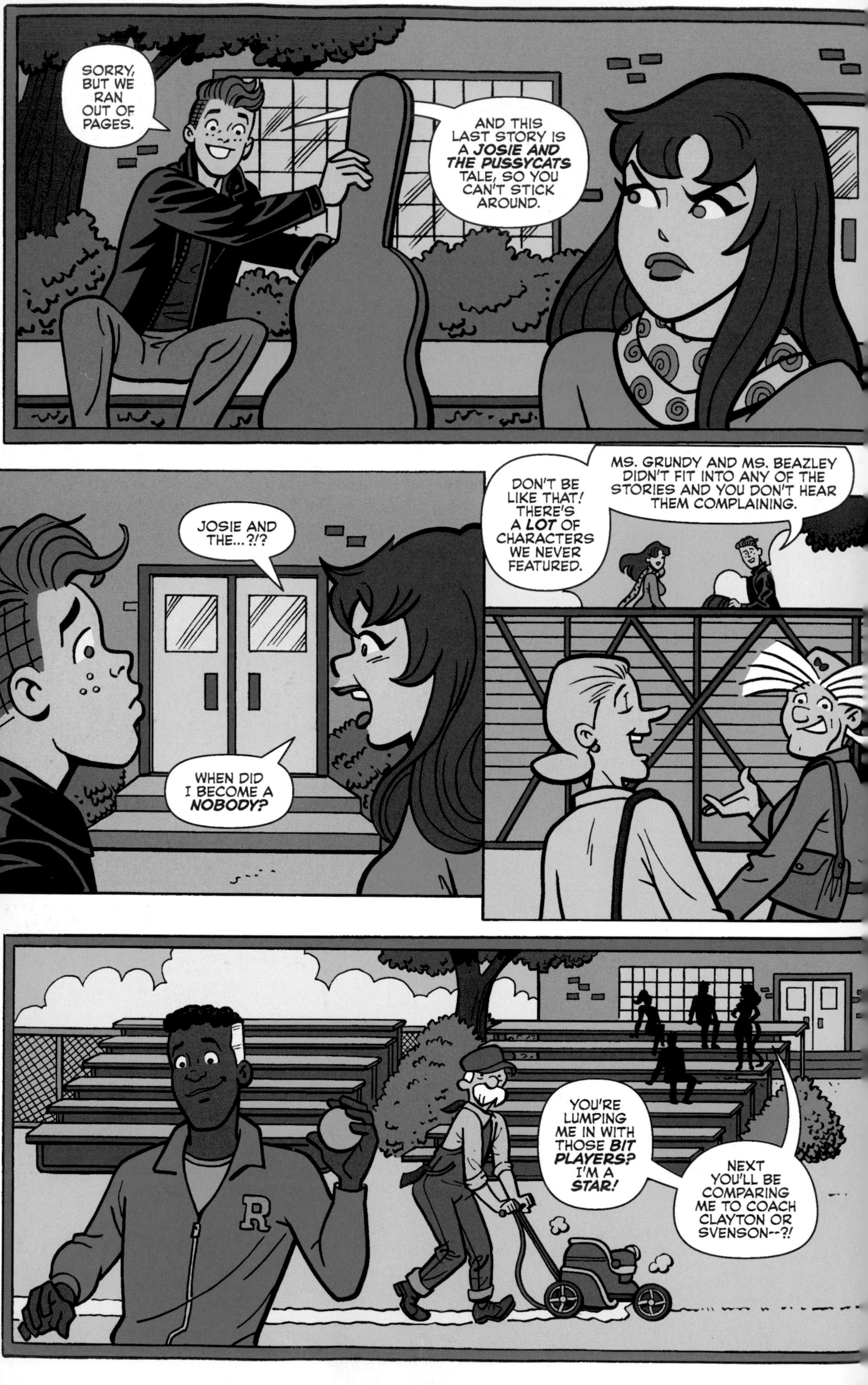
SORRY, BUT WE RAN OUT OF PAGES.
AND THIS LAST STORY IS A ***JOSIE AND THE PUSSYCATS*** TALE, SO YOU CAN'T STICK AROUND.
JOSIE AND THE...?!?
WHEN DID I BECOME A ***NOBODY?***
DON'T BE LIKE THAT! THERE'S A ***LOT*** OF CHARACTERS WE NEVER FEATURED.
MS. GRUNDY AND MS. BEAZLEY DIDN'T FIT INTO ANY OF THE STORIES AND YOU DON'T HEAR THEM COMPLAINING.
YOU'RE LUMPING ME IN WITH THOSE ***BIT PLAYERS?*** I'M A ***STAR!***
NEXT YOU'LL BE COMPARING ME TO COACH CLAYTON OR SVENSON--?!

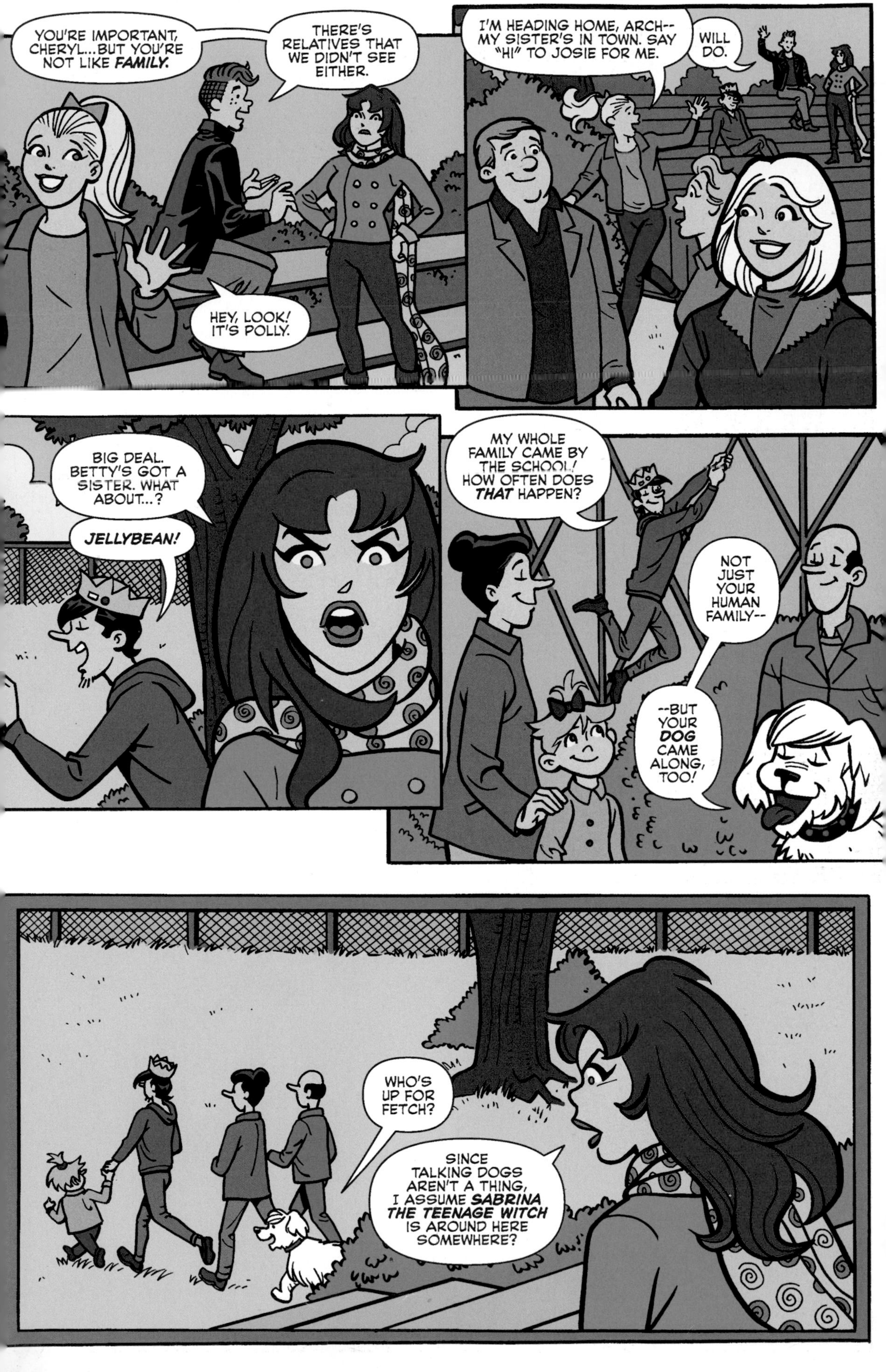
YOU'RE IMPORTANT, CHERYL...BUT YOU'RE NOT LIKE FAMILY.
THERE'S RELATIVES THAT WE DIDN'T SEE EITHER.
HEY, LOOK! IT'S POLLY.
I'M HEADING HOME, ARCH-- MY SISTER'S IN TOWN. SAY "HI" TO JOSIE FOR ME.
WILL DO.
BIG DEAL. BETTY'S GOT A SISTER. WHAT ABOUT...?
JELLYBEAN!
MY WHOLE FAMILY CAME BY THE SCHOOL! HOW OFTEN DOES THAT HAPPEN?
NOT JUST YOUR HUMAN FAMILY--
--BUT YOUR DOG CAME ALONG, TOO!
WHO'S UP FOR FETCH?
SINCE TALKING DOGS AREN'T A THING, I ASSUME SABRINA THE TEENAGE WITCH IS AROUND HERE SOMEWHERE?

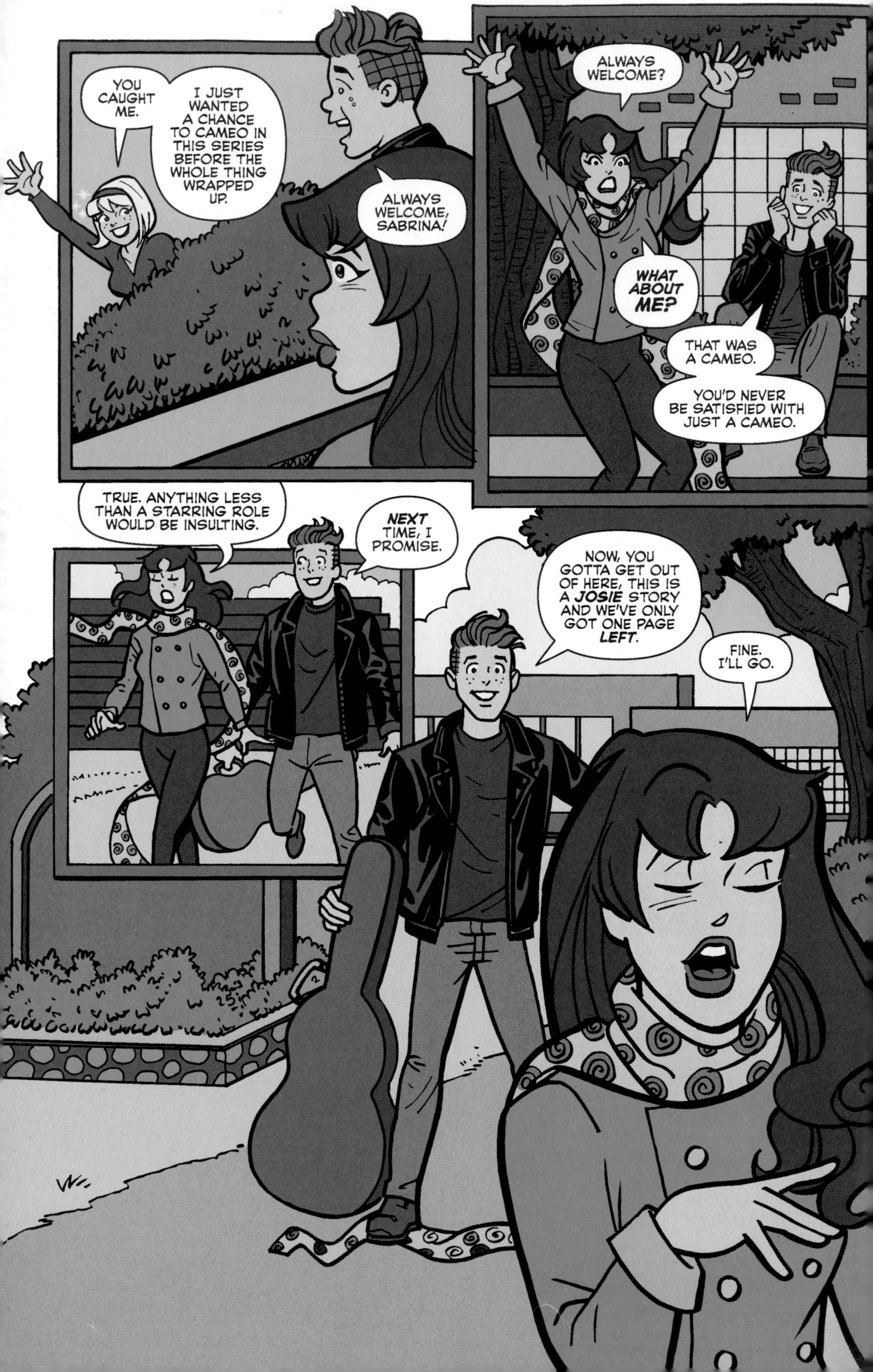

YOU CAUGHT ME.
I JUST WANTED A CHANCE TO CAMEO IN THIS SERIES BEFORE THE WHOLE THING WRAPPED UP.
ALWAYS WELCOME, SABRINA!
ALWAYS WELCOME?
WHAT ABOUT ME?
THAT WAS A CAMEO.
YOU'D NEVER BE SATISFIED WITH JUST A CAMEO.
TRUE. ANYTHING LESS THAN A STARRING ROLE WOULD BE INSULTING.
NEXT TIME, I PROMISE.
NOW, YOU GOTTA GET OUT OF HERE, THIS IS A JOSIE STORY AND WE'VE ONLY GOT ONE PAGE LEFT.
FINE. I'LL GO.

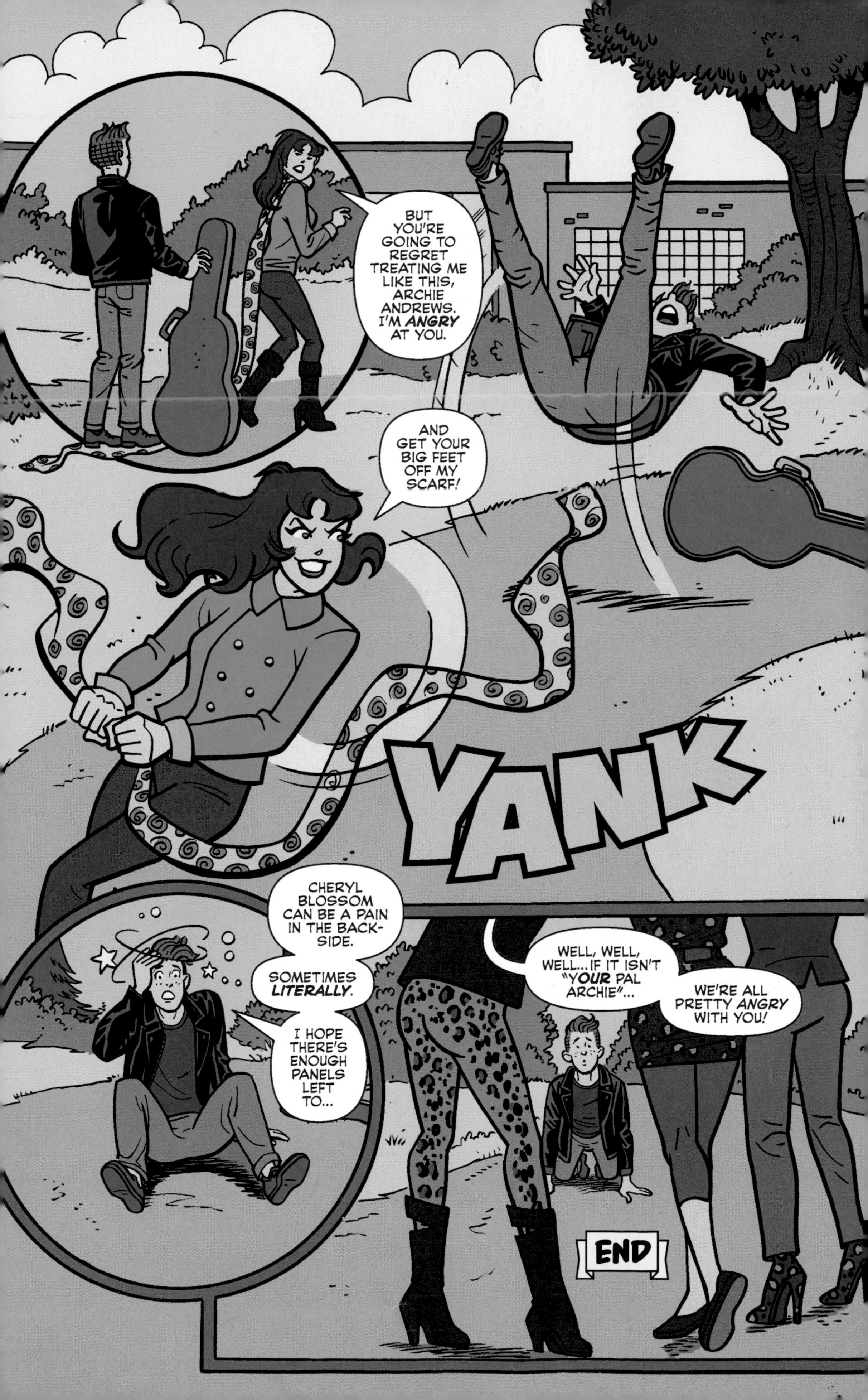
BUT YOU'RE GOING TO REGRET TREATING ME LIKE THIS, ARCHIE ANDREWS. I'M *ANGRY* AT YOU.
AND GET YOUR BIG FEET OFF MY SCARF!
YANK
CHERYL BLOSSOM CAN BE A PAIN IN THE BACK-SIDE.
SOMETIMES *LITERALLY*.
I HOPE THERE'S ENOUGH PANELS LEFT TO...
WELL, WELL, WELL...IF IT ISN'T "*YOUR* PAL ARCHIE"...
WE'RE ALL PRETTY *ANGRY* WITH YOU!
END

Your Pal Archie®

SPECIAL FEATURES

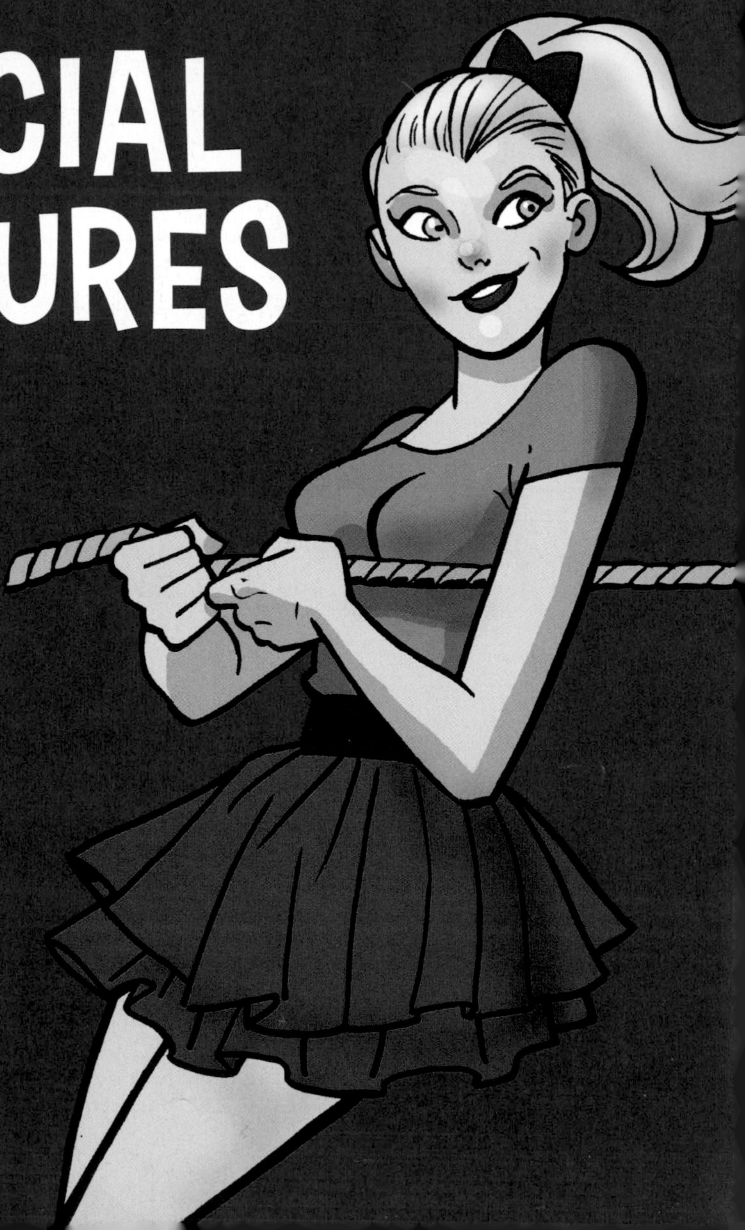

Original promotional sketch for *Your Pal Archie* by Dan Parent and Ty Templeton.

Dan Parent's artwork was influenced from the styles and fashion of The CW's hit new RIVERDALE TV series, while remaining familiar for fans of the classic style.

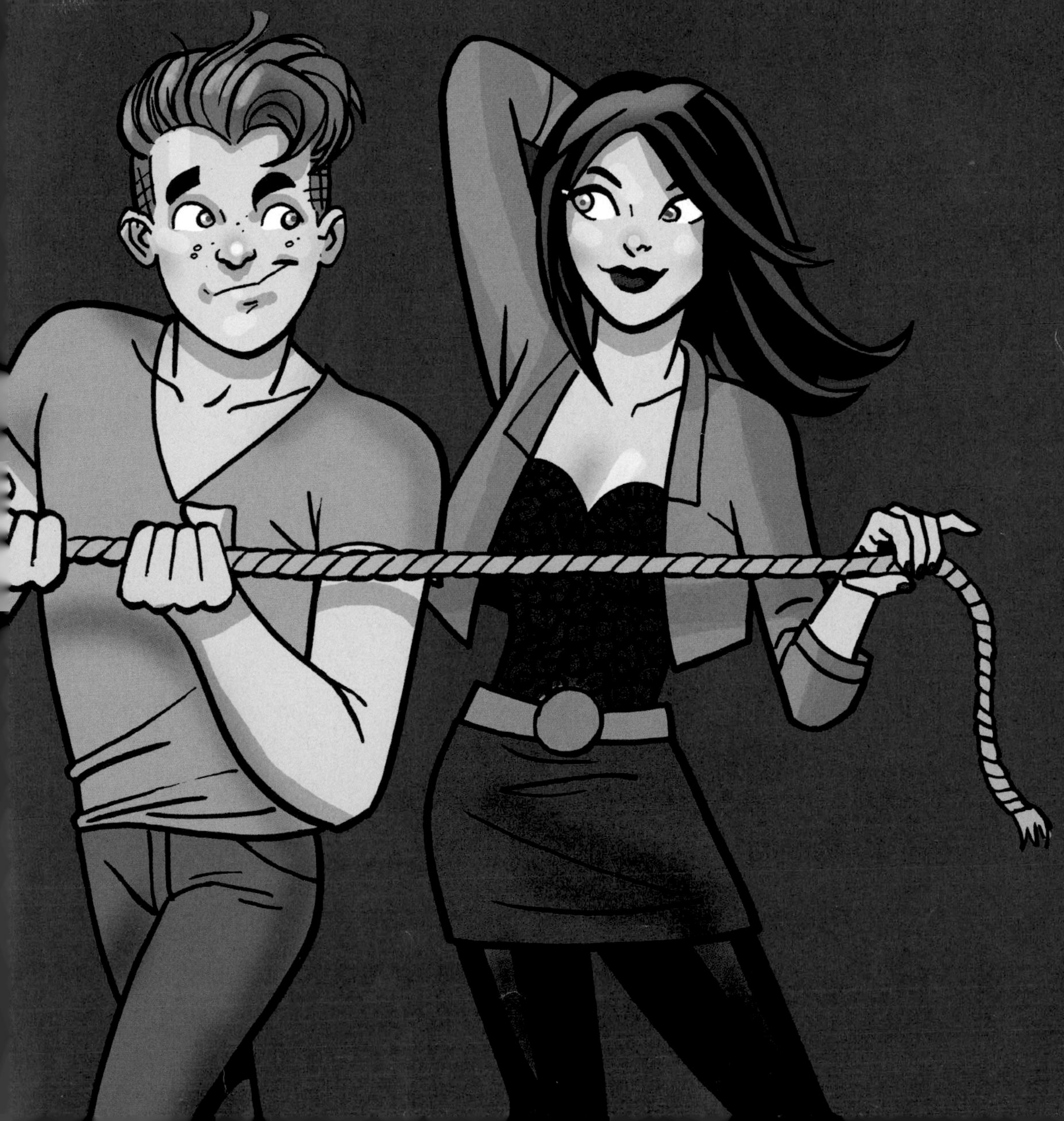

Your Pal Archie®

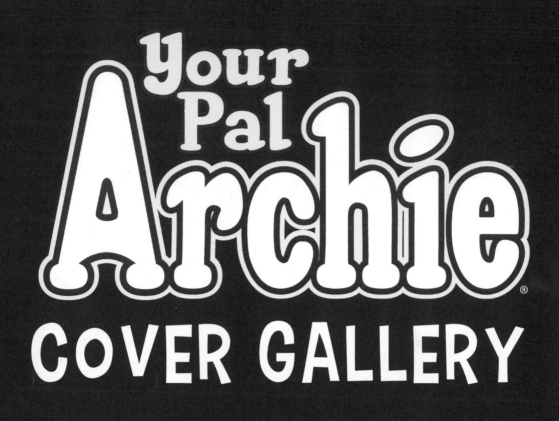

COVER GALLERY

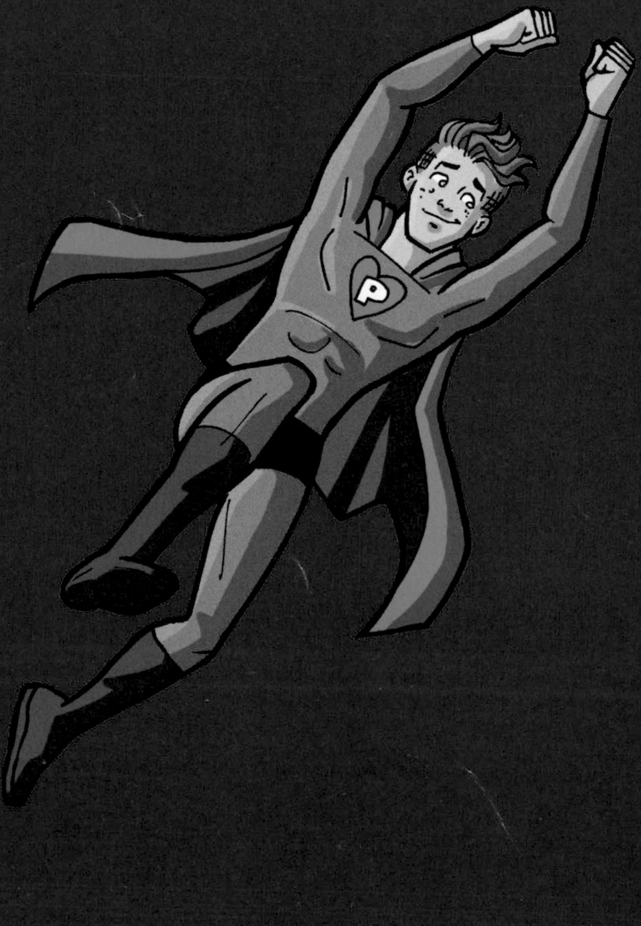

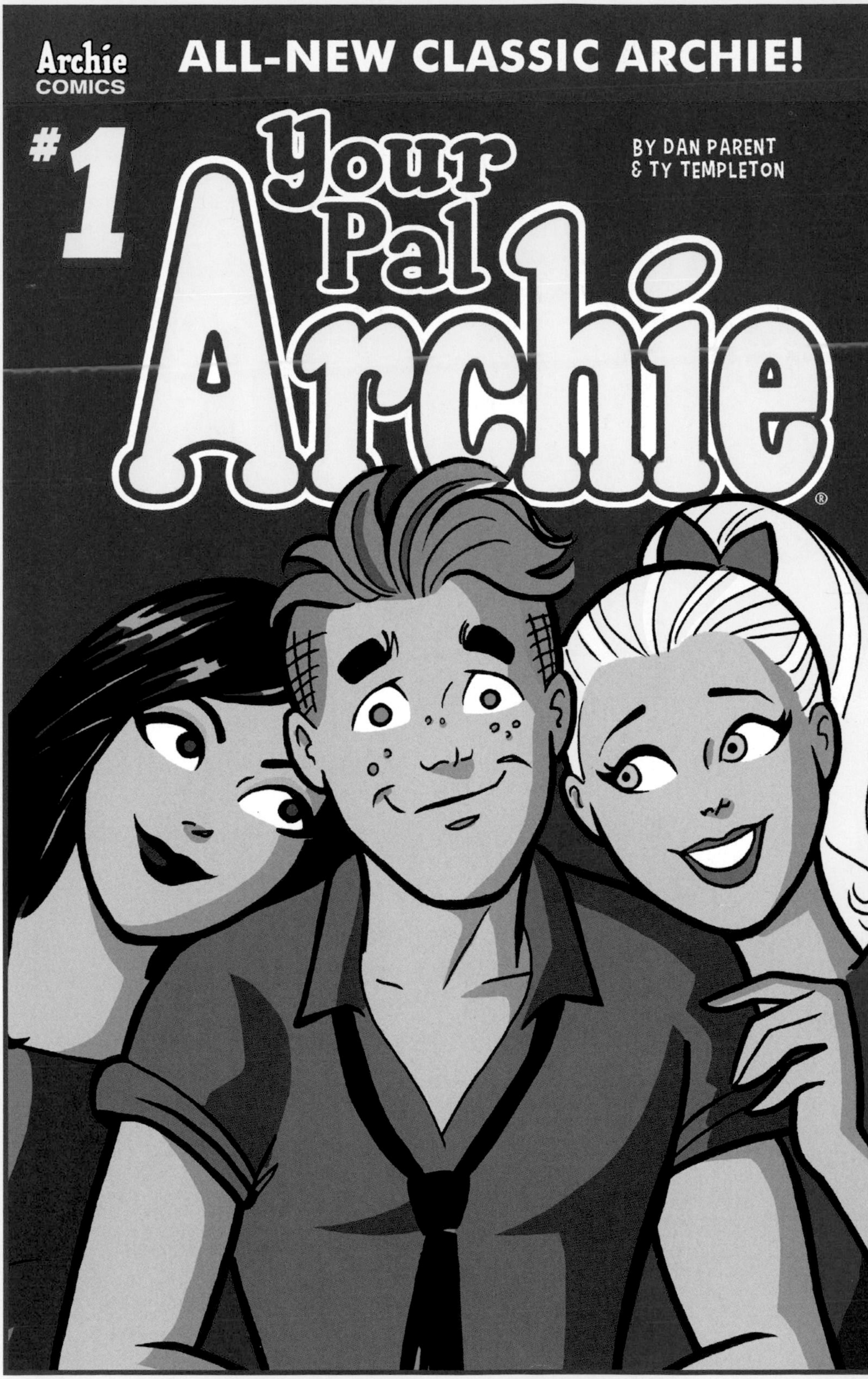
Archie COMICS
ALL-NEW CLASSIC ARCHIE!
#1
Your Pal Archie
BY DAN PARENT
& TY TEMPLETON

YOUR PAL ARCHIE #1 DAN PARENT

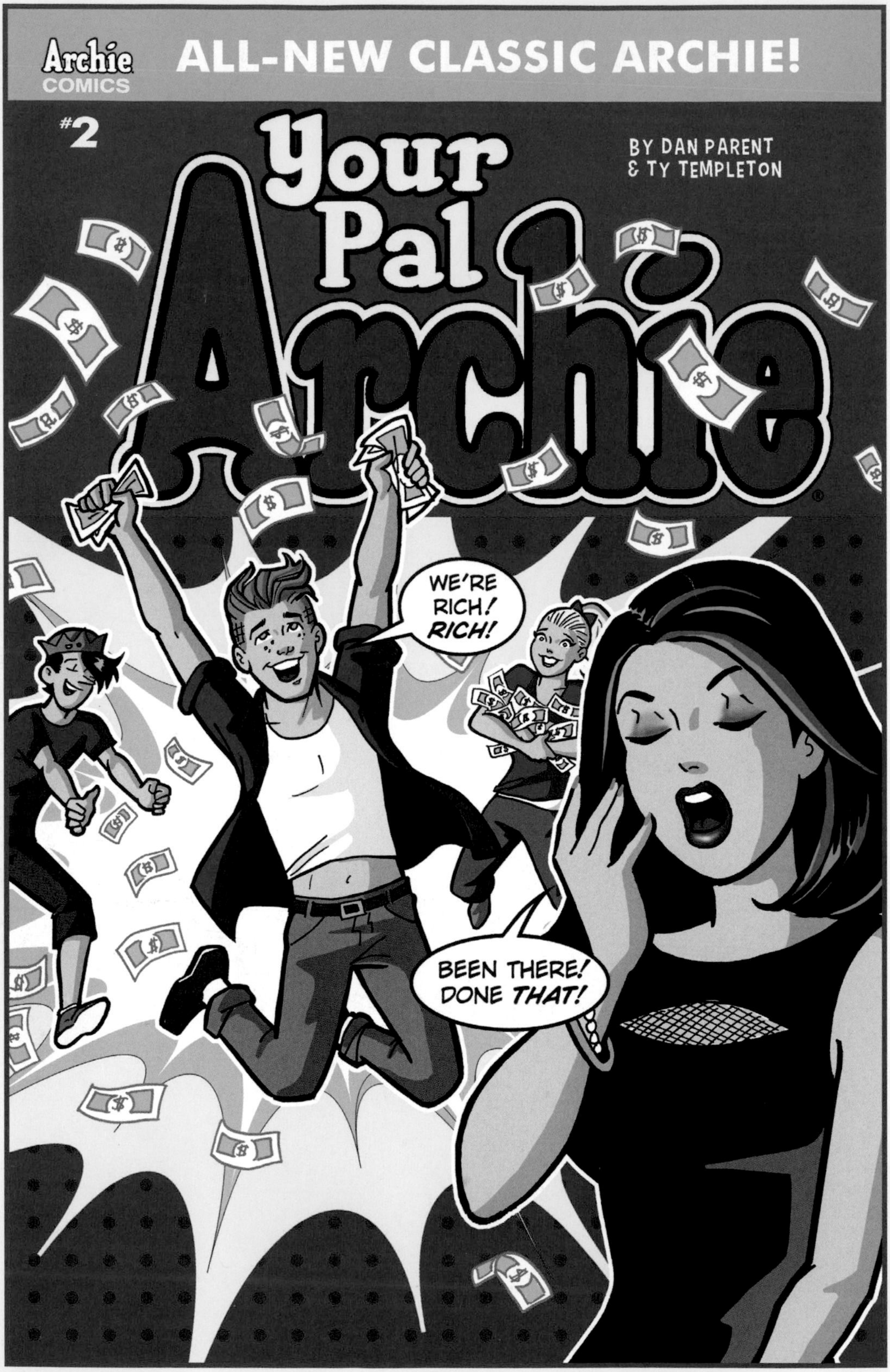
Archie COMICS
ALL-NEW CLASSIC ARCHIE!
#2
Your Pal Archie
BY DAN PARENT
& TY TEMPLETON
WE'RE RICH! RICH!
BEEN THERE! DONE THAT!

YOUR PAL ARCHIE #2 DAN PARENT

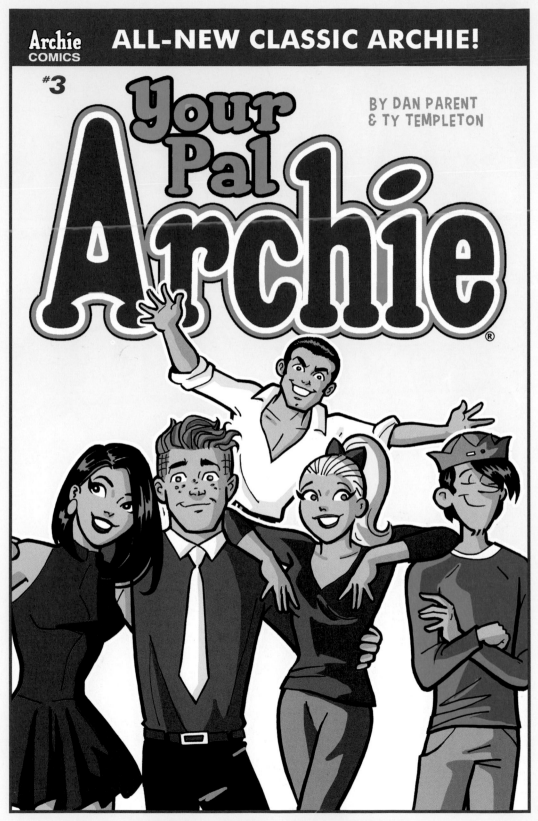

YOUR PAL ARCHIE #3 DAN PARENT

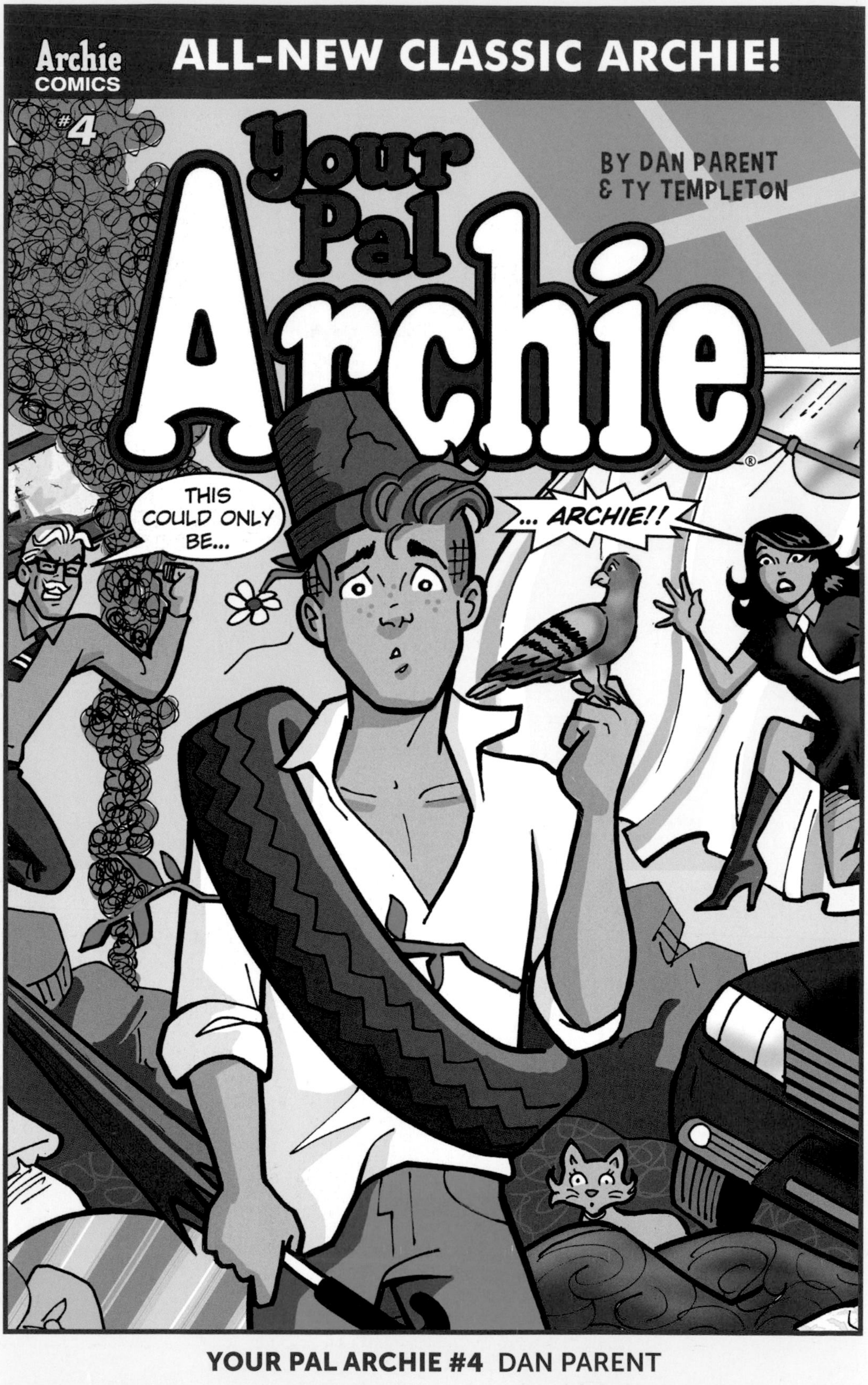
Archie COMICS
ALL-NEW CLASSIC ARCHIE!
#4
Your Pal Archie
BY DAN PARENT
& TY TEMPLETON
THIS COULD ONLY BE...
... ARCHIE!!

YOUR PAL ARCHIE #4 DAN PARENT

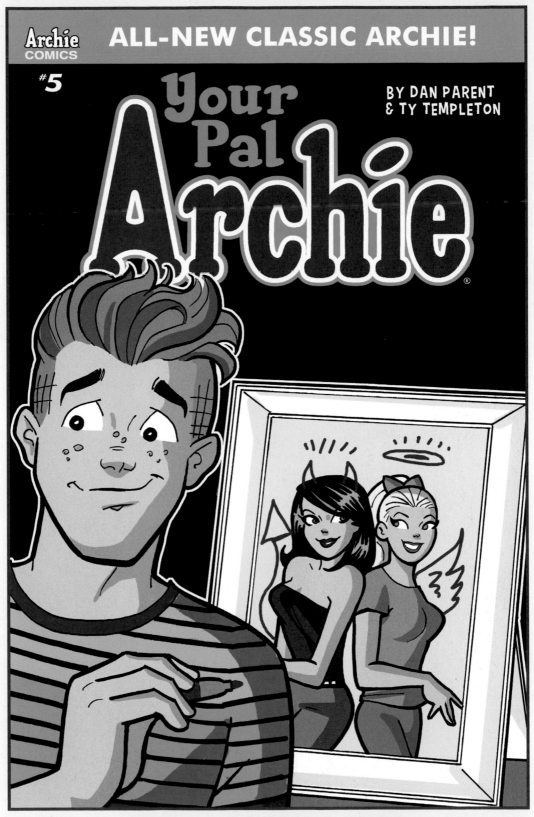

YOUR PAL ARCHIE #5 DAN PARENT

CONNECTING VARIANT COVERS

Issues 1-5 of Your Pal Archie featured special connecting variant covers by artist Les McClaine. These covers form one giant image of Pop's Chock'lit Shoppe featuring Archie Comics' most beloved characters!

Here is a look at the entire spread:

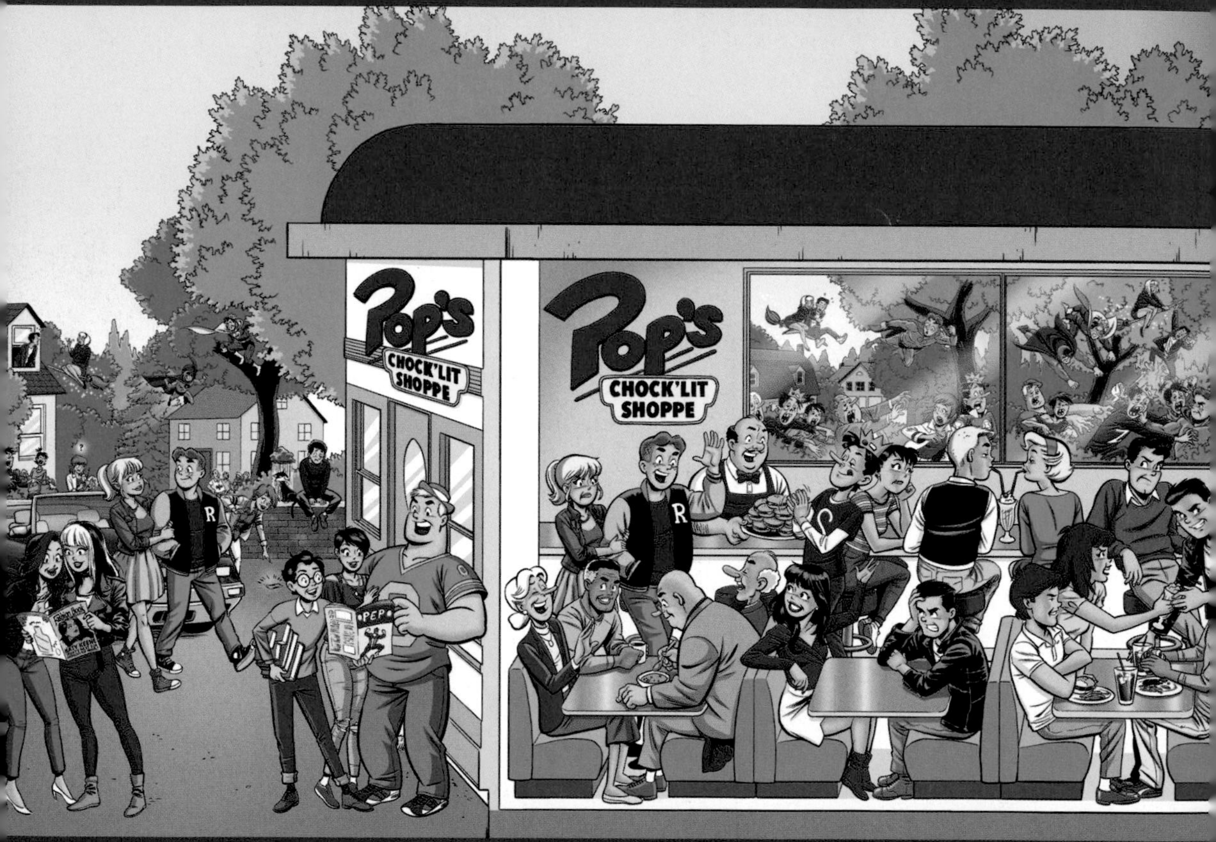
Pop's
CHOCK'LIT SHOPPE
Pop's
CHOCK'LIT SHOPPE
PEP

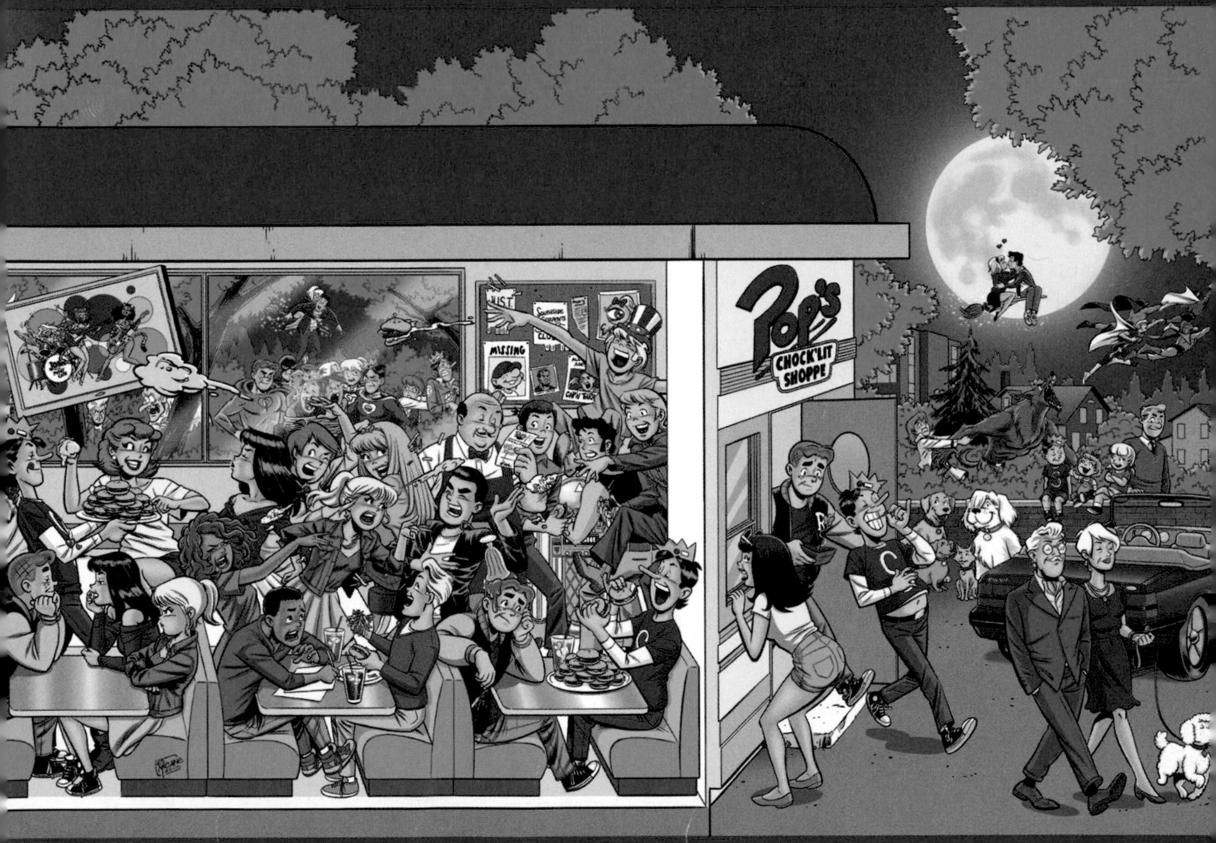
Pop's
CHOCK'LIT SHOPPE
MISSING

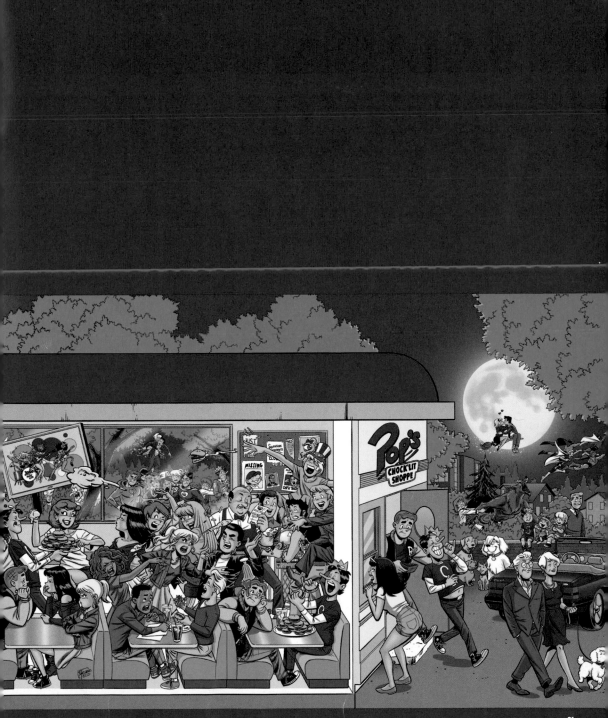

ART BY **LES MCCLAINE** WITH **ROSARIO "TITO" PEÑA**

SPECIAL BONUS ISSUE

COSMO™

Cosmo and his Martian crew are traveling in search of adventure in the deepest corners of space! Their latest mission is about to turn into a much larger adventure as they stumble upon their most unique specimen yet: A panicked human!

STORY BY
IAN FLYNN

ART BY
TRACY YARDLEY

COLORS BY
MATT HERMS

LETTERING BY
JACK MORELLI

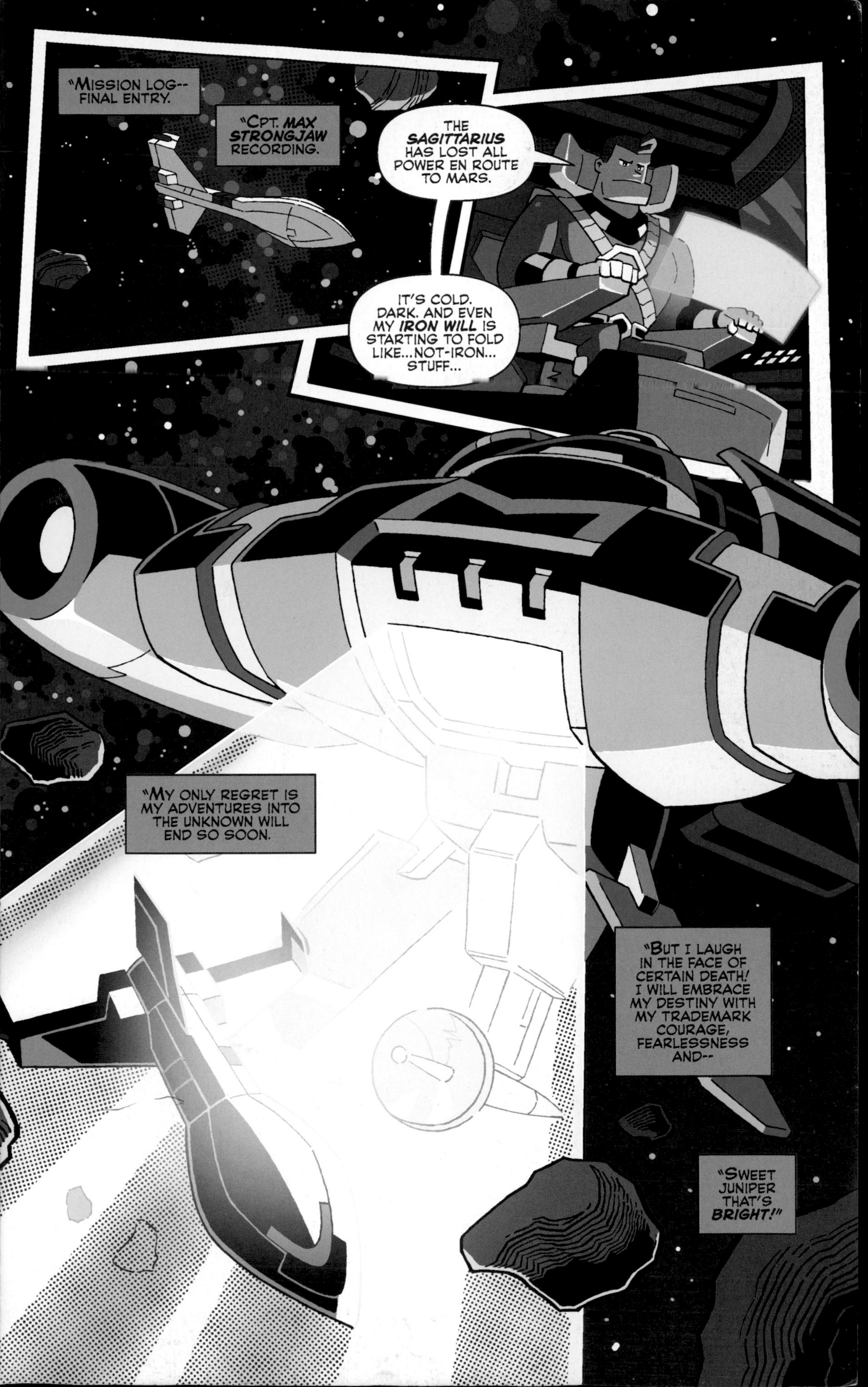
"MISSION LOG-- FINAL ENTRY.
"CPT. MAX STRONGJAW RECORDING.
THE SAGITTARIUS HAS LOST ALL POWER EN ROUTE TO MARS.
IT'S COLD. DARK. AND EVEN MY IRON WILL IS STARTING TO FOLD LIKE...NOT-IRON... STUFF...
"MY ONLY REGRET IS MY ADVENTURES INTO THE UNKNOWN WILL END SO SOON.
"BUT I LAUGH IN THE FACE OF CERTAIN DEATH! I WILL EMBRACE MY DESTINY WITH MY TRADEMARK COURAGE, FEARLESSNESS AND--
"SWEET JUNIPER THAT'S BRIGHT!"

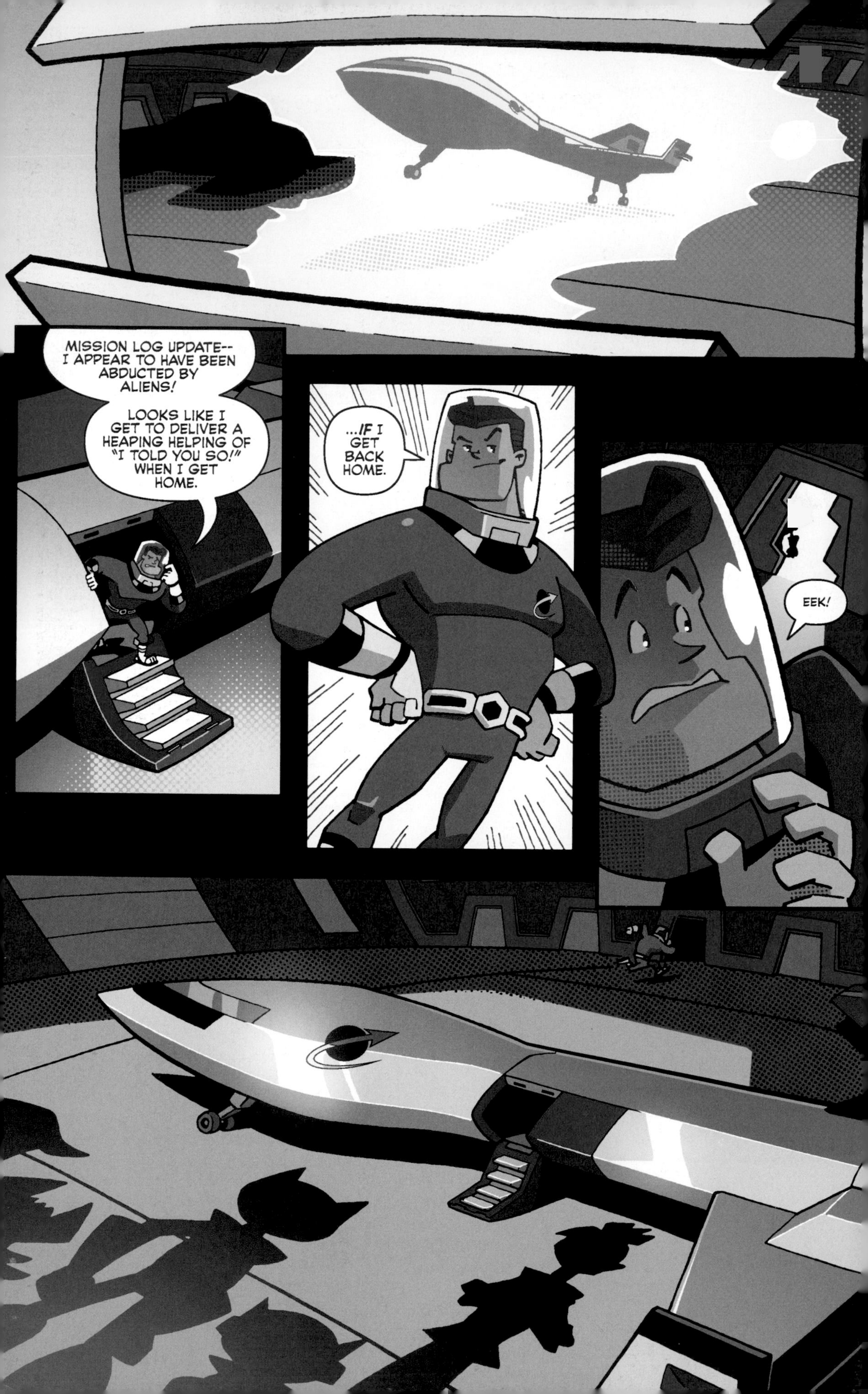
MISSION LOG UPDATE-- I APPEAR TO HAVE BEEN ABDUCTED BY ALIENS!
LOOKS LIKE I GET TO DELIVER A HEAPING HELPING OF "I TOLD YOU SO!" WHEN I GET HOME.
...IF I GET BACK HOME.
EEK!

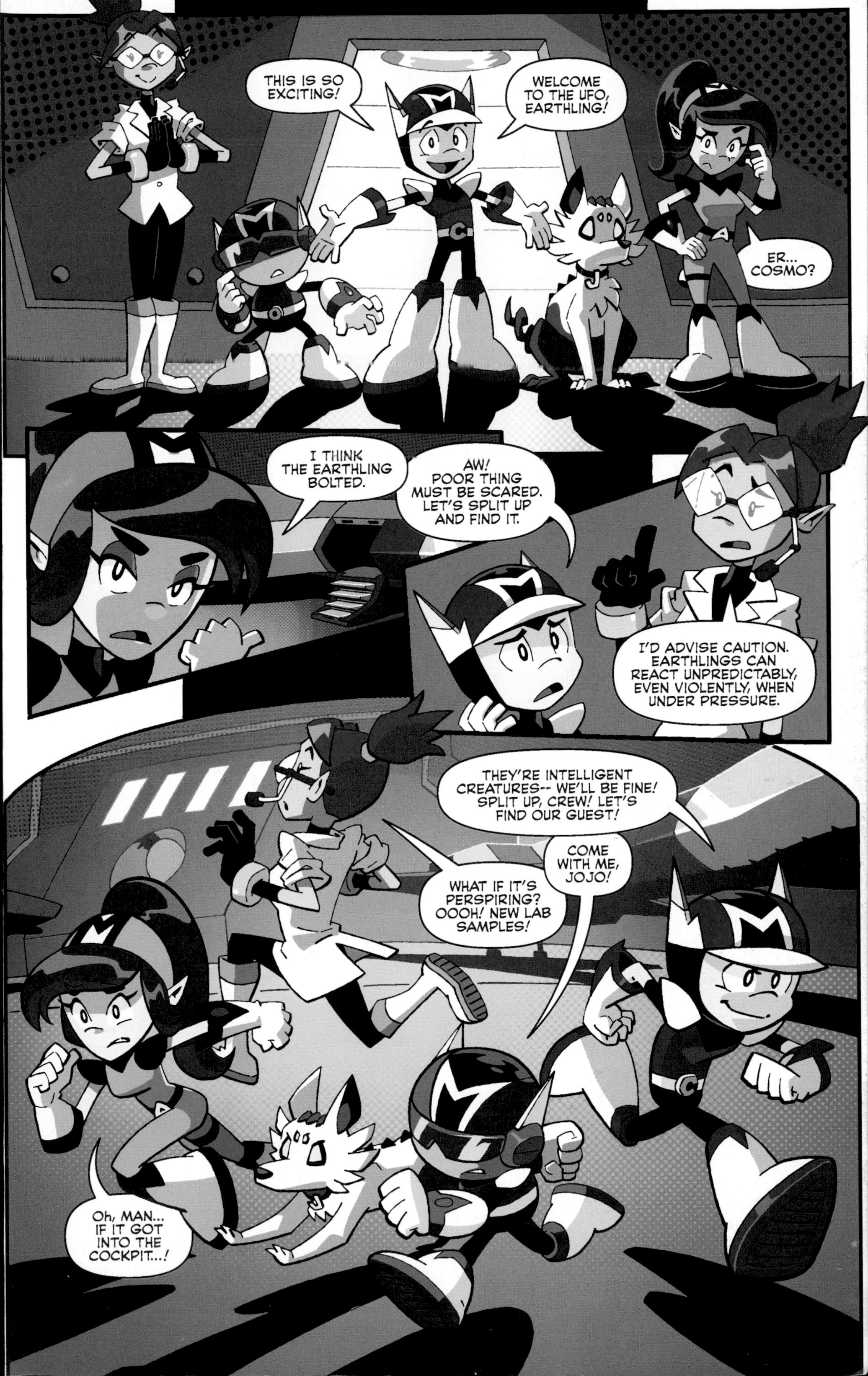
THIS IS SO EXCITING!
WELCOME TO THE UFO, EARTHLING!
ER... COSMO?
I THINK THE EARTHLING BOLTED.
AW! POOR THING MUST BE SCARED. LET'S SPLIT UP AND FIND IT.
I'D ADVISE CAUTION. EARTHLINGS CAN REACT UNPREDICTABLY, EVEN VIOLENTLY, WHEN UNDER PRESSURE.
THEY'RE INTELLIGENT CREATURES-- WE'LL BE FINE! SPLIT UP, CREW! LET'S FIND OUR GUEST!
COME WITH ME, JOJO!
WHAT IF IT'S PERSPIRING? OOOH! NEW LAB SAMPLES!
Oh, MAN... IF IT GOT INTO THE COCKPIT...!

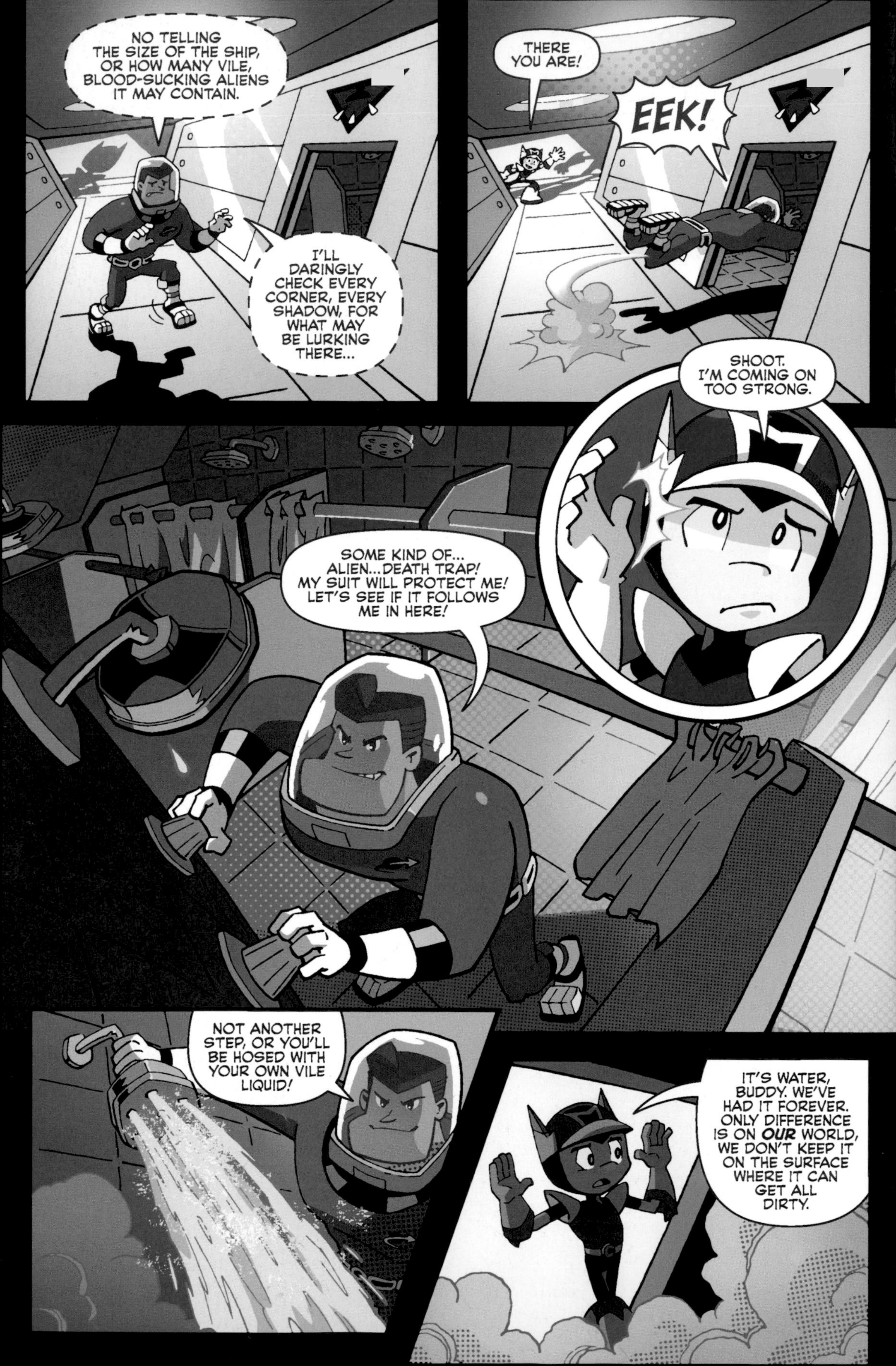
NO TELLING THE SIZE OF THE SHIP, OR HOW MANY VILE, BLOOD-SUCKING ALIENS IT MAY CONTAIN.
I'LL DARINGLY CHECK EVERY CORNER, EVERY SHADOW, FOR WHAT MAY BE LURKING THERE...
THERE YOU ARE!
EEK!
SHOOT. I'M COMING ON TOO STRONG.
SOME KIND OF... ALIEN...DEATH TRAP! MY SUIT WILL PROTECT ME! LET'S SEE IF IT FOLLOWS ME IN HERE!
NOT ANOTHER STEP, OR YOU'LL BE HOSED WITH YOUR OWN VILE LIQUID!
IT'S WATER, BUDDY. WE'VE HAD IT FOREVER. ONLY DIFFERENCE IS ON OUR WORLD, WE DON'T KEEP IT ON THE SURFACE WHERE IT CAN GET ALL DIRTY.

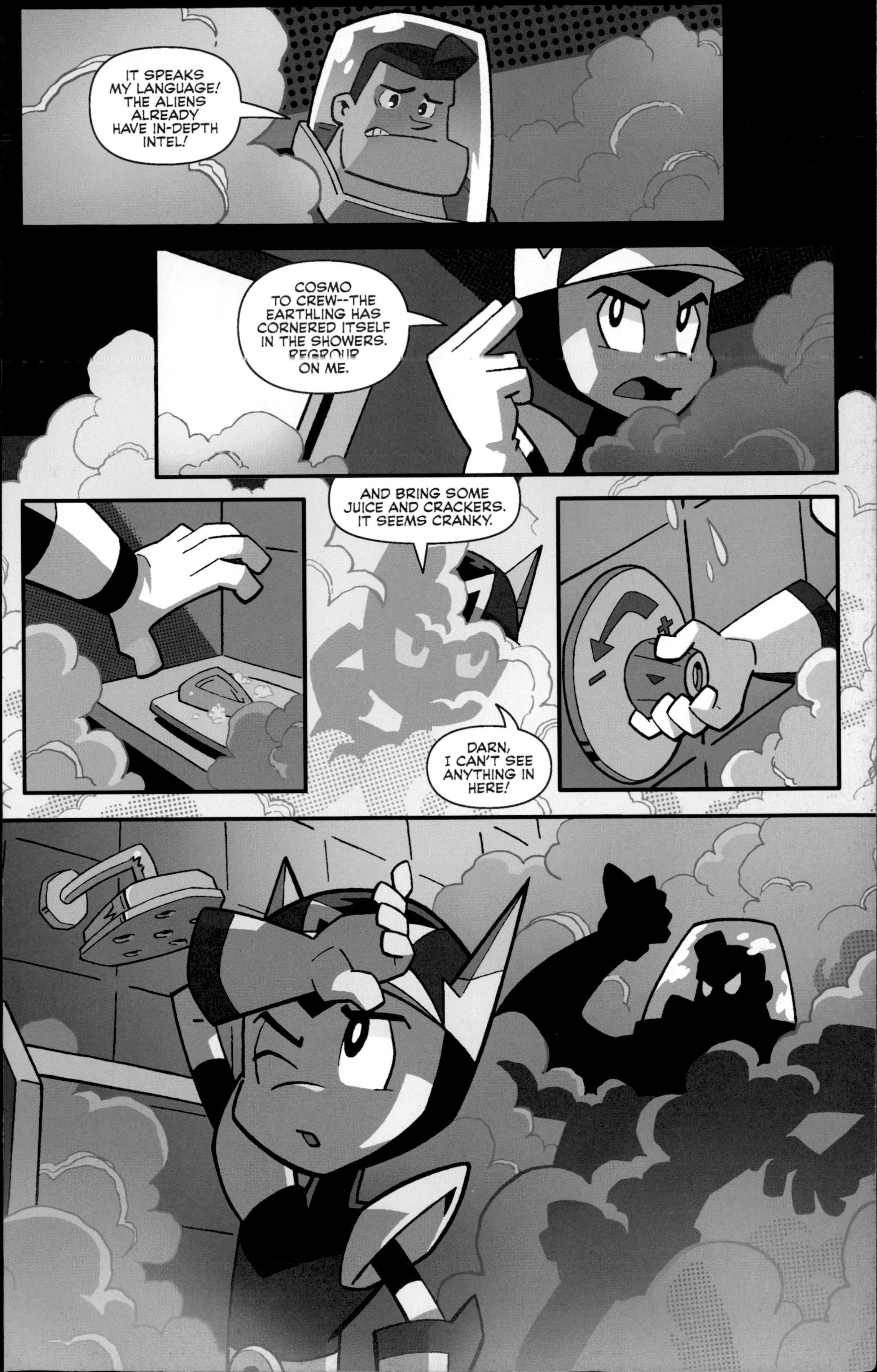
IT SPEAKS MY LANGUAGE! THE ALIENS ALREADY HAVE IN-DEPTH INTEL!
COSMO TO CREW--THE EARTHLING HAS CORNERED ITSELF IN THE SHOWERS. REGROUP ON ME.
AND BRING SOME JUICE AND CRACKERS. IT SEEMS CRANKY.
DARN, I CAN'T SEE ANYTHING IN HERE!

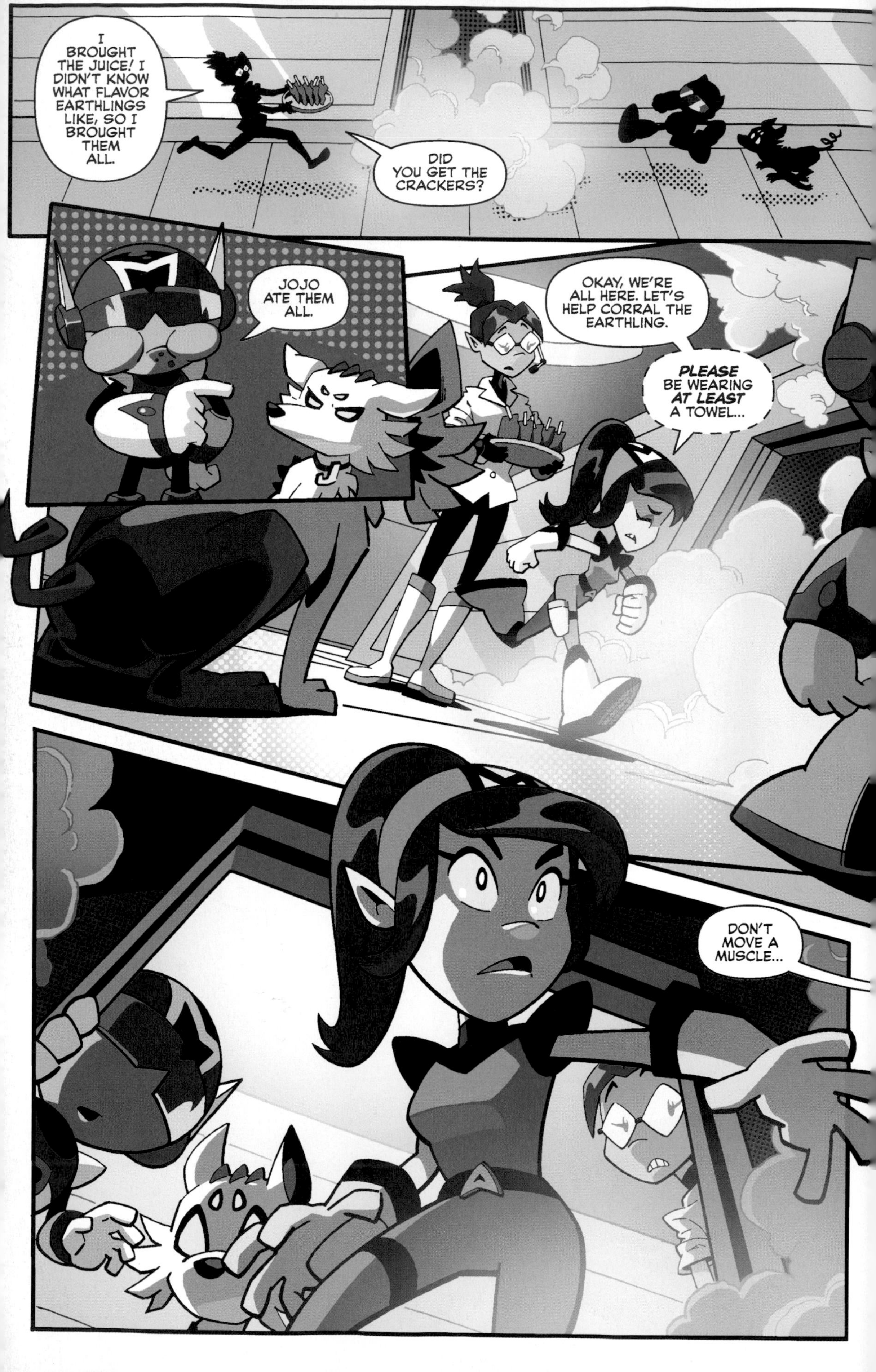

I BROUGHT THE JUICE! I DIDN'T KNOW WHAT FLAVOR EARTHLINGS LIKE, SO I BROUGHT THEM ALL.
DID YOU GET THE CRACKERS?
JOJO ATE THEM ALL.
OKAY, WE'RE ALL HERE. LET'S HELP CORRAL THE EARTHLING.
PLEASE BE WEARING AT LEAST A TOWEL...
DON'T MOVE A MUSCLE...

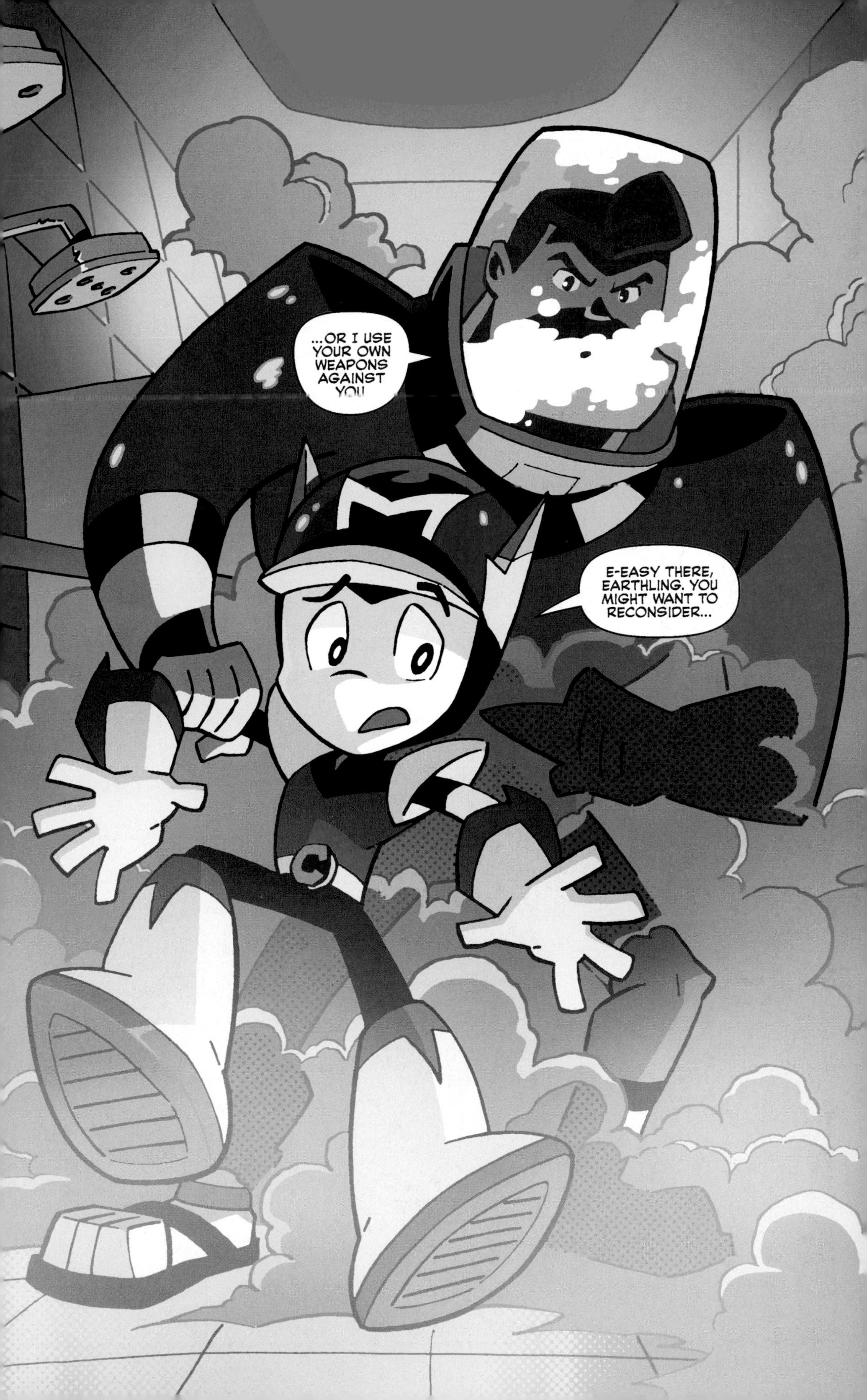
...OR I USE YOUR OWN WEAPONS AGAINST YOU.
E-EASY THERE, EARTHLING. YOU MIGHT WANT TO RECONSIDER...

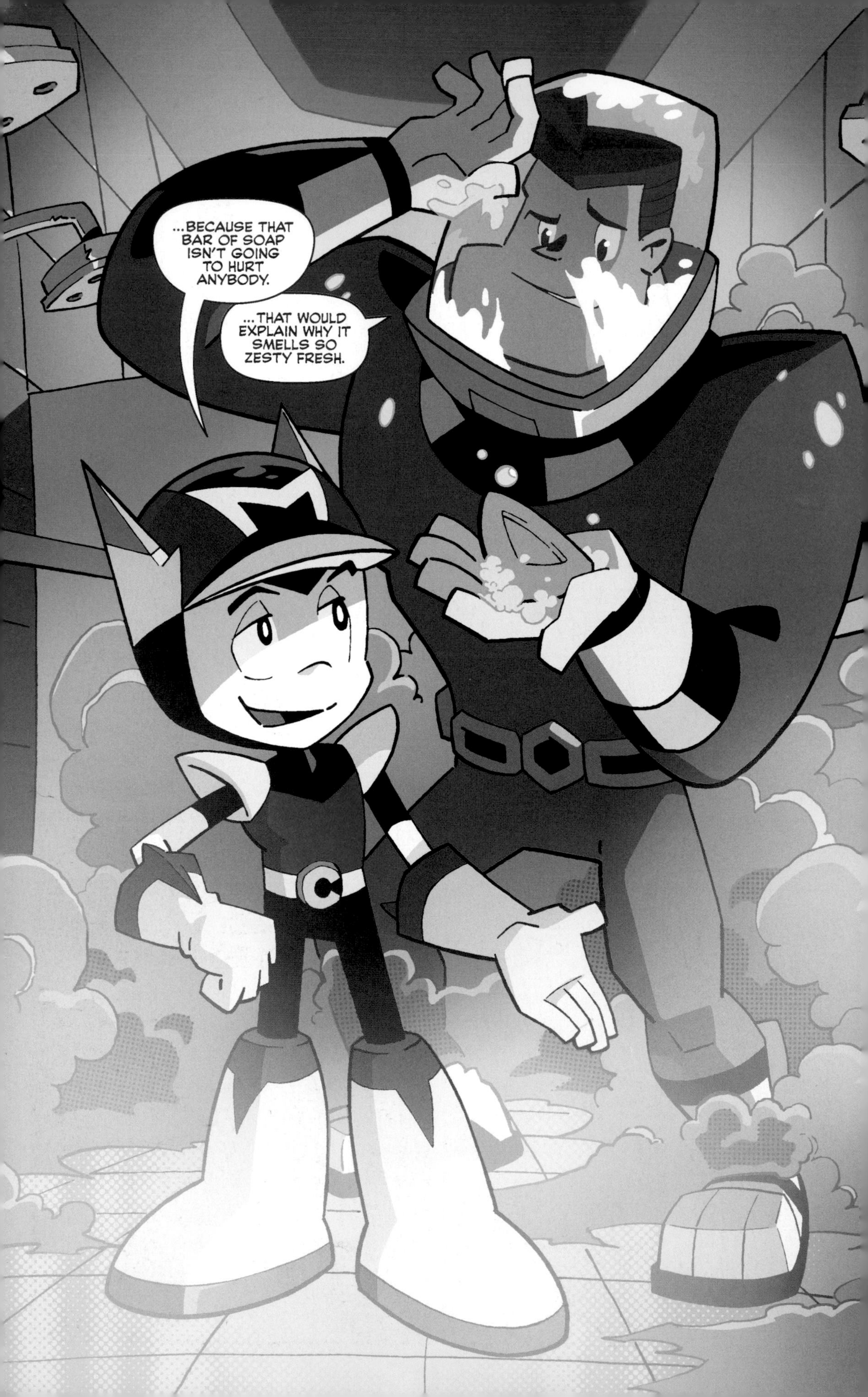
...BECAUSE THAT BAR OF SOAP ISN'T GOING TO HURT ANYBODY.
...THAT WOULD EXPLAIN WHY IT SMELLS SO ZESTY FRESH.

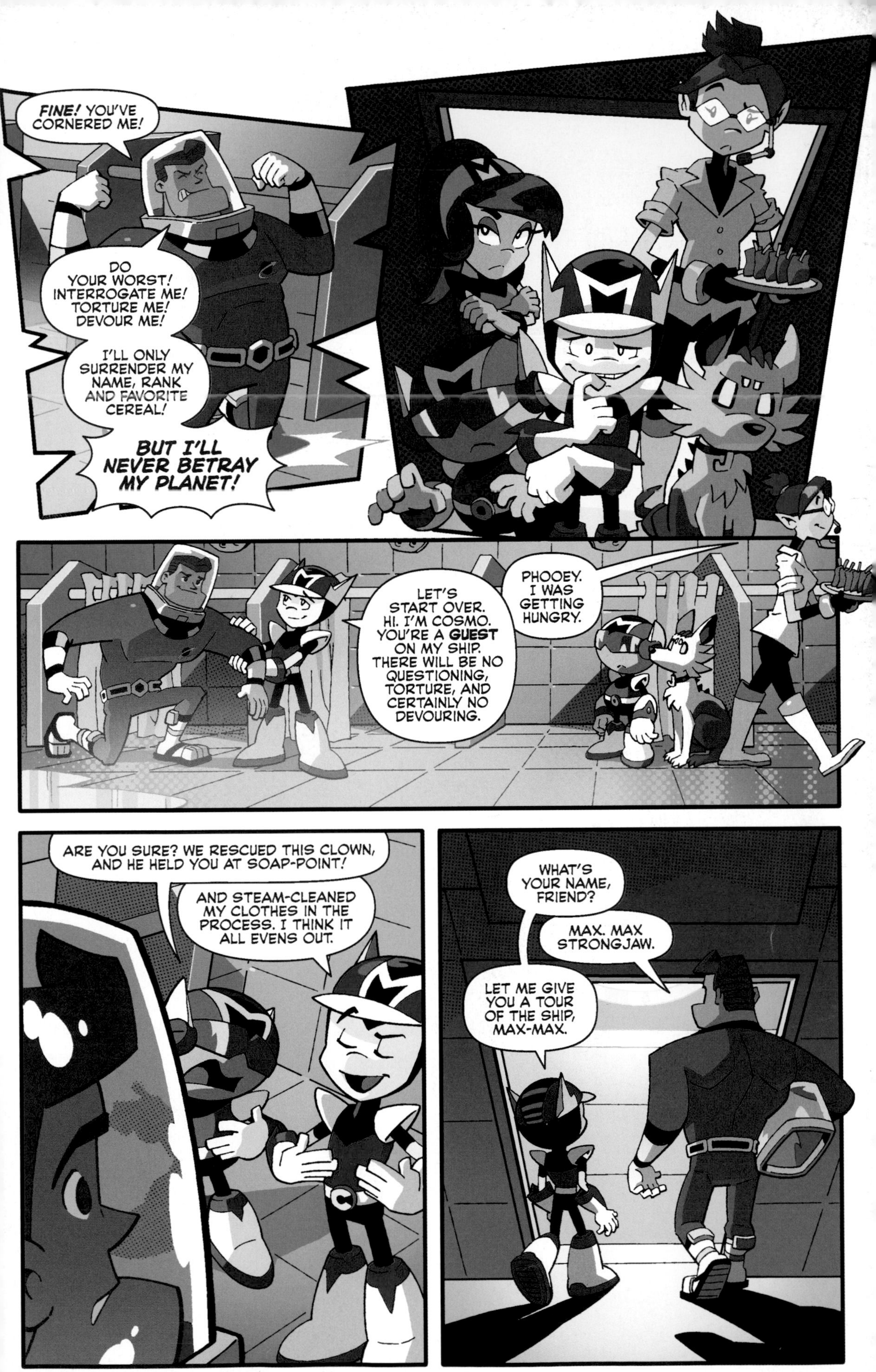
FINE! YOU'VE CORNERED ME!
DO YOUR WORST! INTERROGATE ME! TORTURE ME! DEVOUR ME!
I'LL ONLY SURRENDER MY NAME, RANK AND FAVORITE CEREAL!
BUT I'LL NEVER BETRAY MY PLANET!
LET'S START OVER. HI. I'M COSMO. YOU'RE A GUEST ON MY SHIP. THERE WILL BE NO QUESTIONING, TORTURE, AND CERTAINLY NO DEVOURING.
PHOOEY. I WAS GETTING HUNGRY.
ARE YOU SURE? WE RESCUED THIS CLOWN, AND HE HELD YOU AT SOAP-POINT!
AND STEAM-CLEANED MY CLOTHES IN THE PROCESS. I THINK IT ALL EVENS OUT.
WHAT'S YOUR NAME, FRIEND?
MAX. MAX STRONGJAW.
LET ME GIVE YOU A TOUR OF THE SHIP, MAX-MAX.

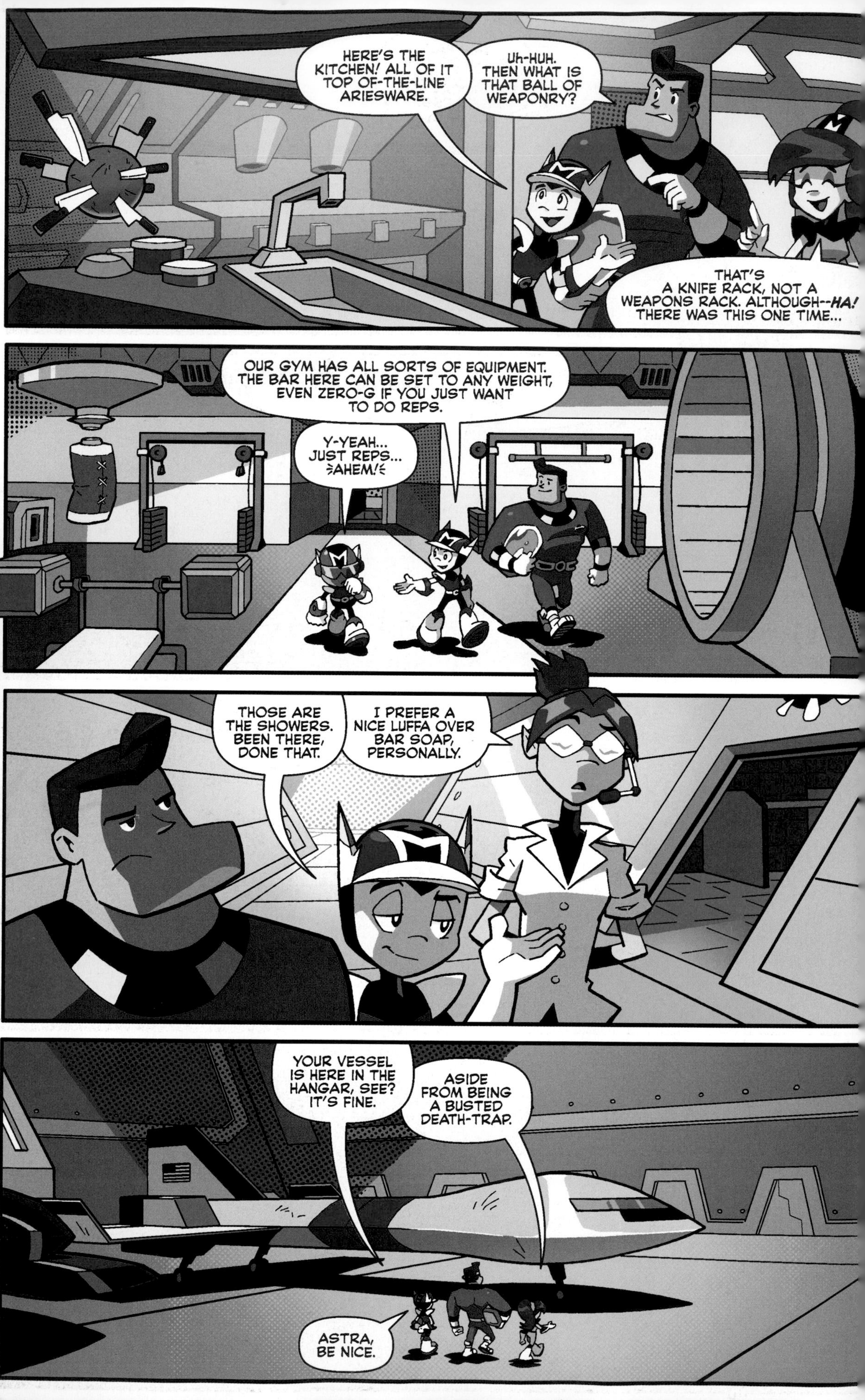
HERE'S THE KITCHEN! ALL OF IT TOP OF-THE-LINE ARIESWARE.
Uh-HUH. THEN WHAT IS THAT BALL OF WEAPONRY?
THAT'S A KNIFE RACK, NOT A WEAPONS RACK. ALTHOUGH--HA! THERE WAS THIS ONE TIME...
OUR GYM HAS ALL SORTS OF EQUIPMENT. THE BAR HERE CAN BE SET TO ANY WEIGHT, EVEN ZERO-G IF YOU JUST WANT TO DO REPS.
Y-YEAH... JUST REPS... AHEM!
THOSE ARE THE SHOWERS. BEEN THERE, DONE THAT.
I PREFER A NICE LUFFA OVER BAR SOAP, PERSONALLY.
YOUR VESSEL IS HERE IN THE HANGAR, SEE? IT'S FINE.
ASIDE FROM BEING A BUSTED DEATH-TRAP.
ASTRA, BE NICE.

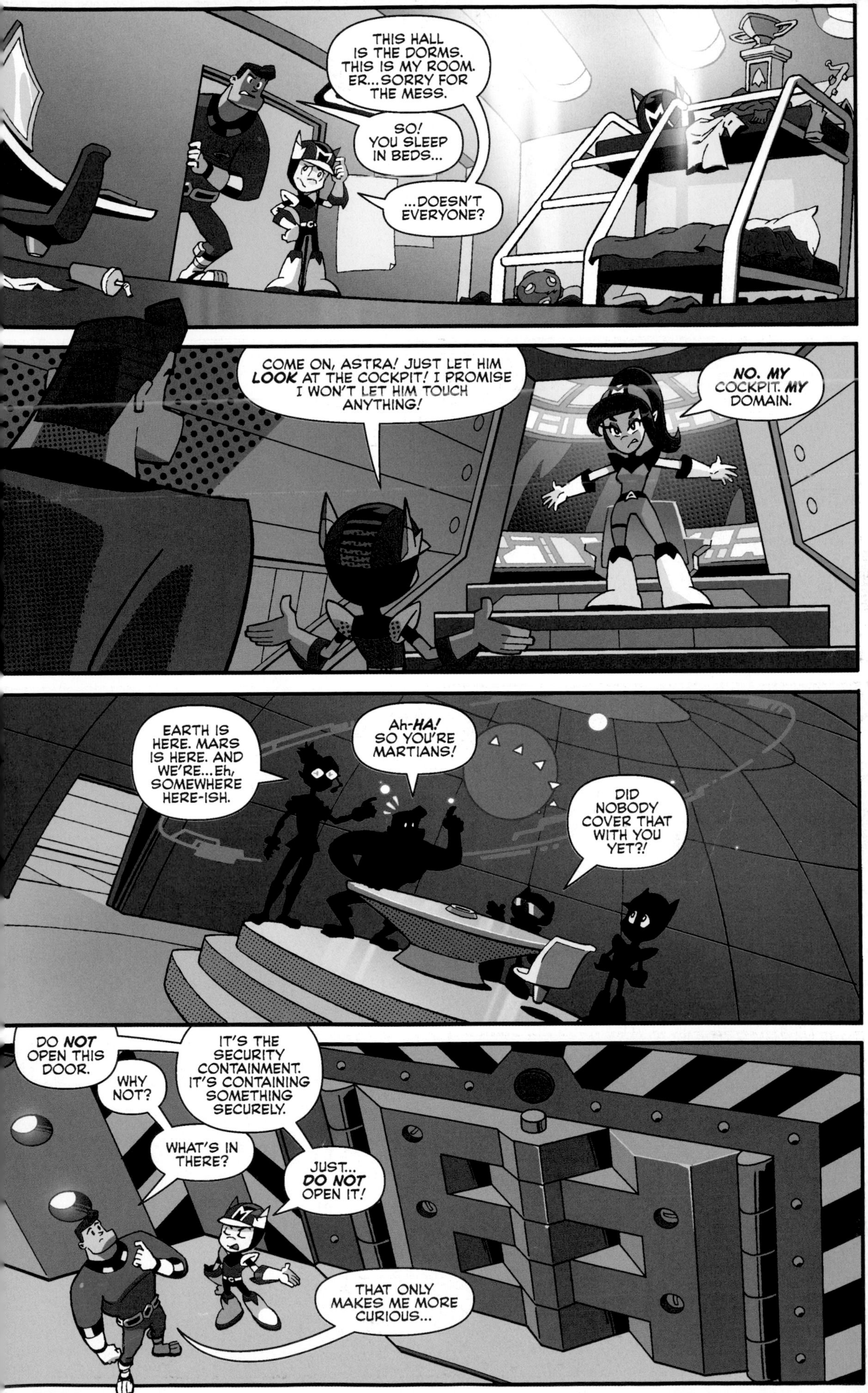
THIS HALL IS THE DORMS. THIS IS MY ROOM. ER...SORRY FOR THE MESS.
SO! YOU SLEEP IN BEDS...
...DOESN'T EVERYONE?
COME ON, ASTRA! JUST LET HIM LOOK AT THE COCKPIT! I PROMISE I WON'T LET HIM TOUCH ANYTHING!
NO. MY COCKPIT. MY DOMAIN.
EARTH IS HERE. MARS IS HERE. AND WE'RE...Eh, SOMEWHERE HERE-ISH.
Ah-HA! SO YOU'RE MARTIANS!
DID NOBODY COVER THAT WITH YOU YET?!
DO NOT OPEN THIS DOOR.
WHY NOT?
IT'S THE SECURITY CONTAINMENT. IT'S CONTAINING SOMETHING SECURELY.
WHAT'S IN THERE?
JUST... DO NOT OPEN IT!
THAT ONLY MAKES ME MORE CURIOUS...

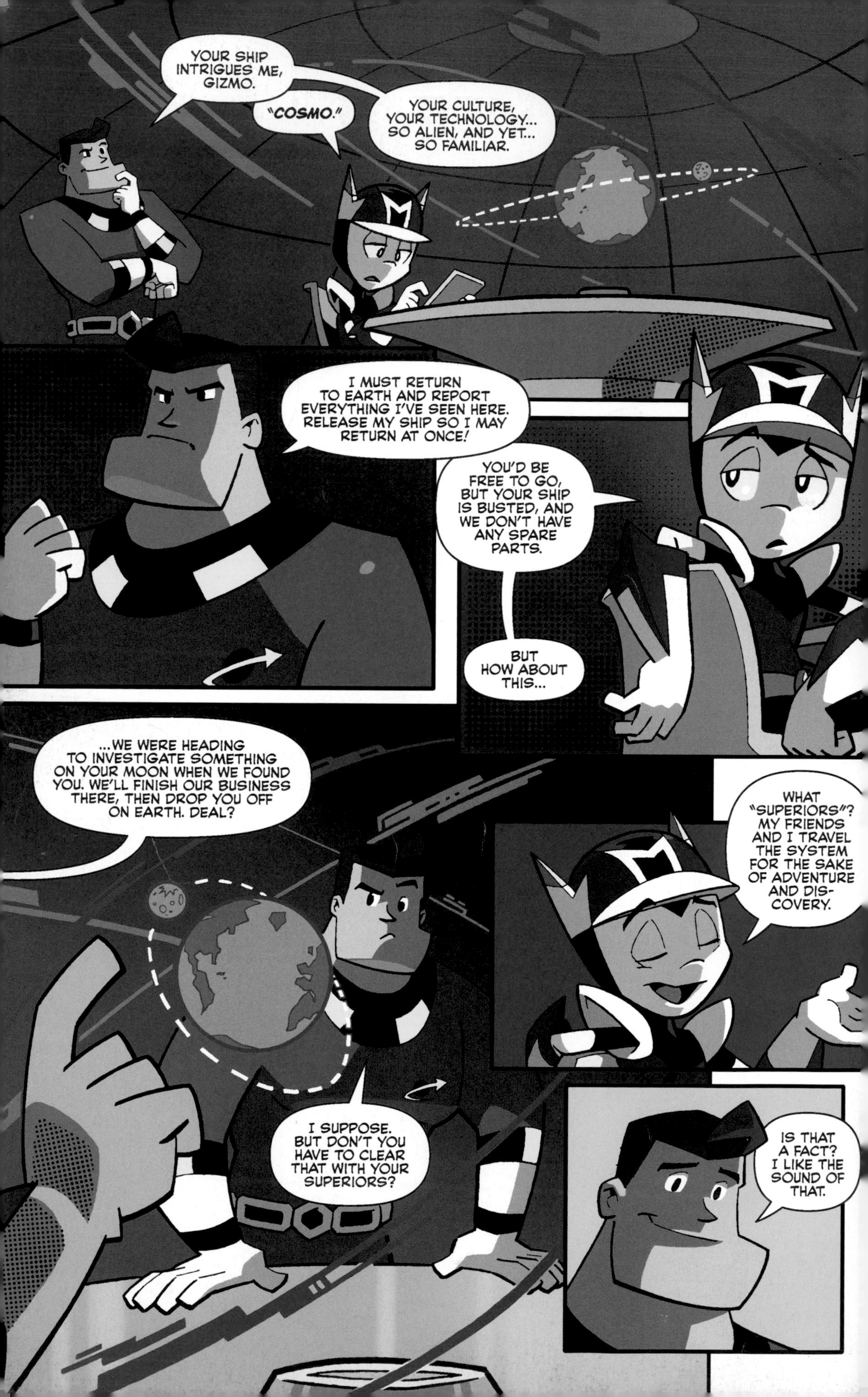
YOUR SHIP INTRIGUES ME, GIZMO.
"COSMO."
YOUR CULTURE, YOUR TECHNOLOGY... SO ALIEN, AND YET... SO FAMILIAR.
I MUST RETURN TO EARTH AND REPORT EVERYTHING I'VE SEEN HERE. RELEASE MY SHIP SO I MAY RETURN AT ONCE!
YOU'D BE FREE TO GO, BUT YOUR SHIP IS BUSTED, AND WE DON'T HAVE ANY SPARE PARTS.
BUT HOW ABOUT THIS...
...WE WERE HEADING TO INVESTIGATE SOMETHING ON YOUR MOON WHEN WE FOUND YOU. WE'LL FINISH OUR BUSINESS THERE, THEN DROP YOU OFF ON EARTH. DEAL?
I SUPPOSE. BUT DON'T YOU HAVE TO CLEAR THAT WITH YOUR SUPERIORS?
WHAT "SUPERIORS"? MY FRIENDS AND I TRAVEL THE SYSTEM FOR THE SAKE OF ADVENTURE AND DIS-COVERY.
IS THAT A FACT? I LIKE THE SOUND OF THAT.

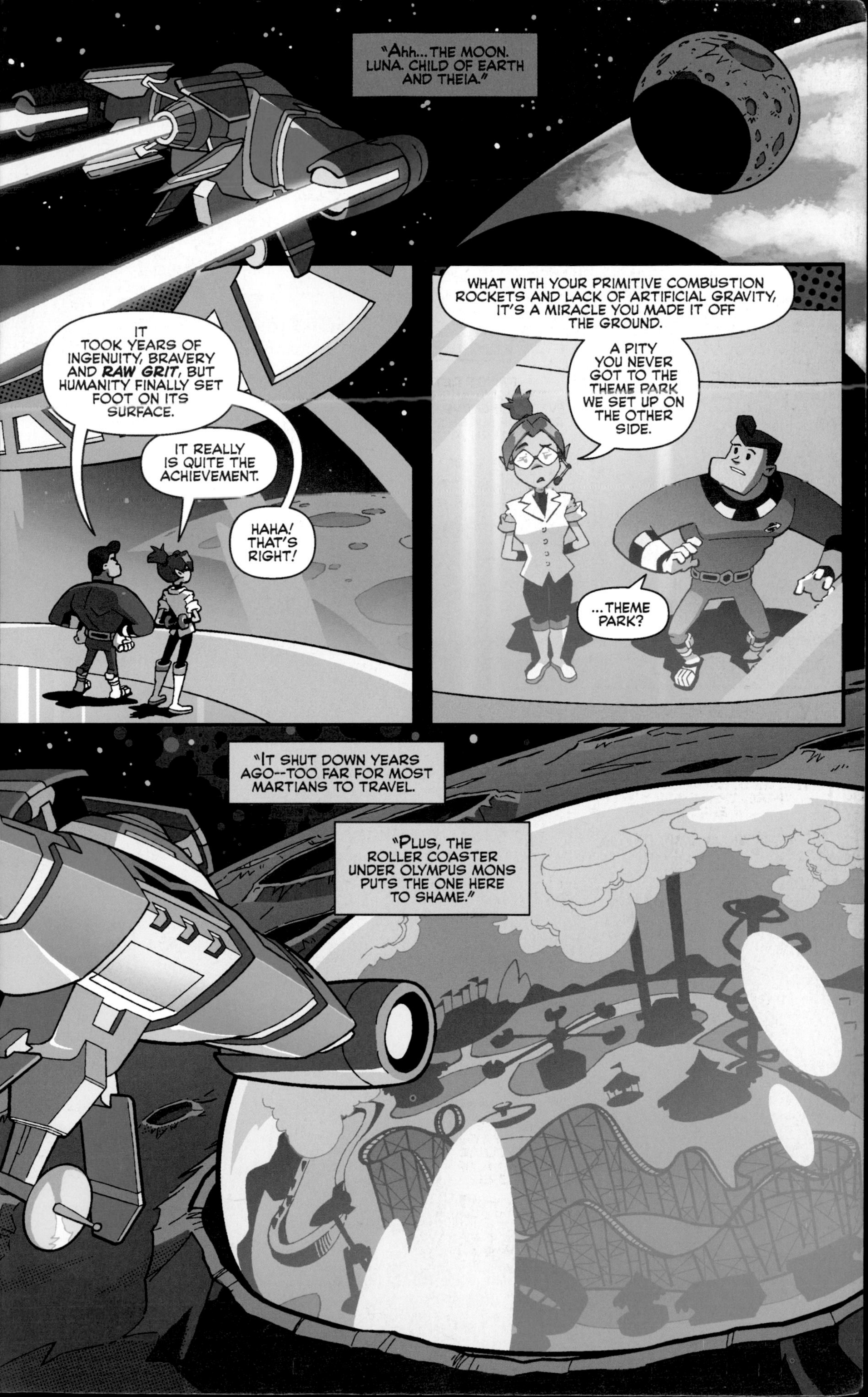
"AHH... THE MOON. LUNA. CHILD OF EARTH AND THEIA."
IT TOOK YEARS OF INGENUITY, BRAVERY AND RAW GRIT, BUT HUMANITY FINALLY SET FOOT ON ITS SURFACE.
IT REALLY IS QUITE THE ACHIEVEMENT.
HAHA! THAT'S RIGHT!
WHAT WITH YOUR PRIMITIVE COMBUSTION ROCKETS AND LACK OF ARTIFICIAL GRAVITY, IT'S A MIRACLE YOU MADE IT OFF THE GROUND.
A PITY YOU NEVER GOT TO THE THEME PARK WE SET UP ON THE OTHER SIDE.
...THEME PARK?
"IT SHUT DOWN YEARS AGO--TOO FAR FOR MOST MARTIANS TO TRAVEL.
"PLUS, THE ROLLER COASTER UNDER OLYMPUS MONS PUTS THE ONE HERE TO SHAME."

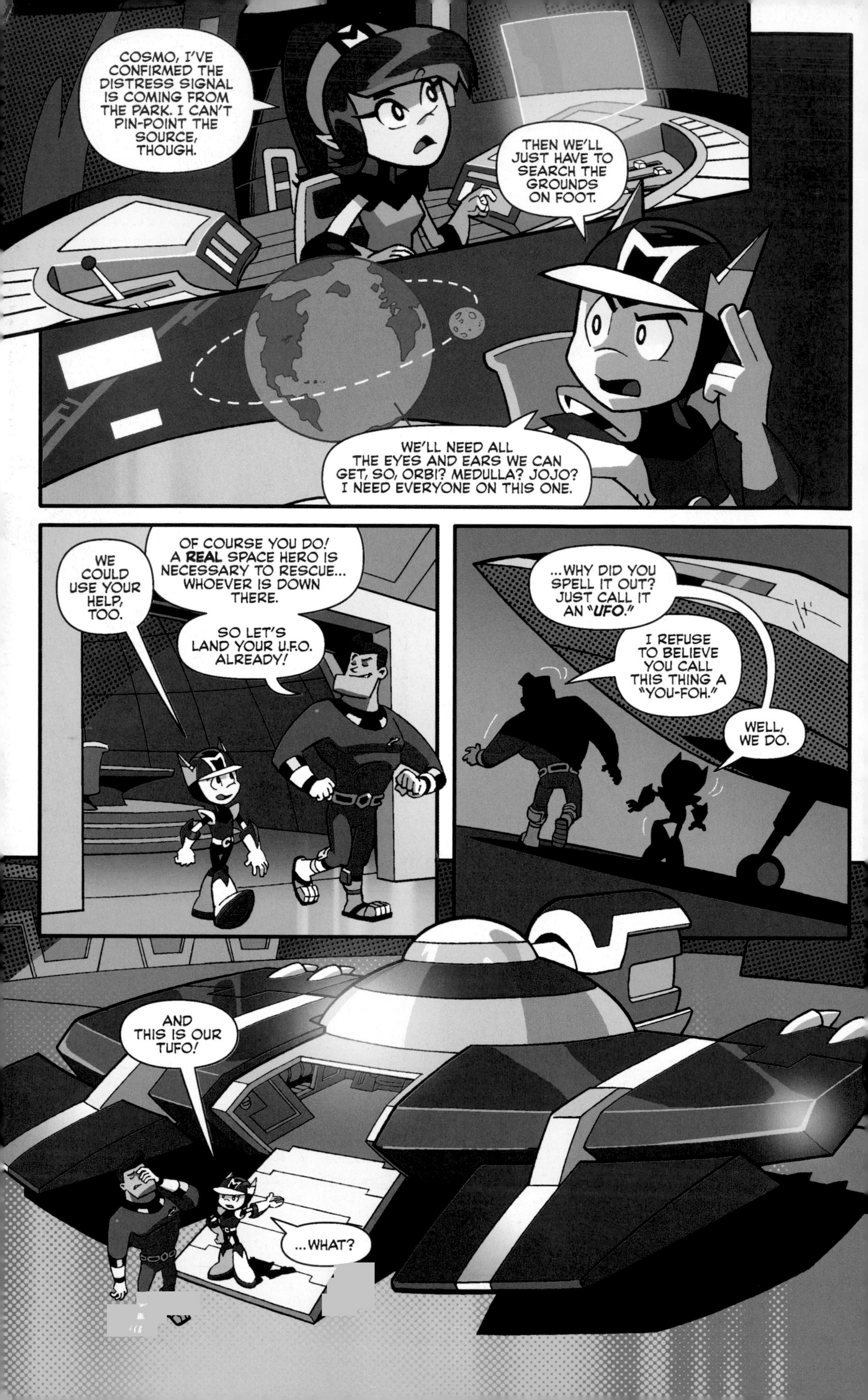

COSMO, I'VE CONFIRMED THE DISTRESS SIGNAL IS COMING FROM THE PARK. I CAN'T PIN-POINT THE SOURCE, THOUGH.
THEN WE'LL JUST HAVE TO SEARCH THE GROUNDS ON FOOT.
WE'LL NEED ALL THE EYES AND EARS WE CAN GET, SO, ORBI? MEDULLA? JOJO? I NEED EVERYONE ON THIS ONE.
WE COULD USE YOUR HELP, TOO.
OF COURSE YOU DO! A **REAL** SPACE HERO IS NECESSARY TO RESCUE... WHOEVER IS DOWN THERE.
SO LET'S LAND YOUR U.F.O. ALREADY!
...WHY DID YOU SPELL IT OUT? JUST CALL IT AN "***UFO***."
I REFUSE TO BELIEVE YOU CALL THIS THING A "YOU-FOH."
WELL, WE DO.
AND THIS IS OUR TUFO!
...WHAT?

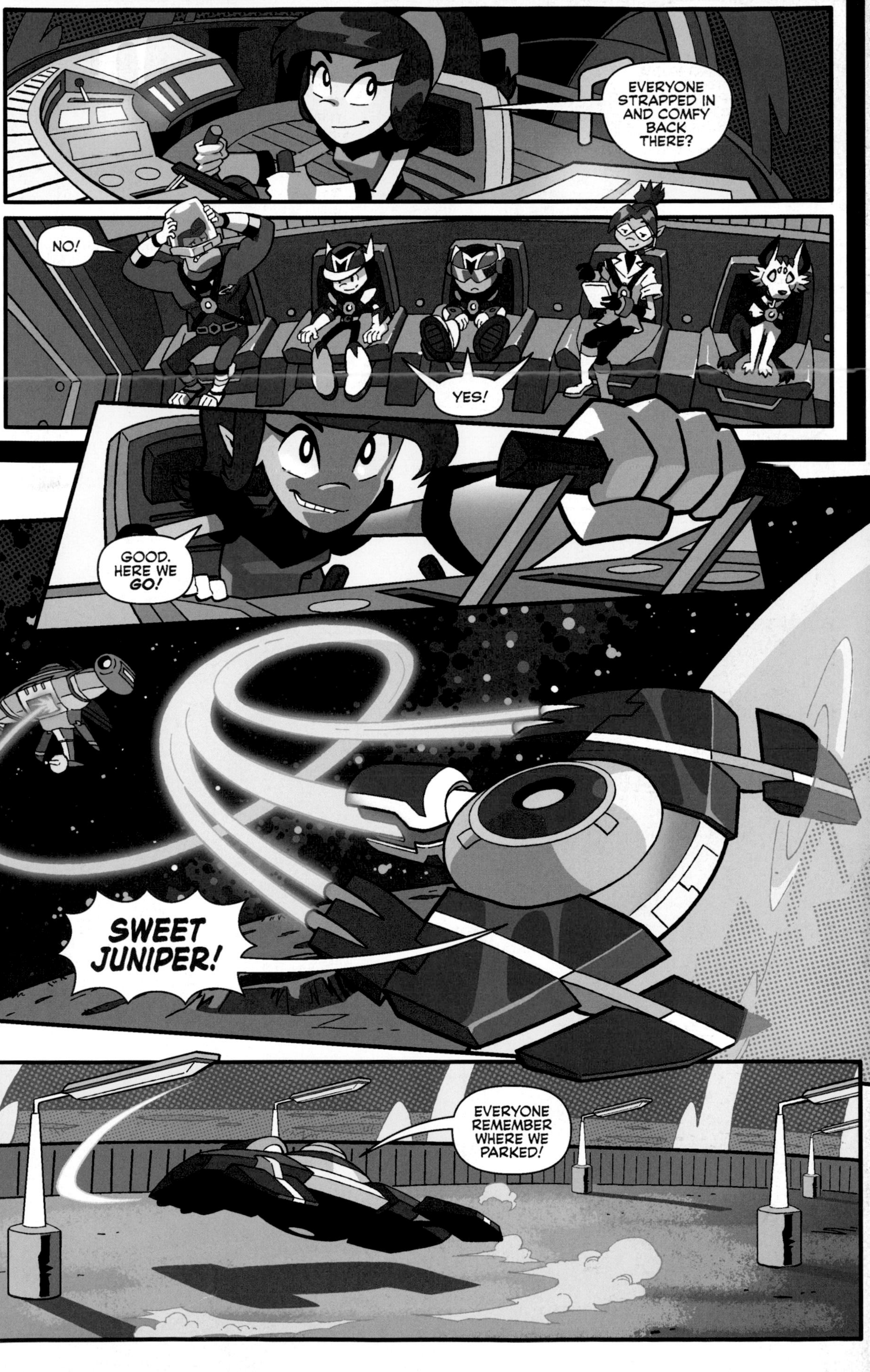
EVERYONE STRAPPED IN AND COMFY BACK THERE?
NO!
YES!
GOOD. HERE WE GO!
SWEET JUNIPER!
EVERYONE REMEMBER WHERE WE PARKED!

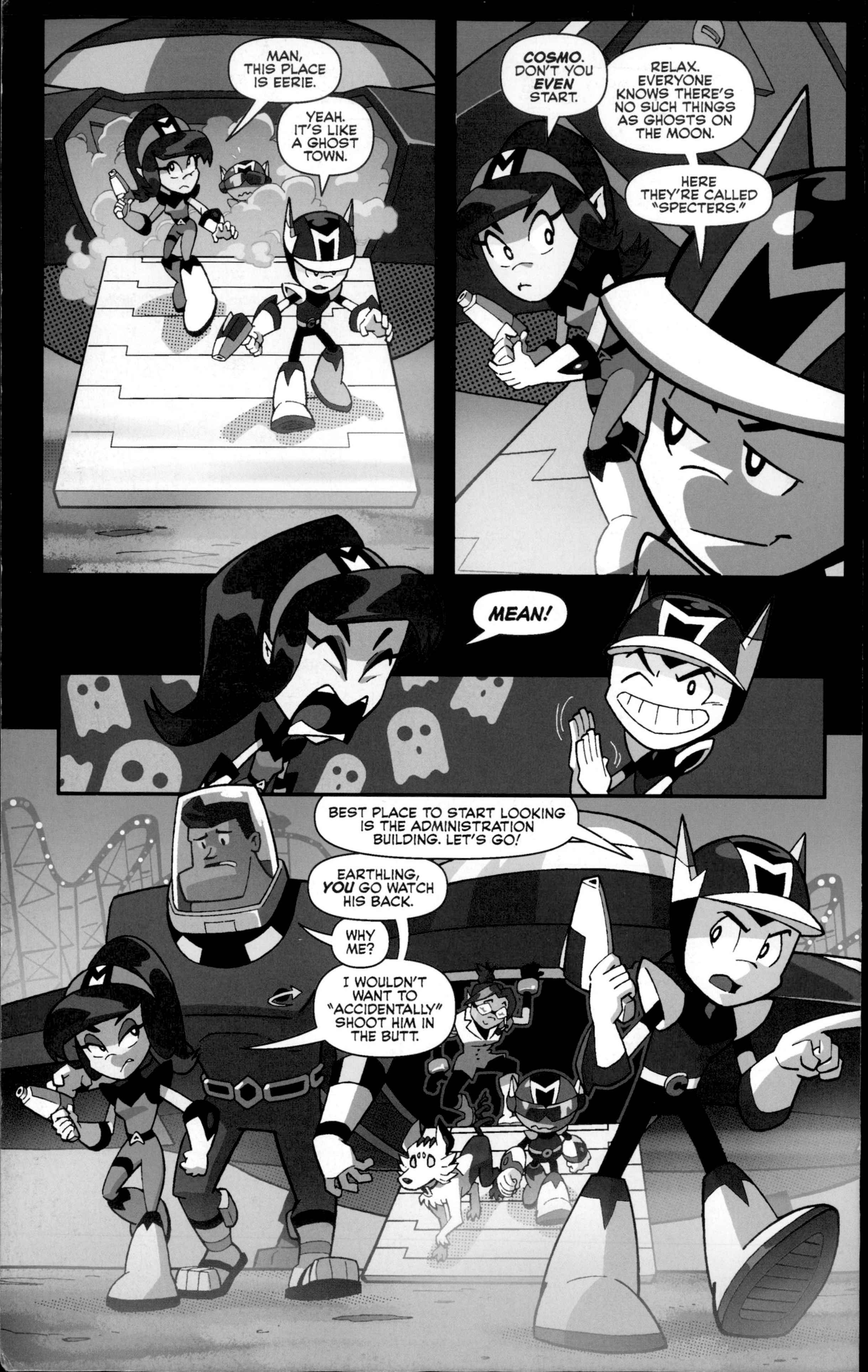
MAN, THIS PLACE IS EERIE.
YEAH. IT'S LIKE A GHOST TOWN.
COSMO. DON'T YOU EVEN START.
RELAX. EVERYONE KNOWS THERE'S NO SUCH THINGS AS GHOSTS ON THE MOON.
HERE THEY'RE CALLED "SPECTERS."
MEAN!
BEST PLACE TO START LOOKING IS THE ADMINISTRATION BUILDING. LET'S GO!
EARTHLING, YOU GO WATCH HIS BACK.
WHY ME?
I WOULDN'T WANT TO "ACCIDENTALLY" SHOOT HIM IN THE BUTT.

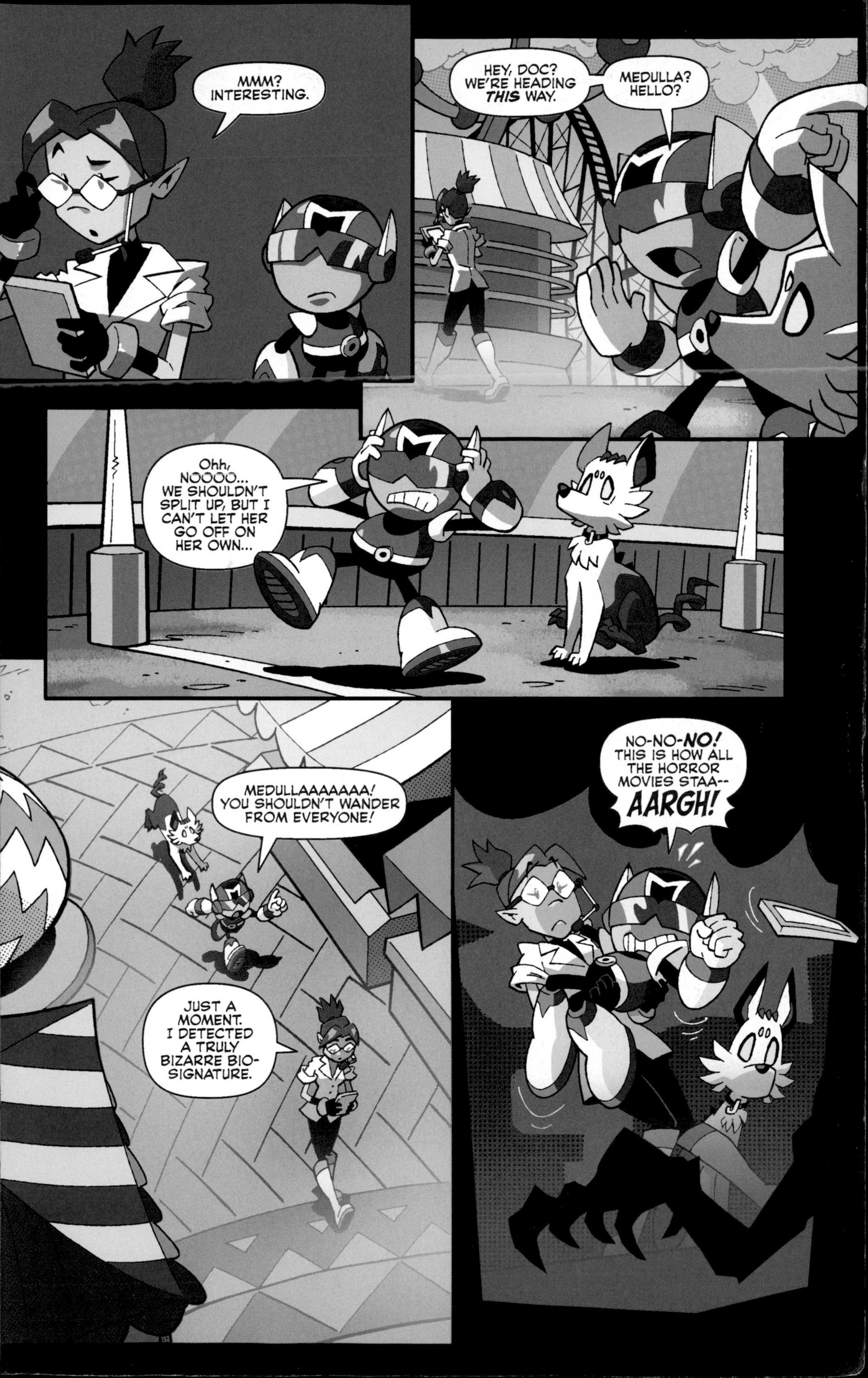
MMM? INTERESTING.
HEY, DOC? WE'RE HEADING **THIS** WAY.
MEDULLA? HELLO?
Ohh, NOOOO... WE SHOULDN'T SPLIT UP, BUT I CAN'T LET HER GO OFF ON HER OWN...
MEDULLAAAAAAA! YOU SHOULDN'T WANDER FROM EVERYONE!
JUST A MOMENT. I DETECTED A TRULY BIZARRE BIO-SIGNATURE.
NO-NO-**NO!** THIS IS HOW ALL THE HORROR MOVIES STAA-- **AARGH!**

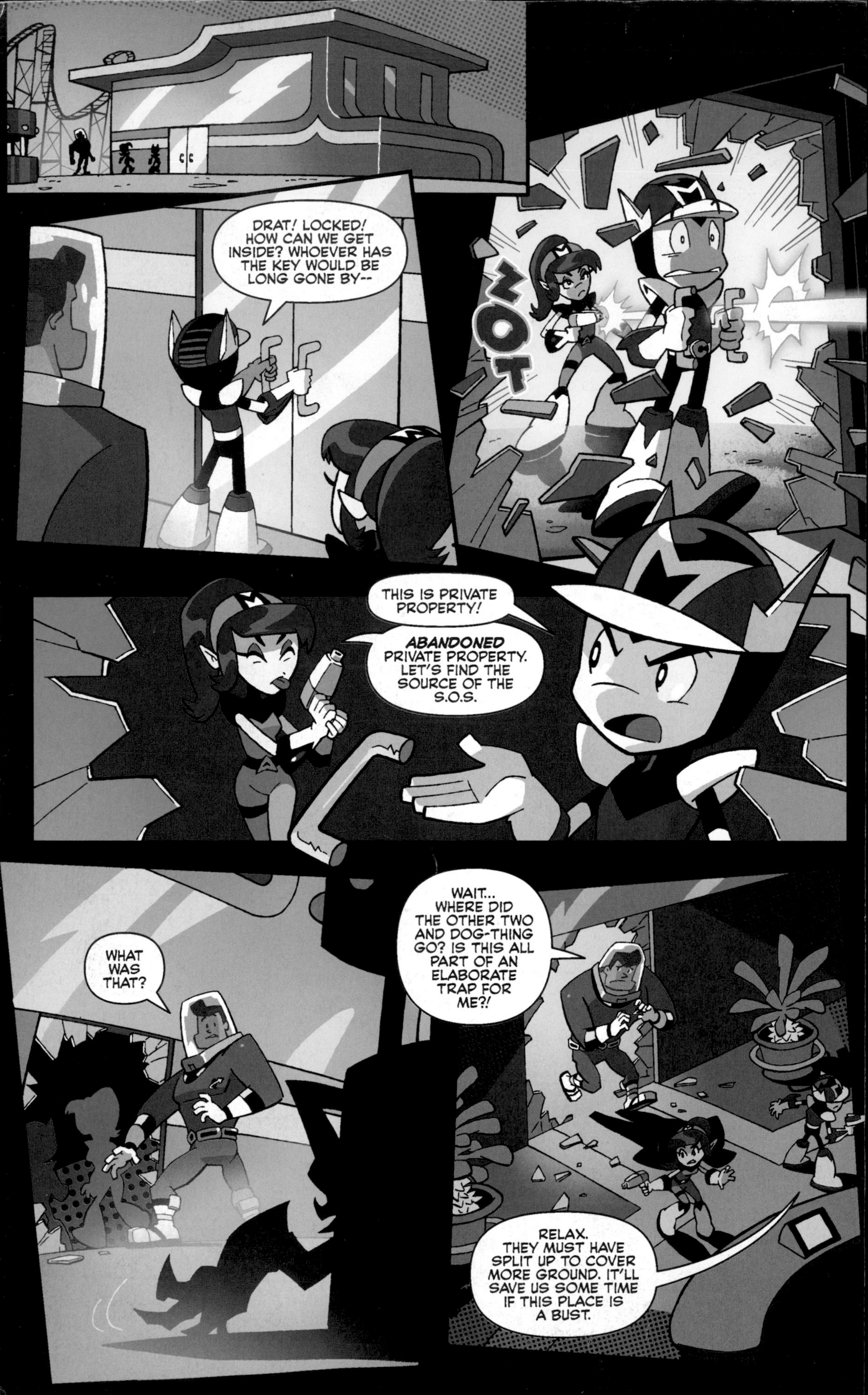
DRAT! LOCKED! HOW CAN WE GET INSIDE? WHOEVER HAS THE KEY WOULD BE LONG GONE BY--
ZOT
THIS IS PRIVATE PROPERTY!
ABANDONED PRIVATE PROPERTY. LET'S FIND THE SOURCE OF THE S.O.S.
WHAT WAS THAT?
WAIT... WHERE DID THE OTHER TWO AND DOG-THING GO? IS THIS ALL PART OF AN ELABORATE TRAP FOR ME?!
RELAX. THEY MUST HAVE SPLIT UP TO COVER MORE GROUND. IT'LL SAVE US SOME TIME IF THIS PLACE IS A BUST.

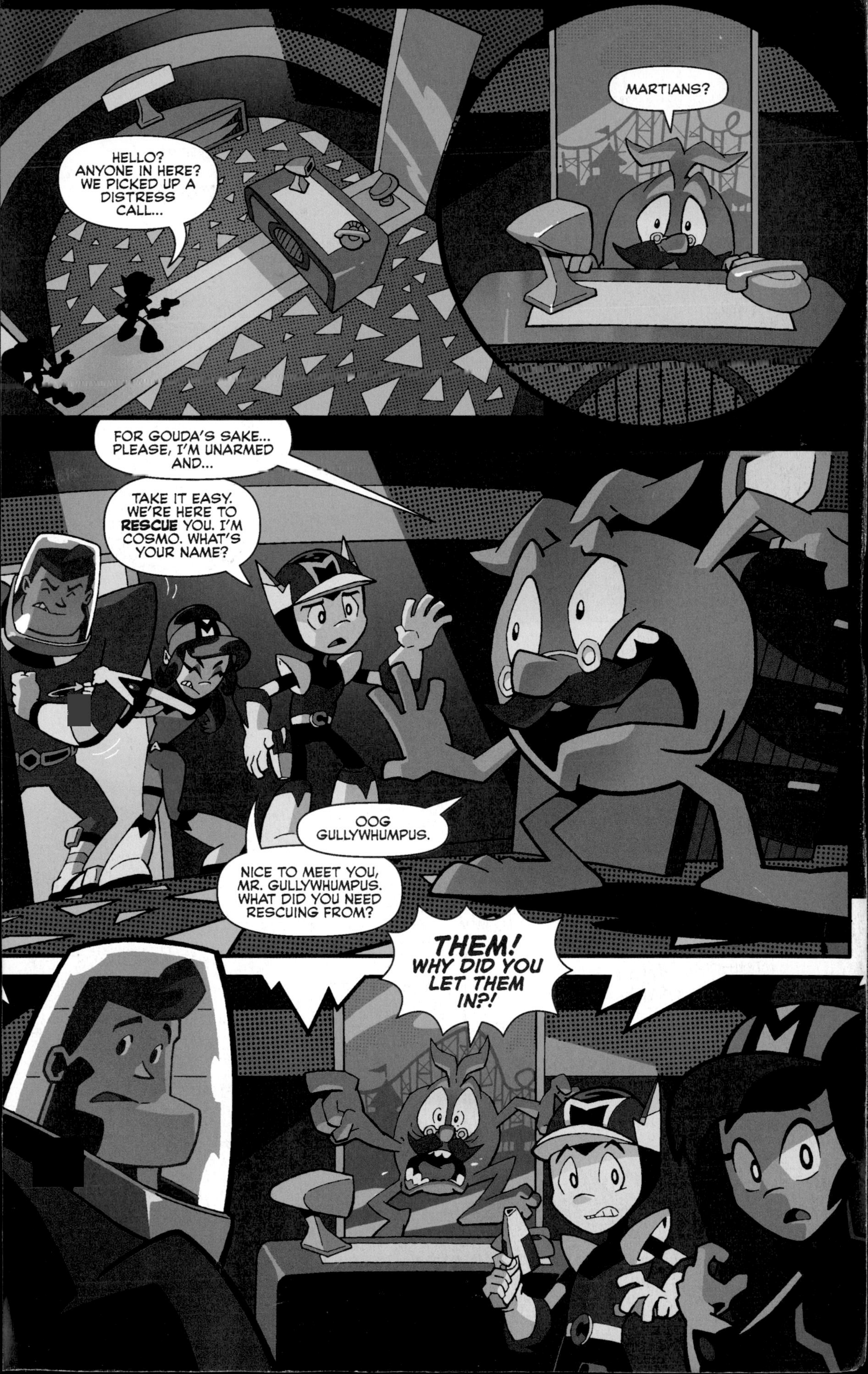
HELLO? ANYONE IN HERE? WE PICKED UP A DISTRESS CALL...
MARTIANS?
FOR GOUDA'S SAKE... PLEASE, I'M UNARMED AND...
TAKE IT EASY. WE'RE HERE TO **RESCUE** YOU. I'M COSMO. WHAT'S YOUR NAME?
OOG GULLYWHUMPUS.
NICE TO MEET YOU, MR. GULLYWHUMPUS. WHAT DID YOU NEED RESCUING FROM?
THEM! WHY DID YOU LET THEM IN?!

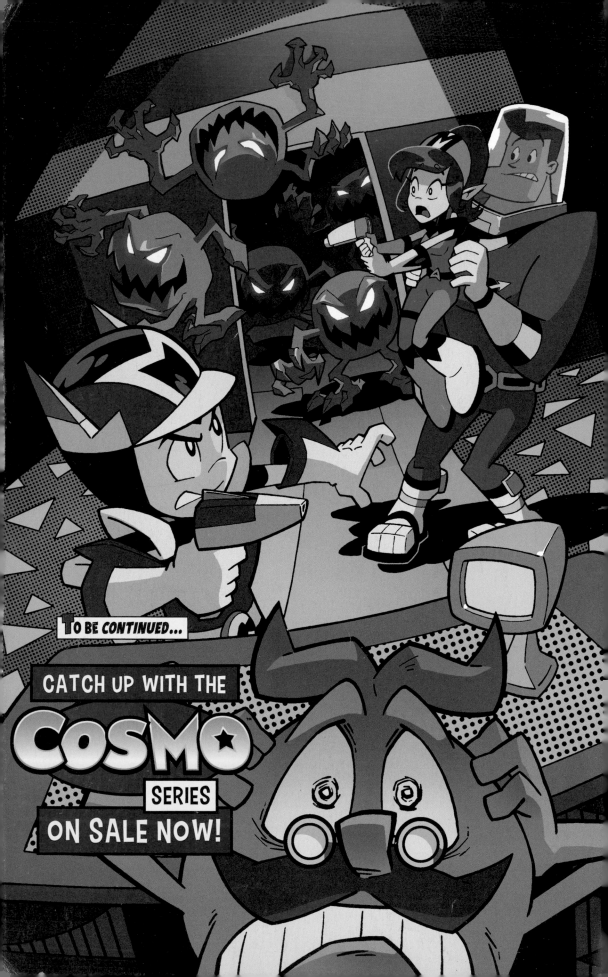

TO BE CONTINUED...

CATCH UP WITH THE

COSMO

SERIES

ON SALE NOW!